MW00737830

PRAISE FOR *A BRIEF VIEW FROM THE COASTAL SUITE*

"In *A Brief View from the Coastal Suite*, Karen Hofmann's richly drawn characters spin in a changing world, tangled up in the messiness of love and family, the pressures of work and success, and the unending search for a sense of self as age and experience shape their lives. This is a novel of stunning elegance, sensitivity, and compassion that revels in the enthralling complexity of everyday life."

—CORINNA CHONG, author of *Belinda's Rings*

"Hofmann's prose is captivating. She excels at writing everyday scenes. Some thrum with tension; others are characterized by warmth."

—JOHN M. MURRAY, *Foreword Reviews*

PRAISE FOR *WHAT IS GOING TO HAPPEN NEXT*

"It's a novel that's as original as it is ambitious, and it works, resulting in an all-engrossing visceral reading experience, and I'm recommending it to everyone."

—KERRY CLARE, Pickle Me This

"As a family saga, the novel is empathetic, compassionate, and expertly paced."

—BRENDA JOHNSTON, *Canadian Literature*

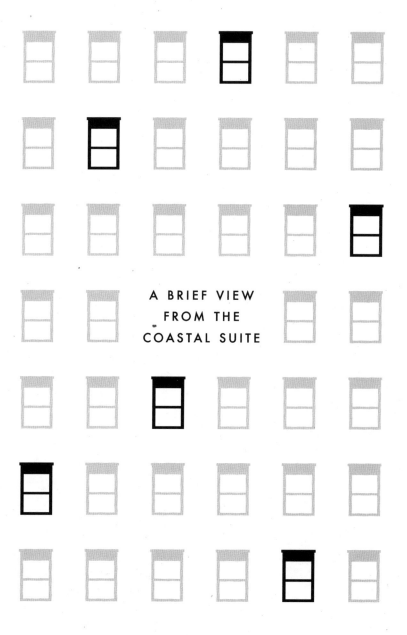

A BRIEF VIEW
FROM THE
COASTAL SUITE

A BRIEF VIEW FROM THE COASTAL SUITE

KAREN HOFMANN

NeWest Press

COPYRIGHT © Karen Hofmann 2021

All rights reserved. The use of any part of this publication – reproduced, transmitted in any form or by any means, electronic, mechanical, recording or otherwise, or stored in a retrieval system – without the prior consent of the publisher is an infringement of the copyright law. In the case of photocopying or other reprographic copying of the material, a licence must be obtained from Access Copyright before proceeding.

Library and Archives Canada Cataloguing in Publication
Title: A brief view from the coastal suite : a novel / Karen Hofmann.
Names: Hofmann, Karen, author.
Description: Sequel to: What is going to happen next.
Identifiers: Canadiana (print) 20200263579 | Canadiana (ebook) 20200267191 | ISBN 9781774390177 (softcover) | ISBN 9781774390184 (EPUB) | ISBN 9781774390191 (Kindle)
Classification: LCC PS8615.O365 B75 2021 | DDC C813/.6–dc23

Editor: Anne Nothof
Book design: Natalie Olsen, Kisscut Design
Cover photo © Ronnie Comeau/Stocksy
Author photo: Julia Tomkins

NeWest Press acknowledges the Canada Council for the Arts, the Alberta Foundation for the Arts, and the Edmonton Arts Council for support of our publishing program. This project is funded in part by the Government of Canada. ⸿ NeWest Press acknowledges that the land on which we operate is Treaty 6 territory and a traditional meeting ground and home for many Indigenous Peoples, including Cree, Saulteaux, Niitsitapi (Blackfoot), Métis, and Nakota Sioux.

NeWest Press

#201, 8540-109 Street
Edmonton, AB T6G 1E6
780.432.9427
www.newestpress.com

No bison were harmed in the making of this book.
Printed and bound in Canada   1 2 3 4 5   23 22 21

For siblings, colleagues, friends

BEFORE

May 18th, 2000

CLEO HAS BEEN EXPECTING the call for a few weeks, and so when her phone rings at two a.m., she's instantly, completely alert. It takes her less than five minutes to brush her teeth, put on deodorant, dress, and grab the bag that she and Mandalay had prepared. She's only delayed a couple of minutes, because she realizes as she's getting into her car that she's forgotten her phone and wallet, and has to go back for them. And then Cliff is awake and wants to come along, and she thinks that through for thirty seconds and then says yes.

She really doesn't like hospitals. Too many bad associations from childhood, she guesses. She'd have thought that those would have been superseded by the occasions of the births of her own two children, now aged three and six, but even walking through the main entrance, she stiffens.

She dispatches Cliff to find some coffee, makes her way up in the elevator. Finds her sister in the labour room, following the nurse just in time to catch Mandalay in the middle of a contraction – eyes squeezed shut, face scarlet, panting.

Cleo is sucked into some vortex of fear that she didn't know she'd been carrying around inside of her. *I don't want to be here. I don't want to be here.* But then the contraction ends, and Mandalay opens her eyes.

The doula can't make it, Mandalay gasps. She's got the flu. Her sub has another birth going on. Different hospital.

The sense of her purpose trickles back, now. What she needs to do. What she and Mandalay have rehearsed. She pulls herself together. It's her job. She has the bag with the back rollers and the music and the sugar-free suckers and the organic lavender wipes.

I'm here, Mandalay, she says. We can do this.

Now the hours of contractions. It's like watching someone overtaken by a violent storm. Cleo is dragged back to the memory of the birth of her daughter Olivia, and after hours of agonizing contractions, the nurse saying, Cleo, a way to go yet.

She watches the two fetal monitors, holding her breath when one heart rate dips repeatedly. She gives Mandalay her hand to squeeze, and then, when it starts to hurt, the rubber ball they've bought for the purpose.

Around five, Mandalay begins to cry, rather than breathe herself back to some sort of stable ground, between the contractions.

Cleo says to the nurse in charge: That's enough. Give her some Demerol.

Do you want Demerol, Mandalay? the nurse asks.

No, no, Mandalay insists.

You should take a break now, Cleo, the nurse says. Go get something to drink. Sit down for a few minutes.

Cleo leaves. She takes off her gown and cap and goes down to the cafeteria, where Cliff is helplessly waiting, orders coffee and a muffin, leaves most of the muffin in crumbs on the tray.

When she comes back and re-gowns, things have shifted. Mandalay has surfaced from wherever she has been, and has taken on animal form. She moves onto all fours, crouching on the bed, rocking.

ANOTHER WAVE COMING, Cleo says, watching the monitor. They'd decided on *wave;* Mandalay has practised visualizing the rollers on the beach near Phuket, where she had once flung herself into the bright aquamarine surf.

The gap between the spike beginning to grow on the monitor and the clamping of her spine and stomach is just long enough for a wild hope to surface that it won't be so painful this time.

It's not a wave. It's a tsunami.

Starting to subside, Cleo says, and the deluge of pain briefly abates.

I can't do this, Mandalay says.

A guttural howl like nothing she's heard before erupts from her innards. Is that her?

Breathe, Cleo says, steadily. Breathe, Mandalay. Breathe.

I can't I can't, she says.

But then she can. Mandalay finds her breath; she pins her attention to it. Her body begins to do what it needs to do. There is much pain, but the pain is not her. She visualizes diving and rolling in the warm waves, at Phuket. The waves had tumbled her over, but she'd learned to give herself over to them, and she would find herself lying in the shallow ebbing water, laughing, after they retreated.

She'd been with Benedict, then. Her last boyfriend before Duane.

Duane isn't here, now. She can't imagine him being here, wanting him here. God, no, she'd said, when Cleo had wondered.

She rides the waves and rides them, but then it's too much, she's being beaten up, there's no space to catch her breath. A vortex. *Roll with it,* she tries to remember, but her body isn't hers now. She's lost her tether to it.

And now the first twin's emergence. There's a sudden cessation of violence. Mandalay feels an astonishing calm.

Cleo's nephew slides out head first in a rush of blood and water, a fish, an otter, a wet, red human. He takes a breath.

They let Cleo hold him in a warmed towel for a few seconds, after they suction his nose and mouth. He looks like one of my own children, like Olivia, Cleo says. The nurse takes him from Cleo's arms and puts him on Mandalay's chest.

WHEN THE NURSE puts her son on her chest, Mandalay feels this: that she and he have been travelling towards each other for all time, and have finally arrived.

She's able to hold to that sweet, calm feeling even when they tell her that the other twin is in trouble, that they can't wait any longer. It's not what she wanted, but she understands. Someone lifts her first-born son from her arms, and Cleo is signing a form, and cold disinfectant is being swiped across her belly and she knows that she is going to be anesthetized and cut and it was not supposed to go this way.

But she knows it will be okay.

IT IS LIKE A BAKERY, Cliff thinks, except for the blood on the bed. Too many people, and he couldn't tell them apart, in their puffy blue caps and their long aprons. Then he recognizes the one on the bed as his sister Mandalay. He's stayed by the door, out of the paths of the others, who were not actually moving erratically, as he'd thought, but working at their business in a couple of quiet little clusters. One group around Mandalay's bed, and one around a clear plastic tub sitting on a high wheeled cart.

One of the figures by the bed turns and he sees that it is Cleo. Cliff, she says. There you are. Come and see the baby.

The nurse who has fetched him wraps him in a gown, pale yellow, and pulls a hat on him. She hands him a surgical mask, as well, and does it up behind Cliff's head. He hasn't seen a newborn before, to his recollection. Cleo's babies had been a few weeks old before he'd got up the courage to go visit. He's thinking, somehow, that it'll be like a pup or kitten – he saw plenty of those, growing up – wet, blunt-muzzled, blind. But what's in the tub, though wrapped up like a loaf of bread, is clearly a person. It looks at him. Its eyes focus on his face. There's a passage of energy between them, like when you recognize someone you haven't seen for a while or see someone you know in a place you don't expect.

It makes him dizzy, that glance.

Do you want to hold him? Cleo asks, but he doesn't want to, yet.

Then there's a flurry of activity near Mandalay's bed, and more people in the room, a gurney, and Mandalay being lifted onto it on the count of three, and a woman speaking brusquely at him to stand back as they began pushing the gurney very quickly toward the door, several people with their hands on it, pushing, running, and the sound of it moving very quickly down the corridor.

Then the bassinette with the baby in it is taken away, and Cliff is left standing in the empty room, by the bed with its bloodstained sheets.

He'd been woken so early this morning, and had come upstairs to the kitchen, from his basement room at his sister's house, to find Cleo dressed and rushing out the door. Then she'd run back in and up the stairs, saying, *wallet, phone, keys,* the way she did when she was overwhelmed and in a rush.

He'd grabbed that chance to go along. Had thrown on a T-shirt and jeans, shoved his feet into his crushed, laceless running shoes, scooped his jacket from the hook in the hallway.

Good, Cleo said, when she'd emerged from the house and seen him leaning against her vehicle. Good; you might be useful. But jeez, Cliff, have some breath mints.

He hadn't been able to be very useful. He'd sat in a waiting room. Cleo had asked him to get her coffee, a couple of times, and he'd done that, but there wasn't much else to do.

Someone comes into the empty delivery room, and tells him nicely where he can go. And now he is sitting and waiting again, in a different place.

He's been in this hospital before. He'd had an accident, eight months ago – had fallen down a flight of stairs, fractured his skull. Well, was pushed, but it was easier to say *fell*. People didn't ask so many questions.

He recognizes the scent of the hospital, which is the scent of his waking up and finding himself safe, cared for. It will be okay, he tells himself. It will be okay.

He's in a hallway, an alcove of a hallway, with chairs upholstered in blue plastic and a painting of ocean waves on the wall, and there are swinging metal doors with small windows at one end, and a sign that says Surgery, no unauthorized persons beyond this point.

It's very quiet. Should it be so quiet? He doesn't really want to be here. It's very early in the morning. He hasn't had breakfast and he would like to go find Cleo. But he sits. Someone has brought him here, said, You can wait here, Mr. Lund.

AND THEN, sooner than he would have expected, the swinging doors with their small windows open and Cleo, gowned and capped and masked, walks through, carrying the swaddled baby.

No, it's a different baby, wrapped differently, more loosely, and as it's offered to him he sees that its head is kind of sticky, wet, as if it's just come out of the sea. This one is paler, its head rounder, its eyes squashed shut in anger or repulsion. He recognizes that expression: it's a look of being unpleasantly surprised. Cleo says, Look, Cliff, and puts the baby into his arms. It's a little smaller and lighter than his cat.

Cliff, Cleo says. We have two new nephews. What do you think of that? It's the Lund brothers, second generation.

1

Appraisal

THE GLASSED-IN ROOM for spin class is brightly lit, and overlooks the parking lot from the second floor of the new plaza, so that even as Cleo parks, she can see the rows of waiting black and chrome machines. She's just in time. At the top of the stairs, she steps out of her boots and laces on her turquoise and white runners, hangs her coat and handbag in a locker, fills her water bottle at the fountain. *Ladies' Only* is painted, in pink flourishes and sketchy grammatical accuracy, on glass double doors. From inside the spin room, it looks darker outside than it is, even at three o'clock on an early January afternoon. The fog folds itself around the buildings, chalks out colours. There's no horizon.

She's one of the first, and takes her favourite bike: second row, right side. Positions the water bottle in its wire holder. Stretches, using the seat for support. The spin bikes around her fill up.

The instructor comes in, carrying her clipboard, her sheaf of release forms. She has a relaxed, confident manner; she's a popular instructor. Welcome, she says. First spin class of 2008. How is everyone's Christmas shortbread sitting?

There are groans, a laugh or two.

Then they are pedalling, slowly, at first, in low gear, a warm-up.

Cleo's hams protest almost immediately. She managed to get to the gym only once over the holidays. Now she will have to pay for her sloth.

They pedal slowly, easily, in time with each other. Cleo looks around, sees familiar bodies. This afternoon class is mostly attended by women her own age, women who, like her, work part-time and have children old enough to be left alone for an hour or two.

Then they're shifting up, and she actually has to concentrate. Let's work on slowing our breathing, the instructor says, as if her attention is on Cleo. Deep, even breaths.

There's the whir of twenty wheels rotating, gear and shaft and disk.

They must all be generating some horsepower, Cleo thinks. Too bad it can't be collected to power the lights, or something like that. Her calves ache.

Let's gear down, the instructor says. But pace up! Now they're racing, the wheels spinning, the whir a higher soughing. Cleo feels her heart rate come up. The bike's readout says her pulse is at 137. That's good for aerobics but not for fat burn. She slows slightly, watches the monitor until the green LED numerals decrease.

Let's keep the pace up! the instructor says. Cleo pumps her legs a little faster. Her machine picks up the vibrations of all the machines as her classmates pedal hard. For a few seconds Cleo has the sensation that they are moving, that the bikes have somehow left their solid platforms and are surging forward, toward the floor-to-ceiling glass, the rolling fog outside.

She slows a little, just ahead of the instructor's call to wind it down.

Everyone's panting. The woman next to Cleo is very flushed, almost bent over. New Year's resolution rider, Cleo thinks.

The pace rises and falls now, but is easier. Behind her, there is conversation. Two of the older women in the class are talking about their holidays. Desert Palms, Santa Barbara, Cozumel, they say. Dehydrated Malibu Barbies, Cleo's friend Lacey calls them.

They talk about how bad the service was, how expensive the drinks, how their husbands ignored their directions, took the wrong overpass, the wrong bridge.

Cleo would like to go on a trip, somewhere warm. They never do, she and Trent. It's too expensive, over the holidays, Trent says. Also, he doesn't like to fly.

Her friend Jennifer, who's on a bike the next row over, had said: I wouldn't put up with that. I would just make him go. Well, she has no doubt of that. But she and Trent have a different kind of relationship. Neither makes the other do anything. They aren't that kind of couple.

They're not the other kind of couple, either. Joined at the hip, one brain shared between them. Cleo can hear one of the sixty-something women, the one with the pewter pixie-cut, the sinewy thighs, now talking about a cycling trip, it sounds like, somewhere in southern Spain. Adrian and I, she says, again and again. Adrian and she had liked the town with the cathedral, the olive-oil region, the wine, the seafood. Had not liked the vendors, the smell of the local cigarettes, the wandering dogs.

Cleo would like to go to Spain, to India, to Peru. She imagines herself drifting freely through a market with spices and braziers and bright pennants of handwoven cloth. She does not think she would like to go there with Trent, or with children.

She pedals and pedals, her leg muscles warmed up now, in her second wind. What if she were to crash through that glass wall, to just keep pedalling? Or if this were a ship's prow, sailing southwesterly through the fog?

Will she travel, when she is older? She's forty, now. It will be another eight or ten years before her children are more or less grown. Will she still be going to spin class?

Her foster mother, Mrs. Giesbrecht, with her tight grey curls, her loose comfortable body, would think it a shocking waste of time and money. She gets plenty of exercise in her garden and ironing and scrubbing floors, she would say. But probably more like gossiping and doing good deeds, Cleo thinks. But never mind that. Cleo's biological mother, Crystal, would see even less point in going to exercise class: Crystal, who at sixty still wears her hair to her waist, is skinny and fey and braless, and gets in her car to go half a kilometre up the highway to the gas station to buy milk. Crystal had a nervous breakdown when Cleo was twelve. She had five children in just over five years, and then lost them all to social services.

Cleo calls and visits both Mrs. Giesbrecht and Crystal, but never often enough.

Last push, the instructor says. Gear up again. Let's cover some miles, ladies. The body achieves what the mind believes!

Outside the bright glass room, the fog thickens, the daylight ebbs.

Except for a brief interlude doing her second degree at the University of Ottawa, Cleo has lived all of her life within a hundred kilometres of the Pacific Coast: has spent almost all of her life in the shelter of the dense cedar forests, breathing the mild moist Pacific air. She has always had access to the temperate green delta, to its January camellias and ironic palms, its glass skyrises and pedestrian sidewalks, its outdoor markets, its artisanal coffee. She would never want to live anywhere else. But she'd like to live further west, in Vancouver itself.

And so, it appears, would two million others.

She and Trent, a professional couple on an income and a half, can barely afford to live on the fringes, the outer ring of the suburbs. Their house has doubled in market value in the last ten to fifteen years, but places nearer the city centre have more than doubled. They are moving further away from any possibility of living in the lively, multifarious core.

Anyway, Trent doesn't want to move. He grew up in a small leafy town in Ontario, where eight-year-olds rode bikes to the five-and-dime to buy Oh Henry! bars with their weekly allowance, and fathers drove to the nearby city to work. He thinks that they can replicate that here, but the satellite city they live in was built to a different scale, built for cars. There are no sidewalks; a six-lane parkway feeds traffic from the residential clusters to the cloned malls. Their street has a walk score of three out of a hundred.

Trent's parents had given them the down payment when they were expecting Olivia. They hadn't been able to get their heads around the idea that the sum they'd given each of Trent's Boomer brothers in the early 80s to buy their cute farmhouses or Annex town-houses amounted to only a down payment for Trent and Cleo. Why do you need such a fancy house? Trent's mother had asked.

It wasn't a fancy house. It was a basic three-bedroom builder's house on a tiny lot, in a subdivision of almost identical houses. But even if they had allowed for inflation and given them twice the sum, it wouldn't have been enough for an inner-city property.

They could perhaps afford a half-duplex in the shabbier East-end neighbourhoods of the city. Cleo's sister Mandalay lives in that sort of place. Precariously.

The cyclists pedal, and pedal, and do not progress.

She misses Lacey, who always went to spin class with her, who got her to try it in the first place. When they cycled side by side, they could chat through the entire hour, and it went by quickly. There's a kind of isolation, going to spin class alone.

In the change room, someone asks, Are you staying for upper body? And another woman replies: No, have to make five dozen cup-cakes for the band trip.

She finds herself heading downstairs with Michelle, whom she has known for years, since their daughters were in kindergarten together. Michelle is changing into a pastel cashmere jogging suit, fastening a tiny diamond bracelet that flashes on her wrist.

Pretty! Cleo says. Christmas present?

Michelle looks dazed for a minute and then smiles her not-quite-focussed smile. Yes, she says. Christmas present.

She looks like she shouldn't be out on the street without someone to hold her hand. Yet Lacey says she was a dental hygienist, before she married Richard.

Then Jennifer returns from the sink, where she's been re-applying her makeup. Where is Lacey? Jennifer asks.

Lacey has taken on a new job, a full-time one with the regional health authority.

Is anyone going to Zumba tomorrow? Michelle asks, although it's just the three of them there.

I have to work, Cleo says.

Oh, Michelle asks, as if stumped. What do you do again? You're an interior decorator, right?

Whenever Cleo explains what she does, people's eyes glaze over. She says, now: More or less, yeah.

God, Jennifer says. What am I going to cook for supper? I think Mike will leave me if I make pasta again, but it's honestly all the kids will eat.

Michelle is searching in the rhinestone-embellished mini-backpack that seems to function as a purse for her keys. Richard's away, Michelle says. So I guess the girls and I are just going to order a pizza and curl up in front of *America's Got Talent*.

Cleo runs through her mental list of the contents of her fridge. Dinner's all ready to go – she made a spinach and cheese casserole this morning – but there are tomorrow's lunches, and something niggles about the last loaf of bread.

Cleo's car starts grudgingly, as if it had better things to do.

▼▼▼

MANDALAY ALMOST HAS THEM ready in time.

Aidan is dressed, at least, in his new jeans with the turned-up cuffs and a green checked shirt, standing still under her comb, when the doorbell sounds. She feels his shoulders square, thinks — she can see only the top of his head — that his jaw tightens. Her own chest clenches.

You're good to go, she says. Can you grab your backpack?

Let me see my hair, he says.

The mirror's hung on the back of the door. She stands behind him, comb at the ready. His clear skin flushed with the bath. His caramel-coloured hair slicked.

It's all wrong, he says.

How?

Look, he says, pointing to the curls forming at his temples, where his baby hair, the fine hairline down, has already dried.

It's perfect, she says.

No!

Knocking at the door now, peremptory. She yells, *Coming!* and then, at the other child, *Owen!* and hurries to the door. A flitting awareness that she's frowzy, her hair sprouting from the twist put in hours before, her T-shirt sopping from the boys' bath. Her sweatpants stained from a misjudged milk pour. The thought that she had meant to have five minutes to tidy up sinking through her, stones in a well.

She opens the door and there he is, his wide shoulders in a (new?) leather jacket half-blocking the light. His head is slightly tilted and he's wearing a faint smirk. She knows he's just won a bet made with himself about how long it would take her to come to the door, or something like that.

Nice jacket, she says.

Thanks, he says. Motorcycle.

She glances reflexively at the lane, almost believing that he would turn up for the boys on a motorbike, but there's only the hulking black suv, as usual.

In the bath all together? Duane asks, looking at her wet shirt. She feels herself flush and scowls. It's been at least two years since she stopped bathing with the boys, in the face of his objections. Not that she had cared whether he didn't like it. The bathtub had just been getting a little crowded.

Then Aidan's at the door, beside her. His damp hair, his glowing fine skin. Hey, Dad.

Heyyyyy, Aidan. How are you?

He doesn't touch the boys, she notices, again.

Aidan looking tense, expectant. How are you, Dad?

Well enough, Duane says. Then, before a conversation can start: Where's your brother?

The sound of thumping in the hallway, like a one-legged creature approaching, and then a more muffled thud, the tumble of flesh and bone. She sees Duane wince, knows she has winced herself. And Owen appears, hopping, in the hallway, more or less dressed, but both of his legs in one half of his jeans.

Did you fall? she asks, reaching for him, but he's laughing, showing the gap where all four front teeth are missing, the lower permanent ones growing in serrated, as if he's turning into a shark.

Aidan has lost and replaced his teeth one at a time; Owen was late, and now losing his milk teeth all at once, scrambling to catch up.

Hey Dad, Owen says, enthusiastically. Guess what? Guess what?

I guess you haven't learned to put your pants on properly yet, Duane says. Get it together, Owen. We're catching a ferry.

Oh, right! Owen says, and sits, or rather falls on his bottom, and starts over with his jeans. She feels Aidan's shoulder blade, like a hard little wing, pressing into her waist, where he is leaning against her.

I'll go get Owen's backpack, Aidan says, and disappears into the hallway.

Okay now, Dad? Owen is jiggling with energy.

Shirt's on inside out, Duane says.

Owen laughs, and Duane finally laughs with him.

Glasses, Owen? Mandalay asks, gently, and he turns, trips, nearly collides with Aidan in the doorway.

Duane says: You had one task today, which was to have the boys ready on time.

She doesn't answer; she will not argue with him in front of her children. She can hear Owen still rummaging around. Your glasses are in the bathroom, she calls.

I know, he calls back. I'm looking for Ed.

In your backpack already, she says.

Oh, he says, reappearing in the doorway, grinning. I forgot.

Who's Ed? Duane asks.

Teddy bear, she says, shortly. Of course he'll say something, make fun of the boys having teddy bears.

He just raises an eyebrow at her.

She goes to help the boys into the SUV but Duane says, No, no — they can do it by themselves. They do, opening the heavy doors, climbing into their booster seats, pulling the seat belts across themselves, and fastening them.

See you Sunday night, Duane says, over his shoulder. There's a piece of a broken toy on the walk, the arm and rotator cuff of some scaly plastic creature — not in Duane's way at all but she sees him nudge it smartly off the path with his left foot, not even breaking his stride.

So now the weekend to herself, except for the four hours she's working Saturday.

First Mandalay needs to talk to someone, to ground herself. The house seems so empty when the boys leave, especially after the happy chaos of getting them ready to go. And then Duane's hostility, his criticism, rattles her. She tries a couple of friends, but neither is answering. She dials her sister, Cleo.

Ugh, Cleo says. I hate dealing with critical, arrogant men. She sounds a bit distant, as usual. How are the lice?

Gone, Mandalay says. But you wouldn't believe how much work it was. Everything had to be washed.

I can believe it, Cleo says, though Mandalay wonders. Cleo's kids have never had lice. But it's good to have a little sympathetic conversation after engaging with Duane.

I think I should tell him he can only take them one weekend a month, she says. Or even once every couple of months. It's so disruptive, you know?

I thought you had a legal agreement, Cleo says.

Well, she does. But it's not really fair. She's the twins' mother. She's the one who has nurtured them every single moment of their lives, since they were conceived. It's just been her. And she alone knows all of their thoughts, their preferences and dislikes, their funny fears and their habits. It's not right that Duane can just swoop in and take them away, every other weekend. She hates it.

But you said you need that time to get things done, Cleo says. You said you never have time to get your house organized or work on your art projects.

Art projects. Cleo has such a way of diminishing her work, sometimes. It's hard to do much on the weekend, she says. She feels disoriented with the boys gone. What she could use, really, is daily after-school care – someone who would come in and play with the boys, maybe do a little light housekeeping and meal prep. Someone who would interact with the boys, encourage them to do constructive play and reading, but also give them their space. Someone who would be *her* for a few hours. It would be good to have a regular schedule, a bit longer to work each day. She could get more done. As it is, it feels like no sooner does she drop the boys off at school in the morning, then it is afternoon and she's picking them up again.

Cleo is silent. (Cleo is judging.)

Well, Cleo says. I have things to do this evening.

Cleo is always busy.

Mandalay should try to get something done this weekend, herself.

She wanders through her house, makes some tea, sits for a while with the cat, in a patch of sunshine. The house has such good bones, and she actually loves the renovations that were done back in the seventies – the emerald backsplash tile in the kitchen, the closed-in porch, the little stove. She loves the wood floors and wide trim, the mullioned windows, the bamboo or paper blinds she has hung on hooks, the paper globe lamps and hanging plants, the claw-foot tub with its familiar chips and rust stains. Everything is a bit dusty and worn, but the house has such good light and proportions that it's just all very warm and cozy.

It's a look that people pay a lot of money for now, in those little boutiques along Granville or even the second-hand stores on Commercial, right? *Shabby chic*, it's called. But she was doing it before it became trendy. There's something so honest and comfortable and lived-in about her place, with its old sofas draped in vintage blankets, its rickety but graceful little side tables. Everything looks worn and inviting and *real*. Maybe it's harder to keep super clean and tidy, but it also doesn't really show the dirt, and she doesn't believe in being anal about it. The occasional stray sock or towel just adds to the charm and layering of pattern, this way.

She drifts down the stairs, to the basement. It's not a bad basement, for an older house – at some point it had been finished, a suite made, and it's partly above ground, and gets decent light.

At some point, she remembers, there had been some talk about renting out the suite again. But she needs the space. All of her art stuff is down here, piled on the counters and stacked against the walls – and there are the boxes and tubs of stuff – items she has collected for potential art projects, clothes and toys that people have given her, or that she and the boys have outgrown.

It's a bit of a mess. Maybe she should clean it up. But she doesn't have the energy to sort it all. The prospect just fills her with ennui. And it's not doing any harm, is it? It makes her feel optimistic, to have her raw materials waiting. She will have a studio again one day.

She likes to come down here, open up the odd box, take out an object that she's forgotten about, and subsume herself in the memories attached to it. She likes to go deep into the moment – holding, for example, this set of preliminary drawings she did for an assignment back in second year printmaking class. It's so many years ago, now, but the memory of her days sketching buildings down on the waterfront – before it was all changed – flood back. It's like she's reliving it. Such a rich experience, it is, to be able to recapture sensory detail like that! It makes her life so rich, gives her such a deep appreciation for her landscape.

Or, as now, she opens a box, and out of it come springing a long batik-dyed silk blouse, in almost iridescent teals and cobalt blues and purples; a cotton T-shirt printed with a drawing of a squid; a stack of irregular shaped pieces of velvet that used to be pieces of clothing, in all sorts of shades; a large clump that she has to move other items to lift out – it's a tangled ball of very crumpled vintage linen table napkins. Under that, folded yardage of wool suiting, charcoal-grey, with a pinstripe. What on earth had she planned for that?

She roots down a bit. She has a kind of tactile memory now of some intricately textured lace she'd found on a bargain table outside a fabric shop in the Punjabi Market, further south around Main and 49th. Where is it? She has had an image of it, within the last few days, overlaid on … what? She'll remember when she sees it. Is it in this box? But the fabric near the bottom feels damp, and a sharp mildew odour rises as she disturbs the pieces piled there. She pulls out a length of pearl-grey satin and finds it speckled black with mildew. Oh, damn.

She'll have to wash everything, now, and throw away the damaged bits.

One day soon, she will go through all of the boxes – there are only a dozen or so – and sort things in some way, maybe by colour or texture … she ought to have a set of shelves built, like the ones that knitting shops keep yarn on, so she could see what's there, at a glance, for inspiration. Maybe she could find something like that ready-made, at IKEA? And she also needs some long work tables. And really, some better lighting.

She leaves the box open. She can't get everything back into it. It had been folded and packed away very tightly, probably by Cleo, on one of her rampages.

She climbs back up the stairs to the kitchen, calling the cat to follow.

Dishes everywhere, but she's not going to waste her solo weekend doing dishes.

Mandalay's house is split into two suites, as are many of the houses in her neighbourhood. She has the main floor. The basement had been rented, when the twins were babies, to a single middle-aged woman who worked for some big company – was it a utility or a grocery chain? – Mandalay can't remember. She was a bit gruff, kept to herself. She didn't seem interested in, or even tolerant of the boys. Once, when they were small, she had knocked on the door to complain that the twins cried too much. She had seemed really upset. It's not very nice, the woman had said, to be woken up night after night.

Tell me about it, Mandalay had thought. She didn't have much sympathy. Everyone was a baby at some point. And her babies didn't cry that much. It was just that there were two of them.

The woman had moved out soon after that. Duane brings up the absence of a tenant once in a while, but Mandalay doesn't want someone living downstairs again. She needs the room for storage. The boys play downstairs, too, during the long rainy winters. They need the room. Duane must see that. The main floor alone is too small. The boys have to share a bedroom and there's only one bathroom.

But it's a great house, and around her a neighbourhood has emerged, over the past few years. That is to say, the neighbourhood has been there a long time, but it has gradually taken shape in her consciousness, like a photograph in developing fluid: the long-time residents of the street, the Asian grocery, doctor's and dentist's offices where she takes the boys; the thrift store and hardware store, the pharmacy, the bus stops, the elementary school, the Anglican daycare, and garage and electrical repair shop, as well the little retail shops. It's older, definitely, but it has so much character and ethnic richness. And now the families of the twins' classmates from kindergarten and first grade, who come to her house to play and invite the boys and her over sometimes. Well, some of them. And she has her old friend Belinda who lives nearby, and Belinda's colleagues and students, other artists. Even some of her own classmates. She is lucky. She knows that she is lucky.

It's a great neighbourhood, despite what Duane says. The incidence of crime isn't really that high, not nearly what the media makes it out to be. They're happy here, she and the boys.

▼▼▼

CLIFF HAS STOPPED at the Briteway Café on Hastings for a coffee and sandwich, his usual stop if he has time. He likes it because it is small and inexpensive and not fancy, but homier than Tim Hortons, where most of his crew like to go. The main waitress/cashier/sandwich-maker, Helen, is a woman of maybe his mother's age. She's familiar and not alarming and speaks clear English. The same food is always on the menu: thick-cut, foamy white or half-and-half bread, Schneiders deli meats, French's mustard, iceberg lettuce. Soups made out of potatoes and chunks of beef or chicken, and vegetables whose names he knows how to pronounce. There are five wooden tables and spindle-back chairs, and a checked café curtain that matches the tablecloths. Nobody else he knows goes there, so he doesn't run the risk of having to talk when he doesn't feel like it. The café gives him a quiet space in the day, a way to drop out of his life for just a few minutes.

Especially, his wife, Veronika, and his business partner and brother, Ben, don't come here. Ben never eats at places like this; he only likes Joe Fortes or fancy places like that, where you have to drop forty bucks for lunch. Veronika doesn't eat lunch.

They are the closest people to him in his life: Ben his brother and Veronika. But even so, he needs a little space away from them, once in a while.

His phone buzzes and he sees that in the time it has taken him to leave his parked car, walk to the café, and sit down, he has four new messages. Three are from people he works with and one is from Veronika, but he won't read any of them right now. This is the small part of the day when he doesn't want to look at messages.

There are no messages from Ben. He suspects that Ben is at Whistler, boarding, or maybe even backcountry. He's been trying without luck to get hold of Ben for a couple of days. He wishes Ben would get back to him. There are a few things Ben needs to be on top of, things that could fall apart, that Ben should handle. If he doesn't take care of them, clients will be unhappy and the company will lose money.

Ben knows this. It's not Cliff's job to tell him, to be on his case. But he wishes Ben would answer his messages. He tries to be polite and give him space, but he wishes Ben wouldn't leave these gaps that complicate Cliff's life.

Helen brings him his food then, so he puts away his phone. Coffee in a nice thick white china mug, with a little stainless steel cream pitcher and sugar bowl. Sandwich on a white paper doily, cut in two, each half stuck through with an extra-long toothpick tipped with a coloured cellophane frill, pickle on the side, glass of water.

He opens and pours in the packets of sugar, then the cream. He admires the miniature pitcher and bowl – especially the pitcher. It's a nice shape, simple and elegant. Sometime if he's passing a second-hand store, he'll go in to see if he can find one like it to take home, but he's never seen any quite this shape, with the same proportion of spout and handle and bellied bowl.

Anyway, Veronika would think it too plain, too utilitarian.

He used to come here with Ray, who had been his boss, but then Mrs. Cookshaw, the owner, had died, and had left the company in her will to Cliff. That was a surprise to everyone.

Cliff hadn't known how to run a business. Didn't have a clue. He thought he would learn from Ray, only of course not making the mistakes Ray did, talking big, promising clients things he knew at the time he couldn't deliver on, screaming at the crews. But Ray had quit – hadn't even shown up for work after the news got out. The dispatcher had kept them going and Cliff had to find a bookkeeper and his sister Cleo had said: You should take a small business course; they're at night and almost free. And Cleo's husband Trent had shown him some computer programs. That was for the accounting end.

What he'd needed was a replacement for Mrs. Cookshaw, who was still dealing with the clients and making the weekly schedules and contracts up to when she died, at eighty-seven. She hadn't taught anyone else to do this. She hadn't shown anyone else. Cliff had to figure it out, to look at Mrs. Cookshaw's coloured charts and lined notebook and find a software program that could do it for him. He'd had to become Mrs. Cookshaw.

Nicki who worked with him had helped him. They had decided she would be the manager, take over Ray's job. That was supposed to be temporary, though. Nicki had anxiety: if she had to deal with people and timetables and conflicts, she would lose it. She only wanted to work with the vegetation. Cliff kind of understood that.

Then Cliff's brother Ben had said he would take it on. He could do it. He needed a job; he liked to work outside. He would sign on for the summer, while they were short-handed. So Nicki could go back to mowing and weeding, which she said didn't tax her.

Ray had said, when Cliff went to see him in the hospital: Of all the dumb luck. I guess you're the luckiest son of a bitch in the universe, Cliff. You can land on your head and come up with violets in your teeth.

Which wasn't funny because Cliff had actually landed on his head a few years before that, and fractured his skull. Mrs. Cookshaw had visited him several times and brought him cookies with Smarties in them, which was kind of weird but somehow just what he wanted, and had told Ray he had to keep Cliff's job open for him.

But that could be what Ray meant. Ray was an odd guy.

He hadn't told Ray that it wasn't all violets. The equipment was all falling apart: there were always a couple of vehicles in the shop. There weren't enough crew to do all of the jobs on schedule; they were always behind, but there wasn't any money to hire additional crew or buy new mowers or trucks. Cliff had started looking at second-hand stores and garage sales for used loppers and pruners and even rakes and shovels. Everything they had kept breaking.

But then Ben, or actually Ben's adopted father, had decided that Ben should buy in and become a partner. So everything had changed.

Cliff finishes his sandwich and coffee and slides a toonie under the saucer and stands up to go. He feels the phone buzz in his pocket, but he'll wait to look at it until he's back in the truck. In the Briteway, it's his time.

Out on the sidewalk, he looks at the sky, trying to see if it will rain in the next couple of hours, or not. He had learned from Ray to do that. Look at the sky and make the call: is it worth getting out the mower? That kind of thing. He'd learned most of what he knows about landscaping from Ray. Ray was a good landscape worker. A bad boss, but good with landscaping.

As he's getting into his truck, he sees, in traffic, a vehicle just like his, moving eastward. His vehicle's twin, white, with the same green tree logo and Lund Brothers Landscaping curving around the tree, in a circle. It gives him a thrill to see that. His company's vehicle.

He watches the other truck until it disappears into traffic further down Hastings.

2

Equity

ON SATURDAY AFTERNOON, after her shift at the bakery, Mandalay walks along East 11th to Commercial, turns left at Commercial, then right onto 15th, walking along the park toward Knight. It's one of her favourite walks, if it's not raining, if the twins are cooperative, or if there's enough time on the babysitting meter. She hasn't done it for ages, though – long enough that she notices some changes: houses being renovated, with new roofs and paint and shingles, new front doors of fresh, heavy wood, with more substantial and modern hardware. New fences and hedges and porches, and builders' vans everywhere. On one street, a row of adjacent houses all for sale, by the same agent, and in the next street over, a row of adjacent houses all vanished, and a construction site.

Is the neighbourhood getting gentrified? But that's not a bad thing, is it? The price of her house might go up, and maybe Duane won't keep talking about her moving.

She's passing, now, a new block of townhouses with lots of cedar beams and huge windows and coloured tile and concrete facades. They're quite attractive, Mandalay thinks: Not ostentatious or monolithic at all. But they look expensive. What will that mean?

On the main thoroughfare, the dry cleaner's and the little diner and the independent travel agent's shops boarded up. She hadn't noticed from the bus, and she usually walks the side streets. There's a new high-rise office block and chain stores going in; in fact, there's a giant billboard announcing this, with an architect's rendering. It's kind of attractive, actually. But it's so much change. And what does it mean for the neighbourhood, those little independent businesses being shut down?

Not that she had ever patronized most of them, she has to admit. But they must be an important piece of the neighbourhood.

She passes the old theatre, the marquee gone, the doors boarded and graffiti-splattered.

Suddenly her house with its back porch and wide baseboards and coved ceilings, even its drafty windows, its buttercup-choked lawn, feels threatened. A vague panic lifts suddenly in her chest, spreads and coalesces. It's a sort of anticipatory nostalgia; she's felt it before, this swelling ache for what has not yet, but will soon change and pass. The familiar shell of the house she has lived in the last seven years, the bonds with her sons, the complete lack of distance or barrier between her sons and herself, the balanced triangle that is her life. All seems, or shows itself, as ephemeral, as vulnerable.

Around her, the soft living air, the cool blue light. The sun is setting over the rise of Cambie Street to the west, illuminating the laurel and the catalpa trees along the streets; the panes of windows and automobiles reflect spangles of pale citron. The sea, which is not visible from this neighbourhood, sends up swathes of blue mist in the morning; the horse chestnuts and maples, giants of trees that have fed on gentle winters and ample rainwater, arch over even the shabbiest street, tint all green. The ornamental cherry trees are in blossom, clouds of pink festooning the streets. Camelia, forsythia, tulips in neighbourhood gardens: the early blooming of the West Coast spring.

Her lungs fill with the good soft air. Her hip and knee joints move freely. Her arms and shoulders relax, let go of the motions of gathering, carrying. Her hands surrender the memory of grasping and pressing and spreading. Her spine re-aligns as a confident supportive column. She can always find the best of herself, walking the tree-sheltered streets of this neighbourhood.

THE BOYS RETURN, as always, Sunday evening.

Owen climbs the front entrance stairs with an exaggerated rolling gait and Aidan says: We went on a sailboat.

Her heart nearly stops. (Sudden squalls; being run down by large boats; hitting the rocks.) She's learned not to ask what they're doing beforehand. So far, rock-climbing at a gym (Owen had pinched a finger badly in a clamp of some sort), kayaking lessons (both boys had been soaked, but that seemed part of the deal), tennis lessons (Owen had sprained his thumb), trips to Science World (Aidan had been lost for fifteen minutes).

She swallows and breathes. Did you like it? What did you like best about sailing? (Whose sailboat? Had Duane taken them out on his own? Had they worn life jackets, at least?)

It's not that she doesn't trust Duane with their safety. Her fears are totally irrational; she knows that. But they clutch at her, gibbering possibilities of maiming, even death. They are so persuasive, so convincing. It is difficult to quiet the insistence of her instincts.

She had not let them go off with Duane, without her, until they were four. She would not have got away with delaying it that long except that Duane had said that he didn't want to do outings with them until they were toilet trained.

It was awesome, dude! Owen says, suddenly lit up, careening around the room with his arms in a triangle over his head.

But Aidan comes over and leans against her. I was frightened, he says. She hears that he still doesn't nail his Rs; he has an accent. Also, Aidan says, I was kind of nauseated.

Nauseated! Owen shouts, gleefully. He mimes retching.

Did you help sail the boat? she asks, fishing.

Yes! Owen screams. Watch the boom! Man overboard!

Aidan says: No; Dad and his friends did all of it.

Yeah? Which friends? But suddenly both boys are wigged out, hollering and running and throwing punches, apparently deaf to her voice.

She's also anxious now about how Duane might be influencing the boys – let's face it, he's more materialistic than she can approve of. He lacks, she thinks, a social conscience. He has a sort of ruthlessness. Basically, he's a bully. It's all going to be pretty corrupting. A sense of imposition, of something bordering on violation, washes over her.

Why had she agreed to the visits? The arrangement hadn't been what she wanted. She'd been unfairly manipulated, in some way. Why had she let him into the boys' lives? She can't see it's really going to do them any good, having a relationship with Duane. Already she can feel them growing unwholesome new aspects of their characters.

She'd been weak. Well, not weak, really – broke. Out of options. She must not beat herself up anymore about it. She'd made the best decision she could, at the time, probably. Her options had been to take Duane's high-handed offer, which had seemed only generous at the time, or move in with her mom, Crystal, and live in the back of beyond. She'd made the best decision she could, at the time.

The boys ricochet around the house, yelling, slamming each other with pillows. Pretty soon they'll start banging into things, hurting themselves, crying.

So much negative energy! This is the kind of influence Duane has on them.

Then the phone: Duane calling her from his car, though he has just dropped the boys off.

I want to talk to you during the week, Duane says. I have a proposition.

Well. She'll have a proposition for him, too. Once-a-month visits.

An opportunity has come up, he says. I think the boys will love it.

She waits.

I'll call you again, he says.

She puts the boys in the bathtub, though they seem clean, though they complain they showered that morning, at their dad's. She pours in a capful of lavender oil, lights candles, turns out the bathroom light. She puts on a CD of monks chanting, but Aidan says it gives him a headache, so she turns it off, puts on an old Miles Davis CD, turned low. Turns her own agitation down, lets her own negativity slip away, froth on a stream.

The bathroom is dim and steamy. She can ride her breath for five, six counts before she's distracted. Aidan calms down first, slides down under the water so that only his flushed cheekbones and forehead, his nose and lips and closed eyelids emerge. Owen splashes around a while longer. Shh, shh, she says, and then all is quiet.

Finally, Aidan stands up in the tub and silently holds out his arms, and she wraps a towel around him and lifts him up, straight out of the tub and onto the mat, and while he turns himself slowly, ritually, she dries the little wings of his shoulder blades, the small ridges of his ribs and vertebrae, his flat belly, his orchid-like, drooping scrotum and penis, his bony knees and sharp shins. She holds his pajama pants open while he steps into them, resting his hand on her shoulders as he lifts one foot, then the other.

Then Owen, who sags against her dramatically, as she begins to rub him down, who says, I could fall asleep right here, and lays his head on her back.

In her own bed, later, she thinks, They're mine. I made them. She knows that they are not hers: your children are not your possessions. But she cannot deny that fierce sweetness, that one-ness with them.

She can barely remember, now, their younger selves. How small they were at birth, five pounds each, barely. She can scarcely remember their wrinkled necks, their stubby grasping hands, the rolled-up sleeves and dangling empty feet of their sleepers.

The twins had gone nearly full-term. Nice healthy babies, the midwife had said. But Mandalay's feet, in the last weeks, had swollen into oblong blocks that she could barely squeeze into extra-wide Birks. After that, she'd completely lost control of her life. She'd barely been able to get out of bed. She'd been overwhelmed, coming home with two newborns, a great incision across her belly, no core muscles to speak of. She'd had no idea. She'd imagined herself having long periods of leisure while the twins slept, time to do yoga, read. Had pictured herself getting really fit pushing the double jogging stroller along the park trails. Her biggest worry had been how she'd deal with the boredom during the six months of EI benefits she was eligible for. Nothing had prepared her for the chronic and progressive sleep deprivation, the forty minutes of breast-feeding out of every two hours, the mounds of soiled diapers and cloths, the inability to do things like have a shower, get groceries, cook a meal. On top of that she was experiencing waves of depression.

Her sister Cleo had come by every day for the first couple of weeks, had thrown the high-smelling cloth diapers in the trash, brought in cartons of disposables. Had brought groceries, made meals, cleaned up, done laundry, held whichever twin was crying at any given time, so that Mandalay could have a shower or eat a bowl of soup. But Cleo lived an hour out, in Coquitlam, and had her job and two small children.

Cleo had arranged for their mother, Crystal, to come and stay for a week, but that had been a disaster. Crystal had wanted only to watch TV. She'd been afraid to take a taxi to the grocery store, unable to figure out the washing machine or to put together an edible meal.

Then Cleo had sent over their brother Cliff, and that had been a little – a lot – more useful.

She'd only survived because Cliff had been recovering from an accident and had moved in with her for a few months.

When the boys were two months old, Duane had showed up. Cleo had talked to him, she knew. Duane had asked to see Mandalay, not the twins, his sons, and that had undermined her resolve to stay independent. She'd said he could. She'd asked Cleo to come by, so as not to be alone.

Duane had made a point of not even looking at the cribs, which were visible through the open bedroom door of her small apartment. That should have told her. He'd sat on her sofa and chatted like they were old neighbours or something. Then both the babies had started to whimper, and she'd gone to feed Owen – it was his turn at the trough – and Cleo had scooped up Aidan, and when Mandalay had come back into the living room holding Owen, Duane had been in possession of Aidan – holding him along the flat of his forearm, Aidan's head cupped in his hand. Duane had been completely expressionless, his gaze completely focussed on Aidan's face. She remembers that, and the way something inside her had clenched.

She'd looked around helplessly for Cleo, but Cleo had disappeared, in the bathroom, maybe, and she'd felt weak in the knees, had sat down, unable to say anything. It had felt that she was balanced on the edge of something momentous and precarious, but she had no idea what it was that lay ahead of her. A one-thousand-foot cliff, maybe. There was a decision to make, an action to take or avoid, but she was completely blind to either her choices or their consequences.

She hadn't been able to speak, overwhelmed by her emotions.

And Duane hadn't said anything either – given her nothing to go on.

Then Cleo had returned, they'd switched babies around, and Duane had ended up with Owen, who had gazed at him in apparent fear, then begun to cry. Duane hadn't been fazed – he'd simply turned Owen over onto his stomach, neatly tucked Owen's legs under him, the way Owen liked, and put his hand firmly on Owen's back.

She can't remember now how long he'd stayed – not very long, she thinks. Only those few minutes she'd thought, he wants us. He wants this.

What had she imagined might happen? What had she expected Duane would do?

Then the phone call, from Duane's lawyer, and the offer: bi-weekly access and shared holidays in return for monthly support. A sum that was not enough to actually live on, but too large to turn down.

She hadn't been able to imagine the twins, at two months and basically mainlining her milk, ever spending a weekend away from her, at Duane's house. It hadn't been something she wanted: it had seemed highly theoretical. On the other hand, going back to work full-time in a few months, having the babies in daycare for eight hours a day, had seemed all too imaginable – and terrifying.

Cleo had stepped in again – suggested that she counter-offer with a request that Duane buy her an apartment instead of giving her a monthly allowance. And he had bought a house, and given her half the title. In this way she had acquired a business partner, and the boys had acquired a dad who took them sailing on alternate weekends.

And they had acquired their names. At that point, she had been so sleep-deprived and disoriented, she hadn't been able to come up with any. She'd actually missed the deadline for registering the births, though, as she had said to Cleo, What were they going to do – repossess? She'd had silly, affectionate names for them that she had used to try to express the slightly different personalities that they had. Owl and Rabbit. She'd considered having those names registered, but everyone had said it was a bad idea. Cleo had called them Thing One and Thing Two, after Dr. Seuss. Cliff had claimed not to be able to tell them apart, though they were not identical.

Duane had suggested their first names. Cleo had approved of them: they matched tidily, both being two-syllable and Celtic. And Mandalay herself had really loved them. They were right; they were just what she was looking for. Similar, but different, holding a balance of soft and harder sounds. Not too ordinary, but containing some history. They were euphonious, their associations both strong and gentle.

Only months later – when it was too late, when they had already been using them and had officially registered them – had Mandalay actually *heard* the names in her mind as meanings. *Aidan and Owen.* Aiding and owing. And there was never any question which one of these states Duane felt a more proprietary interest in, and which he relegated to her.

She has already lost those newborns, the babies and toddlers that had superseded them. They will change, inevitably: one day they will be men, separate, independent. But for now, they are still hers.

▼▼▼

CLEO'S JUST INSIDE THE DOOR, divesting herself of raincoat and boots, and Trent's already at the top of the stairs addressing her: Have you called the school yet?

She is bent over, unzipping one of her boots, and can't see his expression, but his voice sounds hectoring. She steps down from the stacked heel of her boot, her left leg suddenly three inches shorter than her right, so she's hobbled, and bends again to unzip the right boot.

No, she says, very patiently. I've been at work all day.

You said you'd take care of it, Trent says.

I'll do it tomorrow, she says, straightening. Her lower back sends a message of discomfort – well, pain, really – as she adjusts to her new posture, but she disregards it, breathes through it, once, twice. She exerts herself to keep her voice light, even. It's just over eleven hours since she left the house, and she hasn't really stopped moving all day.

You need to follow up on that call, Trent persists. I just want to know that you're going to do it.

Breathe, breathe. She stands in the entryway, at the bottom of the stairs, the effort of climbing up and entering the rest of the house seeming all at once more than she can take on. Trent is standing at the top of the stairs, feet apart, hands on his hips, barring the light from the kitchen behind him.

I haven't had time, she says. I was going full-on all day.

The euphoria of her day's work is diminishing, tiredness seeping into its place. But she's home now, and she has tomorrow to take care of personal chores. It's just about meeting with Sam's teacher, anyway. She starts up the stairs.

You could have found five minutes to make a phone call.

Breathe. Ground. This is just Trent being a bit obsessive, the way he can be. She can do this.

Should we talk about our system? she asks. Weren't we going to leave messages on the answering machine for me to listen to, or write them down and leave them on my desk?

He actually doesn't move as she gets to the top stair.

You said you'd take care of it. His voice aggrieved, now – accusatory.

Look, she says. I take care of this stuff all the time. Now she has to literally push by him to move up to the last step. She feels her hip bone knock his thigh.

Oh, for goodness sake.

Can she smell food? She had been hungry, a couple of hours ago, but has now passed through hunger into that other place, that high octane place, where she doesn't seem to need food. She thinks she can smell pork fat, fried potatoes. It is not appealing.

Suddenly, the house is unfamiliar, its layout and smells strange, not welcoming, not hers.

What the fuck, she thinks at Trent. What the fuck? Do you actually do any fucking work around here at all? But she doesn't say it.

She heads into the main floor powder room, shuts and locks the door. Sits on the toilet seat, counts to ten. This is untenable, she hears a voice say inside her head.

It's okay, another voice answers. It is a calm voice, a reasonable voice, one that might be addressing a child or colleague who is upset.

She is so good at this technique.

It's okay. It's just Trent having a bit of anxiety.

After a moment or two she hears Trent move away, muttering, then hears him treading heavily up the stairs from the main floor. She waits another moment, flushes, washes her hands thoroughly and deliberately.

She heads for the kitchen but Olivia calls down the stairs to her, and she knows to take the opportunity to talk. You always have to be available to teens or they'll shut down, and then you'll lose them.

Olivia needs forms signed, a cheque, a pair of gym shorts. Cleo sits on Olivia's unmade bed, doesn't mention the bed or the piles of dirty – and clean, unworn – clothing on the floor, though that requires an effort. She's sure she sees several things she washed on the weekend, some still with their folds, mixed in with the inside-out and rumpled jeans and hoodies. She sits, because she knows that it's good just to sit sometimes and be available.

What are you working on in French right now? she asks. It should be safe. Olivia likes French class, is good at it, likes her teacher.

It is a good call. Olivia lights up, shows her a comic strip she's making about a family of mice. It's beautifully drawn, the French captions neatly, and as far as she can tell, grammatically printed. There's a bit of whimsy, there, a bit of tender humour in the story of the mice. The little girl mouse is having a tantrum because she has asked for a blue birthday candle, and her father has brought her a red one. Olivia has drawn the sweet funny mice, the birthday-cake candles that the mice hold up like torches. She's talented, Cleo thinks. The father makes a perilous second trip to find the blue candle, and encounters many dangers. In the meantime, the little girl mouse and her mother make a cake and pick some flowers, oblivious or just protected. In the end the father mouse returns safely, and all three dance.

It looks very good, she says. It's delightful. She reads it over again. You are so creative and funny, Cleo says. Tears come to her eyes. That Olivia is this beautiful, original young woman – that she is a whole person, that she has grown out of that infant Cleo produced! And in such a short time.

All of those hours she'd spent with Olivia, when she was small – reading to her, doing craft projects, teaching her to draw. Even after Cleo had gone back to work part-time, she'd still made sure she put in the hours at home, with the kids.

Olivia sighs.

Is everything alright? Cleo asks. She knows she's not supposed to phrase it that way; she's supposed to make open-ended questions, but she can't get her mind around one right now.

Everything's fine, Mom, Olivia says. I need to finish my homework now.

She should check on Sam, before she goes back downstairs. Sam's not in his bedroom. She really wants to change into more comfortable clothes, but she should check in with Sam first. And also she needs to let Trent decompress for a few more minutes. That's the routine. And it works!

Sam's in the basement rec room, which they still haven't finished renovating. She needs to call the drywall guy again about the ceiling, which now has a magical porthole into a space of joists and plumbing and wiring since their old dishwasher sprang a leak six months ago. Sam's playing on the game console that's hooked up to the television. When he sees her, he calls Mom! and pauses the game, drops the controller. He flings his arms around her. He's sticky, greasy, and she's suddenly conscious of her dry-clean-only shirt, but she makes herself not flinch, holds him snugly. His head up to her collarbone. He's warm against her, his arms wrapping her waist. The familiar smell of his head, his still-fine hair. She feels her heartbeat soften and some pressure ease off over her entire body.

Have you eaten? she asks. What did you have for supper? She nuzzles him, feels her blood pressure drop, releases him back to his game.

WHEN SHE GOES BACK UPSTAIRS, she's hungry — desperately hungry, now, as if she's been possessed by an emaciated bear. Trent's supposed to make dinner on her late nights, but sometimes what he feeds himself and the kids.... She finds the end of someone's dinner — one cold wiener and a half-eaten one, and some French fries — on a plate in the fridge, puts the plate in the microwave, pours ketchup over the food and eats it standing up. Disgust rises in her briefly, but hunger beats the disgust down.

When she's finished, she rinses the plate and silverware and pops them into the dishwasher, and then opens the fridge again, driven now by some compulsion that isn't connected to logic or reason anymore, just blindly searching. *What.* The contents of the crisper — green, cold, raw — repulse her. Bottles of condiments. Processed cheese slices in the fridge door. She peels off three, rips one after the other from their wrappings, rolls them into cylinders, and pops them into her mouth. Chew, chew, gone. The plastic texture, the quick hit of fat and salt and umami. *What else?* A box of crayon-orange fish-shaped crackers on the pantry shelf, likely opened a year ago. A handful into her mouth. Salt, again; the quick pasty dissolve of starch. *What else?*

But finally something in her says enough. A glass of water, then. The heavy food in her belly like cement. Beginnings of heartburn. A burp. But also, finally, the warmth and comfort of her blood sugar rising.

She runs again up the stairs to Sam's room, to read to him, as she always does, for half an hour before his bedtime.

MOST NIGHTS NOW she sits up late reading articles in industry journals and trade magazines, addenda to code books. She reads articles online on parenting and on childhood behavioural issues: on autism, obsessive-compulsive disorder and attention deficit hyperactive disorder. She reads recipes and looks at online clothing catalogues. She looks at real estate in neighbourhoods closer to the city (and more expensive) than hers. She looks through home decorating magazines: she has several subscriptions.

She does not read novels anymore. She used to love reading literary fiction, especially, but now she doesn't have the time; they take too long to get where they're going, maybe. Or she needs to learn more practical things. Fiction never seems to be about anyone with a life like hers, and she is not interested in escape.

Long after Trent has fallen asleep, she puts away her magazines and laptop, changes, in the bathroom, into her pajamas. She removes her makeup, and examines her facial features, her skin, in the mirror. She's tired, but not at all sleepy.

She climbs into the king-sized bed, keeping her distance. It's a good bed. It cost as much as her first car. It doesn't matter how Trent flails and flings himself around in whatever violent accounting dreams he's having, her side of the bed doesn't move. She doesn't feel it at all.

▼▼▼

VERONIKA IS WATCHING TV when Cliff gets home, but she gets up right away to warm up his meal. She leaves the TV on. He picks up the remote, asks if he can lower the volume.

But I'm following the show, Veronika says.

I can't hear you talk, though, he says. He understands why she likes to have the TV on when she's alone at home, but he doesn't understand why she likes it so loud, and why she has to have it on when they're eating or talking.

He stands at the counter of the open kitchen, watching her, and when she turns around and sees him, she puts down the dish she's holding and runs over to embrace him. You smell delicious, he says. He thinks: New perfume. Her perfumes are subtle and he can't name what they smell like, but this one is new.

In his arms, she's warm, soft, her flesh comfortable, comforting. He holds onto her longer than she holds onto him, but this is his favourite part of the day. When she lets go, she gives herself a little shake and goes back to her cooking; he sits at the small high dining table, which is made of wood finished in a colour called "Espresso," matched with high upholstered chairs, and watches her.

Her hair, which falls in blonde spirals down her back, bounces a little as she moves. He could watch her all day. She thinks she is fat, but he could look at her rounded chin, her rounded breasts and bottom, all day.

Sometimes he is struck with such surprise that he lives in this pleasant townhouse with its glossy dark furniture and white cabinets, its velvety carpeting, its plush sofa set. He feels such surprise and pleasure that he's almost dizzy.

Veronika puts a placemat on front of him. She's fond of things like placemats and coasters, and what he thinks must be called doilies, things that are layered on furniture, to protect it. She likes to go shopping, and to buy things for the house. She buys a lot of them. Things for the bedroom, things for the dog, useful or not really useful things. She likes cut glass and gilt edges, metallic embroidery. Picture frames with insets of fake tortoise shell or that shell-like material called mother-of-pearl. Furniture upholstered in flowery patterns, and side tables with inlays of brassy metal and marble. She has filled the house with these things.

The things she buys are not expensive: he sees that. Except perhaps for the sofa set and tables. He can see that what Cleo calls her *taste* is not really expensive. He has seen expensive things – in Ben's house, and especially through the windows of some of the houses where he has landscaping contracts. He has seen a different kind of expensive, anyway. Maybe it's quieter. But he likes the way Veronika has built up the layers of comfort in their condo. Everything is soft or shiny, reflecting light. Everything says: This is our house and it exists for our comfort and pleasure.

He thinks maybe she shops too much. He can't imagine that there is anything else that they need for their house, and then she brings home more. It will be better though, when she gets a job. She hasn't wanted to get a job, because her English isn't good enough yet, she says. She doesn't want to work at the kind of job where it wouldn't matter. She did not move here from Estonia, she says, to work in a tool factory or a chicken-plucking factory. Fair enough. She is going to school; she is learning English. That is her job now.

Even watching TV, that is helping her learn English.

It will be good when they have kids, too. He can imagine her pushing a nice stroller with a toddler in it, the toddler with a fuzzy hat and pink cheeks from the damp wind that they get around here. Then him coming home and playing with the child the way he had played with his sister's kids when they were small. He thinks that they should have a baby soon, because Veronika is already thirty-seven, and he will be thirty-six this year. He thinks that it would be a good time to have a baby now, while Veronika is at home a lot anyway, learning English. But she says she wants to have a steady job first; she wants to have a way of supporting herself. He can understand that.

She puts his plate and utensils and mats for the hot containers on the high table, taking several trips. She could do it all in one trip, or he could do it himself, but he can see that she takes pleasure from opening the drawers in the kitchen cabinets and in the sideboard, taking out one thing from the neat stack of things, and carrying it to the table.

He can smell the food, now, heating in the oven. He salivates. It had taken him a little while to get used to Veronika's cooking. There were a lot of onions in it, and doughy things, and meat. It had taken him a while to get used to how it sat in his stomach, but he did not want to complain about food someone else had cooked for him. And now he finds it tasty. He thinks about it during the day, how rich and satisfying his dinner will be.

How was your day, love? he asks. What did you do today? Did you go to your class?

She turns toward him a pouty face. I did not feel like it today. I did not have done my homeworks. I went to the mall instead.

He likes it that she is honest: that she tells him what she feels, and he never has to try to guess or wonder if she is telling him the truth. He is lucky with that, he knows. He tries to be honest too, but he doesn't always know what he is feeling.

He feels lucky, though, about Veronika. He knows he is lucky.

Of course, he had been really stupid. Everybody had explained that to him, after. How it worked. That they weren't really beautiful Russian girls online looking for Canadian husbands. Those pictures, those introductions – those weren't even the girls you would be connected to. They weren't maybe even real girls. Just made-up stories, fake photographs. It was about immigration; they just wanted sponsors. Or worse, it was about prostitution. People said different things to him, but they all showed him how stupid he had been. He would only lose his money. How much did you pay? they asked him. What did you tell them about yourself? What did you promise? Until he saw, yes, that he had done something really, really dumb. Until he had dreaded the future, instead of looking forward to it, thinking happily each morning about the life he was going to have with this girl, when she arrived in Canada.

He had not wanted to answer the first email from Veronika, with its bad English, or to look at the photo attachments, which had seemed real enough. The girl in amateurish, real-looking shots with the captions "With Cousin" and "With Nieces" and "At Little Lake" *did* seem to be the same person as the girl in the studio photograph he had originally seen, but he had become ashamed of his fantasies, of how many times a day he had looked at the posed (and airbrushed, as everyone had pointed out to him) photograph, the young woman with the dimples and blonde curls and huge, long-lashed eyes.

He had been too ashamed of himself to write back, but then she'd written again: *I am feeling angry because you treat me like I'm not important. How can you do that? You must be a very hard and brutal man. Yet I will tell you, also hardly, that I will shine if you give me love, and you will not be sorry to help me. But you must be kind enough to answer.*

She had shamed him, when she called him a *hard and brutal man*. He had never been hard or brutal to anyone. He didn't want to be. It was his main goal in life, to avoid being that kind of person. So it was an unpleasant feeling to have her accuse him of that. It had made him feel anxious, as if there were bad things he had done that he wasn't aware of, as if people knew something about him that he didn't know himself.

It had taken him a long time to work that out, how he felt. At first, he had just been shocked and angry, and had deleted her email and looked up how to block her (he couldn't figure that out) and had decided to call it a lesson learned, as his foster mother, Mrs. Giesbrecht, would always tell him to do when things went wrong for him. And then it had come to him, one evening, while he was trying to figure out the crew's schedule for the next week. He could see, suddenly, that she must be very frightened at what she was going to find. She would be alone in a strange country, far from home, with no money, contracted to a stranger. She had to be very brave.

He had seen too that she would not have said she was angry, and about him ignoring her (he had already paid for her flight and paperwork), if it was all just a scam. He admired, then — as he did now, three years later — her frankness, her boldness. Her ability to say what was bothering her, to just let it all out.

Did you find the homework hard? he asks. I could help you with it, if you like.

She is having a hard time learning English. Well, he can't imagine how hard it must be. He has tried to learn a few words of Estonian, and of Russian, which, Veronika says, all Estonians speak. He gets a phrase down but then an hour later he can't remember it.

Veronika also speaks Finnish, which is related to Estonian, and Latvian. He'd had to look up where Estonia and Latvia were.

It is hard, she says. I have to write something for my class. About a holiday that is important to your family.

Oh, yeah, Cliff says. That would be hard.

Veronika hasn't told him everything about her life before she came here, he knows. Just a few things. Her father drank and didn't support them. Her mother worked several jobs and Veronika had to quit school and take care of her younger sister, who drifted into bad habits and who has pretty well disappeared. Veronika had cried when she told him that. Well, her eyes had been wet. She doesn't really cry.

So family holidays, that might be a hard subject for her. And it's not like he has been able to give her a real family life here. He can tell that she had hoped, maybe, for more closeness with his siblings. But they don't even do holidays together, much. He had explained that Ben had his own adoptive parents, and Cleo was always working, and Mandalay didn't drive, didn't have a car, didn't know how to cook normal food. But he thinks she is disappointed.

You could write about birthdays, he says.

That's not a family holiday.

Well, they are, kind of. Because of our traditions. In Canada.

Or, he says, make it up. Make up a story.

Yeah, okay, she says. Anyway the problem is mostly that is boring. You know? I have to write about boring thing because my English is so bad still. But I don't give a shit about those thing.

He has seen in a magazine or an ad where someone says: After all these years, I love that she can still surprise me. But that is not true for him. He feels like the ground is falling away from under his feet, usually, when Veronika surprises him.

Well, he says.

Never mind, she says. I will go tomorrow. I will write the essays. I will write about how dry and boring is turkey. Turkey, blah blah blah.

That should be good, he says.

She takes the casserole dish out of the oven and puts it on the cork circle on the table. Takes off the lid.

Oh, man, the smell. Oh, man. He is so hungry.

Veronika puts food on his plate. It smells so good. It looks so good. He is so lucky.

In the evening Cliff takes Veronika's little dog out for a walk, beyond the globe cedars in the pea-gravel beds that constitute the condo complex's landscaping, and up the boulevard to the forest park where real cedars, twice as big around as a man's arm span, form an otherworld of exposed roots and shadowed archways. Buster, the dog, is so tiny that walking to the end of the boulevard is a good outing for him, but Cliff likes to go further, and carries him when they enter the canopied trails with their writhing tree roots. Buster's short legs can't manage the distance or the unevenness of the path, and in this borderland between suburb and forest, coyote or even cougar sightings are not uncommon.

It's drizzling a little this evening, but not under the dark dense canopy. It is chilly, though: Buster shivers, and Cliff zips him inside his jacket. The air is different here – not only cooler, but thicker, stiller. In spots where some light penetrates, he sees the white berries of waxberry. They seem to glow faintly with their own illumination.

That would be the thing, he thinks. All of the new places they're landscaping, the owners want in-ground lighting, solar lamps hidden in pavers, and stepping stones and ponds. Even in bushes. Sometimes little copper lanterns hung on tree limbs. It all has to be invisibly wired and solar-powered. When it works, it's dramatic or magical, though he worries about the night creatures that like the dark – things that do better in the dark, growing or looking for food or mates, or places to sleep or hide.

But in here, in this shadowy vaulted space, the white berries seem to make their own light. What if they really could? Could a person cross a shrub with something that glowed? Something bio-luminescent? He remembers from nature shows that there are deep sea creatures, jellyfish for example, that can produce light, chemically. Could it be done with genetic engineering? He bets it could – the genes that make bioluminescence – or is it bacteria? – could be spliced into something like yucca. Holy Moses, that would be some-thing. Imagine a sloping curve of lawn in the shadow of something tall and dark – yew, maybe – and then cold white candles of yucca. That would be something.

He doesn't stay out long. It's late and he's been up since before five. And Veronika doesn't like it if he stays out too long, though she doesn't like to come with him. She says walking is for the poor and the very old. She had enough walking to do as a child in Estonia.

The walks calm him.

At the end of the path under the dark bulky cedars he turns and begins to walk back. He can feel Buster against his shirt, snuffling a little. He had bought Buster for Veronika, as a tiny pup, to give her some company while he is working, but he wonders how much company Buster is. He's kind of feeble, Buster is. He doesn't do much: he eats and cries and wants to be picked up. But he sees by the way that Veronika talks to him that Buster is a person, to Veronika.

He'd had a cat, once: Sophie. She'd been like a person to him. He had understood her, and she seemed to understand him. He still thinks about Sophie, often. He'd lived with her a long time, longer than he has lived with Veronika, if he thinks about it. Sometimes he misses Sophie; he feels a little sadness for her. For his cat. He would never tell anyone that. He'd had to find a new home for her, when Veronika had come to live with him. Veronika did not like cats.

He turns into the driveway, now, between the sign that says Hillcrest Estates and the flower bed where the rhododendrons are already fattening at their tips, already swelling with the longer days and sunshine. He would have done something different with that flower bed. He had wanted to get the contract for his complex, but he had been underbid by a bigger local company.

He likes coming back to the complex, after dark has fallen, seeing the warm light in the windows of his condo. His own windows, the warmth and light inside. That's something.

Veronika asks him if he wants to watch his favourite program on Oasis, the nature channel. He's too tired tonight. Thanks, though, sweetie, he says. Okay; she will PVR it for him. Thank you, he says.

In bed they nuzzle and clamber and hit the sweet point together, which is good. Veronika spoons him until he's almost asleep, then slips out. She sleeps in late and so she'll get up and watch TV late into the night, the sound lowered, but he's happy just to fall asleep. He's so tired. He's happy to feel the leaf patterns over him, forming themselves into worlds he can't decipher, to feel the moss-covered logs of fallen cedars open, to step inside and to fall, fall, weightless, blind and deaf, into the dark calm earth.

3

Offer

DRIVING EAST OUT OF THE CITY, into the suburbs, Cleo sees the moon rise directly ahead of her, huge, yellow, stippled with shadow. The sky, this late afternoon, is a muddy, muted indigo: washed denim at the horizon, deepening overhead. Nice complementary colour effect, she notes. What word for the moon? *Pumpkin* – one of those new pale ones she had seen last fall, carved out with templates, on sophisticated porches. *Lantern* – a rice-paper globe with a candle, set aloft. *Dirigible*. She and her son Sam had looked that word up a couple of weekends ago; she's always trying to make his video games into more value-added learning experiences.

For a moment, as the highway angles upward more steeply, the moon expands even more, becomes what it is, a huge mottled gouda-hued satellite, frighteningly close to the earth. Hurtling toward earth? Cleo briefly imagines the cataclysm, the oblivion. But it is an optical illusion. Like a harvest moon, but it's only March. She's read that the effect is caused by dust in the air. The dust is from the excavation of hundreds of new building sites along the valley, not from summer-baked soil and chaff. It has been an unusually dry winter, with an unprecedented amount of new construction.

The highway dips, and the moon shrinks back a little, into an ordinary full moon. Under the moon, she notices, a star is hanging, like a pendant in a woman's décolletage. No, not a star; a planet. Is it Mars or Venus? She can't remember which. Mars for war and Venus for love. Lucky in war; unlucky in love. Where is that from? The star or planet does not twinkle, but is large and lustrous, a deep transparent amber. It's a gemstone, she thinks, a big yellow sapphire, suspended under the moon. It looks so close tonight that she might reach out and lift it off its invisible chain. Whatever it's hanging from.

Imagine a pendant like that, a big pale stone – opal maybe – set in gold, with the darker yellow gem suspended below it. Would it be a topaz? Maybe a citrine? What is a citrine? She doesn't know, but it sounds yellow. A yellow sapphire? It would be a signature piece; it would dress up a turtleneck or a blazer. It would look smart. She has never owned any real jewellery, or been that interested in it. Her wedding and engagement rings are small dim bands, non-committal. She wears a cheap functional watch.

Yes, a pendant, a heavy gold pendant. She can almost feel the weight of it against her breastbone, a lovely yellow fire in a heavy gold bezel. How it would glow against her skin.

She could buy something like that. Have it custom-made, even. She'd want a good big clear stone, handsomely set. But she can afford it. She's going to be making a lot of money, now. Well, not a lot compared to some people, but more than she had ever thought she would.

She could spend some on herself. She works very hard.

It would be nice to have a tangible reward, something beautiful that she had chosen for herself.

Her boss, Kate, would know what sort of stones. And where to get something like that custom-made.

She takes the highway exit for her suburb, and now the moon is behind her, reflected in her rear-view mirror. It's such a long commute.

An hour in busy times, two hours if she tries to do it in rush hour. Half an hour, if she waits. She's found it efficient to do this, to arrange her work schedule – luckily she is only fifty percent, and has some flex time – to arrange her working day so that she comes in very early or at mid-morning, leaves at three or at seven. Though will she be able to continue this if.... Well, she'll have to make sure it's part of the negotiations.

Also, she uses that evening time to do errands, which is also efficient of her. It's amazing how much you can get done with good time management, careful planning.

A feeling of warmth, of pleasure rises up behind her breastbone.

Her boss, Kate, calling her into her office this afternoon. Or rather, sending her an email inviting her to drop by at 2:15. Cleo had been raising her hand to knock at ten seconds to the hour, not that knocking was necessary; all of the office walls were glass, completely transparent, though Kate's could be shuttered at the touch of a button. Everyone's eyes on her then as she'd walked there from her own desk. Everyone knowing it was a summons, likely, by the promptness of her response.

Kate had leaned back from her and smiled, and she had seen that the smile was on the sunny side of conspiratorial, so it was going to be okay. Not that it wasn't, almost always, especially these days. Cleo is one of the few who have been with the company for more than five years, now, which is surprising, because she had been so junior, so marginal, so expendable, to start with.

She'd been called into Kate's office quite a bit, her first year. She'd seen the darker conspiratorial smile, the one that said, you and I both know you've fucked up, and here are your options, and my options. Of course, she'd thought about quitting, but the job had worked well for her. She was actually quite good at the drafting, even though it was boring, sometimes. She had a degree in engineering, so drafting didn't use the extent of her skills, didn't challenge her, but she was good at it. The flex time had worked; she had two children, and didn't see the point, honestly, of having kids and leaving them in daycare ten hours a day. And the office had what was generally called a relaxed, creative ethos, though what that meant, really, was that the designers wore Lululemon and went for three-hour bike rides on sunny afternoons.

THE OTHER THING ABOUT working here is that the shop is entirely women. Kate was committed to that model. She had gone to all-girls private schools, and said that women did better work without guys around. It's also managed, theoretically, at least, on a collaborative model. Everybody gets input on decisions. There are votes. There are dividends.

Cleo's husband, Trent, who's an accountant, had said that companies that have a collaborative model always fail. They spend all of their time having meetings and power struggles, and make bad decisions that are compromises, that try to please too many people, or they can't agree, and always default to the status quo.

It's true that they have a lot of meetings. Cleo, as a part-timer, can opt not to attend most of them, though that means she doesn't get to vote, doesn't get a say. But she'd figured out soon enough that they aren't really a cooperative. Kate, the principal, makes the major decisions. She's just very good at making it look like everyone's ideas have been considered. It was Kate who had decided to move into the new premises in downtown Vancouver, though that meant a long commute for most of them, who couldn't afford to live in the city. It was Kate who decided to exchange their local furniture and cabinetry suppliers for a Danish company that did mass production of cheap (but sustainable, Kate said) laminated wood product. It is Kate who makes the hiring decisions.

Cleo doesn't really mind. Cleo had been trained in a male-dominated, hierarchical industry, as an engineer. She doesn't mind being at the bottom. She doesn't see that the creatives, the designers who work under Kate, and who complain about her high-handedness, would make better decisions than Kate does. She has not hung out in the washroom exchanging bitter wisecracks when Kate made her pronouncements, over the years. She's seen where that went. Nope; Cleo knows which side her bread is buttered on.

And Cleo has been retained and given a schedule that works for her, while some of the more talented, glamorous, and ambitious people have been let go. This has been surprising not only to some of the women above her, but also to Cleo herself, because she had been so junior, so marginal, so expendable, to start with.

She thinks that her best asset is that she doesn't underestimate her own expendability.

And then Kate's unexpected summons of her today.

Cleo had brushed her hair and teeth, put on fresh lip gloss, checked her black jeans and sweater for lint before going. In her office, Kate with her straight chin-length bob, her makeup-less face, the distressed jeans and T-shirt that proclaimed her privilege. The new handbag, very smooth leather in a shade of green Cleo had not seen in stores yet, on the shelf that had been built for the sole purpose of holding Kate's handbag.

Cleo had admired the bag. It had taken her a few years to learn the proper way to admire Kate's bags, but she's got it now, she thinks. A slight widening of the eyes to indicate that she's impressed, even slightly envious. Then a tilt of the head as if to check the label. Which used to be Gucci or Coach or something recognizable from magazine ads, but lately has become some obscure Scandinavian or Germanic word, with an umlaut, stamped on some industrial-looking aluminum label. Then listening to Kate's story about the bag's provenance, and the finale: Cleo's "May I?" either verbalized or indicated with another head inclination, a lift of her eyebrows, and the slight caress, as of the cheek of a new baby, and the exhalation.

She had admired the new green bag properly, not without a real tinge of envy that she hadn't suppressed, only muted slightly, and then sat back, but upright, in her chair to wait for Kate's news.

The scuttlebutt had been that there would be a merger, which worried a lot of people, but nothing official had been said, and so Cleo had to go into the meeting pretending ignorance, but ready to catch on to Kate's hints, if it seemed that's what Kate wanted.

That sunnily conspiratorial smile. Cleo had waited.

How are things? Kate had asked.

Because she has been working here for over seven years, Cleo knew the correct answer is not a rummage through her personal life, a report on her kids' achievements, but a smartly positive soundbite.

Fantastic, Cleo had said. The new software is starting to show it has legs.

Kate had narrowed her eyes at Cleo. Starting?

Cleo had to tread carefully. There had been some major, major problems with it, at first. It was not a software program that she would have chosen. It was particularly hard to navigate between apps that were frequently used together – about seven windows had to be opened to get from framing to HVAC, for example – and it didn't communicate well with their old software, so she and the other techs have had to upload hundreds of files manually. Cleo had done much of this on her own time, and she'd had to persuade Kate to buy her a third monitor. But the software purchase had been Kate's decision.

On the other hand, Kate isn't stupid. She had certainly heard the complaints. And if Cleo were too positive, and it turned out the software was a complete dud, and Kate decided to toss it, Cleo must not have seemed to have been a fan of it.

Oh, adaptive bugs, Cleo had said. There were always adaptive bugs. But in the long run.... She had made a little gesture with her hands. She wasn't sure that her gesture had conveyed anything. Maybe it had looked too indeterminate? Cleo hasn't been good with body language.

But Kate had smiled.

Cleo, Cleo, she had said. You've certainly come a long way, since you started working here!

That was as much a criticism as a compliment, but Cleo had smiled back. A small smile.

You've probably heard that we're going to be making some changes, Kate had said.

Cleo had inclined her jaw slightly. In the past, she would have given a little shrug, but she had learned – the hard way – that Kate hated shrugging, that she read it as apathy.

In fact, it's very exciting, Kate had said. Completely confidential, still, of course! But we're going to be expanding.

Yes, a merger, then. Or acquisition?

We'll be getting some new clients, Kate had said. And some new colleagues.

Cleo's heart had lurched down her thoracic region. She could see, suddenly, where this might be going. There were certain disadvantages to being a technician in a drafting pool, and to having an engineering, rather than a design school background. Cleo had never felt that she had quite fit in. And although Kate had been a benefactor, a benevolent dictator, if the company were to acquire partners.... Well. It would be hard for Cleo to find an employer that suited her quite as well.

But she had maintained her small smile, and nodded.

It'll mean some reorganization, Kate had said. But that's a good opportunity to revisit our vision of ourselves, and our structures.

It's never good to be too entrenched. Stasis is especially unhealthy in a creative industry.

Cleo had nodded again.

Kate had paused. She had gazed at Cleo. Cleo had tried not to look like a deer in headlights, a rat in front of a boa constrictor. Breathe, breathe.

Kate had looked quite serious.

YOUR CONTRIBUTIONS haven't been unnoticed, she had said. She had leaned back in her chair, smiling. You are really productive, Cleo. Your billing hours are outstanding, and you're becoming more and more the person that the designers go to with their more difficult projects. I'm thinking that there is going to be a more significant role for you in the new structure.

Of course, Kate had said, we'll require a lot more of your time. You'll have to think about that, Cleo. But Sam and Olivia are, what? Ten and thirteen? And Trent is still an associate, not a partner? So you should have some flexibility there.

Of course, you don't have to make a decision now, Kate had said. Talk it over with whoever you need to. Maintaining confidentiality, of course! But I hope you'll consider it.

Thank you! Cleo had managed to say, finally. Thank you for considering me!

It was a big compliment. And a reprieve. That's all that she could think of, for a moment. A reprieve. She had not realized until that moment how much she did not want to go looking for another job.

But it was a big deal to have this affirmation of her achievements, too. She had worked for Kate for nearly eight years – since Sam was a toddler. She had worked part-time, in the drafting pool, not doing terribly interesting things, to be honest, but interesting enough. Drafting building designs – she was good at it; she might even be very good.

Her role was to draft up plans for Kate and her designers, and not only to draft but to redraft them, to present them for review and make corrections, over and over, and also to catch possible flaws, but not criticize them or correct them on her own — just to make them magically apparent to the designers — and then to magically fix them. To interpret the designers' dreams, to make concrete their intentions, to erase their mistakes, while being invisible herself.

She was very good at that.

And she has been very productive — she could see that she gets through a lot more work in a week than any of the other technicians. Everyone knew it. You're a machine, Cleo, the others often said.

NOW, DRIVING HOME, she feels that glow still, but her head is clearing.

Does she want this? She hadn't really thought about working full-time — and full-time in this industry means seventy- or eighty-hour weeks, at times. She's used to having the flex time, the extra hours in the week, to go to the gym, to take the kids to their appointments, to do all of the errands and shopping that make a household really run smoothly. She likes having a home in which there are always clean, folded clothes in the drawers, appealing, nutritious meals on the table at the same time every day, bills and permission forms dealt with promptly, tidy rooms and matching towels and library books and healthy houseplants. It's important. It's stable and calm, which is important for the kids, and it's decent and — well, just proper. It's civilized. And it makes her feel happy, to live in a clean, functional, aesthetically appealing space.

And it takes a lot of work.

But the salary increase. That could do a lot. That could improve things. It's not that they don't have enough to live on, but more money could mean having some of the extras. They've never gone on a big trip. She's always wanted to go to Hawaii or Mexico for Christmas, and they never have gone. Trent says it's too expensive, and she can see it is really expensive, thousands of dollars. And they really need a new kitchen. She has done a lot of redecorating of their house. She's repainted and fixed up the bathrooms, but there are still those eighties kitchen cabinets, melamine with the oak strip at the top. They could have a new kitchen. Even a bigger, more functional kitchen.

She's going to need a new vehicle soon, too.

She has forgotten to ask how much more she would make. Or what her position would be. Trent's going to be impatient with her for not having asked.

She'll just say Kate didn't tell her.

What's the catch, though? And why her? Have Pam or Lindsay or Nancy, the other technicians, been approached? She hasn't noticed them being brought in to Kate's office – but it could have happened when Cleo wasn't around. One of them would likely have said something, though. They all watched her go to her meeting with Kate. She had not noticed any knowing looks. None of them had said anything.

She'll really have to think about it, though. Not make a decision too hastily.

She doesn't even know what she'd be doing. Though she can guess, maybe, if she thinks about it. Not creative. They're not going to move her up to creative. Likely, she'll be given some sort of senior technician position. There hasn't been one, but if the pool increases....

Of course, if they are acquiring or merging with another design company, there is going to be another pool of technicians. And usually, a larger company needs fewer technicians, proportionally. She's noticed that.

So if she doesn't take this, will she be kept on?

All speculation, she reminds herself. (But why hadn't she thought to ask more questions? Stupid, stupid.)

So, she'll just tell Trent that it was very vague, that there weren't specifics. And the possibility of a salary increase, if nothing else, will impress Trent.

A bigger salary could be the answer to quite a few of their problems.

She turns from the arterial thoroughfare onto her own street, and now the moon and its pendant swing before her once more, lustrous, resplendent, just out of reach.

She's going to want a substantial chain.

▼▼▼

DUANE SAYS: It's not like you work, it's not like you'd even have to commute. And the malls there have everything you'd want. Whole Foods. Montessori. You'd be in a new place, with more energy-efficient heating and appliances.

Mandalay can hear that he's on the car phone, the Bluetooth or whatever it's called. She can hear the traffic, the muffling of his words at times.

She says: I work. I have a job. And I don't want to live out there. In Tsawwassen or Delta.

You have a part-time job in a bakery. You could do that anywhere. Surrey, then. Or Ladner. Maybe Richmond, if you want, though there you're getting more expensive.

I don't want to live so far out.

Far out from what? Why do you want to be in the city?

I like it here.

You're just used to it. You could be in a modern place. Cleaner, too. It would be good for the boys' asthma; you're always complaining about that. Also, you could get them into a better school.

Their school is fine. They're in a good school.

Trust-fund hippies and multigenerational welfare families. That's who lives here. That's who the boys are going to school with.

She wants to say that it isn't true; that this area of the city is being bought up by professionals with young families, but she doesn't want to appear to buy into his class hierarchies. The argument is devolving into an old one: Duane has long wanted the twins to be at a private school. She has long refused, on the basis that she doesn't want the boys to grow up with the kinds of kids who go to private school. She realizes her argument isn't really logical, but she knows what she means. It's a deep, intuitive thing. Duane gets speechless with anger about it. Your idiosyncrasies are going to impact them for their whole lives, Duane says. Do you realize that? Your selfish and outdated and baseless prejudices are going to hold the boys back. Why not give them the best of everything?

She knows what she feels. She knows, deep within, even if she can't articulate it, what is best for her children, the children of her body.

You don't even know any of the people whose kids are in private school, Duane says now, picking up the threads of that old discussion. They're people who want really good quality for their kids. They're not evil because they have good incomes. They're people with passion, creative people. People who have good incomes because they work hard and they're good at what they do. They're the people who support the arts and environmental issues, NGO work – all that shit you say you value.

I don't want my children bullied by over-privileged kids.

You have outmoded and inaccurate ideas. So, it's okay if they're bullied by underprivileged ones?

They've been through the pattern of this argument so many times. And Duane doesn't fight fair. She refuses to answer. She won't perpetuate it. She says, instead: There's a feeling, when you live downtown. There's an energy. You choose to live downtown, too.

I live in False Creek. You choose to live in a disadvantaged neighbourhood.

There's more going on. It's culturally rich.

And if by that you mean ethnic gang crime, I'll give you that.

She thinks now that the gang crime is actually happening in the suburbs — isn't it? — she does hear the news, sometimes, sees headlines on the front pages of newspapers as she goes by. But she must not let herself be drawn into his sort of argument. She can't win.

She says: More ethnic mix. More individuality, variety, authenticity.

You can't be authentic in a new townhouse in a decent neighbourhood?

I like where I am, she says. The boys are happy. We're fine.

But you aren't, he says. You've just called me to ask me for more help.

Damn him; he just twists whatever she says to his own advantage.

I asked you if I could have a little more space, she says. For myself and the boys. That's not really asking for help.

Mandalay. We have an agreement. We have a legal agreement. You have part of the house to live in, and the rental space is supposed to be income for me.

The rental didn't really work out. How can she explain it to him? How can she get across the indignity of the situation? The woman in the rental suite drove her crazy. She could feel the tension coming through the walls sometimes. And they really do need more space. The boys need a playroom. And she wants them to start using the downstairs bathroom more. She never gets to have a bath without one of the boys coming in to pee.

She says: Duane. I've really thought long and hard about this. We absolutely need the space. The boys are getting bigger. You have as much space as we do, and you're on your own.

There's a moment of silence, and she thinks she's lost connection, but then he speaks again. Mandalay. We have a legal agreement. If you want more money....

It's not about money, she says. It's just about more space. About the quality of our lives.

How do you not see it is about money? he says then, and his voice is a nasty sneer.

Okay, maybe it does come down to money. But Duane has lots. He makes lots. And spends lots. And she is very frugal. She just wishes he wouldn't use sarcasm. It's the harshest, most disrespectful form of communication. It just puts up walls between them.

I'm ending this call now, he says. I have a meeting.

She gets no help from him at all. It's incredible.

DUANE LINGERS after dropping the boys off one Sunday, and then says: You remember Maxwell Gibbons is a client of mine?

The billionaire ex-hockey player.

That's the one. He's invited us to go to his place in the Caymans. He has twins, too, about the same age as Aidan and Owen. They have started a dolphin and sea turtle reserve, and there's a lagoon where his kids have been snorkelling since they were toddlers, he says. Coral reef. He has invited us to fly down with him early next month.

Just for the weekend? Mandalay asks, stupidly.

No. For ten days.

But school isn't out yet.

They're in second grade, Mandalay, Duane says. They can miss ten days of school. They have passports, right?

Of course they don't have passports. Why would they? She can't afford to take them on trips. It's not like they go to Disneyland every year or something.

Duane says he'll get them their passports, get them expedited. He'll need a permission letter from her. He'll need the boys' birth certificates.

Will you be able to get flights, this short notice? she asks. A straw.

Duane laughs. Private jet, Mandalay.

She does not want this, but she cannot say no. There is no way to turn down something like this, an experience like this, for the boys. Richness of experience: that is what it is. She knows that they will love it.

Maybe she could go along?

Sorry, Duane says. They're full. The plane is full.

Breathe, breathe. (She wouldn't want to spend ten days with Duane and his friends anyway, would she? Even in the Cayman Islands?)

She says: Have you told them?

No, he says. Thought I had better check with you first.

Thanks, she says.

So they wouldn't have their hopes crushed, he says.

Actually, she says, it's a very bad idea. They're much too young. I don't want you to take them. There: she couldn't have been more clear. She pulls herself up, turns, strides toward the house.

This isn't over, Mandalay, he calls to her back.

▼▼▼

THE HOMEOWNER IS on the site today. Cliff can see the black British-made car, its beefy shape, parked in the half-paved driveway. And there is the gentleman himself, short, bulky, with thinning, almost shaved black hair. Mr. K. He's wearing a black raincoat that shines a little, and a smallish young woman, also wearing a black raincoat, is standing behind him, holding a large black umbrella over him. The new asphalt is wet and gleams. They are very still, waiting, not for him. Their faces pale against the black. The young woman changes the umbrella to her other hand, bringing her arm up so that she hardly wobbles it. Her arms must be tired, with that angle.

The contractor and the landscape architect are not here yet, then. He is supposed to meet with them. Should he get out of his truck, or not? He had been so careful to be prompt. He doesn't deal with the homeowner, has nothing to say to him. But it is awkward, maybe impolite, to stay in his truck. Get out and look awkward because he isn't the one who deals with the owner, or stay in his truck and maybe look rude? The kind of slippery situation he most fears. The squeeze in his veins.

Behind the owner is the house, which Demyan, the landscape architect, says is still unfinished, inside. What would it be like? The exterior is all slabs of cantilevered concrete and steel and cedar and some shiny translucent material Cliff can't identify — coloured glass, maybe, a sort of aqua shade. Walls that do not seem attached to other walls; thick steel cables. The one room he can see into is like a glass box, with twenty-foot walls, a poured concrete floor. It's like a room in a museum.

How could anyone live here? And yet it cost several million dollars, Demyan has told him.

And here is Demyan driving up, now, and behind him the contractor, and even the architect, who does not drive, getting out of Demyan's suv. A big meeting, then. Will they all go inside? It is still raining. He will get to see the inside.

But no, it seems not. Cliff gets out of his truck now but the others have parked their vehicles closer to the house, and are already huddled. The contractor is putting up another umbrella, and Demyan is underneath it, and the architect has ducked under the owner's umbrella. They are all wearing black raincoats. Something about the angles of their bodies, the inclination of head and shoulders toward each other reminds Cliff of a TV program about primates, maybe a group of male chimps, not the playful ones but the serious, even murderous ones who raid other troops and eat their babies. Something in the shiny wet black backs, the slightly hunched shoulders. He shivers, walking up to the group. He has only a utility waterproof, the kind with orange visibility stripes. He has left his good leather jacket in his truck. He pulls his hood up.

The landscaping is a complex 3-D puzzle of gabion walls, drainage tiles, waterfalls and pools, and tiny pocket lawns; repositioned, hollowed-out boulders; transplanted full-sized ornamental trees. Nearly a thousand tons of earth and indigenous trees have been removed from the site, and a stream rerouted. Cliff is just glad he's not Demyan. Demyan says it's a nightmare of a site.

Cliff is responsible only for the organics. That doesn't mean the same thing as organic food. It means the vegetation. He's supposed to plant the right things, the things the architect and Demyan have agreed on, and then to make sure they grow.

The landscape architect makes room for him in the huddle, so he figures he's off the hook, today. Nothing going wrong with the project, or not meeting the owner's expectations, today, or Demyan would just be shouting at him over the phone. He can go about his other business, which is to check that a delivery of plants has arrived and that they are correct – that the shipment actually contains the ones ordered, which happens less often than you'd think – and then check out some holes that were supposed to have been dug yesterday for an order of trees scheduled to arrive soon. He likely just needs to say hi, today – show his face, make the team look bigger, like when he used to be pulled into games in high school, made to put on the uniform just to sit on the bench.

But he's wrong, he soon sees. There is a problem. Is it a big one? The men's faces all look a little bit jokey, their eyes wide. Not a small problem, though, or they wouldn't all be here. *He* might be here, looking for his delivery, and Demyan would be yelling at him on the cell phone. But the rest of them, no. Especially not the owner.

And if the owner weren't here, they could go inside the house, maybe. It's like they're all standing under a waterfall. Of course everyone else is under an umbrella. He's only half-under, so the rain from the contractor's umbrella sluices onto his hood.

So you're saying there's some subsidence? the architect asks.

No, the contractor says. Not yet. There's a little slippage below. To the west.

But is it potentially an instrument? I mean, we don't have the data to show that it's even constituent.

Demyan says, I tell you, the fuckin' slope is sliding down. There's water underneath. That wasn't in the geologist's report.

Are we discussing a surge? the architect says.

Cliff notices that the young woman holding the umbrella leans forward, after everyone speaks, and murmurs to the owner. Is she translating? He can't remember if he has heard the owner in conversation. Or maybe she's the wife – or daughter – giving her opinion? But that doesn't fit with the umbrella. The owner's face doesn't change expression and he doesn't speak.

What it is, is that the three of them – the architect, the contractor, and Demyan – are all trying to talk about a problem without admitting it's *their* problem. Cliff feels a thread of anxiety then: will they make it his problem? That happens, sometimes.

But no: he is not going to be blamed. He is going to be the solution. Demyan claps him on the shoulder: Cliff, here, is going to put in more plantings, get the root systems re-established.

The root systems. Those would be long gone, would have been taken out with the eighty-foot cedars, the tangle of arbutus that had been removed from the gully to clear the sightlines from the house. To give it an ocean view. He'd told Demyan, at the time – the first time he'd seen the site, the raw bleeding roots of the bulldozed trees.

What my man Cliff doesn't know about plantings, Demyan says, would fit into a rat's arsehole.

So it will be mediated, the architect says.

Absolutely, Demyan says. He has steel rims around the edges of his gums, when he grins, Cliff notes. Are they part of his teeth, or what?

CLIFF CLIMBS DOWN THE SLOPE, sliding in the mud even in his workboots, to where the new trees will be put in. They're going to have a crane for this, which he hasn't booked yet, not being sure of when the trees will arrive. The problem of timing of crane and trees puts a knot in his gut.

The holes have been dug – by hand, by a couple of his employees; they couldn't get the equipment down here in the ravine – and are full of muddy water. He picks up a lopped branch, tests the depth. They'll do, if the walls don't collapse under the rain.

But the slope is in bad shape. There is a lot of slippage. The trees and bushes have been torn out by the roots. It's a disaster scene, mud everywhere, not good mud but clay, the topsoil already washed down the bank. Broken cedar and arbutus roots, the two colours of red, emerging from the soil like wires, or veins. The ground littered with broken twigs and bark and leaves. He doesn't know for sure, but he's guessing it took a few hundred years for those trees to grow in this gully, and likely they grew up among other trees, among fallen trees, and shrubs like salal and salmonberry, devil's club, that held the soil in place, that kept things stable while the young trees got a foothold.

All wrecked now. The owner and the architect had decided to take out the natural vegetation, to groom the slope into something else. The landscape architect had said: They want a fucking Italian grotto. Everything had to go; everything had to be reshaped.

It's just a mess now. He doubts it will work. Not his mess, though. Not his circus; not his monkeys. He has that on a T-shirt. He's just in charge of planting the new stuff the architect has ordered. He can do that.

Climbing back up the slippery, deforested slope, he sees a possible route, a better route. He swings out over to the east, where the gradient is a bit less steep, and there is a natural spill of gravel to give him traction. Yes, the climbing is easier, this way. When he reaches the house site, though, he's blocked by one of the new dressed-limestone retaining walls, six feet high. He should have remembered – he's seen the plans, enough times – but his company doesn't build the walls. They're contracted out to stonemasons. The limestone is smooth-faced and unscalable. It's like the wall of a castle.

Behind the wall, the house rises above him. From this angle it looks like something from a sci-fi movie, all sheer blank surfaces, walls and overhangs. Inhuman, impenetrable. Like the Death Star or something. Houses shouldn't look like that, like fortresses built by giant implacable aliens.

He can't see Demyan or the architect or the builder. Where have they gone? He will have to tell them that the topsoil is gone, because they'll have to bring some more in, for the groundcover to take root. Nothing can grow in that clay. Not anything domesticated, anyway. He'll have to have a conversation about the topsoil, and he and Demyan will have to calculate how many yards they'll need to bring in.

He can't see how to get up. He can't see up to the driveway level, where the others are.

The homeowner appears in a doorway above him, in a lower floor of the house, but still far above him. Cliff wants to call up to ask if he has a rope, but it wouldn't do him much good anyway. He'll have to backtrack, go up the hard way. He waves, and the owner stares down at him, does not wave back.

When he gets to the driveway level again, his pants are covered with the clay mud, and it has got inside his boots as well. He looks for a tarp to spread on the seat of his vehicle. He can hose off when he gets back to the yard, the space where they park the company vehicles and store the equipment. There's a pressure washer there. Nowhere to clean himself off, here.

Demyan looms up to him, says: Know anything about *Medusa finisteri?*

Cliff does not.

Temperate rainforest shrub, apparently, Demyan says. Grows just below the snow line in the Himalayas, or some place like that. Stuff will grow ten centimetres a day, right conditions. A small twig of it will take root in any substrate with a moisture content over ten percent. Owner's going to bring some in.

Something Cliff has seen on a nature program tugs at him. Invasive species? But they must know what is permissible. Okay, he says.

Get it in the ground, Demyan says. It'll take care of this subsidence shit for you.

4

Market

CLEO ARRANGES on the cute Scandinavian-design trays that she has acquired just for events like this the tiny savoury pastries: the mushroom and the cheese, the crab, and the spinach. They look too factory-made, too store-bought, which they are, but she knows a trick or two, gleaned from magazines: some finely chopped parsley sprinkled dashingly here, a few beads of coral-coloured salmon roe there. Very pretty. Is it good enough?

Last month Mira had hosted, and she had served hand-made cheese and spinach phyllo pastries, and a kind of caramelized onion tart on square, matte black plates decorated with squiggles of intense, colourful sauces: pea-green, red, yellow-orange. Also there were some pale green tendrils, pea shoots, and Greek yogurt piped into rosettes – Cleo hadn't even known that yogurt could be piped – and the time before that, at Michelle's, those shooters of jellied gin and vermouth with tiny pimento fish, cut with a miniature fish-shaped candy tool, suspended in the jelly.

She runs the vacuum over the living room rug and the sectional, dusts, quickly wipes down the powder room and entry, though they look pristine – the every-two-weeks cleaning lady has just been. The guest bathroom worries her. A few years ago, she had updated it, taking apart the orangey 90s-vintage oak cabinets and applying several coats of white enamel paint, adding new handles and door pulls, installing marbled ceramic tile on the floor, new taps and light fixtures, and disguising the dusty pink countertop with a faux-granite finishing kit. It had turned out really well, and had cost only a few hundred dollars, plus her labour. But now she can see that it's not really cutting edge anymore. And maybe it looks a little too DIY?

She could get a new mirror – that would make it look more fashionable, maybe. And new towels. That grey is a little bit two years ago.

Or have the whole thing redone. She could do that, now.

She puts on her new sueded cotton jeans from Aritzia, pigeon-breast grey, and a lighter dove-coloured turtleneck. Silver earrings – fat little hoops – and hair pulled into a ponytail, half-chignon style. The paler ends of her hair stick out at the sides like the crests of some exotic crane, or an ikebana arrangement. Lipstick? Yes, but pale. Her toenail polish is chipped, and there's no time to apply new, so on with socks – the grey pair with a goldfish pattern.

Perfect.

(Good enough?)

How nice everything is; how nice Cleo's house is looking.

Sam comes to find her. Trent and the children have been banished, forbidden the living room, for the evening, the children for obvious reasons: Trent because he tends to want to socialize and subvert the discussion. It looks nice, Mom, Sam says. Do you think your friends are going to be impressed?

It's not about impressing people, she says severely. But Sam has noticed the details: the new velvet pillows that she has artfully tossed on the sofa, the tall vase of purple tulips, the trays of hors d'oeuvres.

He can have two pastries: broken ones that she handled a bit carelessly. And then he has to go upstairs, though he whines a little that he hasn't seen her all day.

And here come the guests, one or two at a time. All of Cleo's friends now are women she met through her children — almost all from Olivia's kindergarten year, who have stayed in the neighbourhood, who have got together for play dates and yoga classes and book club for all of these years. And it is just her good luck, just her crazy luck, that she has found herself accepted, included in this group. She would never have believed that she would be one day part of a group like this. She had met these women, dropping off and picking up their kids from kindergarten, and had thought, I'd like to be in that group — and now she was.

Luck, as well as the fact that she lives in a somewhat, though not extraordinarily, affluent neighbourhood, of course. All of her friends are educated, functional women. They've all got at least some post-secondary — most of them have a degree. They all have partners with jobs. They all stayed home, or worked part-time at most, when their children were small. They're all intelligent, socially adept women with decent conversational topics and pleasant demeanors and good parenting skills and the ability to put on makeup and drink only two glasses of wine and discuss a book.

Which they do, for a little while. There isn't a lot to talk about in this book, Cleo thinks, which is a fictionalized biography of an American political wife that's been on the best-seller lists. She'd gone along with it because she wanted support for her suggestion for the next book, *Lean In*, which her boss, Kate, had asked her to read.

They've all read the book. It's an obvious book club choice, with a "Questions for Discussion" section in the back. They're all diligent about reading the books. They're all good at having a lively, though respectful, discussion.

Cleo passes around the trays, pours the wine. She looks at the group, her friends, sitting on her newish living room suite, their elegance, their kind manners. It's lovely.

Here is Cleo's best friend, Lacey, who is a clinical psychologist, and always so insightful and detached about everything. And then Mira, Cleo's other closest friend, the first friend she made in the neighbourhood. Jennifer, who teaches middle-school half-time. Lisa, also a schoolteacher, but in the earlier grades. Then Stephanie, who Cleo met through Mira, and who teaches sociology at the college. And Michelle, who is glamorous, always perfectly made up and coiffed (is that a word people still use?) and stylishly, expensively dressed. Michelle, who doesn't work, who used to be a dental hygienist, but married her boss.

Cleo's best friends, her gang.

She could almost have scripted the book discussion; she knows them that well. But that's comfortable, too. Jennifer thinks the book is a great portrayal of the family, and the pressures of being in the political arena. Jennifer loves the part about the family cottage compound, and all of the brothers.

Lisa wonders if that part is realistic. Would a really rich political family like that have such rustic cabins? Only one toilet, and that not really functioning? Cleo has spent enough summers with Trent's family at *their* lake compound in Ontario to know that it could. Lisa says she'd felt that she'd have liked to have been part of a big family like that, when she read the book. She loves the parts about the family get-togethers and the interactions between the sisters-in-law.

Stephanie says that she thinks it's a good portrait of the patriarchal structure of the Republicans, but she wanted a sharper commentary on the protagonist's passivity, her silent assent to her husband's and his family's politics.

Lacey says she thinks it's a good portrait of the tensions of trying to reconcile political stance with other values. This statement leads them all to a little open discussion. How did Alice leave behind her younger idealism? Was she just trying to find the middle path between extremes? Does she find it? "I live a life in opposition to itself,"

Lacey reads from her copy of the novel, which is bookmarked with little coloured paper flags.

I think it needed to be much more indicting, Stephanie says.

But the final act of rebellion, Mira says. That is brave. Alice has so much to lose, at that point.

Cleo says that she had difficulty accepting that Alice would choose Charlie Blackwell. Alice had nothing in common with him. It's easy to see that she has this idealistic affection for her teenaged boyfriend whom she accidentally kills, and an intellectual connection with the other guy, but Charlie is such a lightweight. It seemed a little improbable, she says.

There's a moment's pause, and then Jennifer says, in her blunt way: It was sex! Cleo feels herself blushing. Stephanie says: Yes, he is portrayed as sexually confident. I wonder if the author is asking us to re-examine that traditional coupling of….

Michelle says: I wonder if it's going to be made into a movie? Wouldn't Winona Ryder be perfect as Alice?

And it's time for more wine, and more of the little parsley and chive enhanced pastries.

Then the conversation shifts.

Jennifer asks: What is everyone doing about grad dresses?

Michelle says: Oh, we bought Micki's when we were in Seattle, in August.

And Jennifer says: Oh, Vancouver for us. We decided not to go to the States as we wanted to make sure that we were on the registry.

Michelle says, then: Oh, no fear that anyone at the school will have the same dress as Micki. It's by an Italian designer, and they aren't in Canada.

Are we talking about prom dresses for our *grade eights?* Stephanie asks. Stephanie's a little bit hippie – not wholly so, but she home-schooled her adopted daughter, Ocean, until Ocean was eleven.

I know, Jennifer says. It's crazy, isn't it? And we should also talk about getting together to book the limo.

This is ridiculous. Doesn't anyone else think it's ridiculous? Cleo wonders.

Oh, the girls all expect it, Lacey says. They see shows on TV, you know. American reality shows.

I don't watch TV, Stephanie says. And I don't let Ocean watch those reality shows.

Prom dresses and limos for thirteen-year-olds! It's insane. Stephanie is right. But Cleo doesn't want to say anything.

Lisa says: They don't have to be that expensive, do they?

Oh, not at all, Michelle says. We got Micki's on sale for only three-fifty. American, of course.

Lisa's eyes widen.

Jennifer says: I told Maddy her limit was three hundred. And she can borrow my silver Manuelos — our feet are the same size.

Lisa's face has gone pink. Stephanie's silence is becoming eloquent. She's emitting some kind of energy, like an inaudible bat squeak.

Jennifer says, Oh, you know what, Lisa? Maddy actually has two dresses, because her Granny bought her one online, and then we found out it (a) doesn't quite fit, and (b) can't be returned. So Amy can have it, if it's a problem scraping together the cash.

Lisa becomes even pinker. Is she going to have an asthma attack? Cleo glances around for Lisa's purse, which everyone knows, contains her inhalers and EpiPens. No thank you, Lisa says, very coldly. I doubt very much it would fit Amy.

Now Jennifer looks away, but Cleo has seen the shine of moisture in her eyes. Jennifer is surprisingly thin-skinned, given her brashness.

Oh, god. Don't let Jennifer offer Olivia the extra dress. Olivia, too, is much slimmer than Maddy. And for certain she will want to choose her own.

We ought to organize a swap, Mira says, agreeably. (Mira, the first of her friends, whom Cleo had met so many years ago, when she had registered Olivia for kindergarten. Calm, grounded, peaceful, wise Mira.) I hoped Mariah would wear the family prom dress, the one I bought for Zoe, but Mariah's half a foot taller than Zoe was at her age.

That would be great, Stephanie says. Ocean loves hand-me-downs. This Cleo doubts very much.

We should book the post-dance restaurant, as well, Michelle says. I think Micki wants to go to Vij's.

Cleo tries to catch Lacey's eye, but Lacey is looking at her phone. *Vij's?* Come on. Cleo has only been once. It's posh, the food super-nuanced, way too expensive and fancy for thirteen and fourteen-year-olds. Someone needs to say something.

I think we should band together and buck the trend, Stephanie adds. Why don't we all just say no? We could plan an alternative celebration – a family picnic in the park. Hey! We could even organize a volunteer event, doing something for the community event. We could do a trash pickup in Ord Park.

Blank faces all around. Only Lisa says, gently, I *like* your idea, Steph. But Ord Park, I don't know....

I'm not taking my kids to pick up condoms and syringes in Ord Park, Jennifer says. And really, I don't have the energy to fight this battle.

Cleo judges it's time to refill everyone's wine glasses again.

Lacey hasn't been taking part, but instead sitting back with a polite, listening smile on her face. Now she gracefully rescues the conversation.

How is Maddy? That was an incredible goal, Saturday!

Jennifer relaxes, then. Maybe she could come over and see the dress, Jennifer says to Stephanie. It's quite a pretty dress. Though I really need to get Mum to rehab over the online shopping, you know?

I can't believe Maddy helped her get a PayPal account. Or yes, I can. Because who benefits?

Stephanie has relaxed too. Even Lisa is smiling.

WE DON'T KNOW HOW to have a discussion, Cleo says later, to Lacey. We're too polite. So Canadian.

Lacey has stayed a little after the others, to help tidy up. That's the stereotype, Lacey says. But I think it's about protecting harmony. And for what reason?

What does Lacey mean?

It's kind of cult-like around here, sometimes, Lacey says. Don't you think?

Cult of what?

I don't know, Lacey says. Suburban virginity. Something like that.

She's lucky to have her friendship with Lacey, who is so intelligent, so detached. So wicked, sometimes.

Even though it's still confidential, because Lacey is her best friend, Cleo says: We're having a merger. I'm getting a promotion. Full time. Team leader, or something like that.

Whoa, Lacey says. We are going to have to celebrate! Can we find an evening to do that?

That's a sobering thought. Will she have time, anymore, for book clubs, for the Sunday afternoon walks or glasses of wine with Lacey, for any social life at all? Will she have time to pay attention to what her kids are learning and doing, or see that the house is run properly?

Let's do it right now, Lacey says. Let's have another glass of wine. We're way too sober. Haven't Trent and the kids gone to bed?

And that seems like a very good idea, though Cleo has intended to get up very early the next morning and peruse some electrical code books for work. Because Lacey is her best friend, her closest friend. And they hardly ever get to see each other anymore.

▼▼▼

MANDALAY REMEMBERS THAT Cleo had said once, I don't know how you can do it; it's so painfully slow and *small*. My mind just goes numb; it's like I've been turned to stone or something.

But that was just the point. It is a small, safe, predictable place, with a slow pace, calming routines. That was the point.

It's really relaxing, Mandalay had said to Cleo. It's like being in a garden. Or a greenhouse.

Well, obviously, Cleo had said. It's in the language. *Nursery school. Kindergarten.* But it's not really meant for adults, is it? You have to find it kind of boring.

Mandalay doesn't, really. Her brain doesn't go numb. It goes vegetative, maybe, which is a different thing. She gets calmer; she gets creative ideas.

It's like a flotation tank.

Cleo had laughed. Except for the noise. Opposite, I would say.

It is true that the breaks, the lunchtimes, are loud. Cacophonous. But Mandalay can pick out the individual currents – the familiar voices among the dozens in the room, or hundreds on the playground, now that the boys are in second grade, and this is their third year in the school.

The second-graders in Mrs. Chau's class are all lined up down the middle of the rows of desks, ready for departure. Mandalay had worried, desks in rows, already, in second grade? But the children moved around a lot to the back of the classroom, where there were beanbag chairs, and to the front, to use the board. They have on their jackets, their outdoor shoes, their backpacks. They are chattering a little, and presently Mrs. Chau will flip the light switch off briefly and back on, to get their attention, and will lead them out of the classroom, out of the school, to the waiting school bus. There is still some darting, as well as chattering. Erin has forgotten to keep on her outdoor shoes, and has to go to her cubby and retrieve them, and change. Esha has opened her backpack up to find something, and forgotten to rezip it, and its contents are rolling away on the floor as she tries to pick them up. Lunch and pencil only, Esha, Mrs. Chau says.

There is, actually, a lot going on in this room. The walls are covered to the ceiling with posters and charts and the children's art; there are low, brightly coloured shelving units full of books and tubs of items – blocks and art supplies and globes and collecting jars – all around the room's perimeter, and flip chart stands, and twenty small desks with brightly coloured chairs, and the teacher's desk and chair.

Mandalay and the other parent volunteers move up and down the line, tucking in a zip-lock bag here, extracting a book there. (That was Aidan, reading in the lineup.) One of the other parents, Tim, passes a dropped jacket back to its owner. Up and down the line, correcting, listening to stories, tending to the hopping, humming, gyrating second-graders. Tim, the stay-at-home dad, is good at it, attentive, but not too anxious. His younger daughter, a baby still, is in a carrier on his back. Mandalay sees that Owen is looking at a classmate's toy, a contraband DS game. Tim confiscates the machine, puts it in Mrs. Chau's desk for safekeeping.

They know the drill well. They have been volunteering since kindergarten. They are Mrs. Chau's extra eyes and ears and hands. They all live in the same neighbourhood, a dense, small catchment area. They are diverse, but the school brings them together. They see each other in the shops, the older ones, like the bakery where Mandalay works part-time, and at the bus stop, and walking along the quieter side streets.

At last Mrs. Chau returns from her errand to the office, flicks the lights off and on. The chatter sucks itself down some invisible hole. They file out to the bus. Besides Mandalay and Tim, there is also

Mr. Gill, who is Vikram's grandfather (or possibly great-grandfather), and Avril and Lauren, Filipina nannies, who always volunteer together, and Umma, in her ankle-length dark robe and her bright blue silk headscarf. Mandalay has made a point of getting to know them. Umma is very shy and has very little English, but her eyes are observant. The nannies cling together. Who wouldn't? They have older children, too, that they care for: both work for Chinese families. Mandalay has read about the abuse of international nannies and wonders if these two get out much, get enough to eat, get time off, get paid properly. But they have each other. Umma has two younger children, a four-year-old and a toddler. She goes on a lot of the outings. Mandalay had invited her and the other children to come to her house, after school, once, and Umma had said she would but didn't arrive. Mandalay knows that it's important to keep trying, to keep reaching out, to avoid assumptions.

There had been more moms, and some dads, on outings when the boys had been in kindergarten, but they have fallen away, most of them. Moved away or gone back to work. Property prices have risen, it seems, even in this somewhat shabby and unfashionable part of the city.

Mrs. Chau now stands at the front of the bus, swaying quite gracefully with its movement as she iterates the instructions for the day for the third time. She thanks the parents, using titles and surnames. Mandalay is Mrs. Lund. She cannot get Mrs. Chau to call her anything else. It is a conservative milieu. The children clap their thank-you. Owen and Aidan are sitting separately, with friends. Mandalay's seatmate is a little girl called Amber, who always attaches herself to Mandalay.

They are off to the aquarium for the day. It is part of their unit on the ocean. Mrs. Chau divvies up the children among the parents. She is very organized. She has taken grade two classes to the aquarium before. She knows what to expect: this is evident in both her tone and her instructions. It is very reassuring. Mandalay gets Owen and Aidan and Amber and two other children. Five children: that is not so bad to keep track of. She should even be able to help them fill out the question sheet that Mrs. Chau is right now handing out.

The children sway and bob and jitter as if eddies of water were moving them, agitating them in circles, occasionally uprooting them entirely, as if their small shoes had only a tenuous holdfast with the ground. When they get off the bus, they have left behind three back-packs, a jacket, a shoe, and several of the question sheets. The other parent volunteers pay no attention. Tim is one of the first off the bus – he has the most unruly of the girls to corral. Mandalay scoops up the jettisoned belongings.

They wade through the group turnstile and down the curbed ramp to the rooms with their huge glass tanks of water, their reconstructed biomes and fish. Here is the North Pacific, with its golden-brown kelp, lacey sea fans, rockfish with their bored sullen faces, green anemones like monstrous organs, giant oysters and crabs and purple starfish.

Aidan asks: Are all of those things under the ocean, *here?*

Yes, Mandalay says. I've even seen them myself, in the wild. (A tightness in her chest, as she thinks: The last trip I took with Duane. The trip on which the twins were conceived.)

A silent world, teaming.

The children do not want to fill in the answers on their sheets. She reminds them, reluctantly. Aidan and the little girl called Stella confer, write in answers, ask how to spell things. Owen zooms around with the other child, Devon. He'll remember what he has seen, though. Amber clings to Mandalay. She smudges, erases.

Why don't you *draw* the answers, Mandalay says.

Amber looks up at her with her curiously light brown eyes. Am I allowed?

Sure, Mandalay says. I'll mention it to Mrs. Chau.

Amber is of mixed race, unlike most of the children who are clearly European or Asian or South Asian, from tight communities. Amber has caramel streaks in her hair, gold-brown skin, those light golden-brown eyes. She *is* amber. A shy child, not yet conscious of her own beauty. Mandalay helps her, and some others, in Parent Volunteer Reading. She also sees some of the children at the bakery, which is the kind of bakery that gives cookies to the children of customers.

They head to the tropical fish area now, where both boys show off naming the fish – her brother Cliff was obsessed with reefs, had taken them here many times – and then the shark tank, where the boys bump their noses on the glass, gloating at the cruising sharks, whose noses are also bumped – raw and sore-looking.

Then the tropical rainforest, hot and humid, with its sudden strobes of bright birds, its free-range tortoises, its secret sloths. The coelacanth, giant prehistoric fish. The children excitedly pass among themselves the information that the fish in the low tank is four hundred million years old. There are skeptics. Near-fights break out.

The artificial tide pools are nearly identical to the ones she had explored as a child, on the West Coast, but lacking the slipperiness of barnacled and algae-slicked rocks, the splash and sweep of wave. She hardly returns to those shores and beaches, now. Will her children grow up not knowing that space?

The sulky crocodiles. The hyperactive otters. (Are they being driven mad by their small enclosure?) The belugas, likewise, which cruise and turn, cruise and turn, eyeing their watchers through the thick glass.

When she had discovered herself pregnant, she had prepared as for an arduous and dangerous voyage. More than that – a journey of exile from her former free life. But it had turned out more than that. She had become the vessel itself, not the voyager.

In the early months of her pregnancy, she'd been aware — hyper-aware, her doula had said — no doubt because of her leanness and her muscle tone, her years of biking and yoga — of the movements of the fetuses inside of her. She had felt them first twitch on their umbilical lines, then roll over, then wriggle and shoulder past each other in their amniotic pools. She'd looked at images online and in old *Life* magazines so that she could envision them at every stage. She could sense them in her uterus, translucent little beans with huge dark eyes and fan-shaped hands and feet, flippers. She'd felt them flutter against the thick sensate walls of her womb, and had held them in her attention, and had caught, sometimes, their emerging thoughts in her bloodstream: *Hungry.* Or: *Sugar jolt!* Or: *Good Mother Ship. Love.*

Before they were born, she had known them, the individual prints of their bodies, their minds.

She has never told this to anyone, not to her sister Cleo, who would point out that there was no scientific evidence that this was possible; especially not to Duane, who would find a way to use it against her.

In the dark round beluga theatre, with its carpeted benches, watched by the beluga and dolphin, the children unwrap and eat their lunches — the packaged crackers and processed cheese, the steamed buns and dumplings, the flat breads and pulses, the tiny tubs of yogurt or hummus or applesauce. Umma has organized handwashing and the spreading of a plastic cloth for her group — a religious thing perhaps but she's right, the carpeted benches must be filthy. Mandalay's group will have to consume its share of microbes today.

Next to Mandalay, Tim has made a spot for his younger daughter, Zara, a sturdy toddler of eighteen months with the plump cheeks, little white teeth, round eyes and thick curls of a baby doll. He opens a Tupperware box to reveal an assortment of raisins and pieces of granola bar, and Zara's cheeks flush, her eyes sparkle, her teeth part in a wide smile. She claps her hands together. Mandalay laughs; all of the parents and grandparents and nannies laugh, in a moment of spontaneous shared happiness.

She likes Tim, who is a stay-at-home dad, whose wife runs a company. She has been to their house, with the boys, and Tim has brought the girls over to her place. Tim's house is newer, architect-designed, cute and efficient, with cabinets slotted under stairs and rollaway beds. Tim has an almost-finished Master's degree in something – is it filmmaking? – which he will finish once both girls are in school. Unless we have another child, Tim says.

He is interesting, well-read, able to talk about art and books and film. He's good with the girls, patient, aware, balanced. A good father, a good man. What would it be, to raise children with a partner like Tim?

She has gone out with a few men, since the twins were born. A few men, a few times. When the boys had been three or so, she had met an artist at a party at Belinda's, and for several weeks, had been on fire, had glowed like a nuclear reactor, with the fusion of talk about art, and frequent, fervent sex. At some point, she'd thought that maybe this relationship would be it – that the two of them, while keeping their own necessary solitudes (hers with the boys; the artist's with, well, his art) would be able to maintain at least some version of their passionate trysting. But then the twins had got terrible croupy colds from daycare, and the artist had gone to Italy on a research grant....

After that, there had been Steve, an intense, bearded school-teacher, divorced, with two sons of his own, a little older. He'd at least seemed to get it about having kids. He'd wanted to meet the boys, and had taken them on a hike in Lynn Canyon, and had hectored the then four-year-old twins throughout the day – on their inability to keep up, to pay attention, to shoulder their backpacks correctly.

After she'd told him she didn't think their relationship had a future, Steve had said: But the boys and I bonded so well.

Then pretty Micah, with his long butterscotch hair, his chill, his humour. The boys had bonded with him. Had loved him. She can picture even now the three of them rolling around together, Micah right down at their level, his lithe tireless twenty-nine-year-old body buried, like theirs, under piles of toys and books and abandoned projects.

She'd made all of the meals and washed Micah's clothes and stayed up late when he texted her from his friends' places to see if she could come over. And then he'd gone tree planting, the spring the boys turned five, and hadn't come back to them.

That had been tough on the boys.

ON THE TRIP BACK to the school, Mrs. Chau collects the question sheets. Only a few have been completed, but that is acceptable, it seems. Never mind, Mrs. Chau says, taking the seat beside Mandalay for a moment. Some are ready for this kind of work. Some are not. She pauses for a moment, as if resting. Well, she must be tired, Mandalay thinks. She herself is just about exhausted. Then she stands up, and Mandalay notices her slightly extended abdomen. Oh, the bump isn't too big – she should make it through to the end of the school year, Mandalay calculates. But Mandalay feels a slight twinge of dismay. The boys were supposed to be in Mrs. Chau's class for both grades two and three.

Are her sons to be abandoned by Mrs. Chau, now? If she is moving on to having her own offspring will she be able to continue with her care and devotion to Mandalay's children?

Foolish, atavistic thoughts. Where do they come from? As if her boys' well-being is threatened. Next year they will have a different teacher. Owen and Aidan – all of the children – will grow up and move on. And anyway, the boys have *her* – they have their mom.

But she wishes that Mrs. Chau were not leaving. Mrs. Chau, who works many unpaid hours to organize field trips and extra outings for the class.

SHE TELLS DUANE: You have to talk to them yourself.

He hasn't come inside the house for a long time – the last time before today might have been when one of the boys fell asleep in Duane's vehicle and had to be carried in. He never comes in to visit. But now he has invaded her living room.

Duane sits on the sofa, and talks with the twins almost formally – almost as if he's making an actual business proposition. Well, no – it's less of a proposition, more of an announcement. But he does ask them if they'd like to go.

Of course they do. She realizes that she has been holding a last-ditch, improbable hope that one or the other of them would refuse. But they are excited. They want to go.

At least today the house – the downstairs, anyway – is mostly tidy. It had become a bit of a catastrophe over the week, but she had spent some time this morning picking up the boys' stuff, vacuuming. There is nothing for Duane to be appalled at – nothing out of place (except the small grey sock protruding from under one chair; she had seen Duane glance at the sock and then deliberately avert his eyes).

Duane is on his best behaviour, she sees. Only one dig: Aren't you glad, he asks the boys, that you've been taking swimming lessons all winter?

It had been a sore point between them: he had wanted them to have lessons at the Aquatic Centre, and had paid for them. She had to get them to the pool twice a week, though, and hated it: their shivering and complaining, the regimenting, the inconvenience of it. Why couldn't they just learn in the natural way, at the beach, in the summers? But Duane had been adamant.

Maybe it's not a dig. Maybe he is just making an innocent point to the boys.

No, he is not.

Still, the visit seems comfortable, natural. A new experience. Should she invite Duane to stay for dinner? She does have some pasta she was going to cook. But after half an hour, he looks at his watch.

He has to go, he says. Oh, and does she want him to take care of getting sunblock and swimsuits and all of that? And what about getting Owen prescription goggles so he can see things underwater?

There is no end, she thinks, to the enhancements you can give to your life, your children's lives, if you have enough money.

After Duane has left, Aidan hugs her around the waist. That was nice, wasn't it, Mom?

▼▼▼

CLIFF CAN'T TRACK BEN DOWN, so he has to go to the bank by himself, which he doesn't like to do. His customer service representative's name is Donna. He's always nervous in her office. He's afraid that she'll figure out how stupid he is with numbers. He's afraid she'll ask him questions he can't answer. He lets Ben do the talking. But she's been leaving messages for days that they need to come in and go over some fiscal year-end things with her. He wants Ben to do it, but Ben is not answering his messages. Cliff is afraid that something will go wrong with the business if he doesn't go see Donna. That they'll suddenly run out of money.

He knows that it's not how it works: Donna doesn't control the money; he and Ben do. She just keeps track of it for them and makes sure that some of the bills get paid, and once every three months sends them a statement. And once a year they're supposed to come in and meet with Donna and tell her what they want to do.

He parks his truck and walks into the office building with his heart stuttering in his chest. He had seen, on a TV program the other night, a scientist talking about how human bodies respond to fear – the adrenals, which were (he had not known this) little plum-sized things sitting in his lower back, on top of his kidneys – how they were designed by evolution for a fast reaction to danger. Imagine, the scientist on the program had said, hundreds of thousands of years ago, you're walking through the bush, and you hear a noise behind you…. Cliff had felt an adrenalin response just imagining that.

You're going to either fight or run, the scientist had said, and an animation had come up on the screen of a man with bushy hair and beard, wearing a spotted animal skin, turning around and seeing a sabre-toothed tiger crouched behind him, about to jump him, and the cartoon man swinging his club at it. Then they showed the man again, but he realizing he didn't have his club with him (how someone could draw that whole thought in a few lines!) and starting to run, the cartoon puffs of dust at his feet.

In the modern world, the scientist had said, we don't have to face physical danger very often, but our body still creates these responses to our mental fears. Even though they don't help. Even though they might make it harder for us to think clearly, just when we need to.

Cliff takes the elevator up to the third floor of the bank, where Donna has her office. He normally would take the stairs, but he's never been able to find them from the building lobby. The elevator is new – completely smooth and silent. He can't tell when it starts moving. (His heart is stuttering; his blood is rushing to his extremities, away from his brain and digestive system.) He has to trust that the elevator will respond to his pressing the button.

He has put on a button-down shirt and tie, and his cleanest, newest jeans, and the jacket Veronika gave him for his birthday. He had worn the jacket last year; it's the nicest thing he owns, and Ben had said that he looked like a Russian gangster.

The elevator does stop on the third floor. The doors open.

The receptionist smiles at him and says she'll let Ms. Fuoco know he is here. He doesn't sit. He's guessing Donna will be annoyed that he has come without Ben. She'll probably feel he has wasted her time.

His heart is hammering away as he follows the receptionist down the corridor, past all of the other accountants' offices. His sister Cleo works in an office building, too. He's never been to see her office. He wonders what it would be like to work inside all day, in a small space.

His hands are damp. He wipes them on his jeans. He thinks of the sabre-toothed tiger: Rather face that. Laughs at himself. That's better.

If he had been younger when it all got going, he would have liked to do computer animations.

Donna is a tall woman with very shiny hair and nice calves and a comfortable way of talking and moving, as if she spent a lot of time taking care of some skittish creatures – feral cats, maybe. She doesn't comment on Ben's absence. He doesn't either, not knowing how to explain it. She gives him a folder full of printouts of lists of numbers, and coloured graphs, and he looks at it numbly. It's always Ben who reads the reports, makes sense of them, has a conversation with Donna. It's all Greek to him. Or Estonian! He smiles to himself. What sorts of things does he remember Ben saying? Maybe he can just look like he understands what Donna is showing him, deal with it all later.

Accrue, Donna is saying. Assets, amortization, balance. Credit, deduction, equalization, financing. He nods. He looks at the coloured bar graphs and pie charts, and he follows with his eyes, and turns the page when she turns hers, and nods. Sometimes he almost under-stands it all but then he loses it again. He wants to say slow down, start again, but it would be too embarrassing. Fear is choking his brain, like clay silt.

Now she's asking him a question, though. She has pointed out something, and she's asking him a question about it. Ahhh, he says.

He can feel sweat trickling down the inside of his shirt and wants to yank off his tie. He feels he has to take off his tie because he can't breathe.

I'm not sure, he says. He's dizzy. What's the point of being dizzy? He would not be able to run from the sabre-tooth very well, if he were dizzy.

He'd be very happy right now if he could run somewhere, though.

Donna asks if he would like a drink of water. Yes. He loosens his tie. He removes his jacket.

It's just words and numbers. He just has to ask her to explain it again.

Donna says something about amortization, front-loading, over-draft. He shakes his head. Takes a deep breath. You have to slow it down for me, he says. You can't use those words.

He would never have thought to say something like that, but now it's out, he feels his heart slow, his blood clear, as if a big glop of something has been washed out.

Okay, Donna says. Let's look at it this way. You can put down a one-time extra loan payment, and that will help you because you're still paying mostly interest on your loan. Or you can leave it in the account to create a bigger cushion, which might be a good idea – you're having to borrow money about every other month to cover your payroll, and that's costing you.

And then suddenly, it is clear. They owe a lot of money, he and Ben. Mrs. Cookshaw had left him the business, but they had taken those loans out to buy the new trucks and equipment, and they have to pay that money back. He understands that. He gets it about the gap between getting paid and having to pay out, too – he's had to explain that to Veronika. What he hadn't really seen before is how much money he owes, and how much he is paying every month that isn't even loan repayments or equipment or his employee's wages.

It's more money than he pays for his mortgage on his house. It's more money than he pays himself in salary.

He doesn't feel dizzy, now – just cold. How much cushion do we have? he says, and Donna says, Well, you can see, basically none, and he feels colder, like he has turned into a machine. Okay, he says. Put enough in so that we don't run out again. Then put the rest onto the loan.

That seems like a good idea, Donna says.

She will draw up the paperwork. He'll have to come in and sign it, tomorrow. Doesn't Ben have to sign too? No, not for this. They have it set up that way.

Good, Donna says. She has a lot of forms for him. Taxes, she says, and he signs and signs. He signs every year, of course, only usually Ben is there and he trusts that Ben understands what is going on.

The fear grips him again, then. What if he has done something wrong; what if Ben thinks they should be doing something different? But Ben hadn't returned his calls, and it's nearly the end of the month that taxes have to be paid.

What do we usually do? he asks, his face heating with shame. What did we do all of the other years?

Oh, it hasn't been an issue for very long, Donna says. It's only the last couple of years you opted to pay yourselves dividends.

He remembers now, the cheque, the extra money. Placing it on the table in front of Veronika. That had gone for new furniture: a whole houseful of new furniture. He remembers her happiness, describing to him the solid wood dining table and bed and dressers. He hadn't really cared but it had made her so happy. And now he has a house of nice things, and it does give him pleasure.

But the money needed to go back into the business, didn't it? When they owed so much and kept going into overdraft. Didn't it?

Monopoly, he thinks, that's where he knows the word from.

Dividend. It's one of the Monopoly cards that you can turn up: School Tax or Get out of Jail Free. One of the yellow or orange ones that sit in stacks on their own marked spots in the middle of the board. Bank Pays You Dividend of $50.

His sister Cleo and himself, Mrs. Giesbrecht, and one or more of the other foster kids used to play board games at a kitchen table: Parchesi, Sorry, Life. The smell of baking, of cinnamon, lard pastry, buttery, yeasty breads.

It was one of the orange cards: turn it up and you would get money. One of the cards you wanted to get.

He couldn't read all the words but Cleo read them for him. Community Chest; that was it. He hasn't thought about it in years.

It was a strange game, full of strange words. City words, he had thought. Or maybe Mrs. Giesbrecht had said. They lived on a farm, in the valley, the eastern sweep of it, where the mountains began to dip down onto the green plain. Mrs. Giesbrecht had called things that were complicated or to do with money, *city* things: TV programs, except for *Gunsmoke* and nature shows; Cleo's tape deck; a neighbour's tinted hair. The microwave oven. Cleo, after she had left and was going to university.

Monopoly: that was also *city*.

It was a strange game to give to children, if you thought about it.

It was all about real estate, that game. He had not known that, as a child, but he sees it now: Park Place, Baltic Avenue – those were chunks of real estate. City blocks! You had mortgages and people had to pay you rent, and you could buy utilities. You tried to win by buying up things so other people had to pay, to lose money, and then you went to jail if you couldn't pay. A strange game for children.

Cleo had always been the banker. She had liked to be banker. She'd read his cards for him too, the Chance and Community Chest cards: read them to him, slip them quickly back into the pile without letting anyone else see them. He'd won often, when Cleo played with them. Never, when she didn't. His cards had almost always been good ones, when she'd read them for him: Bank Pays You Dividend of $50.

He recalls, now, Cleo's hand moving smoothly between the money tray and his own piles of goldenrod and lemon and pink and blue paper bills; sees the pale yellow hundreds slide out almost invisibly from under her palm to join his stash.

His dividends.

5

Assessment

MONDAY: a meeting with a couple of members of Cleo's team, Tilly, Michael, and Lindsay, and the contractor for a new project. Cleo has booked the conference room so they can have quiet and spread things out on the table. They're getting the routine down; they're gelling. Michael is pulling up some specs from suppliers of a rather esoteric heat pump, in a very organized and thorough way, using the laptop projector. Despite his best-friends-forever, gossipy manner, he is completely focussed at work. He overkills things, Cleo thinks. But it's amazing to work with him. Tilly is busy with some graphs on *her* laptop; she will be prepared with exactly the right information. Lindsay is putting together some printouts of drawings – hard copies. That's discouraged – paper waste. But Lindsay says she likes people to have something in their hands. Cleo thinks she's right.

It's all good. They do their run-through. They discuss. Tilly used to talk too little, Michael too much, but they're shifting. They're balancing out.

Cleo makes notes on her Blackberry. She'd be faster with a pen and notepad, but she has to adapt. She has to set a good example.

When they're done, it's clear that they've all brought in some valuable ideas. Cleo makes sure to say this, makes a few suggestions for small changes, thanks and praises them all, briefly, to let them know that this is really what's expected of them. But she is pleased. They have a new product and a new protocol ready to take forward.

Cleo had been right, of course, that there would be a little purge of personnel. But the whole purge-and-promote process had been mystifying. Well, not the whole process. Much of it. Gwyneth had been dropped — or jumped. Cleo didn't actually know which. She can't imagine Gwyneth doing anything so definite as resigning. That was a mercy — she was starting to make a lot of mistakes, ones that were costing the techs too much time to fix, or even to get their heads around. Nancy had not been dropped — but had gone on long-term disability, to have two knee replacements. There wasn't much sympathy for her among the younger employees. Cleo had heard comments about Nancy's limping, her slowness. It didn't fit the new company image.

Because that's what it had been about, the merger. And the subsequent purge. The new firm's roster looked richer, sleeker, more fashionable. And definitely skinnier.

Cleo has lost a few pounds herself, not intentionally, but because she's so much on the go. And because she works now with Michael, who is so urbanely affable, so elegantly slim, that if he is not gay, he is working very successfully to cultivate that impression; and Tilly, who is tiny and Asian and piquant and doesn't seem to have grown into her adult body yet. Those two live on kale and fifteen-minute workout machines, both of which are now kept in the lunchroom.

It has been six weeks since the merger — the actual consummation, as Lindsay refers to it. Cleo has been billing forty-hour weeks, and putting in probably fifty hours. It's not so bad. All of her old engineering cohort are doing much more. She had negotiated the fifty-hour cap, though agreed to a few weeks of overload per year.

She had been surprised at what she'd been offered. She hadn't even tried to negotiate, which had frustrated Trent unbelievably.

She knew she wasn't a good negotiator. It seemed more important just to have a bottom line – even if that bottom line was quitting the company – and let the others toss the balls.

Associate. She hadn't wanted that title. She'd suggested *team leader*, which reflected what she actually does. But others had wanted titles. And it sounded good, even though, as Trent had pointed out, fifteen-year-olds working at The Bay were called Sales Associates.

They were all associates, now, except for the designers, who were the partners.

The company with which they had merged was about the same size as Kate's. There was a principal, Alex, a few designers, and the usual assortment of draftspersons. They did commercial work, new build. Alex and Adam were engineers. There was a lot of call for engineering in their design work, which focussed on the interiors of very upmarket office spaces.

It had seemed at first an unlikely union: *re/vision*, Kate's residential reno design company (though they'd been doing larger and larger projects lately, massive renovations of mansions on the Endowment Lands, that sort of thing) with the commercial new-build people. But Cleo has seen the logic of it, more and more, as they go along. Kate has been able to access some new projects; Alex's company, *Aeolus*, has got better premises and more design clout. They share a couple of reno teams; there is less downtime for their contractors. Enough work now to book them completely.

Aeolus: she hadn't got that at first. It's made from the sounds of the initials of the two original partners, Alex Olson and Larry Schiff. Very clever.

Kate had said to Cleo: I need you to lead the drafting people. You're the only person who can move comfortably between the designers and the technicians. You're adaptable enough to fit into the ethos of the new place.

What it means really is that she doesn't argue with anyone, Cleo knows. She'd stay up all night redoing work to avoid an argument. So now she is responsible for five other people, as well as her own work.

She doesn't mind it too much. She had been surprised that Pam wasn't given the position, instead of her: Pam had worked longer, and more hours, at re/vision. Cleo's promotion hadn't gone over extremely well with Pam. Lindsay had reported later that Pam had burst out angrily, sputtering and crying that Kate couldn't do that – luckily, in the privacy of Kate's office, not in a larger meeting.

A mystery, for sure, why Kate hadn't given Pam the promotion, Lindsay had remarked. But Pam had stayed, during the purge that followed the merger, and was now, nominally at least, answering to Cleo.

TUESDAY: meetings all day. Cleo doesn't say much in meetings – she realizes that she probably knows even less than she believes she does about issues. She listens and takes very careful notes, not just of techni-cal things she must attend to, but of the way the partners, Kate and Alex and Larry, and the associates interact. How they negotiate, how they persuade, how they form alliances. And how they disagree. Especially how they disagree. But this is a callback with their corporate law firm clients, who seem to be tinkering still with the designer's mock-ups, and want Cleo to explain to them why *this* can't be done, and how much it would cost. They seem unfazed by the numbers she suggests, though she's gone quite high, for safety – she actually doesn't do the costing herself, as she tells them; it'll have to go through the project manager.

They seem to have unlimited funds. She wonders how much they have to spend, how much they make. (Duane, Mandalay's ex, must be loaded.) She bills them accordingly.

The next meeting is a consultation about a different building, a projected reno. This building is old. Pre-1980. There's asbestos everywhere, which is fine if you don't disturb it. She pulls up the new WCB code on asbestos in drywall, walks the building owners through probable scenarios. Double isolation rooms, 30-micron air-cleaning machines, hazmat gear. Unfortunately, the process adds about fifty dollars a square foot to the reno.

She sees the owners exchange what looks like a devious glance. The WCB fine is fifty grand, now, for an infraction, she says.

They say they'll think about it. What they'll probably do is a teardown. They'll still have hazardous waste costs, but it'll come out cheaper to completely rebuild, likely.

What a waste, though – a building that is perfectly useable, if they only didn't want bigger windows, higher ceilings. (She is happy, though, to work in a building with giant windows and high ceilings. No doubt about it.)

WEDNESDAY: a visit to assess the building envelope for a leaky condo. Another leaky condo. Cleo is looking at one of these a month, it seems. They're complexes built in the early 90s, very attractive buildings, with architecturally interesting rooflines, pastel stucco, large balconies. There had been buying frenzies for them, she remembers. She and Trent had thought about buying one so that they could live in the city proper, when they were expecting their first child, but had realized that for the same amount they could get a whole new house further out. Recently, though, inspections have begun to discover that the architectural style, which had been imported from California, wasn't up to the North Pacific coastal climate. Everything about the buildings had been designed for a warm, dry place. In the damp, cool weather of Vancouver, the angles of the roofs, the flashings that sealed vents and outlets and windows, the boxy little balconies, in some cases the pretty peach and terracotta stucco itself – had proven inadequate. What was called the building envelope – the design and technical features that keep a building watertight, and therefore free from rot and mould – had just given out.

It had taken a few years – until the new home warrantees on the buildings had expired, to be precise. But now it's almost a new industry, the assessment, the remediation. It's unlucky for the owners, who have seen their equity collapse, or have had to pay for million-dollar remediations that don't add to the list price of the condo, for which they'll never be able to recoup their outlay.

They're a tricky thing, the assessments. Nobody wants that kind of bad news. Cleo is good at it, though – she's good at the detail, the estimation.

THURSDAY: a meeting about having a meeting. And another meeting with the bookkeeper about some missing invoices. In the late morning, a meeting with a new client. Cleo preps the meeting room, with its glass table, its computer screens. Her team presents. After, the designers and principals and the client go to lunch.

It doesn't matter what they are called: the technicians are never asked to go to lunch.

HER BLACKBERRY ALERTS HER about the one o'clock meeting with Michael at Ballast and Sparrow. Okay, okay, she says. She has time to comb her hair, blot her forehead and nose, apply lip gloss. Taxi to the client's office as they have time neither to walk there nor find parking. She hasn't had breakfast or lunch, so she chews some breath-freshening gum and hopes there'll be coffee.

A longer meeting than she'd anticipated: the clients, another law firm, don't seem to have finalized their own wishes yet for their new premises, and seem rather to have called Michael and her in to give them a smorgasbord of ideas they can later hash over amongst themselves. Not efficient: not a good use of her time, of Michael's time, as they had been over-prepared for the stage they're at. Though she bills it, of course.

She uses the time in the taxi back to the office to book a doctor's appointment for Sam, and an orthodontist appointment for Olivia, via her cell phone. She needs to book haircuts for everyone, a dental cleaning for herself, and an oil change for her vehicle; get the furnace checked, get her laptop looked at — but these things will have to be booked on other days. Or she'll have to take a half-day off. Her phone buzzes, and she sees it's her kids' school. Her mind goes into alert, but she hardly wants to answer in a car with her colleague. Then she remembers that it's an in-service day. Sam's actually at a day camp, Olivia at a friend's. She lets the call go to voicemail.

She listens to her cell voicemail later, while typing out a fillable form, even though she knows that multi-tasking isn't really efficient, that she isn't really saving time. It's just a reminder that she's supposed to meet with Sam's teacher. She calls, books evening slots.

Back at the office, she's just very tired. So tired that she feels like she's floating.

WHEN CLEO HAD TAKEN ON the new job, Kate had said: Think of it this way. You're doing this on behalf of the company. It's not you. It's just a role. You compartmentalize. That's how you do it.

Friday starts with a complaint by Alex about Tilly, which as team leader Cleo needs to deal with. An interview with Tilly ends in sulking. Cleo suspects it's just a case of Tilly's natural intelligence rising up in intense, personal dislike of Alex's professional manner, but it's not useful to say that. She's supposed to follow a script about communication models and mediation. She's supposed to get her technicians to work well with the designers. It would be easier, she can see, if Tilly were to solely work through Cleo. She's sensitive, disinclined to take criticism. Is it that she's a millennial, or were they all like that, starting out?

It's hard to remember. Cleo feels that she would not have dared to argue back with a superior at work the way Tilly does. But even the word *superior* seems out of Tilly's lexicon. And maybe that's good thing?

Then a couple of hours, finally, working on a project at the computer, a satisfying bit of structural problem solving, her own design work, which is pleasing to her in its functionality. *Form follows function*, she thinks, though that ethos is perhaps out of favour in this city or century or just among their clientele. During these two hours, she is unconscious of everything else. She feels completely, steadily, calmly *alive*, and the time goes by far too quickly.

▼▼▼

MANDALAY'S ON HER WAY to a dinner party at Belinda's. It's for a visiting artist. She's always invited to Belinda's parties. They are a kind of lifeline, she has to admit. She can bring the boys, as Belinda's daughter Harriet is the same age as they are, and entertains them efficiently. The three disappear to the upstairs of Belinda's house and are happily occupied until Mandalay wants to leave.

But this evening, she's on her own, and that's okay too.

Belinda opens the door and while she takes off her rain boots and transfers to Belinda the wine and dish she has brought, Belinda asks: How is it going?

Okay, Mandalay says. In fact, she has been having waves of panic, every few hours, as her body remembers a couple of seconds before her brain that her sons are with Duane in the Caymans, a nine-hour flight away, and will be for the next week and a half. It seems ridiculous to feel that way. Lizard brain, on alert for her young.

Getting some work done? Belinda asks.

Trying, Mandalay says. She has made an artichoke dip and brought seed-covered crackers to go with it. It's not potluck, but if she brings a dish and a bottle of wine, she feels more justified in turning up. She is so on the periphery of this crowd: faculty and one or two grad students Belinda's supervising, and a couple of bigger name artists from the city. She always feels on the periphery. But she loves this crowd; she loves the vibe, the colourful personalities, the art talk.

Belinda's husband Joe comes out too, into the entrance hall, which is tiled, a Moroccan pattern in orange and cream and black showing between oddments of rugs, braided and knotted, local and exotic, and tumbled shoes. On the walls is a gallery of framed art photographs and lithographs, and student paintings and drawings by Harriet — some of the artwork that Joe and Belinda accumulate more and more of each year. Invest in, Belinda says, but with a wink.

Joe is a ceramicist, a famous one, in his sixties. He's a small man, with very muscular arms, cropped grey hair, a mild expression like a monk's.

No entourage tonight? Joe asks. Belinda and Joe's daughter Harriet is close behind him.

Kidnapped, Mandalay says. Pirates of the Caribbean. They're sailing the high seas.

Ah, well, then, Joe says. You have a big decision to make, don't you?

It takes Mandalay a few seconds. Oh, yes. Whether or not to pay the ransom. Not at all, she says. I had it tattooed on their bottoms when they were born: Don't bother asking.

Joe says: Seriously, you doing okay? Everything going okay? His eyes are very kind.

Mandalay has to swallow. It's more difficult if people are kind. Fine, she says. Thanks.

Harriet ducks under Joe's arm. What! No partners in crime for me, this evening? Whatever will I do?

Belinda says, I did mention, didn't I, Harry? And Harriet says: I think you did, as a matter of fact, Mother. But my proto-adolescent frontal lobe filtered out the message.

Belinda always says: Harriet is eight going on forty. Used to adult attention, as an only child of elderly parents. She likes the limelight too much, gets above herself.

But Harriet is lovely. She's just the sort of playmate Mandalay would have dreamed of for the boys – an androgynous little girl, uninterested in the latest TV series or toys.

Belinda carries Mandalay's offerings to the long, long wooden table – made by Joe, of course, out of reclaimed warehouse lumber – where a spread is being laid out. Belinda and Joe turned the largest room of their house, what would normally be the living room, into a dining room for their many dinner parties. (They don't give other kinds, Mandalay realizes: They are always feeding someone.) They don't actually have a living room – the smaller room off the kitchen has become an office, filled with bookcases and desks and computers. An enclosed porch off the back contains a couple of old sofas draped in throws and blankets. The main floor bedroom – they've replaced its door with an archway – is Belinda's studio space; it has the best light. Joe's studio is in the former garage. Upstairs, it's impossible to identify who owns what bedroom: there are three bedrooms, each with a large bed, a lot of pillows, large armoires and chests of drawers and overstuffed chairs.

Nothing gendered or conventional in any way. And everything in the house – which has no decorator style, simply wood floors and walls of deep complex colours or white – is beautiful: almost all second-hand, Belinda has said, the furniture and lamps and doors. Mandalay imagines that it must have taken forty years to find and gather everything – she doesn't often, herself, see such beautiful objects in second-hand stores. And then everywhere, art – on the walls, on surfaces. Art and books.

Belinda has been her friend since before the twins were born. She's a painter and art instructor at a college, and maybe the most open and accepting and generous person that Mandalay has ever known. She's like some kind of miracle – a smallish brown woman in her fifties, with short greying dreads and glasses, always dressed in layers of earthy-coloured linen skirts and tunics and homespun wool shawls.

Mandalay perpetually desires, and never can achieve, to be more like Belinda.

She is not the first arrival, she sees with a mixture of relief and disappointment. She loves it when she can have Joe and Belinda to herself for a few minutes at one end or the other of a party, but she also worries about being that loser friend who comes too early, stays too long.

Especially when the boys are not with her.

But here already are the usual guests, the artists and art teachers, the favoured grad students, the guest artist herself, Linda Bartell, a large woman with a grandmotherly bun and flowing dress. Mandalay has seen her work online, though she hasn't been to the show yet. It's multi-media, she knows – abstract collages of roadsides and vacant lots, with their undergrowth, discarded, broken objects, occasional dead wildlife rendered in fabric that she has apparently – it's hard to tell in the photographs – manipulated to create tense juxtapositions of texture and colour.

Belinda introduces her, says: Mandalay has also been working in abstract fabric collages.

This is true, but not really true. In fact, she had done some work for a class in textiles several years ago, and then abandoned it when the class finished. She thinks of it with some shame, now. The term-end crits had been brutal. The other students, and even the instructor had referred to her work as quilts or wall hangings, as in, *What is this, a quilt? My grandma makes quilts,* and *No, it's decorative. A wall hanging.*

Maybe attitudes toward textile work have changed. Or maybe Linda Bartell already has status, a reputation, so she can get away with more.

Linda Bartell asks, now, where she shows her work, if she's an instructor. That's a bit humiliating, too, though she's used to it. I haven't quite finished my BFA, she says. I haven't done anything for years. She'd been in her mid-thirties already when she had quit, pregnant with the twins. She'd barely made it to that last year, sliding in on the strength of two different undergraduate degrees she'd started and abandoned in her twenties and a legal settlement she'd got when a business she'd helped start up was taken over. And then the twins had been born, just a couple of weeks after her graduating show should have been. She'd been short just two courses.

She had thought she would paint, make painting her focus, but hadn't found a style or subject that she could make her own – in a way, she knew too much. She paints well enough that she could do a nice business in selling landscapes in some of the city's little galleries, the ones that are frequented by interior decorators and upmarket tourists, but she does not want to do this. It would seem – a sellout. Totally commercial. Making art for consumption, not as individual vision.

For one class, she had produced a group of prints of the houses in her neighbourhood, working systematically, up and down the blocks: a group of four or five houses in a row, in each piece. They'd been partly photographic, partly architectural renderings, partly abstract colour washes. Cleo had said that those would sell well, if she made more, if she could produce a limited series of prints. She'd thought about that — they seemed authentic to her, her own work. But she hadn't had time to do any more.

What else had she been working on? Some charcoal drawings based on photographs of scenes of public beatings or violence — she'd been trying to capture some sense, with the manipulation of line, of the different tensions in the bystanders. She'd been happy with that work, too. But it's not something she really wants to get into, now, maybe. She doesn't really like to go to that place, the concentrated study of violence and conflict, now that she has young children.

All of the art she produced has been languishing in her basement the past several years. And meanwhile, all of her classmates have finished their degrees, gone on to other things. So it's probably too late now.

There are no jobs, only a glut of artists and art teachers in the city, as everyone knows.

It is a humiliating conversation, and one she tries to avoid. She demurs, asks Linda Bartell a lot of questions about her own work, which is tricky as Mandalay hasn't actually seen it, and then turns the conversation to someone else's recent show.

It's one of the dangers of coming to these parties, of course — that someone will ask her a question, or she'll see something that will trigger in her this sense of being sidetracked, of exile. She'll have to sidestep it, or later at home she'll feel really down. She can already feel that squeezing in her rib cage, a sort of band pressing on her heart.

She makes her way to the table to fill her plate and join a conversation Joe's having about the neighbourhood development — a safe topic. She doesn't know what she thinks about it; she's willing to listen to others. But Joe and the photographer he's talking to have segued already into discussions of the *Bienalle* shows they've been to recently. She hasn't travelled in years. She went to Southeast Asia, once, in her twenties, but she hasn't been anywhere since. She drifts away.

Then Belinda is sweeping her up again. Has she met Alex Wong? Here he is. A very young man with long clean hair and new jeans. He recognizes her, he says. He was a second-year student; he helped set up the year-end show in which she had some pieces, right? A few years ago? He remembers her work. He remembers that they had a conversation about the gallery she had been managing in a café.

He's their new hire, Belinda says. Curatorial studies.

Curatorial studies. That's something Mandalay could do – could have done. If she had her MFA. She had run her own little gallery, once, in a popular Kitsilano café. She'd thought up the idea, taken work on consignment from artists, art students, curated the art. She'd done very well. The café had been written up in a magazine.

This would have been her job. The perfect job.

Damn and fuck it. The absence not only of her degree but also her gallery at The Seagull Café suddenly evoked. She struggles to contain the panic and regret.

THE BOYS ARE DELIVERED BACK on a Sunday night, a little sunburnt and jet-lagged, but hers, and whole. She watches for signs that they are different, that they have been altered in some way.

They have come back from their trip with new carry-on sized suitcases with wheels, one each, completely unnecessary. What was wrong with their backpacks? And a ton of new clothes she hadn't packed for them: not just a couple of pairs of slightly gaudy swim trunks each, but also new shorts and T-shirts and sandals and even underwear.

She is shocked, and hears herself say, too roughly: What's all this?

Aidan says: Oh, Mom, it was so hot there, and our old stuff took too long to dry. And Owen adds: Giselle said there were too many holes in my ginch.

Who is Giselle?

She helped look after us, Aidan says, vaguely.

She was nice, Owen said. She let me have the pink sunblock. Daddy said I couldn't but she let me.

The nanny?

I think she was more a *friend*, Aidan says.

A friend of whose? But Aidan will tell her no more, and Owen just laughs and segues into a rambling monologue about sea urchins.

How can she begrudge her sons a holiday with dolphins and sea turtles and someone's friend who let them wear pink sunblock?

It is just having to let go of them, seeing them leave the little world she makes for them, even for a week.

It's hard to get them up on Monday morning, and she asks if they want to stay home from school, but they are both anxious to go. They want to make it to show and tell. They have brought a bag of seashells as gifts for the class. They are both pumped, she can see, with the prospect of having the class attention, of distributing their largesse.

That's perhaps a difference.

▾▾▾

CLIFF AND HIS CREW have just finished unloading equipment at the British Properties estate when the new Ram pulls up and parks halfway on the lawn.

Ben.

Cliff feels his body tense. The homeowner is particular about not parking on the lawn. He, Cliff, doesn't let anyone park on the lawn. He leaves the group of his employees and walks to Ben's vehicle.

Okay, okay, Ben says. The virgin lawn. Okay. He gets out, goes around to the passenger side, lifts out a tray of coffees, a carton of pastries. Can you get the other tray, Bro, he says. I've only got one pair of hands.

He has not seen nor heard from Ben for a month. He has some questions for him, but he will not ask them here, in front of their employees. He grabs the other tray of drinks, shoulders the door shut, follows Ben over to where the workers are preparing to start. There's a little burst of applause, and voices saying, hey, thanks, man!

So they're going to be even later. They've already had a late start to the morning.

The homeowner has guests staying, asked for the mowing not to start before nine. He's their biggest client, and Cliff tries to accommodate him, even though it meant a blank spot this morning, not long enough to get his team to start another job first, even though they'll have to work now through the heat of the afternoon, even though they'll have to push to get done before evening, when the homeowner is having a barbecue.

If Ben plans to stay, Cliff could go and get onto another job. One of them needs to be here, but not both. There's not enough equipment for another person. Is Ben planning to stay and work today? He's dressed in jeans and T-shirt, but Cliff can't tell if they're what Ben calls work clothes.

Yo, Ben calls. Get those coffees over here, Cliff. You have some needy employees!

But they have already had their coffee. They're supposed to be starting now.

Ben's standing there, handing out the coffee and pastries, the group circling him, Cliff on the outside. Standing there, taller than Cliff by half a head, and taller than some of the workers by a lot more than that. His blond head and close-trimmed beard highlighted by the morning sun. Clustered around him, Cliff's team: Nicola, Jason, Juan, John Seung, and John Vuong, smiling up at Ben. Cliff has to squint at him, the sun in his eyes.

Ben has brought six coffees, six pastries. One short of each. He's already drinking and munching, so Cliff has none. Not that he wants any. He wants to get started.

Nicola notices he doesn't have anything, breaks her Danish in half for him. That's nice, but he doesn't want it. He shakes his head. With Veronika's cooking, anyway, he's up two pant sizes in the last two years. And if he eats pastries in the morning, it's like there's a voracious animal in his gut all day, demanding he stuff himself. He nods his head toward Juan, gesturing for Nicole to give him her extra half. Juan's maybe a hundred pounds, never seems to get filled up.

He begins to organize the equipment by job, load it onto the wheelbarrows. A tidy workplace; that's efficient.

He needs to have a conversation today with Ben. More than one. That's the trouble: where to start? But he needs to say, Stop disappearing for weeks at a time. I can't run a business if my partner is off-grid half the time.

If Ben wants out, that's okay; he's thought that through. He'll make Nicola a manager. She's worked as long as him. Back when it was Mrs. Cookshaw's business. And she'd helped him out, when he got the business and Ray quit. She could take over. But he'd need to raise her pay. He'd need to reorganize things so that she was in charge, so the employees and clients recognized that. And he'd have to hire another worker, at least half-time. Which he could all do if Ben weren't drawing payroll.

He needs Ben to either be on the job or step out. It seems logical, put like that. Obvious. But the fist in his guts tells him it won't be simple, that Ben will talk it into something else, and it won't be simple.

He waits ten minutes for everyone to finish their coffees, shooting the breeze, that's what they're doing, on paid time, and says, Okay, everyone. Let's do 'er. He collects the cups, the cup holders, the napkins. A couple of the workers have already just dropped them on the ground, on the pristine crushed-gravel driveway of the estate they are contracted to groom. Morons.

The cup's logo winks at him. *The Seagull.* Four-dollar coffees; three-dollar pastries. And Ben will, of course, have put it on the company card.

He's going to do the edges around the sweep of rhodos himself. It's a finicky job, hard to get even. It has to be done right to get the look the homeowner likes – clean, like the curved edge of one of the green velvet sofas Cliff has seen through the fifteen-foot-high windows of the living room. One of the living rooms.

But first he has to talk to Ben, because there he is now, getting into his truck, and who knows when Cliff will see him again. He walks up to the vehicle's driver's-side window, trying to hurry without seeming to hurry. Ben has started the engine, looks like he's already putting the truck into reverse, but Cliff leans his arm on the open window edge. The truck rides so high, he's not actually able to lean; he stands awkwardly, his arm hooked up on the truck. Ben is high above him, looking down at him.

Hey, Ben says. He smiles: he has a wide easy smile, flash of white, even teeth that has the effect of relaxing any knot, any tightness, in people. Cliff fights to keep his knot done up.

Hey, Ben, he says. Got a minute?

For you, always, big brother, Ben says, but in a way that seems to say that he doesn't.

Where've you been? he asks. He hears his own voice grate. It's not how he meant to start. He sees Ben's eyebrows go up.

What's this? Ben asks. You keeping tabs on me now?

You've been gone a month this time, Cliff says. I'm working fifteen-hour days, seven days a week.

Ben says, Working way too hard, man. I told you that. Hire some new workers.

I can't, Cliff says. There's not enough money coming in.

So take on some more work. Run the business, Cliff! Don't clip lawn edges.

Cliff says, The problem is that you're on payroll. All the time you're gone, you're on payroll.

Whoa, whoa, Ben says. I'm finding this really offensive, buddy. We have an agreement. We're partners.

I don't think this was the agreement, Cliff says. He wishes, the wish is a thirst in him like a dog's thirst, that he didn't have to do this. He knows he will lose any argument with Ben. Ben can think on his feet ten times faster than Cliff. He always ends up losing, not gaining ground, when he tries to confront Ben.

Stay soft, he tells himself. Stay soft, and tell small truths. (Where does this come from?)

I'm not keeping tabs on you, he says. You're just not around. I can't run the business by myself.

Shit. He sees too late that was the wrong thing to say.

So what you're really trying to say, Ben says, is that you need some more support. We need to hire someone to take on the work you're not capable of.

This is how Ben twists things, always. The panic runs in at his chest now. *Flight response*, he says to himself, trying to stay above it, the cold grey maelstrom of it.

Stay soft. Stay soft.

That's exactly it, Ben, he says, surprising himself.

Then why attack me? Ben says. Come on, Cliff you've got to try harder at this partnership thing, man. If you need another manager, we'll put out an ad. Or maybe I know a guy.

I have someone in mind, Cliff says, but....

Well, go for it, Ben says. Smiling again, now. Putting the truck in gear.

Cliff says: We need to talk, Ben. We need to discuss some things.

You bet, man, Ben says. I'm here to talk anytime, Bro. That's how it works.

The thing Ben does with his voice: as if you're the unreasonable one. Cliff waits, though, arms up on the window sill. He feels like a dwarf but he holds his position.

You know, Ben says. You're doing so well, Cliff. You've come such a long way. I'm proud of you.

But, Ben continues, you gotta admit, Cliff, your forte is the practical side of the business isn't it? When it comes to understanding what we do at the finance and structural level, you're kinda lost. And that's okay. I see that you don't always get your head around that side of things. But you gotta trust me. I'm looking out for the business. I'm looking out for you.

Yeah? Cliff says. Ben's voice is warm, sweet, like chocolate cake. Death by chocolate. It's like Veronika's gravy. He feels the warmth inside his chest; he feels a tear come to his eye.

But. But. The fact that Ben has been gone now a month.

In fact, Ben says, I've been working on a really sweet deal for us. Cliff, you're not going to believe it. It's just great. Wait till you see what I've been putting together. Of course, with your agreement, Bro, but you're going to be blown away. Your life is about to change, Cliff. I was waiting to get all the pieces in place, but it's coming together. It's crazy big, Cliff. And that's why it has taken so long. I've been busting my ass. You didn't really think I'd go AWOL for a month, did you? How would that make any sense? Oh, man. I changed cell phones. Did I forget to give you the new number? Oh, fuck, I'm stupid. But you must have guessed, you wouldn't think I'd ditch on our business, would you? This is ours, our baby! You didn't really, did you? Because if you'd even think that … we have some serious shit to work out. That's serious shit, if you're saying that, Cliff.

Yeah? Cliff says. Something bothering him, like Ben has put a piece back on the equipment backward. Like that. Something backward; it all fits but it doesn't really.

But he has to believe Ben because it's Ben, his brother, his long-lost little brother, miraculously found. Ben knows him. They're tight, him and Ben. Ben is — well, he's Ben.

He says, and means it, I trust you, Ben. He feels his whole body relax into that, feels relief and calm flood through him. The relief of it, the ebbing of all the stress and pissed-off-ness he's been carrying the last few weeks. It flows through him, it calms his mind, it smooths out the angry shards of thought.

Ben reaches out through the truck window, tousles Cliff's hair. Well, it's more of a noogie. A faint ridge on the top of his skull smarts.

Ben backs the vehicle up with a jerk, so that Cliff has to step back smartly. Stay real, Cliff, Ben says.

6

Counter-Offer

OLIVIA CURLS HER LIP AND SAYS: It's stupid. Grade eight. It's not really graduation.

Cleo feels a little rush of relief, is about to say, Yes, stupid; of course you don't need to spend money on a prom dress, and stops herself just in time. Okay, she says, as neutrally as she can. Though she has to work on that neutrality thing. Lately, when she believes she's sounding neutral, Olivia says she has an angry tone.

Do you *want* a dress? she asks.

I *need* one.

Okay, then. Never mind, she tells herself. It will cost what it costs. She'd rather not spend the money, but realistically, she can afford it now. There's no reason Olivia should have to wear something cheap or second-rate.

Cleo had sewn her own grad dress, back in grade twelve, on Mrs. Giesbrecht's old Singer. She'd saved up for some time to buy the Jessica McClintock pattern – Gunne Sax, the line had been called, in an unfunny pun – and Mrs. Giesbrecht had produced from somewhere eight metres of pink satin (intended for bridesmaids' dresses for a wedding that hadn't taken place, maybe?), which Cleo had not loved, but thought would do, and could hardly afford to pass up, given that she was counting every dollar in her bid to go to university, to live on her own. Fancy dresses at that time were still under the influence of Lady Diana's voluminous, be-ruffled wedding dress, and Cleo's had been, similarly, a frothy cupcake of a dress.

She had not liked it, after the fifty or so hours of gathering flounces. She had imagined that every seam was puckered, every flounce a little uneven, the sweetheart neckline crooked. She had felt, in the pink satin, as exposed and indecent as if she had gone to the grad in her underwear.

There are two bridal shops on the main street. Cleo takes a deep breath, and calculates a bottom line for the expenditure, which she tells Olivia, so that she won't have to bargain or plead. She'll save them both that indignity. The saleswoman is businesslike, too, asking, straight up, what the budget is.

She brings out an armful of dresses in clear plastic bags, and hangs them in a dressing room. Do you want to go in, Mom? the saleswoman asks. Cleo shakes her head.

There's an actual bride trying on wedding dresses on the other side of the shop. There are about five women with her – sisters, mother, aunts? The bride is not pretty, and the dresses are elaborate, ostentatious, encrusted with ornamentation. There is a huge amount of conversation, of photo-snapping. A whole saga of gasps, tears, gushing, reservations, retractions, dismissal that happens with every dress. The mother and one of the other older women are substantially built, and subside finally into decorative little chaises. They're clearly all settled in for the day.

Olivia emerges again and again from behind her change-room curtain to stand in front of the trifold mirror. What do you think, Mom?

The dresses are almost all variations on a theme: princess lines in pastels. They aren't very exciting, but Cleo is going to be positive, support Olivia's choice. Whichever one you like best, she says.

Olivia is inside the stall for a very long time, with the last dress. When she comes out, she says: I don't like any of them.

Alright, Cleo says. It's your call, totally. Do you want to go next door?

But the saleswoman is back with another armful. Something different, she says.

Cleo sits back on the little stool she has been given and tries to smile.

And when Olivia chooses, finally (and the dress is under budget, even counting the fee for taking it in a bit), Cleo thinks she has chosen well, and says so. The dress is slimmer, more sophisticated, in a shade of teal that suits Olivia's golden skin.

It's lovely, she says. It's perfect. She pulls out her credit card.

They're not even back in the car when Olivia bursts into tears.

What is it? What is it? If you've changed your mind, Cleo says, it's okay. We can go cancel it. (She must not, she won't, think of the forty-five minutes they've just spent.)

You hate it, Olivia sobs.

What? Why would you say that?

You're just so distant! You're not excited at all. You hate the dress.

Impossible to explain what Cleo has been trying to do.

It's a big day for Olivia, and she hasn't made enough of a deal of it. (A screen with *Fail!* written on it in bright lights flashes in front of her.)

Can she salvage things?

A DETOUR THEN TO THE MALL, to the huge Swedish franchise that has appeared recently, to complete the grad paraphernalia. And here Cleo tries (she feels ridiculous) to be the sort of mother she should be: to speak faster, to raise her voice an octave, to give Olivia all of her attention.

There's an after-party at Micki's, Olivia says, holding up a strapless black bodice with a very short skirt made of layers of silvery black tulle. It's club wear, maybe? Definitely not suitable. But it's what Olivia has decided on. And it's cheap. So cheap that it won't matter if it's worn only once, Cleo thinks. Or if Olivia outgrows it before the end of summer. Though she wouldn't have thought that way, a year or two ago: wouldn't have liked the idea of disposable clothing.

They buy some more clothes for Olivia – a puffy jacket, silver, though she already has a perfectly good fall jacket; some jeans and T-shirts; another dress; some more shoes. Sparkly tights, pajamas, undies.

She buys Olivia a pair of silvery high-heeled sandals. Olivia hugs her, her face ecstatic.

Good mother points, Cleo thinks. Well, she says, your feet look like they've stopped growing, so you'll get some wear out of these. And we didn't spend very much on the dress.

Don't tell your dad how much the shoes cost, she adds, in a kind of reflex.

They grab dinner at a trendy burger place that Olivia likes, before they head back home. They have dessert.

It's easy. Almost too easy. The hardest part for Cleo is not checking her phone for two hours.

On the Lougheed, the car dies. Cleo swears only once. She calls the roadside assistance company, rides with Olivia in the tow truck to the dealership where she bought the car, fourteen years ago now. Olivia doesn't want Cleo to call Trent to come and pick her up; she says she'll stay. They sit side by side in the service waiting room.

Can I have a cell phone for my birthday? Olivia asks.

Maybe. They haven't been allowed at the middle school, though Cleo hears that rule is changing. Olivia will have to travel out of the neighbourhood for high school, so a cell phone might be a good idea.

But not Sam, Olivia says. Sam can't have one.

Cleo would normally retort something like *Well, that's mature,* but she just smiles.

It's going to be okay. Olivia is turning fourteen, and is not generally a barrel of fun, but it's going to be okay.

The vehicle has suffered some internal problem so dire that it will cost a few thousand dollars to fix it. She's had that SUV for fourteen years – they had bought it after Olivia was born, to manage all the baby gear.

Maybe she should just buy a new car? The thought feels shocking.

She calls Trent. Absolutely, he says. Go for it.

They are both good in crises, she and Trent. It's the everyday routine that knocks the stuffing out of them: that numbs and flattens and sours them.

Who would have thought it, that SUVs came standard now with seat heaters and rear window wipers and hands-free setups for phones?

I thought you might get a sports car, Trent says, now that we don't have strollers and things like that to lug around.

That's *your* fantasy, she says.

Now she has a car loan payment, like everyone else.

▾▾▾

THEY ARE ALL IN SUITS EXCEPT HIM. He had wondered if he should change, but Ben had said: Nah, you don't need to. But Ben is wearing a dress shirt and a tie. Only he, Cliff, is in his work clothes, his tan-coloured gabardine.

They are all shaking hands, and he notices the different strengths of grip. The ones who work with their hands. Or maybe just work out at the gym. He likes to give a firm grip.

There are seven other people in the room, besides him and Ben, all in suits: the three developers, their lawyer, their accountants, two assistants of some kind in uniform-type suits with skirts, with the 2010 logo embroidered on the lapels of their jackets. The room has dark grey-green walls with light maple panels suspended on them, high ceilings with pendant lights – glass and brushed nickel. The pendants must be three feet across, each. You couldn't hang them in an ordinary house. They look like spaceships – flattened glass globes with brushed-nickel rings. He's not sure about standing under them.

The room is too big for seven people. He can see it is used for larger crowds, for parties, maybe, or press conferences. It is a room for ceremonies. They're probably using it because the other board-rooms are in use. It's that kind of place. Also, they hadn't been expected. Either someone had forgotten them or Ben had mixed up the appointment day or time, because there had been a kind of confusion at the reception desk, quickly smoothed over, the young lady taking her phone through closed doors to make a call, them coming back, all friendliness: could they wait twenty minutes? So terribly sorry. And get them something to eat or drink?

He'd accepted a soft drink and Ben too, and it had been forty minutes, not twenty, but then they'd been ushered down a long cor-ridor, past all of the apparently full boardrooms, to this kind of ballroom. He was glad Ben was there. It was the kind of situation that made him really uncomfortable – having to go to a strange place to meet someone, and then having some kind of mix-up. It was the kind of situation that twisted his guts up.

But it is all okay now.

There is a large desk or table at one end of the ballroom, pale maple like the floating panels on the walls, wired up with micro-phones, and everyone is standing around it. The lawyer reads out the contract, or part of it, and the assistants put copies on the table, and hold out chairs for him and Ben and the developers. Each of them has a copy.

He doesn't read the contracts. He understands the gist of it, but it's not necessary to understand all the legal talk. He initials *here* and *here* and signs *here*. He wishes he had on a tie, his nice leather jacket. He *has* good shirts and ties. A lot of money is involved, he knows, but he doesn't see figures on the contracts, only some percentages.

Now they are shaking hands again, and then one of the assistants takes some pictures, and then the assistants are organizing everyone to be on their way again. The men and women in suits file out of the big maple-panelled double doors, and begin to disperse, and he and Ben are led to the elevator.

When they are outside again, on the street, Ben fist-pumps and says: Whoot! And Hey, man! Be excited! We just signed on for a slice of the Olympic pie! We're on the team, man! Let's celebrate!

Okay. But he has to be back on one of the sites at three. He said he'd be back by three.

Yeah, whatever, Ben says. Celebrate, man!

Okay, Cliff says. Then, he doesn't mean to but he does it, he says: I wish you had told me I should change into a shirt and tie.

Ah, come on, man, Ben says. Seriously? You're worrying about that? Cliff. You were fine. This is a big deal, man! We landed a contract for the Olympics! That's so cool, isn't it?

I think we should start planning out what we're going to do, Cliff says. The weight of the contract, what they've signed on to do, suddenly presses on his chest, restricts his breathing. Miles and miles of pipe to be dug in, topsoil, organics, wood chips.

Ben laughs. It's two years away, Cliff. We don't have to start planning today.

Actually, they do. They're going to have to work out exactly what this is going to cost them. Cliff had done some planning when they put in the bid, but it was really rough. Now they needed to work out exactly what it was going to involve to build all of those raised beds and to put in trees and turf and underground sprinklers around all of those the sites. They will have to book contractors ahead of time, and put in orders to nurseries, because they can't grow all of the plants themselves.

They'll have to get a loan. How will they pay for all of this? A loan. And they won't get paid, the company won't actually start getting payments for over a year, after the installations start. Also they'll have to hire more staff. It's going to be a huge loan.

Some echoing space opens inside of him, and he feels the heart-shock of vertigo, of falling.

Ben says: We should have a party, man. For the staff and our families. This is such a big deal, man. Cliff! Can you believe it! We're part of the Olympics! We're part of this whole thing! And we're going to make a lot of moolah. Can't you see it, Cliff?

Cliff really wants to see it: an office with lots of maple panelling and futuristic light fixtures, a desk with a really nice chair, and not having to mow lawns when it's raining. Yeah.

We should have a party, Bro, Ben says. This is the beginning of something big. Lund Brothers. One day we'll own half this city. We gotta have a party. Let's book a restaurant, nothing fancy, but let's not cheap out. Let's go with Manhattan Grill or something, take the staff for dinner. Their families too. Get everyone on board.

How much will that cost? Cliff wonders. Dinner for twenty people. Or more, because Ben, when he shows up for company parties – they usually have something around Christmas – brings a few friends. Mostly he doesn't have much to do with the employees; Cliff doesn't think Ben can even name all of them. But he remembers, now, the last company party Ben came to – he had brought his girlfriend and three other couples, and the liquor bill, which they couldn't claim as a deduction, had been shocking.

Ben has the vision, that's true. He's not afraid to think big. Mandalay and Cleo had said to him, when they were all deciding that he and Ben would be partners, that Ben would bring the vision and he would bring the practical side.

He knows he's timid, that he processes things very slowly. He knows he doesn't really understand the way business works, that thing Ben says, *acceptable risk*. It feels wrong to him. It makes things clench up inside of him. But he's thirty-six. He doesn't want to be pushing a lawn mower still at forty, does he?

That's what everyone tells him.

Hell, yeah, Ben says. We'll invite our families, too. Mandalay and Cleo and their kids. This is about them, too. Those kids will probably end up working for us in a few years.

He hadn't thought of that. Olivia, Sam, the twins – they'll all be looking for jobs soon. Getting closer to their teens. Olivia already. The millennials. He was just listening to something on the radio: there might not be enough jobs for them.

Himself able to give back, to repay Cleo especially, by being a benevolent uncle, able to help out her kids. And his own, maybe. That's how the other cultures are getting ahead, the Asians and South Asians he deals with, his competitors. They give jobs to their kids and their nephews and nieces. All in the family.

Yeah, it might be a good thing, a party. He'd have it at his house except it's too small. So what else but a restaurant. He'll just have to suck it up.

▼▼▼

BELINDA SAYS: You could do an MFA.

What's the point? Mandalay says. I'm not going to get a job. There are no jobs. Nobody's hiring. I've heard you say that.

Belinda says, carefully, after a pause: There are all sorts of things, short-term, part-time stuff. But it's something. And it could go somewhere.

Mandalay wonders about that pause. A little. Belinda is her best friend, the one person who really looks out for her and *gets* her, who totally, unconditionally, accepts her for who she is.

The pause is something outside of friendship, something that shouldn't be in their conversation. As if Belinda were walking carefully around her. As if she were someone who had to be walked around carefully.

I'm over forty, Mandalay reminds her. Belinda is supposed to remember this, not to push her. It would take me two years to finish. Then I'm supposed to look for something part-time, temporary?

Belinda says: Well, I don't hear that you have a better plan. And you're a good artist.

Am I? I'm not sure about that, anymore. Anyway, does it matter? It's all about who you know; it's all about being trendy.

I think you are stuck, Belinda says.

Belinda is not being helpful. Mandalay has not intended for the conversation to go down this road, anyway. She had only mentioned her dilemma over her house because she needed to vent a bit about Duane. She hadn't wanted to go down this path of Belinda thinking she should work and offering suggestions about what she could do. Belinda is supposed to be more sympathetic.

Has she caught her at a bad time?

Well, I am really busy, as usual, Belinda says.

She can't imagine the craziness of Belinda's life. But it seems lately that everyone wants that for her.

Maybe she *should* do a Master's. Everybody is saying it's the basic requirement, now, which is such utter bullshit – they're just raising the requirements because they can. To make more money. But she can't get anything in her field without it, apparently. She does look at the ads. And it would be impossible to work at something unskilled – retail or waitressing. Minimum wage, it wouldn't even cover daycare, probably, and she wouldn't ever see the boys, and she'd be too tired to give them her full attention when she was home with them, to be calm and cheerful and energized with them.

She needs to have the time during the day to work on her own equilibrium, her own centredness, and then she can be properly present for the boys.

It's just crazy that society doesn't provide for single mothers. That men like Duane can just pull the money in, hand over fist, and have so much leisure time, when she can't even afford a modest house for her kids to grow up in, even if she spends all of her time working. It's a crazy way that the world is organized.

But if she did her Master's, she could teach, then. She doesn't really want to teach, but at least the hours and salary are good. There's time off in the summer. She could do it.

But would it be worth it? There's no guarantee she'd get a job. Everyone says: There are no jobs. And then all the work of it would have been pointless. Also, she'd be forty-three when she finished, assuming she could do it in the usual two years. Does she want to go back to work at forty-three?

Honestly, she can't even imagine taking on the coursework. Looking after the boys takes up most of her days.

It's unfair. It's a sick society that demands that women work while they are raising young children. That expects everyone to work outside the home. While only a few people seem to have everything.

All true, Belinda says. But in the meantime, hey, it might be fun to do some seminars. Get back into your creative work. Maybe you could just, you know, do it for fun. You can probably get some financial support. I'll write you a letter. You're a good artist, Mandalay.

Is that true? Mandalay does not know.

CLEO SAYS: Of course you should do a Master's. What do you have to lose?

Well, time and money.

What would you do with your days if you had unlimited time and money?

Not a realistic question, Mandalay says, to avoid answering.

No, no. She has left it too long. She would have no idea where to begin.

Guess what, Cleo says. I'm online right now. I'm pulling up the MFA program at the university.... Okay, here it is. Let's see. Applying for ... deadline ... blah blah blah. Portfolio, letters, official transcripts, online application form. Do you have a portfolio? Oh, it says digital. Do you have professional photos of your stuff? No? Know anyone who can do that? What's your SIN, Mandalay? Oh, we'll need your PIN from Emily Carr. It'll be on some form or other. Check in that green Rubbermaid tub in your basement with all of your school stuff. Yup, right now. Actually, bring the whole tub upstairs. You'll need to pull up names for references. Got it? Okay, now you need to create a password. At least eight letters. Something you'll remember.

Done, Cleo says. And you owe me a hundred and twenty for the registration fee, but I'll take it in the form of a nice painting for my office.

I don't appreciate this, Mandalay says. She feels sick; she feels unbearably invaded.

Yes, you do, Cleo says.

Cleo, Mandalay says. I never finished my BFA. I have two courses to go.

She had been so heavily pregnant with the twins, and she had dropped out.

Cleo closes her laptop. Okay, she says. What's your plan?

This is not fair. Not fair at all.

▼▼▼

WELL, I GUESS I SHOULD GO, Lacey says.

They've met for coffee — it's the only way Cleo can see Lacey anymore, with Lacey having moved out of the neighbourhood, into an apartment not near anything. It's June, and beautiful, and they're sitting outside a gorgeous café near Cleo's office — and both in pretty summer dresses, which have been everywhere in stores this spring. The return of the pretty summer dress! What did it mean? But they're lovely, so soft and feminine. Even Cleo's boss Kate is wearing them to work, and Tilly, though not the others.

Cleo has on a fairly simple one in a blue that is not quite pastel blue. Subdued robin's egg, maybe. Lacey, she realizes, is wearing nearly the same dress, only in lavender.

It's a joke between them, how they often buy the same clothes, independently. Cleo will never admit to Lacey that when she goes shopping, she thinks: Would Lacey wear that? before she decides. She doesn't trust her own fashion sense at all.

They've taken off the light cardigans that are necessary inside, with air conditioning, and put on their sunglasses. I love your dress, they say to each other, ironically. Lacey says, also: I love your hair!

That's reassuring. Cleo has had foils put in — lighter-coloured layers. It'll hide the grey, her hairdresser had said. It'll brighten up your face. She's not sure about the foils. Blonde streaks, is basically what she has.

Lacey says: There's something I need to tell you.

Something in Cleo's chest drops about ten centimetres. Okay, she says, smiling.

I think I'm going to leave Calvin, Lacey says.

What? How has this happened?

Cleo literally can't breathe.

How has Lacey got to this point, without Cleo knowing? Haven't they always told each other everything? Even when they didn't tell anyone else.

Cleo is the only person, besides Calvin, who knows about Lacey's little brush with pre-cancerous cells, those star-shaped clusters, in her left breast, a year ago.

This feels even worse. And she didn't know.

Of course, all of these years she and Lacey have been complaining to each other about their husbands' selfishness, their grumpiness, their obliviousness. But wasn't that just venting?

And then there's Calvin, whom Cleo quite likes – though of course she believes Lacey when Lacey talks about Calvin's bad temper, his meanness. Well, she mostly believes Lacey. She's pretty sensitive. It could be that her tolerance for the normal give and take of marriage is low. And all of them complain, don't they?

How is she going to talk to Calvin, when she sees him at their kids' soccer games? And more than that – the four of them – Lacey and Calvin, she and Trent – go out for dinner and movies sometimes. Trent pretty well won't do anything, unless *Lacey* cajoles him ... so that's the extent of Cleo's social life as part of a couple.

Okay, Cleo says, involuntarily. (Oh, god. How is this happening?)

But Lacey is her friend. Her best friend. A certain response is required. Something more than *okay*. Are you going to be alright? she asks, lamely.

Hope so, Lacy says. I'm looking for an apartment for me and the kids. Calvin's refusing to move out, so....

That's going to be expensive, an apartment big enough for Lacey and the two children.

It's lucky Lacey has a job.

But her beautiful house, which has actually been featured in a decorating magazine!

There's something eluding her, Cleo thinks. Something important. I'm here for you, Lacey, she says, but it feels automatic, inadequate.

Something occurs to her, suddenly. How far has this thing gone, anyway? Is there someone else? she asks, and sees something in Lacey's eyes that makes her wish she hadn't. Some door suddenly closed. The questions that she can't ask form a kind of plug, so that she can't say anything at all. It seems unlikely. How on earth would Lacey find time, with two kids and a career? Lacey is so rational and pragmatic. There's no way she would give up her very good life unless she had a good reason. Would she?

But Cleo can't see into it; she doesn't know where to start. How can leaving Calvin, breaking up their successful family life, be the result of rational thinking? It's not like Calvin is a monster. He's not abusive. He's a good provider, a good father. He is lean and fit and clean and well-groomed. Handsome, even. Funny, easy to talk to. Though undoubtedly Lacey would say the same things about Trent.

Dammit, she's known them for years, Lacey and Calvin. She's seen them together. They make it work at least as well as any other couple she's seen. And they have a very good life on their two incomes — skiing and trips to Maui and concert tickets.

Things feel suddenly blurry, unstable.

I'm seeing someone else, Lacey says.

Oh, god. What a cliché. And it feels – disappointing.

Cleo hears her own voice, thin and unconvincing. How exciting! Who is it?

It's Richard.

Not Michelle's Richard? Calvin's colleague Richard?

Well, yes.

Oh my gosh, Cleo says. Then: Do you love him? She feels herself blushing. What a personal thing to ask.

He makes me happy, Lacey says. He cares about me and my interests. He listens to me. He's affectionate. He's not always yelling at me. I feel good when I'm with him.

Do you think it will last? Cleo asks. She does not mean to ask this; it just comes out. She realizes it sounds pretty rude. But Richard! She can't even picture him, right now, though she has met him once or twice at a party or out for dinner with Lacey and Calvin. On-his-second-marriage Richard. Never-home Richard.

Lacey says: He's really – kind and passionate. He makes me feel more alive. He makes me feel good about myself.

Okay. Cleo gets it, suddenly. Kindness and passion. That's what they all want.

But Richard!

What's going to happen with the book club? Cleo and Lacey had started it, but half the members are Michelle's friends.

Richard's going to tell her this weekend, Lacey says. He's going to move out this weekend.

Holy shit.

It doesn't matter if it lasts, does it? Lacey says, later, as they get up to pay. We don't really ever know what's going to happen, do we?

7

Competing Bids

LAST YEAR IT HAD BEEN total chaos, Cleo remembers. Too many people, all crowded into Mandalay's backyard, and not enough food. This year, there needs to be a lot more planning.

Mandalay had said: Healthy snacks only, please, on her emailed invitation, but Cleo hasn't had time to cook, and Sam and Trent won't eat things like veggies and bean dip anyway, so she picks up some cold cuts and ciabatta buns and Family Size bags of potato chips for them. She'd got extra, because Mandalay had said potluck, and she knows what happens at these kinds of things. People bring salad or dessert and then make beelines for the protein. She also brings hot dogs — the expensive hormone- and preservative-free ones — and bakery hot dog buns, cases of sugar-free pop, paper plates and drinking glasses and napkins (wasteful but what can you do, on a picnic), and a watermelon, and fruit and veggie trays, and ice to keep the salads from breeding salmonella quite as quickly. And the cake! She'd volunteered to get the cake, because the best place to get an enormous sheet cake, decorated, is one of the big supermarkets on the outskirts of the city, and Mandalay can't get there.

And she has remembered candles, enough so that each twin can blow out his eight, and folding chairs, and thermoses of water, and the portable propane barbecue, and the lawn toys that her kids had played with when they were smaller – the croquet set and the ring toss set and the badminton set.

The twins' birthday party is at a neighbourhood park this year – outdoors, as usual. Mandalay always invites their entire class as well as the parents. (Only really wealthy people do that, in Cleo's neighbourhood.) The park is a little shabby, like the neighbourhood: there is graffiti on the restroom building; the picnic tables are scorched and hacked, decorated with bird droppings. (Has she remembered the disposable plasticized paper tablecloths? She has.) Some pretty lime trees have been inexpertly pruned – pollarded – so that they look mutated, deformed. The lawn has been worn down to earth in large patches.

And here, she sees, as she and Trent and their children carry in the cooler, the folding chairs, the bags of groceries, here are the Chinese grandmothers with their polyester trousers and layers of sweaters; the South Asian grandmothers in their salwar kameez suits, and the granddads in their white button-down shirts and turbans; a middle-eastern family with a lot of children; a couple with dreadlocks and piercings and tattoos; an assortment of children in bright flounced dresses, embroidered blouses, camo-print cargo pants, and their parents looking ordinary, like people she might work with.

A holiday long weekend, Trent had grumbled. And we're supposed to drive into the city and spend the day in a public park. Not my idea of a good time.

She'd had to think strategically. No point wasting the big-calibre arguments on this one – for example, pointing out that she had been going to his family events every summer for the last fifteen years. For sure those arguments worked, but they could only be drawn on occasionally, or they'd lose their force. She had to find something more expendable, but still persuasive enough.

The problem is, of course, that she doesn't really want to go herself, but she has promised — she can't get out of it without an unholy stink. And she's not going to go to a kids' birthday party without her own kids there, that's for sure. She gets solo weekend outings very infrequently — she's not going to waste one on this. Also, Olivia and Sam will be necessary, to help entertain the twins. And Trent is necessary, to help keep Olivia and Sam entertained. Besides, why should he get a day off?

She realizes that the argument could easily have gone the other way. If she'd said that she was just taking the kids, Trent might have insisted, aggrieved, on being included.

She had worried that without his inclusion, Olivia or Sam might have tried to get out of it. They are past the stage of finding their younger cousins cute — not that Sam had ever really been in that stage, or maybe he had for about half a year when he was seven and the twins four — and she had noticed they were less and less enthusiastic about getting together with them.

She hadn't been able to use that argument with Trent, though, because he was as likely to take the kids' side as hers, say that he didn't see why they should go if they didn't want to.

She'd finally said: Mandalay needs us all there. She's invited the twins' entire class, and god knows who's going to show up.

Yeah, in that neighbourhood, Trent had said. Is Duane coming?

She had hesitated. Sometimes Trent seemed to approve of Duane; sometimes professed not to be able to stand him. They've only met him a couple of times. I don't know, she'd said.

Are we really going to have to spend all afternoon? he asked then. I've got other things I want to do.

Like watch the hockey game? Or is it football, now?

It made sense to take both vehicles: Trent's sedan and Cleo's suv. There was a lot of stuff to bring, and Cleo knows that both Trent and

Sam tend to get bored and whiney long before parties end. This way, they can avoid all of those tedious negotiations about when to leave.

There is really a lot of food. All of the families have brought great amounts – some with elaborate propane-powered chafing dishes to keep it warm. There are curries and wraps and pickles of many types, and bowls of rice and of curious vegetables. It's like a heritage days fair.

So much food, and nobody has thought to bring folding tables, and the picnic tables are dirty, and so far apart. But she has paper tablecloths!

A young-middle-aged man with very dirty dreads and brown teeth (crystal meth? Is that what causes it?) is telling his partner and their child not to eat the buns and cold cuts that Cleo has put out on the picnic table. Stay away from that stuff, he says. It's toxic.

She catches Trent's eye, then. *Oh my god*, they flash between them, silently.

Duane looms up to her, looking, as always, slightly sinister with his shaven head, his disproportionly long legs and broad shoulders. Hello, Cleo, he says, in a tone backlit by relief. I see you've got every-body organized. You're like a well-oiled machine.

He does the thing then that men do with their glance – the quick assessing slide – and his eyes widen slightly. Oh, for god's sake. He's thinking she's more attractive than he remembered. God, men are easy to read. And shallow. Lose twenty pounds, and though last year you were invisible, this year they're gobsmacked by your hotness. (Unless, of course, they are married to you, and then they probably won't notice.)

Still, she doesn't mind Duane, personally. She can talk to him; he's a reasonable human being. He can think logically. She likes, too, that he takes an interest – more than a perfunctory interest – in the twins. It's probably frustrating for him to have to deal with Mandalay. He must wish sometimes that he had just paid out and walked away.

And now here is Mandalay's friend Belinda, with her softly freckled brown skin, her clever artistic clothes, her great smile. And Belinda's small, polite, and doting partner, Joe, also an artist. Mandalay is always referring to them as examples of how people can live ethical, culturally rich, spiritually balanced, non-material lives. But Cleo can see the money behind them, even if Mandalay can't. Belinda and Joe aren't poor, though they live in this neighbourhood. She's been to their house. It's deceptively simple, but it's been completely re-done, stripped to the studs likely and rebuilt, with hardwood floors and high-efficiency heating and windows, custom-milled wood. Cleo knows what that costs. And they're not living off their art, either, as Mandalay likes to imply: both of them have tenured jobs at the big art college. They have decent salaries.

Then she spots Cliff, and Cliff's wife Veronika, whose English is really getting better, but is still not to the level that you can have a scintillating conversation. Cliff doesn't look well, and she sees Veronika glance at him sometimes too sharply, but she doesn't know if they can talk about that. Can she actually say that Cliff isn't looking well? It might be a totally offensive thing to say to someone from Russia or wherever it is Cliff's wife is from.

Latvia, is that it?

Veronika has turned out a better proposition than Cleo had imagined she would, she has to give Cliff that. She had really expected the worst. But Veronika has settled in over the past three years, is taking English classes, looking after Cliff.

What does Veronika think, though? What does she want? That's what Cleo doesn't know. Feels guilty for not knowing.

Shouldn't she have a job by now? What does she do all day?

But when Veronika seems about to say something to Cleo, there's the sound of a motorcycle turning into the park, and they all turn their heads. It's Ben, their youngest brother. She knows him by his slim elegant posture, his well-fitting jeans and leathers, even before he lifts off his helmet to reveal his lean sculptured face, his streaky-blond hair and three-day beard. Her brother Ben. She sees the other guests have all turned to look at him: he looks, she thinks, like a cross between Ryan Gosling and Keith Urban. So perfect, so handsome. The youngest of them all, the baby who was lost and grieved and then returned to them, shining, miraculously whole. His lovely straight back, his pale-caramel hair, his beautiful gaze and his white teeth. He's taller than Cliff, muscular and graceful. Her beautiful baby brother. Here he is now, greeting his extended family with just the right amount of friendliness and dignity, wishing the twins a happy birthday, getting Sam to make eye contact, relieving Olivia of her sulky slouch.

They're all so damaged, so incomplete, she and Mandalay and Cliff, but Ben is perfect. Ben is what they all could be, proof that they have it in them. Ben is the one who pulls them all together, brings out their true whole selves.

She thinks briefly of her other brother, Che, dead so many years ago, at nineteen, but lost before that, spiralling downward on a chill downdraft of substance abuse and petty crime. She blocks the train of thought, as usual. It's not good to go down that road. It just leads to unmanageable sadness.

Then it's time for the gift-opening, and, as she told Mandalay, who hadn't wanted gifts, this ritual has two advantages: for one thing, it fills thirty-five minutes of time, during which nobody is running around with a hot dog in his or her mouth, and it gives people a signal that the party is nearly over, and that they may prepare to depart.

The other children crowd in on Aidan and Owen to help them tear the paper from their gifts. There is some pushing, but no conflict.

She looks over at Duane, who is surrounded by the other men. They are all interested in the boys' gifts from Duane – new bicycles, expensive ones, of course. The bikes are touched, admired. Duane has done it again, she sees by Mandalay's expression.

But they are nice bikes. And the boys are eight. They should have bikes.

She sees suddenly why Mandalay insisted that they come to the party: to counteract Duane, to be some sort of force against Duane, who is all too at ease, all too in command of any situation, all too sure of his power and his rights. How ineffectual Mandalay must feel; how frustrated she must be at her own powerlessness. Duane has too much: he intimidates everyone else, even the other men.

Ben drifts up to her. Hey, he says.

Hey yourself. Does she beam at him too warmly? He has an air of one who is frequently beamed at.

What are the kids' names again? he asks.

She doesn't think she has heard right. Their *names?*

Yeah, he says. I remember your two, Olivia and … Sam. But not the twins.

Aidan and Owen, she says.

Right, he says. Then he laughs.

What? she says.

Ben just shakes his head.

Cleo sees Cliff and Veronika standing a little apart, and makes her way over to them.

Cliff says, predictably: The kids have just shot up like weeds, eh?

That they have, she says.

I was just remembering, he says, looking after the twins when they were little.

I remember that, she says. I think you saw the boys as *cats*. You used to carry one or the other around under your arm, football-style, and when you changed their diapers, you sprayed their bums under the kitchen faucet. You used to put Owen across your lap and balance your game controller on top of him. You used to prop them up in front of the TV and watch your endless nature shows.

Cliff grins.

I liked to take one of them out with me in that carrier with the straps, remember? They liked that.

They did. They had loved to ride in the baby carrier strapped to Cliff's chest, to be taken out for errands.

Cliff says: Women in stores were really nice to me when I had one of the twins with me. They looked at me like I was a movie star. You know, they came up and talked to me, they touched my arm.

Oh, you and your baby story, Veronika says. You tell it all the time. Do women get any looks if they are in a store with a baby?

Her English is really getting better. Are they going to have kids soon? Cleo wonders. Not that it's any of her business. But surely that was the point of Cliff getting a mail-order bride from Russia or wherever it was, and supporting her?

Mandalay is admiring the birthday cards Olivia has made for the boys. They are hand-crafted, each one the product of a few hours with scissors and pens and glue. They feature pop-up scenes and riddles and puzzles, cut-out figures with googly eyes, much glitter. Each one is different, though they are equally elaborate. Each references the individual twin's favourite toys and games.

They're exquisite, Olivia, Mandalay says. Works of art. There's so much design and feeling in them. And they're beautiful.

Olivia glows.

Now, where does she get that talent? Duane asks.

Is he joking? She takes after Mandalay, of course, Cleo says, though her sister is out of earshot now.

Duane looks startled. Oh? Yes, yes.

Is he being dismissive of Mandalay? Maybe. Cleo looks over at Mandalay, who is talking to one of the little girls, a rather odd-looking child – something about the eyes, her specific kind of shabbiness (none of the other children can be called shabby) – who is clinging to her. She sees Mandalay bend to the child, smiling, intent.

Mandalay deserves better than she gets from Duane. And from Cleo, too, often.

Mandalay is incredibly gifted, Cleo says. It's too bad that she hasn't been able to finish her degree.

She doesn't know what has possessed her. Not a smart move, maybe. She doesn't want to get on Duane's bad side, for heaven's sake!

She has to steel herself not to flinch when he draws back from her.

Then his body relaxes. Hmm, he says. And that's all.

Mandalay's looking at Cleo, now, narrow-eyed. Cleo can read her mind: Why are you fraternizing with Duane? He's the enemy.

Mandalay is clearly very imbedded in her community: she looks comfortable, relaxed, interacting with the other adults and children; Cleo has to give her that. How does she do it? But this is Mandalay's milieu. It's dealing with institutions and bureaucracy and money that stymies her.

She needs to do something for Mandalay. What? A trip, maybe. Somewhere fairly cheap, as Cleo will have to pay the whole freight. But somewhere. This summer.

▼▼▼

CLIFF AND VERONIKA STAY until the cake is cut, until the little boys have opened their gifts. They seem pleased with what Veronika has chosen, the giant ball, the giant bear, which she had got at Walmart on the way. He'd tried to dissuade her from bringing gifts, because Mandalay had said, and then relented and stopped, just told her not to spend very much, and she had come out of the store with the giant ball and bear balanced under her arms. They almost hadn't fit into the truck.

The kids are too excited, he can see. It's chaos, this birthday party. Kids everywhere, food everywhere, screaming and running and wrestling and sometimes crying. Mandalay and Cleo and the other parents trying to organize the kids. He starts to say something to Cleo a couple of times, but she is distracted before he can get more than a few words out. It's not a good time.

Ben, then, Ben arriving on a new motorbike, and Cleo distracted by him.

Cliff says to Veronika: We need to go now.

Okay, she says, getting up pretty quickly. He'd expected her to want to stay longer, but she seems happy to leave.

As he turns onto Canada Way, taking the shortcut east to the highway, Veronika says: We should do more for them. Your sister's boys.

Why do you say that?

She shrugs. They are poor.

They aren't, Cliff says. Their father is well off. There's lots of money there.

They were wearing such raggedy clothes. Dirty.

That's just Mandalay. She can't be bothered.

It's a shame, Veronika says. People will judge them.

Some people will, he says. Then: And you still don't want …

No, she says. No and no. It's not a picnic in the park, having children.

He has to laugh.

What? she asks.

It's a saying in English. It's no picnic.

Well, you see, she says. It was not a nice picnic.

He has to agree. He can see that Veronika is pleased to be invited and to attend, though. She finds his family cold; she does not understand that they are not always having dinner at each other's houses, that they do not get together much for birthdays or on holidays, that he hardly ever visits or telephones his mother, Crystal. She had said to both of Cliff's sisters: We will babysit for you anytime; you must let the children stay with us while you have a holiday. Neither Mandalay nor Cleo had ever taken Veronika up on her offer. They had each come once to dinner, and then Cleo, but not Mandalay, had invited Cliff and Veronika in return; after that they had always been too busy to accept invitations.

He doesn't blame his sisters. They are not close, that's all.

Though he feels he could rely on Cleo for anything, in a pinch. She's good in emergencies.

No, it's Veronika who has to adapt, to learn that there are different ways of doing things.

When they'd had dinner at Cleo's, she'd brought gifts, too many gifts: brandy for Trent, who didn't really drink; a vase for Cleo that he imagines her grimacing at – Cleo is not one for knick-knacks; a child's makeup set for Olivia (he didn't know why that was wrong, but it was; he could see it was); a military figurine set, merchandise from some movie, for Sam: also wrong. Oh, goodness, Cleo had said: You spoil us! And made too much of the vase. But he could see her kindness, or maybe her intention to be friendly, struggling with her idea that people should not give her children certain things, that certain things should not be bought – perhaps should not even exist. He had not tried to explain that to Veronika.

The gifts for the twins had been a hit though – three years had made a difference, maybe, in Veronika's sense of things.

Matching his thoughts, as she does more and more, Veronika says: That Owen! The way he shouted and threw himself on the ball and the bear. He is a noisy one, but it is easy to see what he is feeling.

Cliff says: I'm always amazed you can tell them apart.

They are not at all the same, Veronika says. They do not look the same. They are not the same size.

Cliff knows this. He wants to praise Veronika. It seems important.

Aidan, he says, the way he carried the ball around on his shoulders, bent like that. He looked like that statue of the guy who carries the world on his back.

Atlas, Veronika says.

It is something that really does amaze and delight Cliff: that Russians (or Estonians) know about Greek mythology too. That Veronika knew the stories that his dad had told him when he was young, and that he'd looked up and read about later. It was a bond between them. It showed that they weren't so far apart.

And then Aidan sat in the lap of the bear and sucked his thumb, Veronika says. I think he is too old to be sucking his thumb.

Aidan reminds Cliff of himself, at that age. He seemed nervous, afraid of doing something wrong, maybe. He was a little awkward and timid. When Cliff looked at him, he felt a slightly unpleasant recognition, a little impatience. Pull yourself together, kid, he wanted to say. But it was himself he saw.

If he had a son he'd want him to be more like Owen, who threw himself into things and didn't cry when he hurt himself, but bounced up and laughed. Owen was a child people looked at smiling. He was the child that made people comfortable, that people wanted to be around.

▼▼▼

MANDALAY HAD WORRIED THAT only a few people would turn up for the picnic in the park, which, both Owen and Aidan informed her, is a very lame birthday party. But lots of people have come, and it doesn't even look like it is going to rain. And she's invited their whole class, so it's a May long weekend party, as well.

She'd thought maybe no gifts, everyone invited to make a donation to the food bank instead, but Belinda and Cleo had both nixed that idea. They're *eight*, Cleo had said; you're just forcing your ideas on them, if you make them sacrifice something at this age. And Belinda had said: Gift-giving is, after all, an important ritual. Harriet has been working on the twins' presents for a couple of weeks, already.

So she had acquiesced, and the picnic has turned out to be a fantastic idea.

Of course, it hasn't all gone exactly as she hoped. She had thought that most of the people who were coming would bring something, and so had provided some big lentil-and-bean casseroles and potato salad and rolls, but a few people – including, of course, Duane and Cleo's lot – have arrived with portable propane barbecues and coolers full of hot dogs, and everyone seems to want to eat those. And then the games she'd organized, the friendly cooperative relays across the field, had been turned by Trent and Duane and a couple of the other dads into a free-for-all soccer scrimmage, which had ended, predictably, in some skinned knees and bumped heads, and a ball landing squarely in the bean dip.

The gifts, of course, are ridiculous. There are some smart things like Lego and Playmobil, but the gifts that get the boys' attention are the big plastic vehicles and alien creatures from, she gathers, TV shows and movies: they bristle with robotics, fangs, mechanized body parts. They are cheap; chrome bits snap off as they are removed from their boxes. They all require batteries. They roar, or use unpleasantly snarling voices. They convert into different vehicles or creatures, and blur the lines between human and non-human and machine alarmingly.

Cleo says in her ear: Never mind. They break really quickly. Then at night you disappear them.

Cleo has given the boys too much: fancy puppets and a real miniature drum set and a couple of recorders from the expensive toy stores on Granville Island; books; a new pair of jeans and a

Disney-logo sweatshirt each. Cliff has come with his wife, Veronika, and brought a giant stuffed bear and a giant rubber ball, which will somehow have to be transported back to the house (and where will she put them, there?)

And Duane has bought the boys bikes.

There's some confusion, as the bikes arrive at the same time as Mandalay's brother Ben, and she thinks – she even starts to say, and hopes her words were covered up by the general noise – that Ben had brought the bikes. But no. Duane. And without consulting her.

But Ben! It's so fantastic to see Ben, her baby brother, her long-lost brother. He's so slim and golden, so polished. He waits while the chaos over the bikes settles – Mandalay can see that Duane had waited to produce them until all of the other presents were over, for maximum impact; he has to outdo everyone else – but then Ben reaches into his backpack and brings out four small stuffed toys, stylized animals of some sort, that have everyone suddenly excited.

Swag! Cleo says. Olympic swag! How do you have these already? I tried to get some for an overseas client and couldn't. How did you get them?

Ben smiles, raises his eyebrows.

Owen looks like him, Mandalay thinks. Aidan too, but not as much.

Oh, it's good to see Ben. He always gives off so much positive energy.

Cliff, on the other hand, is obviously not taking care of himself. He's only a few years older than Ben, but seems middle-aged, past his prime. He's put on more weight since she saw him last, and his skin isn't a good colour.

Poor Cliff, though. He's probably working too hard. He and Ben are in business together, but Cliff is the type to work himself to death, to not see that he needs to have a healthy work-life balance. She feels some guilt, seeing him, as well, because he is always asking them to visit, and they never do.

She hears Ben and Duane talking about some trip. Ben, of course, has travelled a lot; he's been everywhere. Ben had been adopted out of her family, as a toddler, and raised in a wealthy home. Basically, bought by a pair of rich lawyers who couldn't have kids of their own. Not that she begrudges him that, but it irks her that there are these assumptions that Duane and Ben always find things in common. Sometimes it's as if Duane thinks he understands more about Ben's life than Mandalay does.

She doesn't like Duane talking to Ben.

But then Cliff is joining in – he and Veronika honeymooned in Mexico, a couple of years ago, and are planning to go again. And Trent – *Trent* – who Cleo says won't go anywhere, who hates to fly, is saying that he's been thinking they might take the kids somewhere at Christmas this year, and where was a good place.

It's just so much conspicuous consumerism. And these places they're going – they're not even interesting; they're basically American resorts, and god knows what it's all doing to the environment and the local culture. And who would want it, the sun too strong to stay out in for more than a few minutes, fat tourists broiling themselves on the beach, a lot of drinking, a lot of inane conversation.

She's not adding much to the conversation about tropical holiday destinations, and moves away to see that Cleo and Belinda have begun cleaning up the picnic area.

Don't do that, she says. Let the guys do that.

Well, you know, Joe did the cooking, Belinda says.

And the Duane ran the games, Cleo says.

Okay, okay. But they like that. They like to take over the fun chores.

Belinda says: Cleo has just kindly offered to give Harriet Sam's old skis.

I assumed you didn't want them for the boys? Cleo says. I assume Duane has bought them some?

Assumptions again. But yes, he has. And it might have been nice to be asked.

She's suddenly very tired of this party.

IT TURNS OUT THAT BOTH Duane's and Cleo's vehicles are required to ferry home all of the sizable gifts the boys have been given, and so Mandalay walks back with Belinda and Joe and Harriet. She has suggested that the boys push their bikes, but they don't want to, and they don't know how to ride them yet, though Duane and Ben and Olivia have been giving them lessons in the park, running along beside them, letting go when they seem to have balance. Both boys have crashed several times. She wonders if the bikes were a good idea.

We just need more practice, Duane says, loading boys and bikes into his vehicle.

What a nice party, Belinda says, as they walk along under the flowering chestnuts.

Has Belinda ever said something was not nice?

When she gets home, Duane has unloaded the bikes, and Cleo the other gifts, and they are all waiting on the sidewalk.

Why didn't you just go in? she says.

Didn't have a key, Cleo says.

Oh, goodness. She doesn't lock the back door. Surely the boys know that?

You leave your door unlocked, Duane asks, in this neighbourhood?

She would prefer not to, but she has lost the key, and keeps forgetting to get a new one made.

Cleo says, *sotto voce* but not out of earshot of Duane: You know that someone could just come in.

Well, they could break in, too. There's nothing to steal, though.

If they break in, Cleo says, at least you can see the signs. The broken window or whatever. But a crazy person could just walk in and hide somewhere, and attack you and the boys.

She doesn't appreciate Cleo trying to scare her, or taking sides with Duane.

I don't want to go around believing the world is a scary place, she says.

Duane throws his hands up in the air.

Where should I put the bikes? he asks.

In the yard, she guesses.

Duane throws his hands up in the air again. Please, do not just leave them outside to be stolen.

How about the back porch? Cleo asks.

There's no room in the porch – it's full of stuff. Bottles and paper for recycling, a basket of cool-weather clothes, a fort the boys made out of the box that the new stove came in.

No problem, Cleo says. We can just turf some of this into your basement ... don't you have recycling pickup?

She does, but she never remembers which day she's supposed to put out the blue box.

Can't they just leave, now? This is humiliating. The absolute peak of humiliation, to be judged by both Cleo and Duane, at the same time. She feels violated.

She knows she should be more organized. She just can't stay on top of things. No, that's not it, precisely. It's just not very interesting to tidy things away. They always find their way back, anyway. It just doesn't seem that there's any point. So what if everything isn't done with military order, as in Duane's or Cleo's places? A little disorder is human. Entropy is natural.

Duane won't leave the bikes outside and he doesn't want them leaving the doors unlocked, so Cleo starts clearing out the porch while Duane goes off to find a new lockset and get extra keys made.

She can't believe how angry she is.

Once they have gone, Mandalay rolls out her yoga mat and the boys climb all over her with their toys. She says, more sharply than she intends: Please go upstairs to your room, now.

For some time she takes strengthening yoga poses: tree, eagle, warrior.

She hears the sounds of the house, finally, rebuilding her world, an aural basketwork. The fridge coughs gently to itself; the floor stretches and creaks; somewhere in the walls a creature or maybe just a pipe tries to find a more comfortable position. The cat pads in and settles herself on the mat. In the trees outside, birds, maybe finches, are talking about going for dinner, and below that, the traffic on Main, three streets away, is a steady arterial hum.

She gathers herself and begins, deliberately, to move.

8

Depreciation

CLEO IS FERRYING A CARGO OF DREAMERS: her children, her sister Mandalay, Mandalay's children, all asleep in the SUV. Mandalay is tilted in the front passenger seat, her head bumping occasionally against the window, her neck not really doing its job. Cleo can't stand to look at people's necks when they're sleeping sitting up. Their vulnerability distresses her. In the last rank of rear seats, is Olivia, who doesn't get up before noon during the holidays, and had half-fallen into the van in the sweats she wears to bed, wrapped in her quilt, and carrying a pillow, which she had put between herself and the window and disappeared into before they'd left the driveway. Next to Olivia, Owen, who had been sagging in his booster seat before Horseshoe Bay, is sleeping angelically, his face slightly flushed, his lips parted, the fine blue threads of veins showing in his translucent eyelids. Asleep, he looks like an infant, still, not a boy of eight. Owen had been up since dawn, Mandalay said, too excited or anxious about the trip. Hence his sleepiness now, and Mandalay's.

THEY'D LEFT THE TWO OF THEM, Olivia and Owen, in the van on the car deck, even though passengers weren't supposed to stay there. In case the ferry sank, she supposes. Mandalay had dithered, the way she does, as if she has someone looking over her shoulder, judging her every decision, but Cleo had pointed out that the odds of the ferry sinking during the one-hour crossing were infinitesimally small, and that Owen would likely, if awakened, be precipitated into a daylong spiral of tantrums. And Mandalay, whose natural parenting style is more laissez-faire, had fallen in with the decision.

In the nearer rank of back seats, Aidan has flopped completely sideways in the seat belt, in spite of the cradling design of the booster. He looks uncomfortable, as if (like Mandalay's) some of his bones are missing, or have liquified. She hopes he's not strangling himself. You wouldn't think that an eight-year-old could strangle in a seat belt, but Aidan has injured himself in a lot of ways that have seemed unlikely, or impossible.

Next to Aidan, Sam is pretzelled against the vehicle wall with the hood of his fleece jacket pulled up over his head and half his face. She can see the orange wires of his earbuds trailing out of his hood and meeting in a Y on his chest, but can't see if he is holding his Game Boy or has dropped it, again, in the midden of garbage and toys that he and Aidan have created between them. It's possible that Sam is awake, and playing, though she thinks not. There is not even the faintest clicking or rustling. Maybe she should have got Mandalay to trade places with him after the first ferry. They could have had some rare one-on-one time, she and Sam. But he's too light still to sit in the front; the air bag sensor doesn't recognize him as large enough to be safe.

It's not bad, though, the solitude of driving, the time to just think, or not think, maybe. To just be, to notice the scenery, to let her mind drift and settle. It's mid-week and traffic is light. The steep slopes, thickly forested with cedar and fir and spruce, the grey skies with their swags of rain, the glimpses of grey-green-blue sea: they absorb all thought, all tension. She sees deer, a bald eagle, lets the sightings sink into her, secret pleasures. In the thick deep forest, the slow cycles, the silent creatures, move about their business.

She is suspended, unassailable, as if in a terrarium. She knows this highway well, the road up the Sunshine Coast, past Gibsons and Sechelt, Richards Creek, Halfmoon Bay. And usually it is sunny; the rain that has trailed them today, the opaque, oystery skies are an exception. Time is suspended; she is suspended, insulated from chores or obligations or conflicts. If she could maintain this state, drive on and on? But the state is not interested in whether or not it will be extended. It doesn't ask for extension. It simply exists, in the green landscape, the glimpses of sea between the immense trees, the relaxed swoop and curl of branch and leaf and wave.

She drives onto the second ferry, and her sleeping passengers stir briefly, but settle again into sleep. The promontories and islands drift by, deep green velvet slopes rising out of the fjords and the glistening dark currents of the sound. In one or two little bays she can see evidence of human habitation: docks, boats, houses with bright metal roofs. What would it be like to live in a place like that?

Peaceful, if she were alone. A kind of hell, with the children, who would be bored and underfoot all day. And likely spotty internet, if any at all, and no cell phone coverage.

What if it were her and someone else?

When she turns off the engine, Mandalay stirs and says instantly, I wonder what it would be like to live in one of those tiny remote inlets? She's like Cleo; she wakes up fully in a split second, like a switch is flipped.

Peaceful, with just your paints, some books, a cat, Cleo says. Otherwise, misery.

Oh, no. It would be great to be here with the boys, just me and the boys. We would have these marvellous lives, looking at sea life, digging clams, reading by a wood stove, doing art....

Wouldn't you want some time to yourself?

Oh, no, Mandalay says. We just all enjoy doing the same things. We're on the same wavelength, as long as there's nobody else around to disrupt it. I never feel like I have an inside and an outside self, with my children. I think we have no artificial separation – we can be totally authentic.

I think, Cleo says, that children need more peer interaction as they get older. They need to separate emotionally from their parents, a bit. It's part of growing up.

I imagine there would be a home-schooling network, Mandalay says. On those fjords.

It's a ritual they go through, every year, on this trip: fantasizing about living off-grid, or at least out of the city, in the green, sunlit inlets of the coast.

Then they're driving off the ferry, bump-rattle-rattle, and in the town of Powell River, with its tiered streets and arbutus trees.

Should we stop at the Safeway? Mandalay asks.

Oh god, yes. Who knows whether Crystal will have even the basics, Cleo says. She signals to turn to go up the hill toward the shopping plaza. At least let's get some milk and coffee and decent bread.

This, too, is a ritual.

THE INTERNET KEEPS GOING OUT. Sam had been complaining about it, and then Olivia was asking, and now Cleo herself is trying to deal with some work emails and has lost connection in the middle of responding.

She knows better to ask Crystal, who's always vague about technology, and who is out in the garden with the twins, anyway. But she has to do some work; she can't be off-grid for a week. And Sam's going to have a lot of anxiety if he can't play online.

Isn't it good to be unplugged? Mandalay says. You can enjoy real life. It's so fantastic to be here, away from everything. There's so much nature out there!

Cleo can't be unplugged. She has a professional job. She's responsible for what happens, even if she is on holiday. It's not like being a waitress or something.

She decides to call up the internet provider herself, spends thirty minutes on hold.

Then Crystal comes in. Oh, she says. I didn't know you were still using it. I unplug the thingy, when we're not sending emails.

The modem. She unplugs the modem.

You can't unplug the modem, Grandma, Sam says. It has to reboot every time. It's like crashing the hard drive. You're just supposed to leave it on.

Oh, the internet costs so much money, Crystal says. I thought, if we weren't using it....

Are you actually paying by data minute? Cleo asks. Or megabyte? Is that because you have satellite? Don't you have a flat monthly fee? Or are you going over your download limit?

Crystal looks blank.

Just leave it on, okay, Cleo says. I'll pay for the extra time if it's on the bill.

OF COURSE, nobody wants to go to bed, having slept so soundly in the afternoon, so Cleo takes herself off to the spare room at ten – she's been up since five, as usual – and has just fallen properly asleep when Olivia and Sam come in, turn on the light, squabble, go back out to use the bathroom, come in again, leave again. Mandalay has taken the room with the queen bed for herself and the twins, and the room Cleo ends up with has a double bed and a cot. Sam won't sleep in the cot because it is uncomfortable; Olivia complains that it's too short for her. Their voices are exquisite torture, jerking her awake. Cleo snarls something, grabs her pillow, rolls herself into the cot. It is too short, and also lumpy, but she would sleep in Crystal's rockery, at this point, if she could only have the light off and silence.

Olivia says she won't share a bed with Sam: he kicks and he smells.

She heaves herself up and back into the double bed. Get into the cot, Sam, she says. Orders.

She is going to die if she can't get back to sleep now.

Sam complies, but within twenty minutes there's a nudging at the blankets, and Sam is creeping into bed beside her, snuffling a little. She's too tired to argue. She's holding on to the possibility of sleep for dear life. She edges over toward Olivia, who, thankfully, seems to be asleep already.

But now sleep is lost to her, entirely. She could perhaps retrieve it, find where it has gone, if she could only relax.... She lies pinched between her two not-small children. Olivia's giving off a lot of heat, and also inexorably slipping into the well Cleo is making in the middle of the too-soft mattress. She rolls over and spoons Sam. He does smell. His hair needs washing. He's too old now for her to bathe him, but he's not very good at doing it himself. He twitches, suddenly, every time she feels herself start to sink down again.

Dammit. She's exhausted: she's worked sixteen-hour days to be able to take this week off, and has done almost all of the packing and prep for the trip, not to mention the five-hour drive. She needs to sleep. Dammit, dammit.

She can't continue to lie there, anyway. Lying awake at night sets her up for a quick trip to the pit, the whirlpool of obsessive thoughts: she can't take much of that.

She crawls out of the covers and over Sam as smoothly as she can manage, contorting herself, groping for the floor, stubbing her toe on the rolling caster of the bedframe, feeling for the door in the darkness, blunting a nail painfully against the doorframe in her misjudgment of distance. But there, she's out, home free, in the living room.

She might be able to sleep on the couch? But no; it's occupied already: her fingers touch the stiff hairs of the dog's back.

She pulls a knitted blanket from the back of the couch and opens the door to the deck. Yes, the air is fresh here, full of oxygen and earth and evergreens. A night breeze soughing in the branches, and crickets' sawing a kind of white noise. She curls herself into one of the deck chairs, lets herself drift. Even if she doesn't sleep, she can be comfortable.

In the night sky, stars like chips of opal. The stars are rarely visible, now, in her neighbourhood.

She should come up here more often. No, that would make her crazy, the long drive, the disorganization of the house, the sluggish internet. What she needs is her own place, a little place, maybe just room for her, out of the city. Bowen or Keats Island, maybe. More accessible. How much is real estate going for there, now?

She imagines herself relaxed in a clean, sunny, pine-floored kitchen, just big enough to cook simple meals in. Reading in a hammock. Olivia and Sam unplugged. Mandalay's right; it would be good for them, playing a board game together, or scrambling around on some rocky beach.

Trent would never agree to it. But she's bringing in her own money now: she could do it herself. Could she? Of course, if he did agree to it then he'd want to come there too, and now the picture's changing, the dynamic's changing: it's the four of them in a too-small place, Trent always upsetting the peace, disrupting whatever quiet activities are going on, creating drama with his mocking, his fault-finding. He'd probably want a big TV right in the open-concept living area.

On her own? Or with someone else?

No, no. Don't go down that pathway. Just imagine the smell and gleam of the new pine floor and window frames, the shipshape little IKEA kitchen. The songs of the siskins and crossbills and grosbeaks trickling in through an open window. The clean smells of the trees and the sea.

She knows what she wants. It's how to get it that stymies her. Well. She's good at problem solving. She must learn not to clench herself, but to let her mind open to it.

Mosquitoes are circling her, homing in on her exposed face, the backs of her hands. Then a small dark-winged weight displacing air: bat. Now she is aware of their denser presence in the air, she can see two or three of them wheeling nearby. She can hear their wings as they turn. She stays still, listens for them, watches for their dark shapes moving across the field of stars. Superhero bats, keeping her safe from mosquitoes. Should she wake up Sam or the twins, invite them to this marvel? No, another night. She'll keep this for herself, the bats, their blacker-than-night velvet, their impeccable moves. She will keep the bats company.

But the mosquitos are still managing to find her.

She gathers the knitted blanket around herself, opens her car. The passenger seat reclines almost completely. In her new-smelling, body-and-food odour-free shell, she sleeps.

CLEO NEEDS TO GET TO THE BANK, to a proper drugstore, a proper grocery store. Anybody else need to go into town? she asks. She half-hopes that she can do the drive on her own, half-dreads it. In the end, they all want to come along, except Crystal.

Crystal rummages in her room for something, comes out with a pair of cracked patent-leather boots that she wants mended: a zipper is broken. Can Cleo drop them off at the shoe repair place, that's a sweetheart?

Is there even a shoe repair store in town, still? Cleo can't think of where it is. And the boots are definitely not worth repairing. But she takes them without remonstrating. She's trying.

In town they split up, Mandalay taking the boys to the grocery store while Olivia sticks close to Cleo. Sticks close but doesn't speak to her. It's like having a disapproving emu chained to her, Cleo thinks. A helium balloon with a frowny face bobbing just behind her shoulder. Olivia lets Cleo pay for her purchases, though — some tampons, some raspberry-flavoured lip gloss.

After, they decide to have lunch in town, and go for fish and chips at a place overlooking the water. Cleo picks up the cheque. Mandalay doesn't offer to split it. It's a bit larger than Cleo expected. But things are peaceful, while the kids are eating, and after.

For all of Mandalay's insistence on organic produce and fifteen-dollar almond butter, the way she destroys a kitchen cooking a meal, using every pot and pan, she doesn't really feed those boys with enough regularity, Cleo thinks. No wonder they have so many meltdowns.

They'd be better off if Mandalay could just give them an ordinary peanut butter and jelly sandwich on Wonder Bread, on a schedule. And they wouldn't be such picky eaters.... Mandalay ends up finishing most of Aidan's lunch, and some of Owen's. She must do that all the time. It's like eating a second lunch.

Cleo has the grilled fish, instead of the battered, and salad instead of fries. But when Sam gives her a bit of the battered, oily crust of his order, she almost faints with desire.

Every bit of willpower: that's what it takes to be slim.

Then the last stop at the bank, where she needs to transfer some money between accounts. She hopes — assumes — it will be a quick stop, but it isn't. There are forms to fill out and sign. The tellers seem so slow — as if they're being asked to do this procedure for the first time in their lives. And while she's waiting, Mandalay and Owen come into the bank, Owen dripping milkshake like he's been dipped into a vat of it, and ask to use the restroom.

Oh, shit, her car seats.

Did any get on the car seats?

Oh, quite a bit, Mandalay says. Sorry! Olivia's dealing with it. We should probably bring her out some more paper towels.

Her forty-thousand-dollar vehicle, new this spring. So new it still smells new. The pearly-grey faux-suede seats.

I don't think the paper towel is going to be adequate, she says.

Oh, probably not, Mandalay says, cheerfully. But you can take a damp cloth to it when you get home. It's more important to get Owen cleaned up a bit now. He really doesn't like to be sticky.

Cleo opens her mouth but Mandalay disappears with Owen down the hallway.

She can't breathe. She literally can't breathe.

Is there anything else we can assist you with today? the teller asks.

When she gets out to her vehicle, Olivia is still patting at the seat. I'm sorry, Mom, she says. Your new car.

Okay, Cleo says. Let's just put some of the beach towels over it for now.

Mandalay comes back out with Owen, who is wearing only Mandalay's T-shirt, as a kind of dress. Presumably Mandalay is wearing a bra under her buttonless cardigan?

Owen, strapped into his booster seat, announces that he needs another milkshake.

Absolutely not, Cleo says.

Oh, come now, Mandalay says. It was an accident. We don't punish people for accidents.

People get punished for accidents all the time, Olivia murmurs from the far back.

He was fooling around, Sam says. It wasn't an accident.

Cleo is astonished at the meanness of her children. But not ashamed.

Please let me get Owen another milkshake, Mandalay says coldly.

Cleo pulls the car over, does a U-turn, heads back toward town.

Actually, I think I'd like a cone, Owen says.

No cones in my car, Cleo says.

Mandalay says, in a small tight voice, Owen, shake or nothing.

If we're going back to the restaurant, Sam says....

We're not, Cleo says. McDonalds. And no.

I was just asking, Sam says. His injured voice sounds exactly like Trent's.

McDonalds? Mandalay asks, as if Cleo had said The Toxic Waste Dump.

They're hardly back on the highway when Sam says, Mom! Mom! He has the lid off again! He's just setting the cup down on the seat! Mom!

Cleo pulls over. She gets out, opens the back door. Mandalay is saying something, but Cleo can't hear it. She takes the milkshake container and its lid and the straw out of Owen's hands. She puts the lid back on, presses it all around the rim with her thumbs, methodically, to ensure it's good and tight. Pokes the straw back through the little hole.

Then she rotates her right arm backwards and hurls the weeping paper cup far, far into the brush at the edge of the road.

9

Adjustable Rate

THE ISLAND IS A CALLIGRAPHIC FLOURISH of forest and sand, scarcely a kilometre wide, and seven or eight kilometres long, lying a little off the coast. It extends west to east, a straight brush stroke of basalt, the top of an underwater hill that extends for a couple of kilometres and then breaks off into a cursive squiggle to the east. The sand is white, and flows in dunes, and trails off into long shallow sweeps of pale turquoise, where the returning tide is warm. As they approach by water taxi, the island becomes itself: gathers into a stand of individual trees, of Douglas fir and arbutus and Garry oak pinned with cottages, and a skirt of pale dunes and shoreline.

Mandalay hasn't been here for at least four or five years, and the island has changed – though likely she is superimposing her childhood memories of it onto what it looked like on her last visit – conflating the two. The shape of the shoreline has altered: the tides and currents constantly sweep sand from one end of the island toward the other, in a perpetual redistribution of assets. There are more cottages now, and to call them cottages is a blurring of categories, as they are multi-storey houses, encrusted with windows and decks. Most of them are vacation rentals, Cleo says; only about a hundred people live here year-round.

The boat bumps up against the wooden pier, and the skipper, a deeply tanned young woman Mandalay doesn't recognize, tosses the painter around a metal post and leaps out to tie it securely. Then there is the business of unloading their gear and the children. Finally, they have arrived.

They all troop off across the sand: Crystal, Cleo and her two, Mandalay and the twins, with big straw bags full of beach toys and food and towels, the beach chairs, the big yellow umbrella, the cooler, which she and Cleo carry between them. And after all, they are able to match their strides, to swing the heavy container between them almost effortlessly.

The sand is fine and white and warm; they all pause to take off their sandals and sneakers so that they can plunge their toes in it. Owen picks up only one of his shucked canvas slip-ons, and its mate lies ahead of them, a little olive-green fish on the sand, until Olivia reaches it and scoops it up without breaking stride.

She's so beautiful, Crystal says.

All fourteen-year-olds are beautiful, Cleo says.

No, but Olivia is especially graceful. She's so light and – carefree.

Ten years of dance classes at an average of three grand a year, Cleo says. Plus a few hundred more for recital costumes. Sequins aren't as cheap as they look.

Mandalay hears what Cleo is trying to do, the attempt at deflection. She wants to say: It's okay, it's okay. But it isn't, of course. It never is.

Only, to be here, to spend time with Crystal at all, they have to expect these flicks, these small knife wounds, to keep their shields up, develop thick armour, or become mist and air. Something like that.

We all admire that lightness, that freedom, Mandalay says. We all want that.

The children, big and small, are engaged in an extensive system of fortifications; they have gathered some allies, and now a dozen or so of them are excavating, dumping and shaping the white sand and carrying buckets of water. Olivia, the tallest, seems to be directing operations.

Look at all that industry, Cleo says. Children are a greatly under-valued source of labour.

It's nice that Olivia is playing with the younger kids, Mandalay says.

It's only because there aren't any kids her own age in sight, Cleo says. And it's likely the last summer that she will deign to do this. There must be a teenager beach somewhere else on the island?

More likely that local teens are all working at summer jobs. And summer visitors are still sleeping.

Isn't it great, Cleo says, when your kids are big enough that they don't have to be watched every second at the beach? And look at the boys, so much more confident in the water, since their Cayman trip.

Is that a dig? Cleo is smiling innocently enough. But she knows that Mandalay hadn't been happy about Duane taking the boys off like that.

It is true. Things are so much simpler, so beautiful and natural and low-key. And the island is idyllic. Mandalay lies back on her beach blanket. She is so relaxed. This is so easy.

Maybe they could stay longer, another week. Cleo has said she only has this week off, that her kids are signed up for other activities, computer camp for Sam and a trip with a friend's family for Olivia, but surely those things can be changed. Mandalay will just have to call Duane, see if he'll switch weekends.

MANDALAY LOOKS AT one of the magazines Cleo has brought – an Australian glossy devoted to decoration. Cleo has brought along a whole boxful of house and art magazines, issues that had been discarded when her company had moved to its new premises, and Mandalay finds she is hungry for them, hungry for image, for design, for the new.

Look at these wall hangings, Cleo says, folding a magazine over and passing it to her. They remind me of those textile projects you were doing a few years ago. They're made of recycled fabric strips, see? It says here that the artist sells them for three or four thousand a piece.

Mandalay feels the clenching of her *Manipura*, her personal power chakra. It's crazy how Cleo can always invade her space, make her feel lacking.

Assuming I'd have the time to create something like that, and make it my own, she says, I don't have the connections to galleries, and Vancouver is probably not a big enough market.

Cleo shrugs, again. I think it's something you could do, she says. If you wanted to.

Why is everyone so insistent that she do something? What do they think she does all day? And how is it their business?

But it's difficult to stay clenched here, on the white sand, with the light of sky and ocean soaking into her pores. She relaxes. Her sons play happily with their cousins. She swims with them in the sand-warmed sea, as the tide seeps back into the shallow beach, in a shining bowl of little sand fish and crabs and bright twirling fragments of kelp.

LATER, CRYSTAL SAYS: I always wanted to be an artist. But my family...

Is it Mandalay's imagination, or has she stopped to shoot Mandalay a sideways, squint-eyed glance?

My *family*, Crystal says, put me in a psychiatric ward.

Now Ma, Cleo says. Mandalay looks around: the three boys are in the other room, absorbed in a hand-held video game that Sam has brought. But Olivia is with them in the kitchen, and probably listening, though apparently reading.

Crystal doesn't usually go down this path when the children are around, and her partner, Darrell, can usually distract her, comfort her. But he's away on one of his routes for a couple more days.

Do you mean, Mandalay says, the time you chased me around the house with an axe?

She can feel Olivia's ears switch on, feel Cleo sag.

They have an agreement not to step onto this path. It only goes in one direction, and it's very steep. But Mandalay has started them all on it, now.

Well, Crystal says, you stole my best dress! I came out of the kitchen where I was slaving away, and there you were, wearing my best dress!

Sometimes it's her best dress; sometimes her favourite boots.

Cleo is shaking her head at Mandalay, from across the table.

Mandalay has slid all of the way down the slippery vertiginous path.

She is thirteen; she has reached her height, ahead of most of her classmates, ahead of her dumpy little sister Cleo. She's taller than her mom, by half an inch. Her hair falls to her narrow waist. She has long, strong legs. She likes that not only boys but also her friends, and even adults, look at her and smile and say how pretty she is.

Her mom, Crystal, lets her borrow her clothes sometimes, shows her how to put on mascara and blush and lip gloss. Crystal will put her arm around Mandalay's waist in front of the mirror, and say, What a pair of cute chicks.

There aren't enough dressers in their house, so the clothes are in baskets. Saves putting them away, Crystal says. Other things are in baskets, too – her brothers' toys; the scraps and bits that Crystal collects for them to do art projects. At least one day a month, more in the winter when it's raining, they all go to Powell River and Crystal lets them forage the thrift store, and then at the end sorts through what they have found and lets them keep some of it. Or, if it's a fifty-cents-a-bag day, all of it.

And at home it all goes into the baskets, and sometimes it's not clear what is clothes, and what is dress-up, and what is art supplies. Cleo likes to wear artificial leis and feather boas and long strings of beads to school; she hasn't figured out yet that she looks like she's about eight, when she does that. And Mandalay has come home from school to find that a corduroy skirt she liked, a pretty rust-coloured one, like something from a magazine, has been cut up for crafts.

That had been the context for the clothes borrowing, which had happened often, without reproach, until it hadn't.

And she knows that Crystal had undiagnosed bipolar disorder and postpartum depression on top of that, that Crystal was thirty-two and had five children and no indoor bathroom. And that when Crystal was able to go home from the psych ward, after Mandalay's dad died, two of her children were in what was called protective custody, and she found that she had signed papers giving her baby up for adoption. Mandalay knows all of this, and she's sorry. She's sorry that her brother Che died at nineteen, and that her baby brother Bodhi, or Ben, has apparently turned out to be an asshole, and doesn't want anything to do with Crystal, and that she, Mandalay, when she at fourteen moved back in with Crystal, supposedly tried to seduce Crystal's twenty-six-year-old boyfriend and ruin her life.

She's sorry that when Crystal chased her around the kitchen with the axe used for decapitating their chickens, she ran screeching down the highway to their nearest neighbours.

She's sorry that she can't mute herself.

Cleo has on her paralyzed-rabbit expression. How does she manage in the world? How does she manage running a household and a drafting office? It's clear she's terrified of any explosion of emotion.

Olivia hasn't turned a page in several minutes.

I need a smoke, Crystal says.

They sit as she gathers up the ratty sweater she wears in the yard, her rolling papers, her little bag of weed, opens the screened door that leads to the deck.

Grandma, Olivia says, you *are* an artist.

Her voice is so small. It's possible that Crystal hasn't heard her.

There are bats out there, Cleo says. At night. We should show the kids.

CRYSTAL IS PAINTING on the walls again: there are flowers and sea-scapes and portraits and animals on all of the walls of her house, something that delights the boys, who want, of course, to be allowed to paint on walls, too. It's a naïve style, lacking in shading and perspective, and isn't even original. It's like an imperfectly remembered copy of greeting-card art, illustrative art, from the 1950s, sentimental, predictable. The boys love it. When they had arrived, they almost immediately run to the kitchen to find some slightly anthropomorphic rabbits, which they obviously remembered from their previous visit. Mandalay had been surprised. But she had seen their delight.

Now there's a new mural underway, on one of the walls of the garage. It's a tableau, Mandalay sees, of Crystal and Darrell's wedding. Crystal is working from a collection of photographs, and has carefully laid out a grid in chalk on the wall and sketched out the figures that will appear in the painting. It's not a representation of any one photo, though, and there are apparently going to be figures in the painting that were not at the wedding: all of Crystal's children, for example, at the ages that they would have been at that time – 1980 – as well as, in the background, Crystal's parents, and Mandalay's dead father, who definitely weren't there.

She's also included a view of the sea, complete with the clichés of sailboats and seagulls, even though it's a good thirty kilometres to the coast from this place, and the sea definitely not visible.

Crystal and Darrell are in the centre of the mural, already painted, in their wedding clothes. Crystal has a child's face, a slim, youthful body, long ringlets. Darrell still has hair, long hair – dark blond, it looks like, bleached at the ends – and a boy's beard.

You look so young, Cleo says, peering at the photo of Crystal and Darrell.

I was thirty-two, Crystal says. And Darrell was twenty-six. It was a scandal!

The figures that Crystal has painted are cartoon likenesses. You have to guess who they're meant to be by their sizes, their clothes and hairstyles.

What do you think? Crystal asks.

Mandalay can see the flat, half-size figure that is meant to be her: her hair, with its feathering (hours with the curling iron), her turquoise halter dress, bought from a consignment store in Powell River. She says: You've painted all of us in. And our neighbours. She can sense Cleo behind her sending out waves of agitation, and avoids catching her eye.

I'm including the spiritual parts that you can't see, Crystal says. Look, she says to the children. There's your Auntie Cleo, and me. And Uncle Cliff and Uncle Ben. And your uncle Che, there.

Cleo and Cliff and Bodhi hadn't been at the wedding. But Crystal has painted them in, standing in a group around her.

I was thinking I would paint Aidan and Owen in, too, Crystal says. And Sam and Olivia, of course. But where do I put them?

How about in front? Owen says.

Good idea, Crystal says. I'm not very good at painting legs, anyway. I can draw you in right here.

Crystal is already grabbing a brush, a tube of paint, but Cleo says: Weren't we going to have lunch now, Ma?

Of course, Crystal says. She gives herself a little shake, and says, Holy crap, look what I'm wearing on my feet. Then she holds out her hands to the boys: Well, gentlemen. What do you prefer for lunch: spaghetti or macaroni?

It's a picture of the wedding that never was, Cleo says.

I always feel that I'd die if any of my friends saw Crystal's painting, Mandalay says. She has not meant to say that, especially to Cleo.

You hardly need to compete with her, anymore, Cleo says.

DUANE CALLS: can she switch weekends with him? She doesn't say that she has been thinking of asking him the same thing, but she agrees to do it.

You can take the bus back, I guess? Cleo says. She has no interest in staying longer. Mandalay tries to imagine the Greyhound trip back, at least eight hours. And then what to do about the boys' bikes. But still.

And then it comes to her, like a swiftly-returning tide, that she has stayed long enough. It is time to go.

10

Contingency

ONLY BACK A COUPLE OF DAYS after the trip up the coast, Cleo's domestic space is disturbed by a call from Arnold. He is one of the Giesbrechts' older foster sons, who had stayed in the community, settled, was now stolid and respectable as if he were their own blood. Mrs. Giesbrecht, Cleo's foster mom, is dead, unexpectedly of a stroke. Or perhaps not so unexpectedly: she was in her eighties. Mr. Giesbrecht had also died of a stroke, three years before. (They'd eaten a lot of pork chops and bacon and sausages, Cleo recalls, judgmentally.) She never took a day's rest, Arnold says, piously; then even more piously, Except on the Lord's day, of course.

Arnold wants her and Cliff to come to the service. Will she do that? She feels her loyalty is being tested.

Yes, of course she'll come, she says, trying to counter his patriarchal religious manner with excessive graciousness. Is there anything she can do?

Thanks, but the church ladies have it all under control.

She says: It must be sad for you, Arnold. I know Mrs. G. was like a real mother to you.

Yes, well, he says. She has gone to a better place. He sighs, heavily, with satisfaction.

Cliff picks her up at home and they drive out of the suburbs, east, into the farmland, for the funeral. There are shopping malls further and further out along the highway, and subdivisions like strange excrescences on formerly thickly-forested hillsides. It's raining and Cliff is silent, negotiating the highway through the slash of his windshield wipers and the sheets of water thrown up by other vehicles. They pass a new exit ramp with three lanes at a crossroad that, when they lived here, had led through farmland only, without even a feed store along its straight flat route, to a lake.

I learned to drive on that road, Cleo says. It never had any traffic.

I did too, Cliff says. Everybody learned to drive along Harmer Road. Then he's silent again.

How's work? she asks.

Cliff sighs. He has always been a big sigher. Is that where Olivia gets it from? She doesn't see much of Cliff, these days. She should make more effort.

She wonders how his business is going. It should be doing well. She'd seen her other brother, Ben, recently, and he'd seemed flush.

She doesn't know what to ask, in fact.

But it's not a bad thing to ride in silence with Cliff, on this rainy Saturday morning.

I wonder, Cliff says, who will do the flowers for the funeral?

She has to think for a moment, but then she remembers: That had been Cliff's thing, helping Mrs. G. with the church floral arrangements.

You never let me call her Mom, Cliff says, suddenly.

That's because she wasn't our mom. We had a mom already.

I wanted to, when I was little, Cliff says. I didn't really remember Crystal. And I don't call her Mom, either.

Cliff is getting too sad, here. Anyway, I was the one who practically raised you, Cleo says. Don't you remember? She puts on a bad Darth Vader accent: Cliff, I am your mother!

He doesn't laugh.

You had lots of mothers, Cleo thinks. Isn't Veronika, who is bigger and older than Cliff, and who cooks for him and does his laundry, another mother figure? What Cliff has never really had is a father. Their dad had died suddenly when Cliff was six, and Mr. Giesbrecht had been a hard, authoritarian man — a pig farmer and overseer of a foster home for tough adolescents.

She does not say this.

It's still raining when they get to the church. Cliff fusses with an umbrella and she says, I don't need it; I'll just run, and he says that he's worried about his jacket. He's wearing that strange leather jacket, she notices. She'd seen it at Thanksgiving the year before, when they'd all gone to his house for Veronika's dinner. There was something off about it. It looked expensive, but not quite right.

It looks like it might be walrus hide, anyway, she says. Water shouldn't hurt it.

Cliff grins, elbows her in the ribs. They have, simply by stepping into the church parking lot, been transformed back into locals, Cleo sees.

The chapel is respectably full. Arnold and one of the other foster boys, Eric, who also stuck around, Cleo remembers, who also looks like a Giesbrecht, even though he's Indigenous, have formed a receiving line with their wives and grown children and possibly grandchildren: women and girls in dresses, men and boys with buzz cuts. Cleo doesn't remember their names. Arnold and Eric and their wives remember her and Cliff. They are hugged, elbow-squeezed, patted. Their spouses and Cleo's children are asked after. Cleo and Cliff excuse their absence: Trent is busy; Veronika has a migraine. Arnold points them to a reserved family area at the front of the chapel, and a younger version of Arnold walks them there.

She has not walked down the aisle between those varnished yellowed pews for over twenty years. She can sense people looking at her as she passes the pews, her name whispered. She holds her chin up. She is glad of her hundred-dollar haircut, her tailored black suit and high-heeled boots. She is glad that she is still slim. She knows that she is vain and a hypocrite and a sinner.

In the front pews, reserved for family, are maybe a dozen middle-aged men whom Cleo does not recognize at first. The Giesbrechts' extended family, she guesses – they had no children of their own. And then she realizes: the front section is occupied entirely by the Giesbrecht's former foster children, all of those delinquent boys now grown to men.

One by one, she recognizes a few of them, the ones whose stay overlapped hers and Cliff's. It is as if they are wax and someone has held them too near the heat. Or pressed them in with an outstretched palm. Only Paul Johnny has kept his lean features, and they are even leaner, skull-like, his eyes deep hollows, several teeth missing from his grimace. By the end of the service, she will see the changed faces as familiar, will not be able to pull up in her memory the original ones.

The pastor is a new, younger man, as would be expected. He both officiates and gives the eulogy, as is common in this community of silent, physical, inarticulate men. The women are voluble, out-spoken, but are still not encouraged to speak, or even discouraged from speaking, in church. The pastor has done a good job, though – he's done his research. He refers to Mrs. Giesbrecht as Lila, tells some amusing stories about her personality, segues into how she invested her immense love in her foster children and her church work, espe-cially her flower arrangements. (The things we talk about *investing*, Cleo thinks: Time, energy, money, love. A strange way to think about it.) All has been in the service of God. He quotes the usual Bible passages. (Life, too, thinks Cleo, is believed to be an investment in the eternal future – but how have humans come to think that way? Is there another way to think about it? Trent certainly dwells on the need to put away money for the future – a different future than the pastor is thinking about, but still the future. Mandalay, on the other hand, seems to have no sense of working *toward* anything.)

A foster son reads an old, sentimental poem. A foster grand-daughter plays a piano piece, without mistakes. They are invited to join in a hymn – "Lead, Kindly Light." Lila's favourite, the pastor says, and Cleo thinks she remembers that it was true. She had also liked this hymn, in her early teens, at least. She can remember now the evening service, with its candlelight, the ambiance of voices singing together, the warmth of the light against the darkness outside.

She opens the hymnbook and sings out. She always sings, when required, in public. It is the seemly thing to do, and draws less attention than not singing. And really – how often does one get to sing, to sing out in a group, which is a deeply-grained pleasure?

Cliff doesn't sing, nor do most of the men they are sitting with. Some of them look morose, or ill at ease; a couple are quite notice-ably fidgeting or trembling. They had been troubled boys, and many of them, it appears, are now troubled men. But then behind her, she hears a rich, pure baritone lift above the others. *I was not ever thus nor wished that thou …*

It's quite the voice: professional, she thinks, with a deep feeling for the phrasing, the musical possibilities of the rather dirge-like hymn. It sounds familiar, as well, she realizes, after a few bars.

In the shuffling between the end of the hymn and the pastor reclaiming the pulpit, she can't resist turning around to see who it is. Who is singing like that?

She recognizes him, his formerly sharp adolescent face appear-ing like an apparition beneath the broader, bearded, middle-aged one. *Lee Dobson.* She watches recognition of her reshape his face. A tiny rearrangement of muscles. *Flicker.* His smile, then. A kind of augmented alertness in him.

Lee Dobson. Well. There's someone she hasn't thought of in a while.

She tries to piece together her memories of Lee. He must be three or four years older than her. He had been fostered at the Giesbrechts' a couple of years after she had arrived, aged twelve. She can remember his leanness, his height, his long hair, which had been an unusual colour, a red-brown, not red enough to be auburn, but not quite ordinary brown, either, and a constant source of conflict between him and Mr. Giesbrecht, who had old-fashioned ideas about the hair length of boys, and about personal boundaries. She remembers now how Lee would try to make a polite joke of Mr. Giesbrecht's verbal assaults, as if to say: *We're both forced to act out these roles, but who are we kidding?* and how a sort of dispassionate impatience would grow in his voice as Mr. Giesbrecht persisted. Mr. Giesbrecht had never seemed to be able to drop it, as if Lee's resistance, his insistence on his autonomy, itself were an ineffable affront. And Lee had always ended up seeming the more mature, the more reasonable and self-controlled, the wiser, of the two.

She might be imagining that. Lee couldn't have been very old. He'd been in trouble with the Giesbrechts for more serious matters, and in fact was being fostered by them for more serious matters. A troubled youth, as all of the boys in the Giesbrecht's care had been. They had specialized in troubled youths.

Lee had been too thin to be conventionally good-looking, but had been very popular with girls – girls her own age, even, though mostly older ones. She remembers those girls, now – their rounded womanliness, their thick glossy hair, their careful makeup. She, even at sixteen, when she'd really started getting interested in boys, wanting them to be interested in her, had still been flat-chested, straight-haired, likely still with a child's abrupt, awkward manner. She had not attracted Lee Dobson, smart, irreverent, rule-breaking, mischief-making, disreputable, disaffected Lee Dobson, or any of the other boys. Had not wanted to, and then had wanted to and not known how. Had despaired and disdained, both.

His hair is darker now, cut short, the reddish hue gone, migrated to his beard, where it is spangled with white. He has filled out, as boys do. As men in their forties do. His beard is groomed and his clothes fit him decently, and he is more comfortable in his suit of funeral black than are most of the men in the room.

She had wanted to attract Lee Dobson, and had made herself foolish. He'd been flirtatious with her, she remembers. She won't let herself remember the details, now, but a flush of shame rises in her.

Not fair. She had been an almost feral child, then a teenager desperate for stability, for approval. Not fair that she hadn't had the required social skills, or sense of self.

He makes it to her side within five minutes of the mourners entering the church hall, where the post-funeral refreshments will be served, as she knew he would. She thinks that he might say something like "How is it that we never fucked when were teenagers" to her as an opening line. She doesn't know him, but she knows enough men like him, men who must have been the sort of youth he was, who describe themselves as rebels. She knows just the kind of man Lee Dobson would become. How all that precociousness and anger would have sharpened into something else, a cynical, predatory personality, a construct coloured by defensiveness in the form of aggression, by guilt and shame.

He says: I sort of always knew that you'd grow up to be a super-model.

He says: You broke my heart, you know that?

THERE'S A TAP at the passenger window of Lee's truck. It's Cliff, in his strange leather jacket, under his umbrella, and the parking lot has emptied, and nearly an hour has passed since Cleo left the church hall. Lee says, Oh, crap, and Cleo thinks: *Phone number, email, something.* They both have business cards. They laugh at themselves, and then at each other for laughing. She gets out of Lee's truck and into Cliff's truck. She is full of electricity. It's been pent up in her, but now is flowing freely. It's coursing through her arms and legs and spine. She needs to run. She could run all the way back to the city. She could keep running, probably, for several days.

She holds very still so Cliff won't notice. She asks, apologetically: Were you looking for me for a long time?

No, Cliff says. I met up with some people I knew from school and was catching up. It was a great conversation. I had just noticed people were leaving and wondered where you had gone.

He doesn't say anything else. Will he ask? Will he mention anything?

It's late afternoon. It's darker than usual, with the opaque slate-coloured storm clouds, and to the west, ahead of them, lightning flashes split and annihilate the bowl of the sky.

11

New Listing

A FAIRLY NORMAL WORK WEEK, except for the meeting Cleo goes to with Alex. It's about the design for a new construction downtown, a high-rise in Coal Harbour, everything but the building envelope.

Can they really take that on? Cleo wonders. It seems too big a project for their firm, even with the merger. She doesn't say anything, though — just listens. She gets it. She and the others who've been asked along — basically everyone who could be spared — have been there to look like a big contingent, in the way a town in a Western might have tried to fake a posse with wooden silhouettes of gun-slingers. Only the developers aren't the enemy, are they?

At the Novabilis site, they put on hard hats and are given passes on lanyards. The cranes are gone now, the For Lease signs up. The building is in the architect's signature style, a smaller footprint with lots of street-level glass; pedestrian-friendly spaces for shops; stepped, spiralled levels so that the building rises almost organically among the other towers, breaking up the sheer cliffs of glass and steel. The building is sheathed in ceramic tile in shades of white and cream and buff, and it gleams, even on dull, wet days, like a tropical seashell.

She thinks about the work on the ceramic cladding. The calculations of the mounting mechanisms, the load and wind resistance.

The upper floors of the building are office space, premises for a big brokerage company, a media conglomerate, an advertising consortium, some law firms. About two-thirds of the way up, the outer shell of the building folds inward to make an asymmetrical, rounded cleft, or as the builders call it, an infold. It's beautiful – and luxurious, a non-essential, expensive use of space and materials. And on the other side of the building, facing the water, there's a daring series of three horizontal protrusions – frills, she wants to say – that extend from the side of the building.

It's a seashell, she says.

The developer is pleased. Got it! he says.

Alex touches her shoulder in approval.

Inside the frills, the building envelope is perforated by high glass walls. The brokerage firm is going to occupy the top third of the building, and the six-metre high glassed space is theirs.

They take one of the interior elevators up – the exterior one with the transparent shaft isn't operational yet – and she watches herself in the mirror, in her mocha linen trousers, her white silk T-shirt, the carefully cut and highlighted hair that she'll have to crush with her hard hat.

Her team, working with Alex, will design the interior space for the brokerage firm, from the concrete walls and huge window inward, to the open patio that rests on the topmost frill.

She has been walking around in a kind of dream since Monday, when Alex had called her in, shown her the first sketches, and said, casually, Want in, Cleo?

They will lean towards minimalist, organic forms, to echo the building's seashell shape. The tendency of sound to reverberate in the large space will be mediated with floating, layered wall panels that will evoke limestone cliffs or waterfalls; they will be made of recycled glass. Glass panels will isolate individual spaces, and can be made opaque by the flick of a switch, which will control an electrical current and minute particles embedded in the glass – a technological advance on Kate's automatic blinds.

The lighting will be almost invisible – aluminum orbs, painted grey-white, suspended from almost invisible cords. All LED, of course.

Everything natural, and vertical, and designed not to interfere with the view.

She knows to walk through the space strategically, so that she looks up and sees all at once the immense spread of ocean and sky in front of her.

On the protrusion, the balcony, outside of the glass wall, there's going to be a park. Trees, benches, grass, a pond. The people who work here will be able to come out and eat their lunches, bring their phones and laptops and work. Whatever they want. There will be birds in the trees and fish in the pond. Her team – Tilly, Michael, Pam, and Lindsay – will work on this, particularly. They'll be responsible for every detail.

In the cab back to the office, Alex smiles at her sideways, his eyes slitted.

It's not until the Monday meeting that he gives her the next assignment, though, pulling her aside as the others file out from around the glass boardroom table.

You've got too many draftsmen, he says. Billing hours aren't cutting it. You'll need to cut one.

From the project?

Cut one, he repeats, not even impatiently, just a little absently. We don't need that many in the pool.

Which one? Tilly?

One of the veterans, he says. Pam or Lindsay. Your decision.

▼▼▼

AIDAN SAYS: Mamma, what are you going to wear?

Mandalay has not actually thought of this. How interesting that Aidan would!

I guess my green dress. The one with all of the buttons.

Aidan winces.

What's wrong with it? I thought you loved the embroidery on it.

It's coming apart, Aidan says.

I can mend it a bit. Anyway, it's a nice comfortable dress and it must have been really good quality when it was new. And it's a great colour.

It's the colour of poop, Owen says. He is lying on the floor with the Lego; she had not thought that he was paying attention.

What did you say?

Goose poop, Owen says. It's exactly the colour of goose poop.

She is almost struck dumb.

That's rude, Aidan says. But Mamma, it isn't a nice colour to everyone, and it is a different colour under the armholes.

Maybe my blue dress then? The flowered one?

Aidan scrunches up his face. It looks kind of like pajamas. And it has a rip.

She has not been prepared for this. Where is this criticism, this really shallow focus on superficial things coming from? Well, she doesn't need to ask, does she?

But she must give space to their experience, which is valid to them, if not to her.

Okay, she says. I'll go to the Sally Ann and see if I can find something in better shape.

No, Aidan says. You should wear jeans.

Yes, Owen says. Skinny jeans with diamonds on the butt.

This is not the sort of thing she owns. There's a flick of anger, which she recognizes and allows to move on by.

I think they might be expensive, she says. Diamonds and all.

Mom, Aidan says, urgently. Everybody wears them. Then, more persuasively: They would look really good on you.

She's transported, suddenly, to her ten-year-old self cringing at the sight of her mom, Crystal, braless in a tank top, walking through her schoolyard. That twist in the guts, the sharp yank between the overwhelming bond and identification with the parent and the sudden awareness of others' glances. The boys are way too young to have to take that on.

It's just really too bad that at their age – they are only eight – they should be influenced by shallow, materialistic, sexist aesthetics. Well, she knows who she has to blame for that.

Holy crap, she says. It's a big job just to go to this birthday party.

We will go, though, won't we, Mamma? Aidan asks, and she sees that Owen's fingers have stopped moving: he's frozen in place.

It feels like the slivery edge of something being wedged, very subtly, between her and her children. A hairline fracture of the heart.

Yes, of course we'll go, she says. But she wishes, again, that it wasn't happening, this party at the Gibbons, for their twins, who are just a few months younger than Aidan and Owen, at their McMansion in West Van, which Mandalay must also attend, as Duane has to be out of town.

She takes the bus down to 4th, where she used to shop sometimes in her pre-child days. There's a store now that carries only yoga clothing. Racks of tights and tops, cute, but incredibly expensive. Who buys this? She'd love to have a new yoga top, not that she's been to yoga for years, but that would be a week's groceries. And she has gained a bit of weight on her belly and under her arms.

Above the racks of cropped tops and jackets there are rows of mannequin legs, upside down in bicycle position, showing yoga pants in every conceivable cut and colour. For men, too. The choice is dazzling. But really, who is buying these clothes?

Next to the yoga shop is a store that sells only jeans. It looks promising: she sees some rhinestoned back pockets in the window display. A pierced and tattooed young woman zeroes in on her almost immediately, before she has time to even look around.

She doesn't know her size. All the sweat pants she buys at thrift stores are just "large." Ten? Twelve?

The saleswoman says, unhelpfully, that jeans come in inches.

Then she must decide how high in the rise, and if she wants stretch or no stretch, flare or boot cut or skinny. Dark wash? Distressed? Jeans shredded up the fronts of the legs, spattered with paint.

Technopop is playing from speakers, loud enough to be stupefying.

Eventually she is ushered into a change room whose curtain doesn't quite close.

The first couple of tries are terrifying. A waistband hits at about the meridian of her c-section scar. Rolls she didn't think she possessed balloon out at her waist. One pair can't be pulled higher than her knees.

She should just stop. What is she doing? She doesn't want to do this.

But when did she become a person who couldn't wear fashionable clothes? When did this happen? She remembers the pleasure of getting dressed for the day, even in her thirties – the look of her body in jeans, the pleasure of the roundness and uprightness of her own breasts in a T-shirt, her small waist. Is she not allowed that anymore? Who has decided that she doesn't get to be sexy anymore? (Of course she is just buying into the patriarchal, sexist, image-driven portrayal of women's bodies, comparing herself with that, right? But then, where is the aesthetically appealing alternative?)

Do you, she asks the saleswoman, have something a little more conservative? Maybe not for teenagers?

Like, for a mom? the girl asks.

Okay. Yeah. And let's go up a size, okay?

Now she is brought some items that actually fit, actually look nice on her bottom (though again, is she just buying into.... Can't it be just natural to want to have an attractively shaped bottom?) She looks rounded, definitely heavier than she was seven or eight years ago – but *good*. And, she will have to admit, more like she fits in with the other moms, the ones the boys must see as typical. She wants that, doesn't she? It's one thing to choose an individual style of self-expression; quite another to have an identity thrust upon you because of someone else's choices.

She has a small pile of possibilities. Then she looks at the price tags, and almost vomits. The jeans cost what she makes in a month, working at the bakery.

When she consults Cleo on the phone, she says: But I thought you shopped at thrift stores? Anyway, the downtown shops are much too pricey. You need to go out to one of the malls.

A slippery slope, Mandalay sees.

▼▼▼

IT TAKES CLIFF SOME TIME to track down the crate, tramping around in the clay, which has stiffened to the consistency of rubber in the sun. He mistakes the crate at first for building supplies, because it is not a pallet marked "live plants – fragile" as he is expecting, but rather a plastic-wrapped block, as high as his shoulder. That isn't good, to start with – the stacking and the airtight wrap. Not for live things.

There are stamps in unfamiliar writing – characters – over the plastic as well, and customs stickers, and he is surprised: he had thought that Demyan had ordered from a local nursery, precisely to avoid travel damage and red tape. It's difficult to bring live organic material into the country. He's surprised that the crate has not apparently been opened.

When he slits the plastic wrapping with his utility knife, it bursts and retracts; it's been under pressure from gassing out — and the strong methane smell of decomposition fills his nose.

Okay, okay. A problem. Now he wishes the landscape architect, who had specified these plants, suggested the supplier, were on-site. But he's a tricky person to work with, sometimes, especially when things that were his suggestion to use don't work out.

How many plants, if any, are still alive? At first glance, anyway, it might be easier to just send the crate back to the nursery. He'll have to open it, though, and use his phone camera to document the damage, so that they can get a refund. It's such a waste. A crying shame.

He feels a sudden urgency to find and rescue any living plants.

Inside the plastic wrappings is a wooden box. He'll need a crowbar for it. He walks back to his truck to get the tool.

I could have got it for you, Nicki says.

Nicki grabs the crowbar and hops up on the crate to get leverage on the top panel. She is coyote-lithe, nothing to her but muscle and bone and sinew. Her slicked-back gingery hair is darkened by hat-sweat to mahogany around her boney forehead and cheekbones. She can heft as much as most of the guys. She runs a crew now, does a good job of it. It was smart of him to make her a foreman.

She does half his work, he thinks.

Worse than he thought, at first: the upper layer has been crushed, somehow, so that the little plastic cartons have collapsed in on themselves. He pries one open: the plantlets inside are brown mush. He groans. What are the layers underneath going to look like, if this is the condition of the top?

That's assuming, of course, that this is the top, that the bale has been kept same side up during shipping. This was the floor, Nicki says.

I'm sure of it. It's been dumped upside down. This was the bottom of the crate.

The next layer is the same. He'll have to write it off. It will all have to be junked. He'll have to take pictures of every layer, though, in case there's a dispute. But under the second layer, things are a tiny bit better: a few, maybe a quarter, of the containers are intact, and inside the one or two he pops open, there is still something green and identifiable as vegetable, though apparently also dead.

What are these? Nicki asks, and he says the name, and adds, You won't have heard of it. It's not native to Canada. It's a fast-growing creeper that will help hold the soil in place on the slope. It's native to Asia.

She says: Awesome. Another invasive species.

He says he doubts that. Most exotics, he finds, don't survive long. He tells clients and landscape architects that, but they don't listen.

He opens the fourth layer. Here, only a few of the plastic containers are damaged. And on the next layer down (or up), none of the cartons are broken, and he finds healthy propagations growing. What's even odder is that at this level, the bamboo poles that form the corner supports of the crate have sprouted, growing shoots and leaves and insinuating roots around and between the plant containers, creating a supporting mesh.

Look, Nicki says. The roots are growing upward and the leaves downward. I'm right. The crate is upside-down.

And she is right. The last layer, though now under the weight of the whole crate, is well-overgrown with the bamboo, and very well protected. He pries the cartons out, snaps pictures with his phone. About a quarter of the plants have survived. It's both a miracle and a pointless waste.

He and Nicki separate the living from the dead and build a shelter for the surviving plants, out of the bamboo and slats of the crate and the plastic coverings, to shield them from the sun. They'll need to get them into the ground as soon as possible.

So are these are tropical? Nicki asks. Can I take one home, see if it will grow in my window?

Nicki is a maniac for rare plants. In her apartment, she has a greenhouse window – a pushed-out box of glass, floor to ceiling, that she has fitted up with glass shelves. He has seen it. She has more kinds of rare plants than he has ever seen in a commercial nursery. It's amazing.

But there's a strict rule at the company: no tools are ever taken home or borrowed; no plant cuttings, no single slips of ivy, not even a runty petunia from a flat of four hundred. Nothing. It was always Mrs. Cookshaw's rule, and he has upheld it. Nothing gets taken.

You know the rule, he says.

Yep, Nicki says. How about one that is almost dead. Could I take one of those?

It pains him to say no to Nicki. He doesn't like to think about the mess Lund Brothers would be in right now without Nicki. Who works her tail off. And nobody would know: it's just him and her, out here today. But he has to be firm with himself most of all.

Nope, he says. Sweat runs down the inside of his collar. It's a very hot day, for Vancouver.

▼▼▼

A STIFF WIND off the strait buffets her, gusts thrusting themselves inside her clothing, stuffing oxygen into her lungs. Cleo gasps. He says: Are you cold? Do you want my jacket? His words in the gusts are cries, like the seagulls'.

She shakes her head: he'd freeze without it. Anyway, it would take a steel drum to cut the wind. And she likes it. It's like being thoroughly cleaned. And it's only a summer storm.

There is hardly anyone on the seawall this brisk afternoon: a couple of cyclists have passed them, some solitary joggers. At one point they'd met a family with tricycles going the other way. They have the path virtually to themselves.

They push further into the wind, side by side, keeping pace. His jacket is suede, brown-green like leaf litter or forest shade. It flaps smartly, with a sound like sails. His hair, more auburn in the sun, whips around his forehead and ears. She had tied her scarf over her head against the wind, like a girl from the fifties. She has a tendency to earache. She has on a light summer coat, not really adequate in the wind, linen trousers, a thin silk top.

She has borrowed time from work, this afternoon. She'll have to make it up in the evening. He, too, can book off time during his working day. Thus they have managed today's walk.

You're cold, he says. They walk back, to where he has parked, and sit in the truck. Lee has brought a picnic – some fresh sourdough that he tears with his hands; a kind of cheese she's never heard of before, that tastes of butter and iron; grapes, fresh figs, a bottle of Prosecco.

He feeds her. She can't remember being fed before. Open, he says, and she obeys, and he puts the torn bread into her mouth, and holds up the silvery unbreakable wine glass to her lips.

It seems to her that the right and opportunity to meet anyone, at any time she chooses, is a basic human need.

She feels light and autonomous in herself, and also expansive. She wishes freedom and fulfillment for all human beings.

Oh, it's not very sensible. If she stops to think about it, the thought pops up fairly quickly. What is she doing? What can be the point of it?

She can't remember the last time she did something that wasn't rational, calculated, that had no specific point. She is driven to do this: that is all she knows.

Unfinished business, he said, when he asked her to meet, the first time.

The truck windows mist over with their breathing. He puts his hand on her thigh. She feels the warmth of it there, warmer than a human hand could possibly be. She thinks: It has been a long time since someone has touched me in companionship or tenderness. She thinks: I am forty years old, and have not had much sexual experience.

They tumble from topic to topic, associatively, doubling back, making new connections, moving from the personal and subjective through the theoretical and abstract, and back again.

Only talk. Already, though, they have crossed some lines. What are the lines, though? Does she believe in them? They are social conventions; they are what other people would think were lines. What other people would object to.

He's never been married, has no kids. He says that he has never stayed with a woman more than seven years.

And then you get tired of them?

I think they get tired of me.

Women want you, he says. They really want you, and then you're spending your Saturdays going to IKEA and fighting over whose turn it is to clean up after the dog, and you haven't had sex in three months, but if you talk to another woman at a party, it's punishment by death of a thousand cuts.

We want security, she says.

He doesn't have what it takes, he says.

She tells him that Trent is a decent person, but frustratingly self-absorbed, unable to imagine anyone else's needs. That he has anger issues. That he's insensitive to aesthetic. She doesn't think she's quite getting all that right.

There is something between them that they are deliberately excavating, something that wants to see the light.

He tells her about his band career, first in a punk band, back in the eighties, called Cold Sore; then his segue into jazz; of his trips, to New Orleans, to Barcelona, Buenos Aires; about the clubs where he has played, and the smells and the food and the conversations. He tells her about his former girlfriends. He admits he's still sending money to a couple of them.

You surely wouldn't have to do that, she says.

It makes a difference to them, he says.

She memorizes every detail he tells her so thoroughly that twenty years later she will be able to call it up.

All so natural, so sweet, so inevitable. Is this what is meant by falling in love?

He takes her hand and kisses all of the fingertips, deliberately, keeping his gaze on hers. Presses her hand under his just to the left of his breastbone, where his heart is.

See, Trent would not even think to do that.

She is trembling, now, with what must be passion. She might faint with it. The adrenaline of desire.

He says her name, sighing: Cleo, Cleo, as if all of his life he has been moving toward her.

12

Escrow

CLEO RUNS THROUGH THE SUPERMARKET, throwing things into her basket: milk, cheese, tomato sauce, ground beef. Where is the produce section? Lettuce, tomato, cucumber. What else? Her brain denying her access. Garlic bread: pre-made loaf. There.

But then goes back for a box of pasta. She thinks there's some in the pantry, but she can't swear to it.

Several customers already at each checkout, bad luck. She scans for the shortest, the fastest-moving. The express lines all snake back a dozen people deep, almost all professionally-dressed, with their dinner purchases. But they should be moving faster. She chooses randomly, and at first her line's a good bet, but then as she nears the front it slows; there's an elderly woman with more than the maximum items, chatty, fumbling. She feels pressure build in her jaw. Of all the times this person could choose to shop and to choose the wrong line.... She glances at her, meaningfully, but the woman is cheerfully oblivious, taking her time. Then needs a price check. *Gah.*

At home she puts the meal together as quickly as she can, moving about the kitchen quickly, chopping, rinsing, stirring. Scrubs the cutting board, wipes the counters down, while stirring the sauce. She's a surgeon, precise, fast. An emergency surgeon, a war-zone surgeon. Fast and clean, choreographed. Hawkeye Pierce, that's who she is. Complete dinner on the table in twenty-seven minutes from pulling into the driveway. She should have her own cooking show.

At the table Trent says the sauce is bland and Olivia turns her nose up at the pre-made garlic bread. Sam puts a few strands of pasta and a teaspoon of sauce on his plate, and moves them around. Clearly, they've all snacked heartily, in spite of her message that she was running late, but that she would be cooking a good meal.

Trent scoops more food onto Sam's plate, gives a shove to the back of Sam's chair. To Olivia he says: You could try making dinner once in a while instead of complaining. Olivia lowers her head over her plate, forks her food in with a studied robotic lifting, making a metronome of herself: I'm just marking time.

Then there's a squabble between Olivia and Sam, and Trent wades in, keeps the conflagration going, escalates it, even, by tossing in general criticisms after the initial subject has been dropped. There are tears, by the end of the meal.

She's so tired.

I'm so tired, she says. I feel like I could just die, but it would be too much effort.

Trent says: I'll clean up. Hey, Sam – give me a hand.

Cleo lies down on the couch. She puts her feet up.

She has to do some laundry, she remembers. No clean towels this morning. It would help if people would hang up their towels and re-use them. She's bought each person in the family a complete set of towels in a different colour, so that they can do this, but still there are towels on the damp floor. Her spare was damp this morning; Trent had grabbed it, his own being unusable.

She gathers the load, takes it downstairs, starts the machine. She's bought a new set of machines – the old clothes dryer took about two hours to finish towels, and she didn't want to keep buying one appliance, having a mismatched set. She has bought a new set, front-loading, stainless steel. She has paid cash for them.

The washing machine plays a little tune when she presses start. She likes that.

What she wants to do is put her pajamas on and crawl into bed, but she may not do this. Anyway, Trent is always watching TV in their bedroom. She must find the children, whom she hasn't spent quality time with all day. She feels another instinct, not to seek them out, not to make a move toward either of their bedrooms, or the basement TV room, where they'll likely be at this time of evening. To move away from, not toward them as if she's a lightning rod for menace, as if she might lead danger toward them.

Foolish. She runs lightly up the stairs, knocks on her daughter's door, finds her sprawled on her bedspread, ears plugged, both her music device and laptop on, typing messages on her keyboard.

How was your day? she asks. She can't smile: she wills her facial features to relax, her eyes to soften and meet Olivia's.

Olivia removes one earbud with exaggerated patience. Fine? Olivia says, the rising inflection adding a veneer of insolence. She is getting tall; stretched out on her twin bed she looks almost too long for it. She doesn't look at Cleo, which means she's possibly still angry from their argument this morning, which Cleo has forgotten about until now.

She doesn't intend to say it, but she does: Have you done your homework?

Now Olivia rolls over, sits up.

Yes, I have. Can I please have some privacy now? The tone, too: exaggerated patience. So that there's nothing to reasonably point out, object to. No obvious rudeness, just the implication. Cleo sighs. She doesn't mean to sigh, but she sighs.

Cleo puts her head around Sam's bedroom door. He's got head-phones on, is playing one of his games on his computer. When he looks up, she motions from the doorway at the headphones, and when he slips one off, she says: You didn't eat much, Sam. Do you want me to fix you something else? She says it quietly. Trent disapproves of indulging Sam over his eating.

Sam shakes his head. Not hungry, he says.

She goes back to the kitchen, finds the dishes untouched, food still on the table. Geez. But faster, more peaceful just to clean it up than to ask someone else to. If she asks Trent, he'll just try to pass if off in an argument with Olivia, who'll protest she needs to finish her homework, and then he'll chivvy Sam out, and Sam will stand at the sink and sulk.

She needed to get the kids into the habit of cleaning up after supper when they were younger. When she'd tried, though, Trent had just barked at them to do the dishes, not seeming to realize that they needed to work with an adult, to learn how. And when she'd suggested that they should take turns, he'd kind of freaked out, saying he didn't want job rosters, he was an adult. And she'd left it at that. Sometimes he'll do them, but usually he forgets.

She always does them if he cooks, and it's a lot more work, because he doesn't clean up after himself as he goes.

She hasn't managed things well. No, she hasn't. Somewhere along the way she's made a lot of mistakes, let a lot of things slide. But she's too busy to address it now, and maybe it's even too late.

They probably need a bigger house, too. It's crazy that they need so much space, that a family of four needs two living rooms and three bedrooms and four bathrooms. But their house isn't even large, by neighbourhood standards. The trouble isn't that their house is too small. It's just badly laid out. There's no flow. Or maybe, there's too much flow. There's no central core to this house, no heart, no place they all come together.

Also, she doesn't have any office space.

Maybe it would be easier just to move? Imagine, if they lived in an apartment or townhouse closer in – now that would be cramped. But then, of course, they'd all have more things to do – they wouldn't be at home all of the time, on top of each other. Maybe she could walk to work.

She's always had this image of herself and Trent and the kids living in, say, Kitsilano, or off Commercial, and spending weekends going to the outdoor market, to a kids' festival at the park, to the library, stopping by a café where they'd always go for coffee and croissants. In the evenings, they'd have a leisurely late meal at a patio restaurant, sit with a glass of wine....

But Trent doesn't want to move; he's pretty resistant to the idea. She'd gone through the whole business three years ago – getting him to agree to list their house, which wasn't a picnic. She'd taken some books out on negotiating, and had worked through them for months, memorized the acronym, BREAKTHROUGH – what had it stood for, now? Belief, Recognition, Evaluation.... She'd staged the house and kept it spotless for months and months so it could be shown; had looked at and convinced herself of the potential of half a dozen other houses, on two occasions even taking measurements and drawing up detailed renovation plans, only to see them sold out from under them. They hadn't been able to carry two mortgages.

They couldn't afford the kind of house then that wasn't a great deal.

Now, maybe they can. Almost? Her salary has gone up considerably. Though she has just bought a new vehicle.

For a moment she feels a kind of lift at the prospect of change, but then imagines bringing it up with Trent, his usual objections, his propensity to shoot down all of her reasons. His outbursts of anger, even. So really, there's no point.

She loads and runs the dishwasher, scrubs the pots that don't get clean in the machine, wipes down the kitchen, and is just putting out a clean dishcloth when Sam materializes in the doorway. Can she make him some food?

Oh, man, I just finished cleaning the kitchen, she says.

He could do it himself but he'll destroy the kitchen, and it's his bedtime. She puts together a peanut butter sandwich, a cup of hot cocoa, a sliced apple. Not brilliant but could be worse. Cleans up again.

Trent comes downstairs from whatever he was doing, says, disapprovingly: Are you making Sam food?

She hears herself saying, defensively, placatingly, that Sam needs to eat, he's so thin. You should take him to the doctor, Trent says.

She wants to go for a run, but it's dark out now, and quite late. And she's too tired to drive to the gym. She should buy a stationary bike, maybe? She picks up the paper, skims the political and business sections so she won't seem ignorant at work.

It's eleven before she gets to bed, crawls into the small space Trent leaves. Even then, just as she's settling, her mind and muscles easing, she remembers the laundry, and has to go back down to the basement to move the towels to the dryer.

Then she can't sleep.

She elbows Trent. Shakes him awake.

You said you'd do the dishes, she says. Then you just disappeared.

I wanted to watch the news! I was going to!

I need you to do things more quickly, she says.

You woke me up to tell me that.

It's true: that was slightly crazy behaviour.

I can't do anything right, Trent says.

▼▼▼

IT TAKES MANDALAY a few extra minutes to get to the class – after she drops the boys at school and catches the bus, she's a bit behind – but the instructor isn't there yet. When Mandalay comes into the studio, the other students, sitting at the long tables, glance at her with expectation.

They think she's the instructor.

There are the usual very thin students, male and female, with layers of baggy organic-cotton clothes and ropy bleached dreads. There are the two or three in black, with pasty faces and piercings. And then the chic ones in expensive, unobtrusive jeans and T-shirts and leather jackets. Only their styles have changed a little in the last eight years since she was in the classroom. But they look so very much younger. Possibly, now, some of them are young enough to be her offspring.

She smiles and shakes her head a little, and finally moves into the room. She finds a spot at one of the long tables and puts down her bag. She is almost shaking. The others will all know each other, she thinks, as she had known the other members of her cohort, eight years ago.

Here is the instructor coming in now – a woman in her thirties, in a sensible smock and work pants. Mandalay knows her from one of her shows. She is a very good printmaker, Mandalay knows: she has already got a national reputation, has had some prominent shows. And has just started teaching here, on a four-month contract. (What hope is there for herself, still working on her Bachelor's at forty-two?)

She is going to be the oldest person in the class.

They are fourth-year students, and so are expected to dive right into the work the first day. There's the mandatory safety and first-aid review – they work with some toxic solvents – and then they are all going around the room, discussing methods and techniques and intentions. Many of the students have spent the summer, it seems, hostelling in Kathmandu or Patagonia. One of the nondescript-looking students, who she knows will turn out to be one of the most gifted and focussed, speaks in a barely-audible monotone of galleries and artists that nobody has heard of except the instructor. Amanda listens to everyone equally, asks a few questions, is not visibly impressed with any of their accounts.

It will be her turn soon. She has to think quickly because she has scrapped her original plan already. She can't remember enough of the theorists she might have been exposed to in her classes eight years ago — her mind has gone blank. She had meant to say something about the body and liminality and texture and porousness, but she has forgotten that language: that is, she can call it up in her mind but not readily to her tongue.

Dammit, she has to say something.

Images from her life experiences rise in her mind: of the dreadful, disputed rat's nest basement room that she calls her studio; of the Emily Carr setting of her childhood, under the high dark dripping cedars; of the concrete-and-glass high-rises with their steel security gates going up all around her home with her sons; of the no man's land that they make in the neighbourhood.

But also of her hours and hours walking through the public art gallery on Hornby on the free days, since she was sixteen. Of the thankfully un-remediated streets she still walks, shepherding her sons to school, of the mom and pop store with its plastic barbecue duck in the window, where she buys vegetables and rice and beans. Of the shapes of the many-patched sidewalks and the roofs still hoisting broken TV aerials, the bedraggled camellia bushes, the lines and textures of them like calligraphy.

She says: I'm interested, in, like, I guess, textiles and distressed materials.

Oh, god.

After the instructor has moved onto the next student, Mandalay can hear in her head, what she wanted to say. That she's interested in exploring the maternal body, in its lack of boundaries, its simultaneous organic growth and decay. That she'd like to combine techniques to create multiple layers.

So, texture and body and landscapes, Amanda says. Do you all know the work of Roslyn Swartzman and Anne Meredith Barry?

Canadian printmakers of the sixties. She does. Her professors, in the eighties (before many of these students were born, perhaps) had talked of them. She has seen slides of their work: fields of colour and texture, fresh and sharp with accessible lines and shapes, landscapes that hum with references to the body. She doesn't have time to pull together an answer, though, before the instructor (who clearly didn't expect one) has moved on.

They look at some slides.

Then they are all at it, bringing out their materials, their notebooks. They are to do a first project with light-sensitive emulsion and one other medium of their choice. They are to work from preliminary notes and research, which they had been instructed to bring to this first class, which has to be handed in with the project.

Mandalay had almost forgotten this, had scrabbled this morning through boxes of photos, her drawings, her scrapbooks of images cut from magazines, built up over the years. She hadn't had time to think about content, had looked only for something that had interesting form and texture, that would work well in black and white. She'd brought a few things to the class, unstuck them from the pages of her scrapbooks, slipped them into the envelope that the telephone bill came in, and into her notebook, more or less as she was going out the door.

Now she chooses one, an image from a photo essay she'd seen in an old *Life* magazine, some years before. It's of a small mountain of discarded clothing, tangled and twisted and yet displaying the odd recognizable feature: the neck band of a T-shirt, a button placket, a logo. It'll work in monochrome, but she might try to do something in colour, too, because the colour in the heap is so volatile, the splashes of carmine and cobalt and viridian.

Will it work? She has to remind herself how to begin: to learn the image, to absorb in detail its movements and patterns. To make notes. She has forgotten the photojournalist's name, so she'll have to go to the library. She sees an ink-mixing chart hanging at the front of the room. She'll have to note the shades and tones she'll need.

Amanda walks around the room, speaking briefly with each student. You need to have a digital file of that image, she says, looking over Mandalay's shoulder. Camera phone is probably good enough. You have an iPhone? (Mandalay doesn't.) She walks on.

Mandalay thinks: I have no idea how I am going to manage this. How I am going to find the time and energy in my life.

Or how I am going to step away from this, ever again.

▼▼▼

HOW WAS YOUR DAY? Cliff asks.

Fine, Veronika says. How was yours? She doesn't come to sit with him as she usually would, waiting for his food to heat, but leans against the countertop, crosses her arms. His insides sink a little.

Mine was very busy, he says. Crazy-busy.

Maybe that is why you don't take care of the thing I ask you, she says. She's showing her dimples, those tiny bottomless wells that appear at the corners of her mouth when she smiles, but her eyes are not smiling, and her voice is just a little bit sharp.

Your text, he says. I answered it. Didn't you get my answer?

She turns her back, now, opens the oven door, looks in. She does not trust that the microwave reheats food properly. When she straightens and faces him again she says: Cliff, I ask you to put some more in the account. It is very important you do this. I cannot get money myself and if you do not put money in, I cannot take care of the house and things.

He feels, now, a pressure build up in his shoulders, like a vise grip, but he keeps his voice calm. I can't put money in if I don't have it, Veronika. I told you that it has to last until the end of the month.

She looks at him with wide eyes, now – bewildered. Are you angry at me? Do you not want to take care of me anymore? You're tired of me?

The vise has begun to move up his neck. Veronika, it isn't about love. I've literally given you all I can spare this month. There isn't any more. He doesn't say that the amount he put into their joint chequing account at the beginning of the month surprises him with its size. But what does he know, as Veronika often says, what it costs to live nicely? And then he had put in a top-up a week or ten days ago. But maybe, he thinks, he had also given her a little cash between those days, too – something about a birthday present for a cousin.

It's not fair, he thinks, suddenly. He works so hard, and Veronika just spends and spends. And he knows a lot of it is just frivolities. She's spending money faster than he can make it. But if he tries to discuss what she spends, she gets very angry. That's why he had set up the joint account. She is not supposed to ask for more, when that is gone.

He feels the unfairness burn through him, but he tries to keep his voice soft and friendly. She is his wife, after all. He says, Veronika, we've talked about this. You have to keep to your budget. Just don't go shopping all the time.

Her eyebrows shoot up; her mouth drops open: a clown face of outraged surprise, he thinks.

You think it is my fault? she demands. You blame this on me, that you don't take care of things?

He is taken by surprise that she would say this. I take care of things, he says, quietly. He sounds defensive, sullen, to his own ears.

I don't believe this, she says. Her shoulders and chest are heaving, now; her voice is very loud.

Please don't shout, Veronika, he says. They share walls with neighbours, and he doesn't think that this is the kind of place where people like to hear shouting.

The stove timer goes, then, and she flings the door open, yanks the casserole dishes out, crashes them down on the glass stovetop. He winces.

You think you can treat me bad because I'm an immigrant and don't speak English well and have no family to protect me, she shouts. You bring me here and expect me do all your cooking and cleaning and not pay me. This is not what you promise me. But it doesn't matter to you, because I have no power. I am just foreign woman you can throw away.

Veronika, he says. Veronika. She has to see that she has enough. She doesn't need to keep buying things.

She seizes his plate, then, begins to move food from the oven dishes onto it, with sharp raps. She puts the plate down in front of him with some force, so that the contents jump a little. There is some potato dish, running now with yellow grease; a glob of white sauce stuck with vegetable lumps; thick, fat-edged slices of greyish meat.

Eat! she says.

He's not hungry anymore, but he picks up his fork and knife and cuts a bit of the meat. Delicious, Veronika, he says.

She sniffs.

He can see that she doesn't mean it, that she's scared. Just a few more days, he says. Then I'll get some payments in.

She says: Maybe you need to get paid quicker. You say to them:

What is this? You think I run a soup kitchen? You pay me sooner. Thirty days.

He has explained to her before how it works. That to get the contracts, he has to offer ninety days. It's what everyone offers. Meanwhile he has to make payments on the vehicles and materials and cover payroll every month.

There's lots of money coming in, and going out, and it should work out, only the amounts and the timing of it make his head ache.

What is she spending so much on? Well, there's food. She buys big roasts, expensive cuts of beef and pork from the butcher, not Superstore where there are sales; fancy sausages; imported cheese. They do not need to eat like this. Even at the Giesbrecht's, where they raised livestock, they did not eat like this.

And there is more new stuff in the house every day, he thinks. Always a new gadget or household item. Toothbrush holders, candles, fancy pillows. Nothing they need.

She shows it all to him when he gets home, and he doesn't say anything.

13

Default

MANDALAY HAS TO INVITE her sons' classmate Colton over to play. There's no out.

She doesn't like the child. She's not sure that either of the boys really likes Colton, either, though at eight they aren't too discriminating, yet. Can be placated, anyway, with promises of new or favourite activities. Or maybe they're just more tolerant, more accepting.

How can she dislike a child, a little boy, an eight-year-old? She thinks of herself as open, tolerant, accepting: the kind of parent without silly social boundaries or agendas, one who teaches, by example, inclusiveness, compassion, non-judgment. But this kid flicks her irritation switches; he's somehow glib, selfish, manipulative. She suspects he is destructive, pitting one twin against the other. She hopes that his unappealing traits are not going to rub off on her boys.

But Aidan and Owen have been to Colton's house three times now over the last few weeks, and each time Mandalay has unscrupulously angled for the invitation in order to have a few more hours to work. She must now reciprocate. There's a social contract among primary-school parents. She wouldn't care, except that she doesn't want the boys to suffer, to be excluded in some way, for her actions.

They have to invite Colton over – probably at least twice – maybe double that, because there is only one of him, and two of the twins.

And Candice will only too happy to have Colton invited. She has told Mandalay, more than once, that Colton is unpopular. Or, more precisely, that the other kids bully him by ignoring him. Mandalay suspects, from things that the twins have said, that ignoring is a natural form of social control that the other eight-year-old children are using on a child who is not very easy to get along with – perhaps a bully, himself – but she doesn't think she can suggest that to Candice.

She had imagined, when the boys started school, that she would befriend the children who were the outsiders: the shy, foreign, over-looked ones who were excluded because they had shabbier clothing or spoke imperfect English. It had not occurred to her that the only sidelined child in her sons' class, the one who was always left out and therefore always available, would be an outcast not on the basis of unfair discrimination, but rather because none of the other parents liked his behaviour towards their children.

A different kind of discrimination. She's not sure if the responsibility of being a parent requires her to include and accept the child who is excluded because of his unpleasant behaviour. How does that work?

But anyway, she must repay the debt.

Colton walks home with her and the boys after school, on this day: he is to stay until dinner time. She doesn't let the twins walk home unaccompanied; they have to cross Main.

Colton, apparently, hasn't got the message. He asks, Where's your car? And when Owen says, We don't need a car; we walk, Colton laughs, with an adult's incredulous, mocking bark of a laugh. At the first corner he tries to turn left where they are to turn right. I know a better way, he says, confidently. The twins look uncertain.

Do you know this neighbourhood well, Colton? Mandalay asks, rather than directly contradict him.

Of course, he says. My cousins live just around the corner. I know it like the back of my hand.

(Hadn't Candice said that she had no family in town?)

Well, Mandalay says. Today we'll take this route.

Suit yourself, he says, shrugging.

It's like he's imitating an obnoxious adult.

Then, in quick succession, he urges Aidan to run ahead with him and leave Owen behind; announces he's left something important at school and needs to go back. If you have, Mandalay says firmly and untruthfully, you'll have to get it tomorrow; the teachers will have gone home already. Then he tries to break a limb off a small tree; asserts that they're lost and demands to consult the GPS on her phone, which Mandalay says she's left at home; pretends to be afraid of a pigeon, claiming that pigeons spread Avian Flu; tries to cross the street against the crossing guard's directions; and then, as they enter their yard from the back lane, looks up at their house and declares it haunted: he's seen it featured on a scientific TV show.

Mandalay wonders under what circumstances she could justify calling his mother to pick him up a little early – like within five minutes of their arrival at the house.

Once inside, Colton runs all over, trying doors, going into all of the rooms, opening closets and drawers. She can hear the sound of his invasion from the main floor. She can't imagine either of the twins doing something like that, not since they were toddlers.

Owen follows Colton, a little less precipitously. Aidan comes and stands close to her.

Is our house haunted?

Nope.

Are you sure, Mom?

Aidan. Have I ever lied to you?

He shakes his head, looks stressed.

Sometimes people like to make things up, just to get attention, she says. Dammit, dammit. She hasn't brought the twins up to be used to lying or teasing; Aidan doesn't know how to deal with it.

The pigeon thing isn't true, either, by the way, she says.

Aidan looks at her steadily, and, as is often the case, she feels his thoughts; she doesn't even need him to speak. *Why do I have to play with someone you don't trust? That you probably dislike?*

Breathe, breathe.

Aidan, she says. We all have different quirks. She rubs his ears gently. Sometimes when people are uncomfortable, they behave in silly ways.

She is not going to get any work done this afternoon. Cleo had told her once: Play dates are win-win. You get time to yourself when your kids are at someone else's house, and you get time again when kids come over and occupy your child.

Cleo had obviously not run into Colton.

The clatter of shoes on the basement stairs, then: Colton running headlong up, Owen following. Colton flies into the main room and stops stock still in the middle, gazes all around him, turning his head and then his whole body. His eyes grow very wide. His jaw drops.

Wowie! he says. This is the messiest house I have seen in my whole life!

And then he falls to the floor, laughing. He laughs and laughs, not faking it this time, but helplessly, till tears run from his eyes and he's out of breath.

He reminds her of someone, she thinks.

She means to forestall Candice from actually coming in the house by having Colton ready to leave, but loses track of time, and is surprised by her knock, and has to let her in. Would she like to stay for a few minutes?

I've got the other two in the car, Candice says, wistfully.

She hadn't known Colton had siblings. Had the twins mentioned them? But they don't talk much about Colton's house, do they?

Bring them in, she says. Might as well go whole hog. She's lost the afternoon, and it looks like her boys will be too wound up to have supper for some time.

There's a little girl of about five, and a baby. The baby is lovely. Candice unzips him from his fuzzy bunting bag and gives him to Mandalay to hold. She has not held a baby for so long. He fixes his round eyes on her and laughs and waves his hands around and grabs her fingers. That baby-smell is seductive.

He is so lovely, she says, repressing a pang of longing for another child.

Yeah, well, Candice says.

And then it comes out, over tea: the baby that was supposed to fix the relationship, the disappointing behaviour of the husband, the growing realization of negative patterns in his behaviour. It's like he can't see that the rest of us exist, Candice says. His eating the last of the bread for toast is just a symptom, you know?

What a litany it is: grievances both large and petty. Mandalay is helpless, trapped. First World problems, she thinks.

I always wanted to be an artist, Candice says. I think I have an eye, you know? I always had the best marks in art.

You should paint your front door, Candice says. And new kitchen cabinets would really change the place. Do you want the name of my contractor? He's really the best.

We're just in this school for the year, Candice says. I've got Colton on the wait-list for Stewart. That's the science and technology school. We're just on the edge of the catchment area but I can drive him. I'll put Cayla into the fine arts school when she starts next year. It's really important to get your kids into alternative schools, don't you think?

There's just an edge…. Cayla's doing dance already. Can you show Mrs…. Can you show Mandy here a pirouette, Cayla?

I sell packaged gourmet foods, Candice says. Out of my home. It's all mail order. Really good quality sauces and spices. And flavoured oils and vinegars. If you're into high-end cooking, you'll really like these products. And I just love being able to work from home. Of course the income helps, too.

We're getting priced out by the Asian influx, Candice says. That's why we live in this crappy neighbourhood. But it's turning around. More people like us are moving in, fixing up the houses. There's going to be a Starbucks in the new building on the corner of 14th, did you notice? And a supermarket with a parkade, thank god.

I'm sorry, Candice says. I hope you weren't offended by me saying the neighbourhood is crappy? Of course, it's getting better. I've met so many women like myself, lately, who have just moved in. Would you like to come to a Chef's Secret party?

▼▼▼

I JUST WANT TO BE WITH YOU, Lee says. I want to wake up and find you next to me and pull you closer. I want to see your eyes last thing before I go to sleep. I want to give you all the pleasure you deserve.

Cleo's whole body goes electric. All of the cells in her body have desired this. She thinks: Only a few months ago I could not have felt this. Two months ago, she had still been able to consider Lee dispassionately.

It is not what she experienced meeting and dating Trent in her late twenties. That had been more like simultaneously interviewing someone and being interviewed for a pretty great job. There had been some kind of elation, but it was similar to the satisfaction she had got at the breakthrough point in her thesis, when all of the pieces began finally to line up and she had glimpsed the happy possibility of not having to work on the damn thing any longer. She, at least, had been driven by a desire not to have to wonder if she was going to meet a guy with whom she could have kids, acquire a good garlic press and cheese board, and a room for her drafting table. It had been a very strong drive. She had been determined, she knows that now, and winces. So determined, perhaps, that she had not done due diligence about Trent. Or rather, about her own feelings about Trent.

On the other hand, she *sees* Lee. She sees his flaws, for sure. The gaps and biases that pock his personality. Not only the cynicism and the clichés, but also the small dark voids within his normal good humour. She knows so much more than she did fifteen years ago; there's more of her to understand and connect with another person.

It's as if she has woken up from a long sleep, woken up to find that her mind has doubled or tripled in capacity.

He picks her up and takes her for drives in the middle of the day, and feeds her lush exotic picnics of foods she's never had before. He puts music on her iPod, music that she then listens to at the gym or running, feeling his sensibilities inside her brain: Arctic Monkeys, Arcade Fire, The White Stripes, The Killers, Amy Winehouse, Beck. She reads the songs as both sensory gifts and messages. She hears Ben Harper's country-ish "Diamonds on the Inside" and knows the lyrics are meant for her. She hears Regina Spektor's light, breathy voice singing about sweet downfalls and the hairs along her spine tremble. It's an education: somehow, she's missed the last decade and a half of music, except for maybe the very mainstream stuff that's on the radio.

They have only met in public, or nearly public spaces. Cafés, restaurants, the seawall, for walks. It has been all talking. Almost all. Personal things, but also movies, books, politics, philosophy. They don't always agree – Lee is maybe not so left of centre as she is – but they can respect each other's views. She has not been able, ever, she thinks, to have this kind of conversation with Trent – informed, open, analytical. Passionate, and yet detached – maintaining a sense of situation – of humour and mutual respect – even when they were diametrically opposed. Most people won't engage this way; they politely change the subject, if they sense disagreement. And Trent either tries to shut her down, or shuts down himself: turns the argument personal.

With Lee it's not personal. Is that it? And yet there is this openness, this trust.

He *sees* her. He sees *her*.

He says: I suspect we would never run out of things to talk about. He says: I don't like you for your *attributes*.

The desire that washes over her sometimes. She must be with him. She must *have* him.

It frightens her, to feel like this. It's like a flu: her body and her mind in the grip of something that feels external, but that has infiltrated her, altered her being.

Some of the time she feels so euphoric that she can hardly bear to sit or walk; she wants to be airborne. She is bursting, supercharged on some kind of high-octane brain chemical. Lightheaded, full of adrenaline, full of good energy, full of hope and positivity and universal love. She loves herself; she loves everyone. She gets it, now: religious or drug-induced euphoria. She feels a hundred times as alive as she has ever done before.

And some of the time she feels an overwhelming sadness, a kind of grief, even. That she hasn't had this feeling before in her life, that she is forty years old and has not had a life of passion, of intensity, of beauty. Her life has been inauthentic, shallow, shaped by others' wishes. There are decades missing. She can't get them back; she can't ever be young again.

She has become a channel of pure desire, and some of that desire is for her own missed life.

▾▾▾

CLIFF'S GETTING OUT of his truck when he sees it. He's after a birthday present for Veronika, taking time out of the day. Which he can't afford, but there's no opportunity later: the shop will be closed. The parking on Broadway is closed off, some construction going on, and so he has to park on Venables, and as he's shutting the door, he sees it: one of his vehicles parked in the southbound lane, the other side of the street, facing him. The Lund Brothers logo, the Helvetica script he'd helped pick out, the graphic design of the spreading green tree. It's a jolt of pleasure and surprise, no matter how often it happens. The pleasure: one of *his* vehicles. One of his little fleet. And then curiosity: he doesn't know who is driving it, or why they've parked here. There are no jobs in this neighbourhood, as far as he knows. Maybe they've stopped for a sandwich and coffee.

He owns several vehicles, now. For all the jobs.

Well, technically, it's the bank's van, he knows. They'd used a big part of the new loan to buy a couple more.

He had listened to Ben, and now all over the city, his little fleet of vans and trucks, marked with his logo – his and Ben's.

Veronika has told him to go to this jewellery shop. She has told him what to buy, within a few options. He does not really mind this. Of course, it is a waste of good money if he keeps buying her things she doesn't want. And he is bad at guessing.

Old-fashioned jangly bells hang from the door's mechanism. There are other customers: two women in robes and headscarves, whose age he can't guess; a man trying to sell an old gold, or maybe not gold, necklace; a woman in an ankle-length skirt and jean jacket that the shop owner keeps glancing at out of his naked eye, the one not hidden behind his loupe.

He has to wait. But then it is his turn, and the jeweller shows him the pieces when he reads the names from his list. The filigree and pink tourmaline necklace, the two art deco bracelets, the seed-pearl ring. He has been worried that the jeweller won't know what he means, but he produces the pieces right away. It's as if Veronika has given him a coded message, but it works.

He does not like the ring, which has many projections and claws. He can only imagine it getting snagged on everything, breaking apart. The necklace is nice, the pink stones in the swirling gold. But it looks too small. He imagines it around Veronika's sturdy neck. No. Not the right shape. Another circle under her rounded jaw. No.

The bracelets: one seems clearly prettier, more pleasing in its twining gold and platinum structure, the arrangement of the winking little diamonds, but when it is taken away to be cleaned and boxed, suddenly the second comes into its own, seen properly, the subtlety of its design and colour. Hold on, he says. He must look at it again. Then the other bracelet again, which must be taken out of its box, but not laid side-by-side with the second bracelet.

His mind goes from one to the other. The second bracelet now seems to him infinitely superior in its design, but the first has more impact, is bigger, showier. He suspects Veronika would prefer it. The jeweller doesn't show any signs of impatience, but keeps glancing at the young woman in the long skirt, who is still in the store, just browsing. Her skirt is muddy at the hem; her hair, twisted into dreads and then pulled up into a bunch like a handful of snakes at the top of her head, is dull, dry, dirty-looking.

Cliff runs his thumb over his short mustache, which is softer than it looks. The textures: the smooth even soft bristles, the warm fine leather of his upper lip. His jacket, which is real leather – that is to say, hide – that has been softened and dyed and expertly cut and sewn. How it squares his shoulders, gives his torso a solid, streamlined look. He straightens his shoulders, in their leather carapace. He tries to look like what he is, a successful businessman buying a nice piece of antique jewellery for his wife.

Perhaps he should take both of the bracelets. Though they should not be worn together, and he isn't sure that Veronika won't wear them together. Maybe he should buy all four things. Wouldn't that be a surprise for Veronika? Wouldn't he make her happy, then!

But it is so much money.

A middle-aged woman in a blue sweater with a sort of lacy design and a rigid-looking grey skirt comes out of the back room, dabbing at her lips with a flowered cloth handkerchief, as if she has been eating her lunch. She strolls up to the young woman. May I help you? Her tone is harsh. She glances back at Cliff, as if including him in her hostility.

He thinks then: The shop owners think we're together. They think I'm trying to distract the owner while the woman shoplifts something. Shame creeps up his scalp, as if he has really been contemplating theft.

The bigger, showier bracelet, he decides. That's what Veronika would prefer. He would like to buy the second, too, but for whom? Anyway, the bracelets are very expensive. He can't afford both. Even one of them is about twice what he has budgeted for Veronika's birthday.

He has never before imagined himself spending this much on a little bracelet.

Living the high life, he says to himself as he leaves the shop, clutching the handles of the tiny dull-green paper bag. It's awkward, foolish for a man to carry – like a tiny purse would be. He'd put it into his jacket pocket, but it might get crushed.

When he's heading back to his car he sees the company truck again, the bright new late-model styling of it nose, the green logo catching the eye. Who is driving this one? He should have a log of the numbers on his phone, maybe. Or would that be micromanaging? It doesn't matter. Just idle curiosity.

But he crosses the street without even thinking about what he's doing: his vehicle is around the corner, the other direction. Maybe he's thinking he'll see one of his employees in a shop, though what is on the other side — a home decorating store, a dry cleaners, a billiards place — don't seem like places where they would need to stop.

He tries to look casual, like he's not spying. Glances into the shop windows, but doesn't slow his step or crane his neck in an obvious way. Glances back at his shining new truck.

The rear offside corner, the one he couldn't see from the street, is completely dented in, running board hanging, tail lights smashed to red shards.

It's a shock. Or rather, he can't process what he is seeing, and then, as he stands there, the shock-reaction kicks in. He's light-headed; he's going to pass out. He can't get the air in. Or he's sucking it in but there's no oxygen in it, nothing useful to him.

He sees that he has put his hand on the head of the old-fashioned parking meter and is leaning on it.

Who has done this? It hasn't been reported. Whoever it was is probably in one of the shops along the block right now, just goofing off. Smashing in the company vehicle and then just goofing off.

He makes a quick decision and begins to check the shops, opening the door and stepping inside to scan the joint before trying the next one. Beauty parlour: the door jangles loudly and a few faces turn to him. It could be one of the women: he does have female employees. But he doesn't recognize anyone. Two older ladies, hairdressers in pink smocks, and three more ladies in the chairs, their hair in various stages of coiffing. Their thin, arched eyebrows: surprise.

In and out of a few more shops. Nobody he recognizes.

He goes back to look at the damage.

What to do? But his phone is buzzing, and he remembers he has to get to the site soon. In his driver's seat he pulls the belt across his chest, feels the paper jeweller's bag, takes it out and locks it in the glove compartment.

Sits for a moment, until he's calm enough to drive.

It's only a ding. It's a ding in a truck. It happens. Insurance will cover it. Whoever is managing this group, Nicki or Ben, will look after it. They'll mention it next time he talks to them. Maybe they don't even need to.

His breathing, like something sharp, broken plastic or something, in his chest. He should take care of himself. He shouldn't let himself have these panicked reactions. How many times have people said to him, Cliff, you're overreacting. And it's true; there's something not manly about it.

He remembers Ray, his former boss, the way Ray's face would turn purple-red, the colour of the cheap corrosive red wine of the neighbourhood drunks of his former life, and Ray would scream in his face, spit flying from his mouth, whenever something went wrong. He is so not Ray. But it feels like he has Ray inside him, trapped, screaming and purple inside of his chest, right now. What has happened to him?

▼▼▼

HELLO, IT'S LISA, says a voice Cleo doesn't recognize as her friend Lisa's, over the speakers of her car. Do you know where Olivia and Amy are?

I think, at your place? Cleo answers. She can feel the hairs stand up all over her head. Surely that's right – Olivia goes home with Amy after school on Tuesdays, and then they take the bus to ballet class together.

No, Lisa says. Her voice is so tight it's a squeak. And then, before she can explain, it's like a tumble into a nightmare, while Cleo's memory and her imagination fill in the detail. Olivia missing. Missing because felled in the schoolyard by an aneurism, her silly giddy pack of friends lacking the sense to call a teacher, the teacher lacking the sense to call an ambulance. Olivia kicked accidentally by another girl in ballet class, maybe that tall clumsy kid who doesn't belong in the class anyway, a freak tumble, a crack of her delicate neck. Olivia hit by a car, walking from the bus to ballet, no doubt chattering with Amy, oblivious to the distracted cell-talking maniac ramming through the intersection. Olivia abducted, tortured, murdered, like the girl in that horrible novel they read for book club.

Just let her be alive, Cleo begs whatever is listening. Just let her be alive and I will take care of her, I'll look after her, I'll put her back together.

Um, Lisa says, and now Cleo can tell it's her, only her voice is about an octave and a half higher than usual. Um, Amy just walked in the house and passed out on the kitchen floor. I can smell alcohol on her. I need to know how much she has drunk. I need Olivia to talk to me right away and tell me how much Amy has drunk. I called the dance studio, and Olivia didn't show up today either.

Lisa, Cleo says. Your daughter is *fourteen*, Lisa, and *unconscious*. Hang up and call an ambulance, Lisa. I don't know where Olivia is. I'm on my cell. I'm in my car, in traffic.

She hangs up herself.

Holy fucking mother. Where is Olivia?

She will murder her, herself, when she finds her. Only please please please let her be okay.

She speeds the rest of the way home, using up her speeding good luck for the whole year, likely. Floors the car up the curving suburban streets, nearly taking out several pedestrians and getting three fingers – that she is aware of – and literally screeches her tires turning into her driveway.

Where is Olivia?

In her bedroom, apparently, with Claire, listening to Amy Winehouse on Olivia's laptop. Cleo knocks, puts her head around Olivia's door. The room is strewn with all of the clothes that Olivia has worn or tried on since the laundry was done.

Cleo does the thing she has always believed she wouldn't do, the thing that only a bad, manipulative mom who deserves to be hated would do. She smiles and says, in a mild, friendly voice: How was ballet this afternoon?

Mm, fine, Olivia says. She looks up from her keyboard and regards Cleo with her usual detached, considering expression. As if she were weighing Cleo up and finding her wanting.

It's Claire who answers. It was fine, as usual, Mrs. Lewis, Claire says, and gives Cleo a little, lazy grin, a very un-Claire-like grin.

It might interest you to know, Cleo says, in a conversational tone, that your pal Amy is unconscious and on her way to the hospital in an ambulance. Her mom would like to know, please, how much she drank, and what?

If there's one tiny bright spot in this whole misery of a day, it's the looks on Claire's and Olivia's faces at that moment.

It's Claire that cracks, Cleo is proud to see, and not Olivia.

CLEO SAYS TO TRENT: I felt like murdering her. There have to be really serious consequences.

It's pretty normal to experiment with alcohol at their age, Trent says. And Claire and Olivia were fairly sensible about it. It was Amy who drank half a mickey of vodka. That girl has some problems.

Cleo says: Are we going to survive parenthood?

Oh, I'm sure there's worse to come, Trent says, laughing. And Amy has probably learned something from having her stomach pumped.

Cleo thinks: Trent needs to see how serious it is. How can he not see that? She thinks about her brother Che, dead at nineteen, his spiral into drug use.

She's swimming in something viscous. Not exactly drowning, but not anticipating being able to move very fast, if she needs to.

14

Crash

THEY HAVE AN EXTENSIVE ART COLLECTION, Duane had said. It's
mind-blowing, really. Their whole house is full of art.

What kind of art? Mandalay had asked.

A real mix, Duane had said. Some West Coast stuff, masks and
so on. Some abstract art from the fifties. Modernist, I guess. Lots of
sculpture. Lots of paintings. *Lots.*

She had bitten her tongue. Duane has a more educated taste
than most people she knows, and he gets it about form and style
and media, but she can imagine the sort of stuff his stupidly-rich
developer and investor friends might acquire – the sort of paintings
you see at juried art shows in the community hall and in tourist-area
galleries, thick giclée and Impressionist-knock-off splashes of whatever colours are currently popular in living room upholstery, coy
nudes, bronze or glass sculptures of leaping porpoises.

Duane had said, as if she had spoken aloud: You might be surprised. You should withhold your judgment.

Okay. She will withhold her judgment. There will be plenty of
time for judgment, she is sure.

At the door, Aidan and Owen are leapt upon, hugged, dragged
inside, by two small, very clean children – boys, she thinks, though

their hair is longish and fashionably shaped, and they are wearing cuffed narrow jeans and floral-print shirts. She has forgotten their names again, or they never really registered with her. The woman who has come to the door with them, who turns out to be their mother (well, she could have been the nanny, right?) seems to refer to them as Malty and Galty, but those seem improbable names.

Taylor Gibbons is wearing stiletto mules, extremely snug pants that look like the illegitimate offspring of an affair between a pair of jeans and a pair of ballet leggings. Her slightly too-generous bosoms are exhibited by a low neckline, and a lot of very blonde hair is teased out and up and clipped with glittery rhinestone barrettes. She has the face of a lingerie-catalogue model – which, Mandalay remembers, Duane has said that she once was – a long oval with huge eyes, a wide, full-lipped mouth, a small, slightly pointed chin. A Barbie face.

There's a slightly awkward lack of choreography as Taylor Gibbons goes in for a hug, and Mandalay extends only her right hand, but then a laugh, and she's drawn inside, into the magazine-lovely marble and cedar and steel entryway, big as her entire suite, of course, and a glass of wine seized from a tray and put into her hand.

Mandalay squeezes her eyelids shut for a moment, in relief that she is wearing her new jeans.

All of the parents at the party seem very lean and stylish and expensively, though informally dressed. (She notices the brands of their jeans, in her new consciousness, and feels a little embarrassed and ashamed about this kind of voyeurism. The thin edge of the wedge.) She'd thought they'd all be young, but in fact they range in age from their late twenties to sixties. There's a mix of racial backgrounds, even a pair of dads. She'd expected them all to be superficial and arrogant, but they almost all seem slightly geeky, sweet, self-deprecating, considerate. Maybe rich people have got more complicated in the last decade? Or maybe they're just more covert with their powers.

The kids, too – she'd anticipated entitled little hellions, but they all seem more well-mannered and polite, on average, than Aidan's and Owen's classmates.

About half the younger party guests seem to know her twins already. She recognizes names that the boys have mentioned at home. That's a bit of a shock. She hadn't thought – of course, that on those weekends when Duane takes them, they socialize with other kids, other families.

Something like a hole opens up just under her breastbone.

But then she is drawn in. Everyone is so charming. Are they all making an effort to be charming to her? Taylor introduces her, in charmingly different ways to different people as the twins' mom, Duane's baby mama (She has not heard that term before), an artist. (Is this even true? Is she comfortable with Duane telling people that? Is he packaging her that way to make her – their whole situation – more acceptable?)

She's drawn into a conversation about independent schools, another about music classes for infants (on which, surprisingly, other people seem to agree with her). The party is a kids' party, but the adults are marshalled into helping out, which they do with apparent enthusiasm, serving food, facilitating games, escorting kids to the bathroom, and dealing kindly and discreetly with mishaps. (As at every function for eight-year-olds, one of the dads says, someone's gonna overestimate the strength of their urethral sphincter.) It's as if all of the adults at the party have second lives as team leaders or motivational event planners. It's like everyone here has invested a huge amount of money into this event – this life, really – and they're damned well going to make sure it is a success.

Okay, she has it a little wrong. Money, no. But time. Everyone here has a meter on his or her personal time, and wants to get the best value for every second. Is that it?

Okay. Judging, judging.

But this kind of hyper-organized life doesn't leave space for creativity or emotional growth, does it? Because those processes can't be structured into time. Those things just take vast amounts of unstructured time.

All of these children are probably regimented little machines – they're all probably so tightly wound that they'll crack open as adolescents. Even if they aren't showing signs of it yet.

And all of the cheerful, energetic, apparently engaged parents – they're probably all on antidepressants, right?

But the party – a big party, in a very big house – hums along in a kind of organized chaos. That, or the glasses of wine that keep appearing in her hand, is making her feel pretty good.

It's later – cupcakes decorated and consumed, professional story-teller leading some interactive performance in the media room – that Duane's friend Max Gibbons, their host, materializes at Mandalay's side. It's good of you to come, he says. There's some intonation that subtly suggests that Duane's non-attendance is unforgivable, and a bond between them. He wonders, in a slight shift of tone, if he can get her another glass of wine. No? Water, then? Sparkling or still?

Unless she's really not picking up on things, he has become slightly deferential.

She's an artist, he has heard. She demurs. He implies that her demurral is to be expected of a genuine artist.

He wonders if he could ask a favour. He's completely uneducated, completely ignorant, a total philistine, but he can't resist picking up things that please him, on his travels, or at local functions. He's afraid he's got a lot and he doesn't know how to organize it or even list it for insurance. Would she.... Of course, he couldn't impose on her time, but maybe she would advise him as to how to look for someone he could hire to help him?

She's pretty sure, given his normal conversational vocabulary, that he's familiar with the terms "curate," "appraise," and "catalogue." What's he up to? Well, she'd flattered, so maybe that's his intent. But why bother flattering her?

He shifts tone again. Now he's slightly abashed, slightly embarrassed, ploughing ahead while astonished at his own temerity. Would she, ah shucks, it's such an imposition, but could he show her some of the stuff right now?

What is he playing at? He has put her into the role of benefactor, expert, though, and she can't refuse without looking, without feeling unfriendly, mean-spirited.

Duane used to play this sort of game with her. What fun it was, sometimes. A titillation. These days Duane's about as subtle as a burning bag of dogshit. But wouldn't it be more pleasant if their sparring could be more playful?

Duane wasn't exaggerating. Max Gibbons's art collection is huge, and hodgepodge. There are the abstracts that Duane mentioned, names that she remembers from her art history courses: Lyman, Pellan, Borduas – Canadian painters of the 1940s and 1950s, post Group of Seven and not as well known, but important to Canadian painting. The strong geometric shapes, the rich natural colours. There's a Prudence Heward that she'd like to own, a Marian Scott that she has a feeling nobody knows about. (One of her profs had been obsessed with the Contemporary Arts Societies movement, so she had learned a lot about paintings of that era.)

Sculpture, on the other hand, isn't really her area, but she's pretty sure most of the stuff here is museum quality – originals, not the decorative kitsch she'd anticipated. There's a kind of cleft obelisk of ebonized concrete and iron, intersected with glass, that she remembers from a slide. Many strong, edgy pieces by contemporary West Coast artists – a Brian Jungen dinosaur skeleton made of disposable clinical instruments; a spindle whorl, a circular plate of carved and inlaid glass, by Susan Point.

And then the masks. The real thing, Haida or Salish, museum quality, some very old. A dozen of them, powerful, expressive, carved and polished and painted, inset with abalone, singing voicelessly at her, as they always do. They should be in a museum. No, not a museum. Where? She knows, of course, that much art is held in private collections – there isn't enough room in museums and public galleries. Artists wouldn't survive without private and corporate collectors.

What she sees is that Maxwell Gibbons – or someone he hires to do his shopping – has a good eye. And that Max is very, very rich. Which she sort of knew already, but hadn't really understood fully.

Of course, there is some not very interesting stuff mixed in with the real stuff – some of what she expected. The banal, the referential, the very easy. There's a group of leaping orcas in bronze, rather a lot of coy female nudes in all media, a Swarovski crystal polar bear, for which Maxwell Gibbons probably paid the price of a minivan, and which is, in her opinion, junk. And some nice stuff that is just a little mainstream – a Robert Bateman, for example, that her host seems particularly pleased with, and, she guesses correctly, was his first purchase.

All of the art is mixed together, as Duane said, in no semblance of order, room after room of it, hanging on walls, propped on mantels and shelves, plonked on granite plinths. They walk through the house quite quickly, and even then, when they get back to the party room, the entertainer has wrapped up, and guests are organizing themselves to depart. She sees Aidan looking for her. She must have been gone nearly an hour.

Well? Maxwell Gibbons asks. His tone has changed again. It's businesslike.

She knows what's required of her, hears a little authority, a deeper tone, a harder sound enter her own voice. You have some fantastic pieces, she says. And some expensive crap. If you want it catalogued, I can give you some names. For appraisal, you might be better off contacting an auction house.

This is all hearsay, of course. She is parroting her curating class prof.

You'll have to teach me how to tell the difference, Maxwell Gibbons says, but he's smiling. He has got what he wanted. And what is that?

Do you like any of it? Taylor Gibbons asks. She's helping her twins pass out loot bags to the departing guests. Unlike her husband, she sounds completely authentic, and curious.

Mandalay lets herself say warmly that she does, she especially likes certain paintings.

On the way back across the city, south and east, Aidan watches the scenery through the taxi windows. Owen has emptied his loot bag out on the seat. Mandalay can see that it is worth more in movie vouchers, gift cards, the requisite candy (but organic, naturally-sweetened, locally-made, hand-decorated artisan lollipops that she knows retail at six bucks apiece), and novelty toys (but again, hand-made, from the fair trade import shop) than the birthday gifts that the boys brought.

Aidan asks, Mamma, did you have a good time? And Owen, who she didn't think had glanced up from his loot once to look out of the windows says: Everything gets uglier the more closer we get to our house.

We could get a bigger house, Owen says.

That's the trouble with hobnobbing with the rich and famous, she says, as lightly as she can. We get dissatisfied with our own lovely house and toys.

What does Maxwell Gibbons want from her? For clearly, that interchange, the tour and the conversation, was a performance of some kind. But maybe a better question is what has Duane put him up to? And why?

But then suddenly she sees it. It's a message from Duane: not even a very subtle one. *Art is for the wealthy, Mandalay.*

It's his usual method. She ought to recognize it by now.

▼▼▼

CLEO GOES TO ALEX'S OFFICE RELUCTANTLY. She has to do the ethical thing. She can't keep up. Every time she takes time off for family, she falls further behind.

She's going to have to ask to step back, to be demoted, essentially. She'll lose the chance to do all of the interesting, creative stuff, but she just can't keep up. Oh, she's going to be so sad about the Novabilis project. She has done so much research on that; she has so many ideas. She's really passionately excited about that project. She even daydreams about it.

But she can't do it all. And if she can't, they need to give her job to someone who can. And that means her projects.

Alex says: I've asked Kate to be here too, as she's more familiar with personnel issues.

I know, I know, Kate says. It's impossible, hey? But we have so much work right now. Hey, I'm going to share my great secret with you! It's saved my life so many times. You'll find it makes all the difference, I promise! And while you're here, do you think you could just give these a tiny once-over? I think there's something not right, and you're the only person who might spot it....

Oh, she is such a good negotiator. She leaves Alex's office with two fat file folders and a brochure for a catering company that delivers a cooked gourmet meal to your house every night.

Kate has no time, right now. Her new project? It's featured on a TV series on HGTV. It's been kept hush-hush but now it's going to air. Kate is going to design lane houses, small second houses to be built on the larger lots in some of the more expensive areas of town: Kitsilano, Shaunessy, Kerrisdale, Point Grey. The city is going to start issuing permits for lane houses in a few months, Kate says. They're such a great idea! Urban infill.

(Cleo thinks of the lovely generous older yards, with their large trees and ponds and hedges, their little worlds of wildlife.)

Kate will have a crew who do the actual work, but she will come in with the ideas. The drawings will be done by the technicians' pool, but will appear to be done by Michael and Tilly. Who will appear in each show as Kate's assistants.

Sidekicks from specific demographics, Kate says, not quite apologetically. It's what the producers want. Apparently, they test really well with audiences.

CLEO BUMPS INTO LACEY at the school one evening: she has gone to talk to Sam's teacher, been called in, and Lacey has too, it turns out, though her son is in a different class. She has seen so little of Lacey the last few months, partly because Lacey has moved out of the neighbourhood, partly because of Cleo's crazy work schedule, and her heart does a funny little twist when she sees Lacey's tall, slim silhouette, her twist auburn hair, at the end of a hallway.

You're looking pretty skinny, Lacey says.

You're looking pretty skinny, Cleo says. She has on her new jeans and new blue leather jacket, and Lacey is wearing similar jeans and leather jacket in a shade of dull orange that Cleo hasn't seen in shops yet.

How's it going? she asks.

Oh, you know, Lacey says. The apartment is too small; the kids just want to go home. Jake is rude to Richard. Claire is impossible.

Richard's kids won't see him, and Michelle is going to take him for every penny.

And Calvin still refuses to move out?

We're working on that. She's smiling, as she says this, her perpetual movie-star smile.

Lacey would never spill in a public setting, or even divulge anything really personal.

Cleo still hasn't got over that it is *Richard*, their friend Michelle's husband, Richard, for whom Lacey has left Calvin. She can't see that he is much different than Calvin. A little older. Is he very much better company? Lacey had said he was very passionate about her, but not much more. Does that mean he makes her feel really appreciated, or that he is good in bed?

Lacey isn't someone who talks about her sex life at all, and Cleo has difficulty even imagining Lacey has one. Lacey is so private. Cleo has never seen her without her clothes on, even when they've gone to the pool or clothes-shopping together. Not in the ten years that she's known her. That whole thing about the core biopsy was almost impossible to get her head around. Lacey has really high privacy boundaries. It's one of the things Cleo admires about her.

How is Richard worth it? That's what Cleo would like to know.

But at the same time, she sees it, sort of. That he is someone *new*. Someone Lacey hasn't been having the same conversations with for the past fifteen years. Someone whose body, whose gestures, whose mannerisms, whose entire ways of being aren't so familiar that she can't even see them anymore. Can't even see herself anymore.

Sometimes she gets it, and she wonders if it might be worth it, yes, worth whatever guilt and fear and loss and pain might have to be endured, to be able, for even a short space of time, a blink of existence, to break out of the stone encasements that they have built, together, out of every banal decision, every mundane act.

ARE YOU KIDDING ME? Cleo asks. A whole weekend? How would I manage that? How would *you* manage that?

I know, Lee says. I know. But we never have any time together.

I can't, I can't, she says. I never get time off. I work all week, and I spend all weekend and all the evenings catching up on work or doing things with the kids, doing things for the kids and the house.

Really? he says. No spa weekend with girlfriends, shopping trip, lunch and drinks with your sis? He says this knowingly, in a tone that he has sometimes that is cynical or mocking, one that chills her a little. He is describing someone who is not her – someone on TV, maybe, or the wife of a client. He is not seeing *her*.

I don't take breaks, she says. I'm always working.

Almost always, she amends. For one thing, the past few weeks she has taken several lunch breaks – something she never used to do; she used to work through so that she could get more done. There is always more to do than she has time for. She has taken breaks to meet Lee, and then she has had to put in extra time to make up for the breaks. She can't subtract any more from what she puts into her job or her kids.

Okay, he says. Coolly, she thinks.

When a gap between them opens up, when he seems to be looking through her, past her, like this, a little despair comes over her. A little death, as if by suffocation. How has she got to this point?

It has come to her that a decision is to be made, by her, in the future. She must choose between two things, but she doesn't know what these two things actually comprise.

Lee has not ever said anything about a future. She can think of a long list of questions that he has not asked. Suggestions or plans that he has not made.

Okay, she says to Lee. Okay. I'll try.

BUT I HAVE BEEN HOME by seven every day except one for the past two weeks, Cleo says to Trent. She says this in a reasonable, calm way, but the button has been pushed: she can sense the misery elevator ascending to pick them up. I spend every evening with the kids, and the weekends too. And I've cooked meals from scratch at least eight times.

Do you think I haven't too? Trent shouts, though it's not a logical comeback: he had started the argument by saying that she was never home. He's changing the issue.

What are you talking about? she asks, still reasonably.

He says: Forget it. Just forget it. He stomps upstairs. Cleo can hear listening, from the house. Or maybe it's a careful shutting out.

She's been really practicing lately meeting his accusations and his defensive reactions, his outrageous rants, by calmly saying, I don't think that's true, or I don't see it that way. Practicing not reacting angrily or just letting things go, silently.

But Trent has begun to respond differently to her efforts at calm, rational, respectful responses as if she has wounded him severely, as if she is the aggressor. He has started playing the victim when the kids are within earshot. And he's careful not to yell at her when the kids can hear, only to make subtle, referential digs. She used to let even his most egregious slights and insults go, so as not to drag the kids in – so as not to make them witnesses to parental conflict. But he has turned the tables on her. He acts wounded, when she calls him out on things. He says, pained, resignedly, as she never did, as she would never have stooped to doing: *Let's not make Mom mad.* Or: *I guess I just need to let go of this as you're determined to control it.*

Trent the other day, eyes downcast, murmuring: *I guess I've offended your mother again. I just can't get it right.*

That after he'd complained about the dinner that she had cooked, and she had remarked, in a calm, even voice – she'll swear it was a calm and even voice – that it was disappointing to have someone criticize a dinner you had just spent two hours, after a full day of work, preparing.

She sees the beginnings of his strategy working – Olivia saying: Poor Dad, he was just trying to remind you he doesn't like that much garlic, and Sam withdrawing into himself, blank-faced.

On this day she has come home bearing a nice takeout meal from the local shop that serves what is really gourmet cooking. She's been stopping there at least once a week. Kate was right in her recommendation: it's great, though incredibly expensive, not much less than eating out, but she gets a break from the casseroles she makes on the weekends, the KFC Trent picks up on his nights to cook. It's a temporary solution, but maybe it will help. Maybe they just need to get through the next few weeks.

But even though she had texted her ETA precisely, she has come in with her briefcase full of work she will do later tonight, with her two heavy bags of warm food to find Trent ensconced in the bedroom, the table not set, remains of the kids' snacks – peanut butter, cereal, the last of the avocados, intended for tomorrow's breakfast smoothie – littering the kitchen, the kids on their computers, homework undone.

You have to keep an eye on the things! she shouts. You can't be oblivious! She doesn't mean to; she means to keep her voice reasonable, but she is shouting.

Trent shouts back. His eyes are bulging, his face purple, spittle flying from his mouth. Talk about oblivious! Do you even know how long it's been since you had sex with me?

At that moment, she's aware only of Olivia and Sam, completely able to hear this. It's only later that she thinks of what she should have said: *Right. And that's another of my chores?*

SHE NEEDS TO DO SOMETHING. She is going crazy. Because nobody will talk about these things. Nobody will help. And she can see what is happening in her family, but she doesn't completely trust her own sense of things. They can't be this way, because she is trying so hard. She is doing everything she can do; she is always working on getting better, and still things just get worse and worse.

▼▼▼

CLIFF SAYS: What do you mean, we aren't insured? Of course we're insured. All of our vehicles are.

The woman on the other end of the line at ICBC says: Your driver didn't have a class 2 licence, as the conditions of the insurance agreement for this vehicle specify, so the insurance contract is void. Do you understand?

He understands with terrible clarity, actually. He feels that he is standing too close to a giant HD TV screen.

It's one of the company rules that all of the employees' licences are checked and kept on file. Company policy. The insurance company had said to do this and he had always carefully done it. And now this kid, this recent hire, has gone and dinted up not only one of their trucks, and the estimate a few grand to fix it, but also another vehicle he backed into, with some force, in a parking lot. A late-model BMW. And there is no coverage. The estimates for both vehicles come in at just under twenty grand.

When he tracks Ben down, his brother says, only: Shit like that happens. That's why we have insurance.

We don't have insurance. The driver wasn't qualified.

Well, insurance for things like that happening. Insurance for uninsured things.

Cliff isn't sure that there isn't such a thing. Anyway, they don't have it. He has talked to their accountant. He also knows — he looked up the records, saw that Ben had hired the kid that was driving, and Ben didn't do a licence check. Yes, he knows that. He knows it a hundred percent. There's no question this time of there being some perfectly reasonable explanation. Or of him not being sure of his facts.

But his lips won't open to say: Ben, you screwed up. You need to take care of this now.

It's *twenty grand*, Ben, he says. We're maxed out, credit-wise, he says. We're not going to make our payments.

That's what accountants always say, Cliff.

You were there, Cliff says. You know it's true. We don't have any more credit room.

But Ben isn't really paying attention. He's kind of sprawling in one of the oversized leather chairs in their new office, busy with his phone.

He can feel his chest tightening and his brain starting to choke up. *Breathe. Articulate what it is you want. Focus on that.* He wants Ben to take responsibility. To admit he messed up and to come up with some way of covering the financial hit.

Ben looks up. Yeah?

It's twenty grand, Ben.

Ben shakes his head. Man, those luxury car companies stiff you, don't they. Just for a couple of door panels. Hey, maybe you could talk to the owner of the BMW; see if he can get it fixed somewhere cheaper, you know? I have heard of a guy in South Surrey, does a little cash business auto body stuff.

No, Cliff says.

No what?

No, I'm not going to tell the car owner to go to a place in South Surrey.

Ben shrugs. Don't say I didn't try to help. He goes back to his phone screen.

Cliff makes himself take a breath, which doesn't seem to reach a third of the way down his lungs. Ben. You made a mistake. You broke company policy. It's your responsibility to take care of this. You hired the kid and didn't do the checks. I think you should make up the loss yourself. You need to personally come up with the money, Ben.

Now he has Ben's attention: Ben stares at him for a moment, then laughs.

Whoa! You're really freaking out about this, Cliff.

He has not freaked out. His voice is calm. Almost calm.

It's a reasonable thing, Ben.

Ben looks at him, head tilted. I'm trying to understand you, he says. I guess I'm a bit shocked that you would want to take this out on me. It was an accident, Cliff. It was sheer bad luck that the kid, whatever his name is, didn't have his full licence and got into a parking lot accident and dusted some overpriced foreign model. Sheer, random accident. Don't take your anger out on me.

The way Ben has always been able to stay cool, to tilt his head that way and stay objective. How Ben just listens and doesn't say much, but then slices through things with one detached comment and they kind of unfold for him. He sees it now: it's one of the things he has thought so good about Ben. And now.

Not an accident, if the rules were not followed, he starts to say, but Ben cuts him off, talking above him, talking faster.

Are we really going to do this? Is this how it's going to be? Because maybe, then, Cliffie, this partnership isn't working out for me.

Ben has said this a couple of times before, and always, hearing it, Cliff's guts start to turn inside out. He always backs down, ends up apologizing for whatever he was trying to call Ben on. He can't stand it when Ben's angry at him. He kind of collapses, inside.

But not this time. He needs to stand his ground. Well, he is standing in cold sucking black mud, but he needs to stay there.

WHEN HE GETS HOME, he goes to his den and turns on his computer, and he's shaking while he waits for it to boot and connect to the internet. The internet is so fast, now – it's only a matter of seconds. But he hears it's going to get even faster.

He had been half-afraid, half-hoping, that the bank website would be closed for updating, but it is not. He keys in the password and there it is, the list of accounts. The line of credit, the business charge card, the chequing account, all with their balances showing next to them. And without even drilling in, he can see what he should not be seeing, that there is a balance on the credit card.

He had said: Let's just shut the card down, freeze it; and Ben had protested that it wasn't necessary, that it would be too hard to get another one down the road, and the loans woman at the bank had said they might find it inconvenient. She didn't recommend it. That had been Thursday. They had not needed anything. He'd made sure the supply shed was stocked, and they used a different card for gas for the vehicles.

But here, already, was a balance of several hundred dollars on the credit card. And something else. The car lease balance was higher, too.

Okay. Okay. There's an explanation. Because he has to believe what he is seeing, though it seems impossible. There will be an explanation. and things will be dealt with. He will call the branch now and get the explanation. Maybe he should go it alone: one Lund brother in Lund Brothers Landscaping.

WHAT IS HAPPENING, explains the loans officer, is that they have maxed out their business loan. They are making the minimum payments but there is so much interest that they can't pay off the principal. And they can't get any more loans.

Ben says: We have lots of money coming in, though. This is stupid. We need people to pay us faster, that's all. It's the stupid lag between us having to make payroll and our loan payments and buying supplies, every month, and us not getting paid by our jerk-off clients for three months.

Cliff says: It's always worked like that, though. If we hadn't maxed out the loans we wouldn't be in the squeeze. We shouldn't have laid out so much. Ben must be right, but he can't get his head around it. It seems to him that they know they have those expenses, they come in every month, and so do some of the cheques, and they ought to be able to make it balance out.

You're not helping things at all, here, Cliff.

Actually, the loans officer says, you are bringing in a lot of business. You really just need to get a little extra cash in here. Maybe refinance, get rid of the high-interest stuff. That's what's creating drag.

Refinance?

Let's see, she says. What do you have as equity?

Try to get your head around it, Cliff, Ben says. You're just sitting on the equity in your house, which is increasing like crazy. It could be put to work. In the long run, you'll get such good return that you'll be doubling your money. You can get out of debt in no time and then things will be great again.

But what if it doesn't work? What if I lose my house?

That's not going to happen. You heard her. Business is going great! Do you want to miss out on the opportunity to let it grow even more because you're too timid to lose what you have?

But what if it doesn't?

It will work. Cliff. You can do math. We're trading debt at twenty-four percent interest for debt at only six percent. Can't you see that's eighteen percent savings. Do you know how much that is?

He can actually do the math. He knows what they'd save a month, yes. It's not going to make a difference, though – the difference isn't going to pay off the debt. Even he can see that. It'd be like scooping water with a beer can out of the Fraser when it's in flood.

We need to cut back our spending, Cliff says. We need to give up the office space and the leases on a few of the trucks. Those are the things we don't need.

I dare to contradict you, Ben says. The new vehicles and the office space are investments in the business. They'll help us look more professional, be more efficient. You can't really run a business anymore with some old pickup truck out of a shed, Cliff. You have to project the image of what you want to become.

There is always a kind of glow off Ben – he has a confidence, and ease to him that Cliff will never in a million years have. He knows that he, Cliff, is being narrow and timid. He grew up with very little, and he doesn't have the right attitudes about money. It's not something to worship. It's just a tool. He has to learn to see money with more detachment. He's recently read a book about this. But he has a bottom line.

I'm not going to put my house up for collateral for a business loan, he says.

That's not what we're talking about, Bro, Ben says. It's a refinancing. When you bought your house, it was worth so much, and you had to borrow, what, eighty percent of that. But now your house has probably tripled in value.

He understands that. He also understands about corrections, that the markets have done a correction, and his house is not worth three times what he paid for it. It is maybe worth a little less.

But he needs to make Ben happy. He needs Ben to feel happy with him and this feeling is running through his body like an electric hum; it's so loud he cannot hear anything else. Ben is turned away from him now, his arms folded, shaking his head. He can't stand it that he's disappointed Ben. He has to think of something. He has to fix it. He has to start fixing it now.

I sense that you're blaming me for something, Ben says. I feel that you're blaming me because I was the one who wanted to expand things, only you just won't just come out and say it. Look, Cliff. We have to be honest with each other.

Well, he does blame Ben, in some ways. It's always Ben who wants to spend the money, and it's spending the money, money that they don't have, that has got them into this trouble, as far as he can see.

You have to tell me what you're really thinking, Cliff.

He feels suddenly very tired. He always loses at these arguments with Ben. Ben just argues circles around him. Now, if he is to say that Ben always pushes for spending, and actually doesn't work very hard, Ben will show him how he is wrong, again. And he'll be forced to admit it, but then later, he'll see things differently again. He'd save himself a lot of trouble if he just – what? Gave it up. Gave up trying to make decisions where Lund Brothers Landscaping is concerned.

But he can't, because it's his name on the paperwork for the loans, too. His job to try to work this out.

But he won't put his house up for the loan. It's all he has. And it's not his, only: though he pays the mortgage, in his mind it's always half his wife's. That's how it works.

I'm sorry, Ben, he says. The house isn't negotiable. I couldn't do that to Veronika.

Ben sits in silence for a few seconds and Cliff feels the dread opening inside him, inside his chest, like a big sucking hole.

Then Ben jumps up and without a word, is out the door, gone.

What has he done now? What will he do, with Ben angry at him?

Then the thought comes to him out of nowhere, insidiously, like an insect crawling in through a crack he can't see: It doesn't really matter if Ben doesn't come back. Things will go better without him. Cliff can do what he wants, which is to cut back, get the company out of trouble. Cliff was just fine with his two trucks and aging mower and one and a half employees, what he had before Ben became his business partner. He was never going to be rich, but he didn't owe anything and he made enough to live on and to put money away.

He is probably just not smart enough to have a big business. But Ben isn't either, maybe. And Cliff works hard enough to have a successful small business.

Everyone had said it would be a good thing, for him and Ben to join forces. Cleo and Mandalay and Ben's adoptive parents, and his mom, Crystal – and the people at the bank. He's listened to them, of course.

But, the insect whispers, maybe it was just easy to listen. Maybe you had your own reasons for listening, and they had their own reasons for encouraging things, and maybe they weren't anything to do with reality.

He realizes that he needs to move: he's still sitting in the office with the loans officer, and she must have somewhere else to be. In fact, she has made a little cough, or something. He stands up, so that she can move. She is a stranger to him: she has said to him, often, I'm on your team, I'm there for your life, not just your business. But he looks at her now, her neat haircut and careful makeup, her nice suit, and he does not know who she is at all.

Why don't I look into some small business solutions for you, she says, and we'll talk in a couple of days.

Yes, he says, with great effort, as if he's just awakened from a heavy daytime nap. Yes. But he doesn't believe anymore what she is saying.

▼▼▼

WHEN CLEO GOES TO BED, Trent's watching his evening news report. It's not on the regular news channels, but some more in-depth, nerdy, weekly cable program that Trent follows on financial trends.

Well, it's his work – he's an accountant, he should be following this stuff. Though maybe he could PVR it, watch it when no one else is watching TV.

The panellists' voices seem more excited than usual, and she sits on the edge of the bed and watches for a few minutes. It's about some financial services firm in the States filing a Chapter 11 bankruptcy. She's heard of this group, she thinks: Lehman Brothers. And she'd heard, on her way to work the other morning, on the car radio, something about a big Dow Jones drop, but hadn't followed up. She doesn't really follow the market, though maybe she should. Kate, her boss does.

Lots of pundits putting in their two cents' worth about what it means, and whether there should be a bailout by the US government. Trent is watching intently. She'll ask him about it later.

15

Foreclosure

THE BOYS HAVE SOMEHOW persuaded Duane to attend their school concert. Autumn Concert, it's called. They are very excited, both about the concert itself – they have done nothing all month, it seems, but practice songs and cut out orange and yellow construction paper leaves – and about Duane coming. They pointedly don't refer to his coming, but she sees one or the other of them suddenly remember, while they're talking about the concert, while they're singing the songs for her, to practise them, and suddenly become charged, shining.

Mandalay does not know what she feels about this. She doesn't mention it: she will just take her cue from her sons, and try to act nonchalant. But it's not easily overlooked. It fills the house, their. excitement. It's a kind of electrical disturbance.

It's like having someone in the house who's in the throes of falling in love.

She can't believe Duane is doing this. It's totally the sort of thing he always said he wouldn't do. He didn't want to be a family man: wouldn't go to boring family things, be tied down. She remembers his adamant refusals to even meet her sister, when they were dating. Only high-quality entertainment for him.

And now, apparently, he's coming to the concert. He's going to sit on uncomfortable metal folding chairs in a school gymnasium for an hour and a half while a couple of hundred young children whom he doesn't know sing and tootle their recorders, off-tempo and off-key.

Presumably, just to please the boys, to be a good father to them, he has agreed to go.

And so maybe....

Maybe what? Maybe he wants them to be a family, after all? Get real, she tells herself, rudely. Anyway, she wouldn't want that to happen. It's a bad idea. Duane is not dad material, and they really, really would not be happy living together.

Could she compromise a little, if it were good for the boys?

It wouldn't be good for the boys. Duane would be a very bad role model. And he would be inaccessible to them, most of the time. They'd notice that, if they were sharing a home.

Put any thought of a reunion from her mind. It's not in the cards. It's not what she wants. And almost certainly not what Duane wants. He's still barely civil to her.

Duane comes straight from the office and meets them at the school, finding them in the lobby, before the boys have to go to their classroom to be costumed and readied, and parents have to go take their places in those rows of folding chairs in the gymnasium. He greets the boys, jokes a bit with them about recognizing them later, follows her into the gym and sits next to her. She is acutely aware of him. Maybe she wishes he hadn't come? She'd be able to enjoy herself more? As it is, she feels anxious that he's going to be — well, not impressed. That he'll just see the flaws. That he'll make her see them.

He looks around at the coloured paper decorations and the lop-sided crepe paper streamers on the wall, says: This takes me back. Says: Aidan looked a bit seasick, back there. Nerves?

Duane's very relaxed. A few parents who had met him at the boys' birthday party greet him from their seats, and he nods back in a friendly way. He looks at the program; he seems to know which classes the twins are in, who their teachers are.

The concert progresses as all elementary school concerts must, with songs by the kindergarten class in felt elves' hats, their baby voices rising and falling, their little bodies shifting and twitching, jostling, turning right around, hopping, shimmying, completely without conformity or self-consciousness. Then the movement up through the grades, with recitations and skits and recorder playing, accompanied by a volunteer mom on the piano and much good-natured emceeing by the vice-principal in an oak tree costume, all the way up to the seasonal selections by the grade six band, accompanied by a dad on the trumpet.

Mandalay weeps surreptitiously through the whole thing. She knows that Duane has noticed, though he doesn't say anything. She can tell he is noticing by the uncomfortable way he is holding his shoulders.

Though that could just be the chairs.

Owen and Aidan, as third-graders, have both a play and a song.

Aidan has the lead part in the play. She had not known, helping him practise his lines, that it was the lead part. Duane literally sits up a little straighter. Aidan is line-perfect and very funny.

He *owned* that part, Duane says, during the applause at the end.

Owen gets to do a solo verse during the song, and his voice is tentative at first, but then rises, clear and – she hates to say it, but it's the only word – angelic, out toward the dim rows of parents, the thin line of teachers at the back, the streamers and the emergency light and the low, folded-back basketball hoops. There are gratifying little gasps and murmurs from the other parents. Mandalay doesn't look at Duane, because if she does, that's going to be it for her, no matter what his reaction.

As if they were a real couple.

After he pulls into their driveway, Duane says to the boys: Run and get into your pajamas, and to Mandalay: Stay for a minute; I need to talk to you.

So she stays, sitting in the passenger seat of his powerful and expensive vehicle, as she used to so many years ago, waiting to hear what he would say.

Mandalay, he starts. I want to put the boys into a better school. I'll pay the tuition. Their whole lives are at stake here – who they'll be friends with, the attitudes toward achievement and the arts and doing things in the world. They need to be exposed to these things now, while they're developing. They need to see that the world has a lot of possibilities for them.

She can hear his frustration, but what he's saying goes against everything she believes – everything she knows. The boys need to grow up connected to the real world, not to have lives of privilege, to think that everything in the world is theirs for the taking.

They're fine where they are, she says. Didn't you see that, tonight?

Duane shakes his head. You are one stubborn... he says.

Did she hear the beginning of the "b" sound?

Were you going to call me a bitch? she asks.

No. He looks shocked. What kind of person do you think I am?

She doesn't know, anymore.

Nine years ago, she thought that she knew Duane better than anyone else, and that he knew, and understood, and accepted, and liked her, equally. She does not understand how they have become enemies. She must have not really seen who he was. She must have been completely deceived.

He takes off his glasses and with the fingertips of his other hand, rubs the skin around his eyes. (As if she's being difficult. As if she's the unreasonable one.)

Look, he says. Life is dog-eat-dog. I for one want to give my sons every advantage I can. It's just irresponsible not to do that.

He has chosen the wrong word. He's used that word against her before; she's well aware that he considers her irresponsible.

A compromise, he says. I'll help you rent a nice condo nearer their new school. You'll still have a nice place to live, but you'll free up the equity in this house, before the market corrects even more.

No, she says.

He says: It's not about your *whims*, okay. It's about a chance to change the boys' futures. This is the real world, Mandalay.

She can feel her own anger, now, little flicks of hot fluid in her arteries, spreading. She must let it pass through her without igniting her, though — let it simply flow through and out, not react.

Their futures are fine, she says. They don't need your version of the real world.

He lets out a long inarticulate groan and when he speaks again, she can hear his teeth grind, as if he'd like to be grinding her up between them. If you were actually working and contributing, he says, you might appreciate what money means, a little more.

They've had this argument before, too, but he's never come out and said it so overtly. Has he thought that, really, all these years? Now she feels herself crumbling, her stout non-reactivity giving way. Because Duane is not a philistine, actually. He gets art. He values it. So what he's saying is that's she's not going to make it as an artist. That what she's working on is not art.

She feels her throat swell, her sinuses tingle, her body releasing histamines. Soon the tears will spout hot from behind her eyes. Don't fight it, she reminds herself, but she doesn't want to cry; doesn't want to be humiliated in front of Duane.

She looks through the car window up at her house, sees Aidan at the boys' bedroom window, looking out at them.

I have to go, she says, and grabs the door handle. The door doesn't give, stupid automatic locking system, and the handle springs back, catching her fingernails painfully.

She leans forward to pick up her handbag from the floor just as Duane reaches abruptly across her to release the lock. It's an accident, a complete accident, but his bent hand collides with her cheek, the knuckles catching her on the nose and lip with the combined velocity of their movements.

Her head snaps back; for a moment she can't see or breathe. Then the fierce stinging begins, and with it a surge of rage.

Fuck you, fuck you, she says. She can feel blood trickling from her nose and lip, the taste of salt blood in her mouth, the blinding pain in her sinuses, the smart of the lip split against her own teeth. She spreads her hands over her face.

Duane's apologizing, he's sorry, sorry. He tries to pull her hands off her face. Let me see. Let me see, Mandalay.

She fends off his efforts to touch her, lurches from the vehicle, makes for the back door.

Aidan. She glances up to see if he's still at the window. He's not, but there's a movement of the curtain.

Splotches of tears and snot and blood fall from between her hands onto the steps of her house. She is trapped: she can't stay outside, and she shouldn't go in like this. She shouldn't go in like this and frighten the boys. Fuck, she says, fuck, fuck, as if language has left her.

▼▼▼

ARE YOU FUCKING STUPID? Veronika asks.

Cliff has expected this and not expected it. He notices that she pronounces the "ing" sound, unlike native speakers. He notices that it is the first time he has heard her say *fucking* in this way, using it as a swear word.

She has put his dinner in front of him, and normally she would be starting to clean up from the cooking, or sit and eat with him, but she does neither. She stands in front of him with her hands, still in their oven mitts, on her hips, her face screwed up with anger.

A child would know not to do those stupid things, she says. A child could run a business better. Eat your food.

He can't eat, with her standing there. He puts a forkful of potato into his mouth but he hasn't enough saliva to chew, let alone swallow. She has never spoken to him like this before. She seems like a different person, a stranger.

You don't understand how it works, he says. It's the interest, and the recession. They've cut down the profits. Otherwise there would be no problems.

Her faces changes again, to a look of something else he has never seen before, but has known in other people, all his life: contempt.

How dare she. How dare she.

He rises from his chair without meaning to. Don't talk to me like that, he says. Don't you talk to me like that.

Are you shouting at me? She steps closer to him, leans over the counter, puts her face near his. Gives him a shove, her hands on his shoulders. Sit down and eat.

I'm not hungry anymore.

I cooked this. You eat it, stupid man.

She pushes his plate – a steak, mashed potatoes, mixed veg, all covered in gravy, toward him.

He has told her over and over not to pour gravy on his food. He pushes the plate away roughly and it slides over the breakfast counter and off the opposite edge, to the floor. Breaks in two, distributing steak and spuds and peas.

Ahhh, look what you've done, she screams. It's a guttural scream he hasn't heard before, that is like someone banging him on the ears.

He stands, looks over the countertop at the mashed potatoes and gravy splashed across the floor and up the sides of the cabinets, the fronts of the fridge and stove and dishwasher.

Buster slinks into the kitchen, whines, sniffs the gravy.

Stay out, dog, Veronika says, pushing at Buster with her foot.

Please don't kick Buster, he says. He's afraid she'll hurt him. I'm sorry about your dish.

Veronika screams again. The dish! You are sorry about the dish?

She picks up another plate, a clean one, from the dish rack, and lobs it to the floor. This one doesn't break neatly in half but explodes into several shards. Buster yelps and whines again and backs up. Veronika is reaching for the heavy skillet now. She'll crack the ceramic tile flooring if she heaves that. Or she might even aim at him. Or Buster. He lunges for it across the counter, catches her wrists. When her fist connects with his nose, the pain, shooting up into his skull between his eyes, is like a switch being thrown. He slaps her hard, as hard as he can, on the side of her head.

They both stop dead then. He is breathing hard; his chest hurts. Veronika stares at him, a small, secretive smile stitching her lips together. His handprint white against red across her cheek, her earlobe welling blood. His wedding ring must have clipped it.

You go, she says. Go. Now. Don't come back or I call the police.

Okay, he says. Okay, Veronika. But listen —

She screams and bangs the skillet, which she is still holding, against the countertop. There's a cracking sound.

Then a knocking, as from a broom handle against a ceiling, below them.

It's too much. He stamps on the spot, shouts Fuck off, though he knows the floors are too thick to let through the distinct sounds of words.

You had better go, Veronika says.

He says: I won't. This is my house. I pay for it. I pay for it all.

Well, fuck you, Veronika says.

They stare at each other in mutual panic.

CLIFF WAKES IN THE NIGHT and is dying. A monstrous beaked creature is remorselessly trying to tear out and swallow his heart. He's clammy; the pillow and duvet that he has taken out to the sofa are soaked with his sweat. His pulse is galloping and stumbling. His fingers and toes are numb.

He knows what this is. He's seen enough ads, enough documentaries on TV. His dad had gone like this, died in the night of a massive heart attack.

He's thirty-six years old and he's having a heart attack.

He knows he must wake up Veronika and get her to call an ambulance and get him to the hospital. He needs someone to stop it, to get rid of this beaked thing that is tearing at him. He needs to do this before his heart stops working well enough to send blood to his brain, or before the pain is so bad that he passes out from it.

But in spite of the pain, he hesitates. The creature that has gripped him is not, maybe, his absolute enemy. It is not the worst thing that could happen to him. That is what occurs to him right now. That there is a kind of twisted solicitude. Because it knows something.

Maybe this is what he needs. Maybe this is best. He can't, in fact, think of a good reason to interfere with what the creature seems intent on doing to him.

Tears come to his eyes, but then he can't think of why he should deny the creature. He will not, then, have to deal with the mess of his company. He will not have to deal with Ben, or Veronika. He could get out of all that.

His sisters and mom would be sad, but wouldn't miss him for

long. He hardly sees them. He's not really part of their lives. He has no children, no close friends. Some of the people who work with him, Nicki, Juan, they might feel sad. They'd lose their jobs, but could find new ones. (They're going to lose their jobs anyway, it looks like.)

Veronika would be alright. She knows her way around, now. The mortgage on the townhouse is life-insured.

So no reason, no reason.

Only the pain, which is unbearable. He's panting, now. Surely it will stop in a moment. Or he'll pass out.

He thinks about his trip to Mexico last winter with Veronika, snorkelling in the reefs. He recalls the bright improbable yellow of the tangs, the way the water swirled, full of bubbles, as the current spiralled through the narrow openings in the reef. Of how he felt afraid, at the suck of water, its pull on him, and then saw that he could swim with it: a few strokes of his flippers and he was free, in control again. People aren't supposed to feel that it's okay to go under, to drown.

He'd like to do it again, someday. Swim in the reefs. He'd done it once before, much younger, with his brother Ben. He sees the ebb and flow of the currents around the reef, the barber fish, the parrot fish and butterfly fish and bream, the spiny black poisonous urchins, the sea fans and anemones like chrysanthemums, and ribbons of algae winding, swaying, over the reef.

Ben had taken him on that first trip. It was soon after they had met, had rediscovered each other as brothers, after years of separation. Ben had been to Hawaii many times, had been snorkelling many times, but Cliff never had. He had been afraid of drowning but had not drowned.

Now, he's afraid of the pain, that's all. He's seen the TV documentary. He's afraid of the pain and then not being able to breathe. But it will not last long.

He doesn't think that he moves or makes a sound, but Veronika wakes up, is suddenly in the living room, next to him. What is it? Are you sick? What is wrong?

The squeezing intensifies, and then relents a little. Okay. Focus on the space around the pain, the space where the pain isn't. Count the breaths.

But just as he begins to lift his head there's a new pain, shooting like a meteor through his chest, his upper rib cage. It's a whetted knife, a white-hot dagger. It obliterates the old pain. There is nothing in him now but this slice to his heart, and the hot tail of it through his shoulder and neck.

▼▼▼

CLEO HAS TO CANCEL TWICE before she can see Lee again in the afternoon, and it feels like a chore instead of a treat. Not a distasteful chore, just a chore. Some kind of pain rises in her when she realizes this – it might be grief or it might be nostalgia. It has a bittersweet quality, and she can't define it. Doesn't have time to define it, right now. She gets to the room first. The Coastal Suite, it's called. It's the kind of place neither she nor Lee (she suspects) could afford, but Lee has a friend who manages some big names, who keeps the suite booked, and lets Lee use it if nobody is in it. It's on the twenty-first floor, and has a bar and a Jacuzzi and a flat-screen TV that comes down from the ceiling, and a view of Coal Harbour and Stanley Park and the north shore mountains beyond, and of course a king-sized bed.

When he comes into the room Lee looks tired, some puffiness around the eyes and jaw.

He sits on the bed and unlaces his shoes and takes off his belt as if he's just going to bed, as if she isn't really there. He says he's worked some late nights, doing some gigs. He's setting up for a big show:

Madonna is playing BC Place. It's not going well; there are some issues. He sounds a bit distracted, not present. His voice is kind of raw, too.

He says: How are the kiddies? How is Dickhead?

He says: Have you got lawyered up yet?

Okay. She knows he's tired. And she cares for him, right? Nobody can make her feel the way he does. It's just a bad day. He's not fully present. And he's just reflecting the kind of social domain that he comes from. Which normally she finds kind of hot.

Oh, it's not that he's irredeemable. But it would all be so much work.

She comes close to orgasm, and again, and then fakes it to be done. She really, really needs to get back to the office.

On the way through the underground parkade, back to their vehicles, she knows.

She shivers.

Cold, babe? Lee asks.

I don't like parkades, she says. This is true: the ceilings are too low. They don't seem safe.

Afraid of Jack the Raper? Lee says. I get it, babe.

No, it's not that, in fact. In her engineering program, she remembers, the prof had been scolding the class after some generally poor test results. Seventy-five percent might seem acceptable to you, he said, but if you get your calculations seventy-five percent right on a parkade, you're going to have a concrete-and-automobile panini.

That had stuck with her. She thinks of it, when she sees very low ceilings. When she's in parkades.

She knows that she's not going to see Lee again.

For a moment, the sense of what this will mean flashes in front of her. The way that over the few months they have connected so perfectly, so seamlessly, that their minds have seemed to complete each other. If she is never going to have that again?

But to go on, she would have to undo every other part of her life. And for what? She's not a girl anymore. She knows this: that intoxication fades, that after six or twelve months there would be a difference.

That one angry, middle-aged man will be exchanged for another.

That she can't keep doing this: can't keep staying up till midnight to finish work, can't keep rushing home to spend time with one child or the other; can't prop herself up to listen to Trent talk about his day so that he won't feel neglected; can't knock herself out hour after hour so that nothing, nothing, in her life is suffering as collateral damage in her pursuit of whatever she is pursuing, which she seems not to be able to remember, right now.

If she had thought about where this was going – she had tried not to think about it – she had imagined to herself a kind of fading out, an arc of passion followed by some sweet secret memory, like in some French film. She had imagined (when she wasn't imagining a kind of ecstatic, miraculous future in which she and Lee become a couple, which she rarely allowed herself to do) that things would reach some sort of natural end, and it would be clear that it was time to break it off.

So maybe it's just that time, now.

She cannot go on. Or, she doesn't see the point of going on, which is maybe not the same thing.

It's like something is collapsing inside of her.

Lee walks her to her car. His is parked very close, but he walks her right to her car, stands by the door, ready to open it for her after she has pressed the fob. He is chivalrous, always.

She has no time to make up a story. She says: Lee, I can't do this anymore. She tries to look at him but she can't: there is something wrong with her neck.

Hey, he says. I totally understand. Totally get that, babe. It's a huge imposition. I mean, you have so much going on.

His voice so easy, so casual. So maybe she's been agonizing over this for nothing. Or is he just good at hiding his feelings?

They go through what feels like an empty, scripted thing: a few phrases of good will, a hug.

She can't help but glance over at him, before she backs out of her stall. Thinks, then — all of the things she knows about him, all of the things he's said, running through her mind in a rush, the way people say their lives flash before their eyes when they are in terrible danger — thinks, then, of his essential loneliness. If it is all distilled, that's what is left — it's the recognition of some shared window onto the world, some small lens that by strange coincidence belongs to both of them.

On the way home, Cleo turns off the highway at the mall and goes into Walmart. She has it in her mind that they are out of toilet paper or dishwasher detergent, something like that, but she ends up in a kind of trance, drifting up and down the aisles. It's not somewhere she goes often, for reasons aesthetic or ethical or both. Quantities of objects, of temporary, disposable, unbeautiful, mass-produced objects, made too cheaply in countries without decent environmental or labour laws. But this evening, it's an easy place to be, like those places (she's watched this on TV with Sam) where sharks or giant manta rays go to have their parasites removed by little tropical aquarium fish.

A kind of zoning out, of no-being. Possibly, she is delaying going home.

She wheels up and down the brightly stocked ranks of shelves (like coral reefs, she thinks), she also picks up a package of the bar soap Trent uses, a birthday card for Trent's mom, some hair elastics and a box of Band-Aids. A six-pack of drinking glasses — the kids keep breaking them — some triple-A batteries for the remote and the kids' game controllers, coffee creamer: that's on her grocery list.

And a bag of individually wrapped packages of crackers and cheese. Incentive for the kids to make lunches – Olivia has been walking up to the Safeway near her middle school a few times a week. Some athletic socks for Sam, whose feet smell – she must make him change more often, throw his old ones away.

Up and down the banks of shelves she drifts, as if carried by some sort of current.

Little boy's jeans: now there's something. Mandalay's twins are always so – shabby. Where on earth Mandalay gets their clothes, she can't imagine. Last time she saw them, Owen was wearing a pair of stained sweatpants cut off just below the knee, like he was in costume for a production of *Oliver Twist*. She holds up a pair, name brand, decently made. Size eight, slim. She suspects Mandalay doesn't even know that little boys' jeans come in three fits, now.

Mandalay doesn't like her to buy things for the boys. But maybe she'll take off the price tags, pretend they're hand-me-downs from Sam. Yeah? Or, Christmas is only six weeks away, as the store's gaudy displays remind her. She could give them the jeans for a present. It's mean to give little boys clothes as Christmas presents, she knows. But she'll add in some big toys – the jeans can be a side thing.

Up and down the aisles, looking at the shelves and shelves of cosmetics and cleansers and emollients, the brightly coloured towels and plasticware, the frying pans and laundry baskets and step-on garbage cans, the toasters and vacuum cleaners and artificial flowers and framed prints and ceramic Buddhas, the tents and fishing rods, the Barbies and Pokémon cards, the paint and extension cords and acrylic yarn, the locked cases of video games and sale bins of video movies, the mops and disinfectants and paper towelling, the stacks and racks of cheap shoes and clothing, the millions of items of every description, all mass-produced and interchangeable and without meaning.

They had recognized each other, she and Lee, beyond the accumulation of external things in their lives.

Something that feels like the weight of all of the dust of the world settles over her.

She should really go home now.

She pushes her full cart out of the line for the cashier, walks away. There is nothing in it that she needs.

16

Refinancing

CLEO DREAMS SHE IS WALKING THE SHORE at Powell River, where she used to go with her parents and Mandalay and her little brothers when she was very young. She's collecting the flat, pearly, c-shaped lower valves of jingle pot oysters. They are currency. She collects more and more, but then the plastic grocery bag she's using splits, and she keeps collecting more, though they spill out. She's trying to be inconspicuous, in her collecting, at the same time: she doesn't want others on the beach to notice, to get any jingle pot shells for themselves.

In her dream Cleo and Mandalay are their adult selves, but Cliff and her brother Che, her long-dead brother Che, are children. Bodhi, the baby, is not there, not yet born. Her parents are in the background. In her dream she realizes, suddenly, that her father is still alive, and the jingle pot shells become irrelevant. She runs toward him, and wakes up.

She wakes to find her face wet. Grief over her father fresh again, thirty years later.

When Crystal had been admitted to the psychiatric ward, Cleo's dad had said: Mandalay, Cleo, you have to take care of the house and your brothers now.

She can see this scene in her head, though maybe she has imagined it. Mandalay says she has no memory of it. But Cleo has a clear picture, whether it's real or false: the five of them in the car, the old Chevy, Bodhi on Cleo's lap, and it was dark, and they were getting KFC at the drive-thru, the old one on Joyce in Powell River. In her memory they are in their pajamas, and the sodium vapour lights from the parking lot are shining orange in the raindrops on the car windows, and they have just left Crystal at the hospital.

This can't be quite true. They wouldn't have all gone along to take Cleo's mom to the hospital. Mandalay says that the RCMP took her, which sounds more likely.

But this memory of the car feels very real, and she has a clear impression of her father making his pronouncement. His green John Deere cap, his beard, his arm reaching back over the seat as he turned to face them.

You have to be the grown-ups. You have to take care of the house and your brothers. You can't be children anymore, just thinking about yourselves. You have to be good. You have to be grown up.

She remembers herself nodding, her chin going up, her shoulders going back, the importance of her job filling her, stiffening her spine.

She wakes again as usual just before her alarm, which is set to six, but with the sensation that her head has been nailed to the bed with nine-inch spikes. Crown, temples, back of the neck: she feels the blows, the impaling of bone. Thinks: Maybe I'm having a stroke. An aneurysm. A moment of sadness flattens her: the fine network of neurons, the silvery webs of synapses that comprise her, flooded, extinguished. Her *self* ceasing to be, all the thought and experience that have made up her life, that make up her mind, erased, wiped out as if they never existed.

She feels a deep sadness about this.

Then it occurs to her: If I'm having a stroke, I won't have to go to work today.

Oh, come on, now. Her job isn't that bad. It's just – exhausting. And as of the last few months, completely chaotic and unmanageable.

As she moves, now, she becomes aware of the lassitude of her body, the grittiness of her tonsils, the ache of her submaxillary lymph nodes. She's brewing something, if not already sick. She should stay home.

No. Slacker. It's only a cold; she's just picked up Sam's cold, the one he's been nursing for a few days. She just needs to pop some extra vitamin C, some ibuprofen, and get on with it. And quickly: she has an eight-thirty meeting.

But when she sits up, there's a kind of off-kilter spin in her head, and her body drains of something necessary. At 8 a.m. she's vomiting substances she has no recollection of taking in. Chunks of furniture, feels like. Hot acid. She crawls back to bed, longs to pass out.

Slacker, she thinks again. She imagines the meeting she was supposed to be at dissolving, ineffectually; deadlines then not met; a project running over time, running into complications. The company running a deficit, this year, because she didn't go to work.

Sam's home again this day. She thinks he's malingering, but he cries, miserably. He says: I can't, I can't, please don't make me, Mommy. I'm so sick.

She's too sick to argue with him. More than that – she can't decide, can't read, if he's really ill or just wanting to miss school. She swings back and forth, feeling for him, seeing logically that he can't possibly be sick so often, and always well by two-thirty in the afternoon, always well on weekends.

They're both too tired to fight him, she and Trent. They're all in a kind of limbo right now. Sam's been through a battery of tests, in the offices of a children's psychiatrist, at the school's recommendation. They're waiting to hear.

Poor Sam; poor baby. Had she put him in daycare too early? He'd seemed fine, though, and all of the literature said that children who went to daycare part-time, as he had, really thrived. It's something else going on with Sam.

She half-dozes through the day, watches a TV show with Sam about coral reefs. Rising temperatures, something called *catastrophic bleaching*. Whole colonies giving up under stress, ejecting the little symbiotic algae that keep them alive.

▼▼▼

MANDALAY HAS SUCCEEDED in finding some chores the boys could do – outside of their usual ones – so that they can earn some cash, and in taking them to Chinatown to buy Duane birthday gifts, has remembered to have them wrap and pack the gifts.

That had been an excruciating undertaking. The boys had not much money to spend each, and had become painfully conscious of this. It seemed a kind of torment. They had somehow decided that they wanted to get him gifts this year. Since they had started school, they had become aware of gift-giving as an important ritual, and they had made Duane some sort of craft involving their class photos, popsicle sticks, and glitter; but this year, they announced that they need to go shopping, to get their dad real gifts. And then they'd told Duane, and he had said – this was the hard part – that they were only allowed to spend on him what they had earned themselves, doing chores. They didn't really have much of a sense of money for their ages, Duane had said, when she had remonstrated. She didn't *want* them to have a sense of money.

Use your imaginations, she had said to the boys. Think about what kinds of things would be useful or amusing to him. (She had offered, of course, to help them out, but they had been adamant about keeping to Duane's rule.)

Aidan had originally planned to buy Duane new shoes – perceptively, he had picked up that Duane liked nice shoes – but had managed to earn about a fiftieth of what a pair would cost, to his extreme disappointment. He'd settled, painfully, for a pedicure set.

Does she think his dad will like it, he asks, now.

She imagines that Duane likely possesses pedicure tools that cost several times what her son is spending, but says, honestly: He does care about his feet, a lot.

I don't know if he'll like it, Aidan says, doubtfully, miserably, but I think it's something that anyone could use.

She doesn't say: It's the gift that counts. She thinks: Men cop out of gift-giving, out of the insight and empathy work that is required to give appropriate gifts. It's good for Aidan to struggle, to learn that. (It hurts her in the throat and chest, to see him struggle. And for what? Duane's determination to make them into capitalists, that's what.)

Owen has bought for Duane a toy monkey on elastic strings stretched between sticks. When the sticks are squeezed, the monkey does somersaults. The monkey is a caricature, with a fez and possibly a racist physiognomy. Owen is confident, delighted with it. Dad's going to love it, he says. She thinks Owen might wear the toy out before he gets it to Duane: he has taken it out of the gift bag, again, and makes the monkey flip over and over, laughs himself hoarse each time.

Duane had better express appropriate gratitude and delight.

Aidan had asked her the other night to program Duane's number into the home phone. (He had wanted to give the boys cell phones; she had managed to persuade him that they would get lost or broken, and the boys would suffer unnecessary stress.)

Daddy says he will call us, and we can call him whenever we want. *Whenever.*

Okay, she says.

But I like to wait, he says.

It's better if Dad calls first, Owen says.

Yeah, I wait for him to call first, Aidan says. You know? I try to see how long I can last.

Like holding your breath under water, Owen says.

She has to turn away.

The twins are ready at half past six, Friday evening, sitting on the stairs, scrubbed and packed, glasses and stuffies and puffers in their backpacks.

And she herself has found time to shower, to put on her new jeans and a flattering jacket that Cleo has given her. She can at least look presentable. She won't let him find fault with her appearance.

So she is presentable, when Duane's knock comes at six-thirty.

She opens the door and blinks, because he isn't alone. For the first instant she thinks: He's brought a babysitter, but then realizes: No. The girl-woman with him is not a teenager. She is perhaps around thirty, very slim, fine-boned, with straight black hair almost to her waist, a smooth, completely unlined face, half-hidden behind enormous sunglasses, plump lips, a tiny nose. She's wearing what Mandalay would call jogging pants and a jacket, except that they look like they're made of cashmere, and high-top sneakers in a style Mandalay hasn't even seen in shops.

The girl-woman is introduced as Giselle. She puts out a slim, smooth-skinned hand. Mandalay's own hand, grasping it, is meaty, with prominent veins and tendons, and freckles: a peasant's paw.

Oh, Giselle. She recognizes the name, now. And the glossy hair and the small heart-shaped face, from the photos of the trip Taylor had emailed her.

Hi, Owen, hi Aidan, Giselle says, as the boys come out. Of course, she knows them already. Giselle from the Cayman Islands trip.

Her voice is quite deep, but also cool, detached. Mandalay has not imagined that a woman who is a stranger to her is spending time, close family time, with her sons. It doesn't seem possible.

Duane doesn't volunteer their weekend plans, and she doesn't ask. Of course she knows that Duane dates, but he's never brought one of his – friends – along to pick up the boys, before. Maybe he does take women on his outings with the boys, but she's never known about it. Duane isn't into the whole family concept; she knows that better than anyone. It is very unlike him to mix his dating and parental lives. She thinks.

He's just brought this girl, or woman, along because.... Well, for some reason that would make sense and be non-threatening, if she knew it.

When the boys go to the SUV, Giselle uncoils herself from her cool stillness and follows them. Mandalay thinks that she will open the rear doors for them, help them with their seat belts, but she doesn't; she just walks around to the passenger side and waits for Duane to come and open her door. Which he does. The boys open their own doors, scramble in with their backpacks.

They had greeted Giselle as if they were quite used to her.

▼▼▼

THE DOCTOR AT EMERGENCY SAYS: It wasn't a heart attack.

He knows that. The pain had started to fade even in the ambulance; had in fact disappeared so quickly that he had felt fine within a few minutes of being lifted onto a hospital bed. But they had run tests on him all night: had drawn vial after vial of blood, and stuck wires to his chest and hooked him up to monitors on which he could see his heart going along as normal, or what he thought must be normal, a repeating motif of a coastal mountain range.

You do need to take better care of yourself, though, the doctor says. She is about twenty-five, he thinks. No, she must be older than that. But young.

Get your weight down a bit. Lower your cholesterol intake. Do something to reduce stress.

He bows his head. He means to nod, but then keeps his head in place on the downward nod. His chin tucked in. She is just saying what she's been taught to say, and he could have told himself all of these things, but he has to go through this.

He has had an anxiety attack, not a heart attack. But he has plaque in his arteries, his blood pressure is high. There is a wait-list to see a stress counsellor. So they will refer him for his heart.

▼▼▼

OKAY. NOTE TO SELF, CLEO THINKS: When you're sanding drywall compound that's directly over your head, keep your eyes shut. Goggles would help, except if they don't work because they get steamed up right away. Why is that? It feels like the dust mask funnels her breath right up into the goggles. They overlap, or something. Swim goggles! Those might work. But to find them, she'll have to get off the ladder, go upstairs trailing clouds of plaster dust, and root through Sam's closet. She has an idea where they are — she keeps Sam's stuff pretty organized — but if she pokes her head out of the basement, she'll be mobbed by demands for this or that. Better stay here, tough it out.

She lets her arm drop for a few seconds — her triceps and deltoids are screaming, after an hour of reaching over her head to scrape at the ceiling — and looks around. She might be a third done, now. More like only a quarter, though, if she's honest. And after this sanding, she'll have two more coats of plaster to glop on and sand, according to the videos she has watched online.

Scrub, scrub, at a half-metre square piece of ceiling. The old plaster has fossilized, apparently. In the videos, the sanding looked like a few swipes, like removing makeup. She lets go of the top of the ladder so that she has both hands on the sanding tool, and somehow throws her body weight upwards through her arms. There, that's doing it: the lumpy patch starts to melt away.

But she teeters a little on the ladder, and the dust both falls and floats around her. And there: it's in her eyes again. Her lashes feel weighted, as if with stage mascara, and individual particles seem to be hitting her corneas like tiny missiles.

Sweat trickles down the back of her neck. Her breath smells stale under the dust mask. She's dehydrated, maybe. Her shoulders burn.

Also, it's boring.

It shouldn't be boring. She should be able to get into a zone, let her thoughts run free. How often does she get space to actually think creatively about decor? (The grey sofa that's on sale at Jardines? Grey and cream, for the room. Touches of black ...)

She can hear feet above her: Trent's heavy, flat-footed gait; Sam's light padding; the sharp knock of Olivia's high heels. Dammit, she's wearing them in the house again. On the new hardwood floor. Is it worth going to the top of the stairs, opening the basement door, calling out a reminder?

She hears Trent's voice, then, just the sound, not the words, and Olivia's sharp-toned reply, and next a thump-thump that may or may not be two shoes being tossed across a room.

Slamming of fridge and cupboard doors, now. Knife drawers, pan on stove. Trent's making lunch: good. But god, he is loud. Can he not move anything without slamming it? He'd better clean up after, too: there's no way she should have to come upstairs when this is all done and have to clean up after everyone.

Chairs scraping now on the hardwood floor. Trent and the kids both like to hitch the dining room chairs closer to the table with all of their weight on them. It sounds like some of the felt pads are missing. Grind, grind. Can't they hear that they're gouging the hardwood?

Now her eyes are smarting and her lashes are clogged too much to see. Down the ladder again. In the small high utilitarian mirror of the basement bathroom she sees she has been whited out: only a triangle of flesh remains where the dust mask covered her mouth and nose.

This stuff can't be good for her complexion. Probably sucking all of the moisture out of her cells, permanently.

Also, is the dust mask effective enough? She'd bought the better-quality ones from Home Depot, thicker, with two elastics and a metal strip to pinch the bridge of the nose. But was it enough? The next step up was a $120 gas-mask thing. That seemed excessive. But how much of the dust is getting through the paper masks? What is in the plaster, anyway? Hopefully not something that will lodge in her lungs and give her emphysema or lung cancer down the road.

If she did this for a living, she would definitely get a gas-mask thing. But this is a one-off. It should be okay.

She climbs back up the ladder, begins to scrape.

Now it's winter, and they really need the room. They're all inside more. The sound of the kids' programs and electronic games is driving her insane, and Trent is always tripping on the wires, always watching TV in their bedroom, because the kids are using the living room. The kids refuse to go downstairs, to the gloomy, shabby, semi-finished basement room, and who can blame them?

Then this spring, when her salary had gone up considerably, she'd brought it up again: Could they look at a new house, now? But somehow the possibility of moving had got turned into refinishing the basement and keeping the house. How had this happened? Oh, yes: the realtor had said they needed to finish the basement, to sell the house; people absolutely wanted top-end basements now. And then they'd bought some new furniture, and the new SUV.

And then over the spring and summer, they'd gone through three contractors who had said they'd do the work on the basement, and then not shown up. There was so much new construction. Nobody needed work.

And Lacey had said: Why don't you do it yourself, Cleo? You're really adept at home reno stuff. And so this weekend she has found some videos and DIY manuals, and gone for it.

What a negotiator she is! Three years at it, and she has moved from her objective – buying a new home in a downtown Vancouver – to standing on a stepladder on a Saturday afternoon wiping, with her shirt-tail, plugs of Synko low-dust spackling compound from the corners of her eyes.

She is not doing a great job, she can tell. She has been much too generous with the mudding compound – she sees now why the people in the videos she'd watched over and over said things like: You'll learn to be more sparing with the spackle when you have to sand it down – and something had gone terribly wrong – but only in some spots – with the joint tape. There are bubbles, which do not go away. She should probably peel off the tape and start again, but as she has no ideas why there are bubbles in some places and not in others – she can't see what she has done differently – it probably won't be better next time. It could be worse.

It is horrible. Not only so unpleasant, physically – the closest thing she can think of would be working in a mine while plucking chickens – but she's no good at it. She can't seem to get it to work out. She must have been crazy, to think she could do this. It's not possible.

And yet she has to. Finishing the ceiling is the thing standing between her and getting on with the basement reno. She can't move forward until the ceiling is done. And it's improbable that anyone could be found who would come in and complete it now, the mess she's made of it.

She climbs down from the ladder for the tenth or hundredth time to wipe the dust from her eyes. In the bathroom mirror now, a plaster statue. Plaster saint?

Three-quarters done this round, now.

Just think ahead to the ceiling being smooth and finished. How easy the painting will be, compared to this job! And how beautiful the room will look, with cream walls and crown mouldings, the muted blue-grey of the sofa, the red-brown laminate floor, the built-in book cabinets and TV stand, the subtly patterned rugs and throw pillows.

She holds it all in her imagination, the perfect balance of shapes and colours.

Though really, she might just want to move out.

Because she's done with this, now, maybe. (The idea emerging, forming slow bubbles, in her mind.) Maybe she's done with all of this, the two-hour commute and the parent association committee, the kids' soccer games, and the nightly spaghetti or pizza. Done with the endless negotiations with Trent. Done with the landscaping company and the neighbourhood book club and the trips to Walmart.

Sell the house and take half. Split custody of the kids.

Her mind has trouble going there – trouble looking at the mountains of effort and recrimination that going through this process will take. And yet, lately, she can't imagine that it won't be necessary.

At least she needs to have options.

The joint tape is still bubbled up in several places. But she'll keep working at it. She'll keep smoothing it out. This room will make such a difference to everything.

▼▼▼

VERONIKA SAYS: You start over. Just you this time. You have best knowledge, and you have, what you call it, *clee ant bass.*

Client base. Customer base.

Yes. Customer base. That is worth a lot, yes? And you sell some of trucks, you lay off all but two hardest workers, you cut their wages.

I can't cut their wages, he says. They wouldn't be able to live on less than they're getting.

And you give me accounting. *The* accounting. I learn, you pay me. I keep under control.

He needs to think. It is a Thursday morning, but he has not gone to work. At mid-morning, he is still in bed, sitting up beside Veronika, talking.

Start over without Ben. Can he imagine doing that?

What he needs to do is separate his feelings for Ben as his brother from his conflicts with the way Ben wants to run the business.

I know Ben is your only brother, Veronika says. That is hard, right? And more hard because he is lost for many years. So you feel he is precious thing that you have to hold onto.

That is it; that is it.

He remembers lying in bed with Veronika – in this bed, in this condo, though it feels now like history – telling her about the loss of Ben. It was after some dinner that Ben had blown off. Veronika had said: What is it, you all think the sun kiss his ass. But he is just a brat.

He had told her then about his dad dying, his mom being sick, the five of them being split up among different foster homes. Ben – Bodhi, he was called then – Ben, the baby, being adopted and lost to them for the next twenty years. He hadn't told her before because her English wasn't good enough; he didn't think that she would understand properly. Though she knew about the foster homes. They were married, by then: Veronika had met his foster mother.

After he told her about Ben, Veronika had said: So he grew up with the rich family and that is why you think he is better than you.

That was too simple. That's why he hadn't wanted to tell her. But now she seems to get it. Now she understands.

But at the same time: does he want to run the business without Ben? And with Veronika?

It wouldn't be the Lund brothers anymore. Though Ben of course wasn't called Lund.

If his brother Che had not died.

He doesn't know if it will work without Ben. Of course, Nicki would be much more competent, in lots of ways.

No more Lund brothers. That is a sad thing. Unless he has sons who can take over the business.

He says to Veronika: We must have two sons. So that the business can keep being called Lund brothers.

Veronika snorts. Yes, we have two babies. And feed them what? If I am working there is no babies.

It's as if she's just feeding all of his dreams into a chipper, that's what it is.

Anyway, your nephews, the twins, they are Lunds, yes?

He hadn't thought of that. But it's true. Mandalay's sons, Aidan and Owen, are Lunds. Of course, they are very young. He remembers holding them, in the hospital, so recently it seems just yesterday. But how quickly time passes; how quickly they will grow up.

He remembers gardening with Mrs. Giesbrecht, his foster mother, when he had been the same age as the twins are now. The spring sun pleasantly warm on his back. He had not liked working with the animals and with Mr. Giesbrecht, so had been happy to escape that, to be conscripted to help with the garden. As soon as he was big enough he had taken on the heavier work, digging out the weeds, digging in the composted manure. Happy because of being outside, helping, being useful and competent. They had grown blue-berries, raspberries, strawberries, potatoes. Other vegetables, mostly carrots and turnips and cabbages, things that could be stored in the root cellar over the winter. Mrs. Giesbrecht also had a big flower garden: gladiolas, peonies, tulips, roses, delphiniums – lots of big showy flowers. She was always apologetic about it, as if some-body were accusing her of wasting the garden space, or her time, though Cliff had never heard this happen. Well, I need my bit of beauty, she would say. Or, The Lord made the flowers to remind us of heaven.

She had supplied the flowers for the church. He remembers carrying the armfuls of cool perfumed blooms into the building, from her car, Saturday afternoons from early spring till late fall; filling the big vases, which looked like cut glass, but sort of milky, greyish, and were plastic, at the sink in the church kitchen, carrying them into the enormous meeting room, with its big arched beams of varnished light wood, its rows of varnished wooden pews.

He had not liked that so much, being at the church at the wrong time, when the business parts, the behind-the-scenes parts, were hap-pening. The organist and soloist might be practising, running over and over through only a part of a song. The pastor's wife checking that the hymn books were distributed evenly among their wooden pockets on the peer backs – and randomly flipping through them to check for notes or vandalism inside – the churchwardens organizing the donation envelopes, going over accounts.

The business of it. The part that wasn't meant to be seen. On Sunday it was different: all serious and full of grandeur and cere-mony, the service progressing smoothly, as if under its own energy, sweeping everybody up in it, altogether. But on Saturday, helping Mrs. Giesbrecht with the flowers, he'd seen the other side, the machin-ery that made it all work.

He thinks of Mrs. Giesbrecht dying of her stroke back in the spring.

He hadn't gone to visit Mrs. Giesbrecht in a long time, and then he had got the phone call that she had died. He tries to picture her, which is difficult, but seems a necessary act of respect. Her brown-grey hair, a soft colour, like the fur of wild rabbits, one you don't see on women anymore. Her long braids wound around her head and pinned like a crown, her large breasts, which had seemed one solid protuberance, he remembers, without cleavage, a broad solid shelf that began below her armpits and ended steeply at her waist. Her flowered dresses and aprons.

She wasn't his real mother, but he had lived with her for a long time, from the time he was seven until he was eighteen. He has a sort of ongoing vision of himself at that big table: the games, but more the making of food, and the talk, which was a kind of background murmur, Mrs. Giesbrecht telling little stories – not rambling, but somehow boring anyway – of her childhood, her relatives, people she had known – or making plans for the garden or the housework. It hadn't seemed to matter if he was listening or not, so it was just nice background noise, like having a radio on. Comforting. (Like Veronika with her endless TV, maybe.) He had done his homework under her eyes – first, hers and Cleo's; then just hers. (The endless homework: he had felt like being an ox – or a little mule, maybe – tethered to a post, driven round and round to grind the corn.) Mrs. Giesbrecht had taught him to cook, too, before he had left home: she didn't want him to be one of those bachelors, she said, who always had a skillet of lard and fried potatoes on the range, and that was it.

She had expected him to be a bachelor, always, but he was not. He had taken Veronika to meet Mrs. Giesbrecht, and invited Mrs. Giesbrecht to their wedding. He had thought that they would become good friends, that they would find in each other a mother and daughter. They had not. Mrs. Giesbrecht had not approved of Veronika, the way she dressed, maybe, or her long tumbling yellow curls. And Veronika had said that Mrs. Giesbrecht was a judgmental old peasant woman. But there was something practical, something single-minded about both of them. Like you could wind them up and let them go and they would travel over any terrain, through any barriers, to get where they intended.

He didn't visit Mrs. Giesbrecht after that. He thought about her sometimes, but he didn't visit, even though Mr. Giesbrecht was dead. Out of the picture.

Maybe he should have visited, by himself, or even insisted Veronika get to know her.

He has not thought often about Mrs. Giesbrecht, about living there, maybe because it had not been pleasant at the end. He'd felt bad, at the end. He doesn't think about that time. He doesn't encourage thoughts that lead to it.

He'd learned to cook from Mrs. Giesbrecht, and to prepare soil for growing, and to plant and tend green things, to tuck plant slips and seedlings into pockets of earth between stones, to leave space for things to grow much beyond their original size, to know almost by feel, by the texture of leaf and stem, whether a slip of green stuff would need strong sun or thrive in deep cool shade, whether it will need the thick clay gumbo or sandy, airy ground.

And he had learned to plant light against dark, fine against coarse, glossy against dull, yellow-green against blue – to see the plants as not only as living things each with their own way of thriving, but also as spots of colour and texture and shape.

He had taken a diploma in landscaping, but he had known in his eyes and hands already how to coax the earth to grow.

▼▼▼

BELINDA SAYS, LATER, as they follow their customary neighbourhood walk: How unchivalrous of him.

Yes, exactly, Mandalay says. Although she has doubts about the significance of chivalry for women now. She says, again: I just think he should have warned me.

Do you think he brought her along so that you would meet? To let you know?

Yes, maybe. But he should have asked my permission. Before he began bringing his girlfriend on outings with the boys. But how would she rationalize that to Duane? In what universe would he ask permission from her to invite any of his friends on an outing with his sons?

She says: He pretty well acted like she wasn't there. I had this first thought that she was some kind of nanny. But that's totally Duane's style – he doesn't do public displays of affection.

I see, Belinda says.

A thought, then, of Duane and herself, the months they had dated. That public decorum, almost never touching. They had never held hands in public, let alone kissed. The ineffable currents that passed between them when they did brush hands or exchange glances or even moved in close proximity; the graze of Duane's hand on her shoulder as he guided her into a seat: a kind of electromagnetic force.

She had both floated and burned, those months.

Remembering, her body does a swan dive into arousal and fierce longing. It's that unexpected, that immediate, that clichéd. And that painful and humiliating. She lists, on the sidewalk, almost loses her footing.

Okay? Belinda says, putting a hand under her elbow.

Okay, okay. She doesn't want Duane anymore, really.

He's not kind to you, Belinda says.

And it's true. Duane really is not nice to her. He barely conceals his impatience and disdain. Which are real. This isn't like one of the romance novels she devoured when she was a teenager, in which the male love interest seemed disdainful and contemptuous, but it was all a misunderstanding; he was just trying to hide his true attraction to the heroine. No – Duane is mean-on-purpose, mean when he doesn't need to be. He really just doesn't like who she is.

It's just that, she says, when we were dating, he had made me feel *on*, alive, full-throttle all of the time.

Are you okay? Belinda asks. They've made a big expedition, today, are walking along the waterfront in a brisk wind. There's a smell of salt and old creosote; the gulls are circling, screaming.

I'm lonely, she says. I'm forty-two. I'm afraid that I'll never be in a relationship with a good, whole man again. Is this true, what she has just said aloud? It feels like an insight. But it also feels like a thought that might pull her backward, now, into a whole realm of narrative revision that she doesn't really want to make. A whole universe of second-guessing herself. She will not. She will not.

Tears sting her eyes.

Now, now, Belinda says. She wraps Mandalay into an embrace. It's comforting to be held, to feel another adult human hold her. She is reminded that she has not been held by another adult for a long, long time – years, now.

They have walked a long distance today, she and Belinda. Her legs are starting to ache pleasantly.

She *is* forty-two years old. She's a single parent, living below the poverty line, on the generosity, or lack of it, of her children's father and social assistance and a part-time job and some student loans. She has crows' feet and she now needs a bra to hold her breasts up, and she has stretch marks on her inner thighs, and a scar like a thin, silvery ribbon across her belly, just above her pubes, from Owen's emergency exit from her body. Some days, between trying to look after the boys and house and her efforts to finish her degree, she doesn't even have time to wash her hair.

But she can walk ten kilometres without breathing heavily, can carry a twenty-kilo package of kid up a flight of stairs, can control a pencil line on a sheet of pressed paper with not a wobble, can manipulate scores of sensitive tools and media with a muscle memory that makes her fellow students stand around and gape when she's working. And in her new jeans (she thinks) she still has a pretty fine bottom.

Are you going back to campus? she asks Belinda. Are you going to your studio?

Yes. Belinda has some work to do.

I'll walk back with you, Mandalay says. I have some studio work to do, too. She feels herself calm, centred, as they turn and begin the familiar trek through the neighbourhood.

17

Title Insurance

JUST LIKE OLD TIMES, Lacey says.

She is wielding a roller; she is getting some drips on the floor and has made a couple of smudges on the ceiling paint in her rec room, but Cleo doesn't say anything. They can be touched up later.

Remember, we painted *my* rec room, a hundred years ago, Lacey says.

Cleo hasn't forgotten that. Back when Olivia and Claire were in kindergarten and Sam and Cory toddlers, she'd helped Lacey fix up her rec room. They'd painted it the deep blue it is now, stencilled on glittery stars, put up Harry Potter posters.

I guess it's going to need repainting, Lacey says.

Lacey is moving back, taking her kids and moving back with Calvin. When Lacey had told her, Cleo had been horrified for her. Wouldn't Calvin hold it against her forever? What would it be like for Lacey? He had anger issues before, for god's sake. Now what? Lacey had just raised her nicely shaped eyebrows. Calvin's had to agree to a list of things. An anger-management course is one of them.

I'm thinking a media room, Lacey says. Projector screen, instead of TV. Console chairs. Strip lighting on the floor. What do you think?

The kids will love it, Cleo says.

Kids? Lacey says. I'm thinking Cal. He can just spend his time down there, out of the way. She winks, but Cleo is not sure how far the irony is meant to go.

Speaking of kids, Lacey says.

They can hear, upstairs, the sounds of cupboard doors, of pans and utensils, the mixer. It's a PD day, and Lacey and Cleo have booked the day off as well. Sam had an appointment early in the morning, and anyway, it seemed like a good idea. She'll check into the office later, have a conference on Skype.

Great that they're all hanging out, together, just like old days, Lacey says.

Maybe great, Cleo thinks; maybe not. In fact, Claire had turned out to be the instigator of the girls' little alcohol experiment the month before – the one who had purchased the mickey of vodka from an older teenaged boy. Cleo isn't going to go as far as Lisa, who has forbidden Amy from talking to Claire, but she wonders if she's going to be a good friend for Olivia. Who had said: Mom, you don't really know anything about Claire.

And then the two boys had been best buddies when they were small, but now seemed to be going in opposite directions: Sam inward, spending more and more time on his computer, and Lacey's son Cory getting more and more into sports, playing hockey now, and basketball, as well as the ubiquitous neighbourhood league soccer.

But she doesn't say anything about that. She says, instead: I haven't had a chance yet to hear how you decided to break off with Richard. How you decided it wasn't working out.

Because that is something she really, really needs to know.

Oh, a conversation for another day, Lacey says, in the light, breezy voice that means her shutters are all down. Maybe some evening over a glass of wine.

Cleo had thought that Lacey had escaped, unlocked herself from the double contract of household and marriage. Or that she would manage to unzip those two things from each other – to keep one: her house, into which she had put so much of her energy and style, and which her children had pined for. How had that not been possible? It did not bode well for anyone, if Lacey couldn't manage it.

Or maybe there was another way of looking at it – the way Lacey seemed to be choosing. She had simply – well, probably not simply, but without very much talking and perseverating – moved back with Calvin. Moved back home.

▼▼▼

CLIFF HAS TO GO to the heart clinic at the hospital. They make him weigh himself in his boxers, his white belly hanging over the elastic, and they measure his waist and make him go on a treadmill.

They tell him and Veronika to go to a nutritionist to learn how to eat. The nutritionist shows Veronika how many almonds in a little bag equals one hundred calories, and gives her recipes for fat-free muffins and omelettes made from egg whites.

Veronika is not impressed. She already knows how to cook. She is not going to feed Cliff or herself this idiot food. But she gets books; she goes online.

Apparently, in Estonia and Russia, right now, health food is a big thing. Healthy hearts.

Veronika makes granola; she buys hemp hearts and chia seeds and flax seed and pumpkin oil. She has to buy organic everything. It is amazing: hemp hearts are actually more expensive than prime rib roast, per gram.

He comes home sometimes to find that the oven is dark and cold, and there is no hot meal. Make something yourself, she says. I am studying.

He thought that Veronika would be angry about him losing the business. But this: it is as if with every new phrase she learns, now, she becomes more different.

I am not a soft place for you to land, she says.

He goes to work. It is late fall, but there is still some work to do: garden beds to clean out, pruning and leaf blowing. Endless leaf blowing.

What Cliff would like is for everyone to be in a room together — himself, Ben, Veronika, Donna from the bank, Ben's adoptive father. The salesman at the auto dealer, the accountants. Maybe Cleo and Trent. Then he would like someone to explain it all — to explain how it was not Cliff's fault that it all fell apart. That Ben spent the money but did not do enough of the work, that Cliff tried to hold it together as long as he could, but was undermined all the way. He'd like someone in charge to explain this so everybody understood what had happened.

This does not happen. He tries to make it happen. He goes to the bank to talk to Donna, but she has moved; she has transferred somewhere else. There's a new guy in charge of their loans. He's young, and he doesn't know them. He looks at his monitor and uses jargon and doesn't say anything beyond the statements Cliff can read himself in all of the fine print on all of the forms that have his signature.

He thinks about phoning Ben's dad, who is a lawyer, to talk to him alone, but he doesn't. Instead they have a meeting, Ben and his adoptive dad and Cliff and Ben's dad's accountant friend. Ben's dad says: You boys have been having a bit of a party with this, haven't you? Bad time for it. There's a recession.

They have lost a couple of their big clients, and they are having difficulty getting paid by others. This is not their real problem, Cliff knows. The problems started before that. But everyone seems happy to blame the recession for their business failing. There is the Olympics contract, but they will not start on that work until the spring.

Four of the trucks are going to be let go. This means that they go back to the car dealership. They are not worth as much as the loans still on them, but that is how it works.

Ben's adoptive father will own Lund Brothers now. Or he and some other guys will. The name will stay on the trucks and Cliff will manage a crew but he won't be the owner. Only a couple of guys will be kept: the rest laid off. Maybe they'll be hired back in the spring.

And then there is the lease on the warehouse space where they store their equipment and vehicles. You go talk to the property manager, Ben's dad says to Cliff. I noticed three vacancies in the building. You go tell him he needs to give you a break on the lease, or you're out.

It doesn't seem possible that Cliff can do this.

Everyone but Cliff and Juan will be laid off. Nicki will be laid off.

Cliff says: We keep Nicki on over the winter. She's a great crew manager; we keep her year-round.

You cut her salary, then, Ben's dad says. She's picking up prunings, she doesn't need a crew boss salary. Put her on hourly.

Cliff doesn't know how he's going to do that.

Ben is not going to be involved. He's going to go to business school. He's going to do an MBA.

Cliff phones Cleo. She is busy. She says: What do you need right now from me, Cliff?

He can't answer that.

He can't get his head around the idea that he doesn't own the business, anymore.

He says to Veronika: I feel like someone has died.

Bullshit, she says. Bull-*shit*. You go to work the same every day. You service customers the same. You work too long and take calls on weekend. Only difference, you don't have heart attack every payday.

She doesn't get it. She doesn't get it.

Veronika has taken to wearing a kerchief on her head. To hide the roots, she says. That's an accusation. There is no money for her *touch ups*, which, he has learned, cost a hundred and fifty dollars, and have to be repeated every six weeks. She has taken to wearing a flowered scarf on her head, and below the scarf her eyes are permanently narrowed, her mouth pursed, her dimples overcut by the creases that run from the corners of her mouth up to the sharp buttresses of her nostrils.

He doesn't look at her, if he can help himself.

▼▼▼

CLEO IS HOSTING THE BOOK CLUB AGAIN, though it's not her turn, because that's the only way, it seems, that they can pull one together. Nobody else would host. For a while it looked as if the book club was going to fold, because neither Lacey nor Michelle would likely come, naturally, and Lisa was still angry at both Lacey and Cleo about Amy's near alcohol-poisoning.

This month the book's a quick read that's been on the *New York Times* bestseller non-fiction list for a couple of years, about a mountain climber who set up a charitable organization to build schools for girls in Afghanistan, in Taliban country. Cleo had read it in a couple of sittings, waiting for Sam at the dentist; it's not terribly challenging. But innocuous, and worthy, she guesses. Not likely to be too controversial. It might even be one of the books everyone likes. She'd had to come up with something quickly. She'd sourced the book, on sale at the big-box bookstore, and emailed everyone to let them know where to get it, and then had actually picked up copies and dropped them off at her friends' houses.

The group is going to read *Pride and Prejudice* next month, Mira's choice, which should not arouse any controversy. Cleo does not know if she will attend next month.

Everyone has come, except for Lacey. Cleo had invited her, but then had to tell her that not only Michelle, but also Jennifer and Lisa would boycott the evening if Lacey came.

Lacey hadn't seemed upset. Somebody has to be sacrificed, she said, and it will be me, naturally, as I have violated the code.

What code?

But it seems this book will be a good choice. Everyone will find it heartwarming, optimistic. It's something that all them can approve of, building schools for, and educating, young women. After all, the thing that links them all is that they have teenaged daughters.

But do we know that it's a good thing, really? Mira says. I mean, the whole premise of the book is loaded with the assumptions that Western values are superior to Afghani ones. Who says it's okay for one culture to impose its values on another? And do we know that the people sponsoring this have good intentions?

She speaks quite mildly, but her eyes are unusually serious.

Jennifer says coolly: What do you mean by Western values? Like, teaching girls how to read and write?

Stephanie, who is Mira's friend, and always supports her, says: But we don't know what the girls will be taught in the schools. Are they going to be taught to be good employees and consumers?

Jennifer again: I don't get it. Are you saying there's some ulterior motive here? This man, the author, went through a lot of personal inconvenience, not to mention danger. He lived in Taliban households. He saw things first-hand. Do we always have to talk about Western capitalist takeovers?

Lisa says: I don't agree that every culture is equal. Some have really backward ideas. Like genital mutilation of girls. I don't think I want to jump on any politically correct bandwagons about intercultural respect, here.

We're not talking about genital mutilation here, Stephanie says, perhaps too sharply; and simultaneously, Michelle, who Cleo thinks is a little less on the ball than everyone else, says, Oh, I was reading about that. Those immigrant people from wherever are trying to keep doing it in Canada; they caught someone in Toronto....

(Oh, where is Lacey, to exchange glances with?)

Then everyone speaking at once, or not quite at once: there are two or three arguments going on, cutting across each other.

And then, an abrupt falling off, mid-sentence, a trailing away.

I thought it was a sweet book, Lisa says. Her eyes are a bit glittery. I thought it was about hope, and hospitality, and generosity. I thought we could talk about those things. I thought it was interesting that the girls in the book want so much to have an education, and we could remember what that means.

Yes, absolutely, Jennifer says. I thought I would give it to Maddy to read.

Well, at least it's not a book about going shopping, Stephanie says. Or about sexy vampires going shopping.

What's wrong with shopping? Michelle asks.

What on earth has happened to everyone? She can't do it. She can't do this book club thing. At least, not without Lacey.

(But what if they were to keep going? What if they continue, let everything crack open?)

▼▼▼

MANDALAY HAS SEEN THE HEADLINE in the business section of *The Province*, which someone across from her was reading on the bus, and tried to decipher the details from where she was sitting. No good. (She needs reading glasses, the optometrist says.) But the header and the photo were clear. "Local Real Estate Magnate Files under BIA." And the familiar professional headshot of Max Gibbons.

Duane says: It means the business has gone bankrupt.

Will they be okay? I mean, will they lose the house and stuff? She has buttonholed him, as he's dropping the boys off – asked him to come inside, and he has, though she can see that he's impatient, ready to bolt.

She has offered him a beer – she has beer in the house, for once, because students from her class had come over; they'd had a little Christmas party. She and the boys had decorated for it, and she thinks, now, how lovely her living room looks, with the lamps in their paper globe shades, the many plants, the new (new to her) throw on the sofa, which is a rich burgundy, and now the vintage glass ornaments that they have hung – there really is no room for a tree – from fishing line suspended from the large branch she has attached to the ceiling and wound with clear lights.

It's really magical. Her fellow-students had gaped at it, and then seemed transported.

She had not thought they would come to the party. She'd offered, because she had the most space. Many of them said they were living two or three to a room, so exorbitant the rents these days. But they had come, and seemed at home. It had been a happy evening.

Duane says: The business was incorporated, so their personal holdings are exempt.

So, they just write it all off, continue on as usual?

Duane says: You know I can't discuss it. Max is my client.

Client and friend, no? Something else occurs to her.

Duane. Did you invest in Max's company?

He sighs. No, that would be illegal, as I have inside information. There's a pause. Then he says: But I did invest in some of the same things that Max did, in the States.

He doesn't look at her now, and his voice is casual, but something, some vestige of their former closeness, tugs at her perception. He didn't have to tell her that. It's bad news, for him.

She remembers Cleo saying to her recently: The one area Trent and I trust each other in is finances. We're always scrupulously honest about the big money. She had laughed: it was ridiculous, a tenuous and absurd connection. But Duane has that streak in common with Cleo and Trent: for him, money is the big event.

She says, softening her voice: Did you lose a lot?

Yup, he says. Quite a bit.

She says: I'm sorry. Are you going to be alright?

She means: Will he be able to keep his condo, his sailboat, his seasons' passes. That's all she means, truly, at that moment. But he laughs, shortly. Don't worry. I can still take care of my responsibilities.

I really just meant, she says, are you going to be okay, yourself?

Sure, he says. I just would like to have more.

And then: Here's the irony, Mandalay. The housing market has tanked in the States, but it has only corrected a little, here.

What does that mean?

If we'd sold this house back in May, I would have invested the equity in what looked like a good thing, and would have lost most of it. As it is, the value has probably only gone down ten percent. It might drop further. But it's not the worst case right now.

He didn't have to tell her that.

She wants him to say that it's only money; that he has everything he really needs in the world right here. But he will never believe that, and never say it.

Why can't he feel it? Why can't he feel that this is enough, that this is more than enough, the two of them sitting here, with the mellow light of the vintage lampshades, the deep forgiving comfort of the shabby quilts and shawls layered over the sofa, the toys and books (and okay, odd piece of clothing) scattered in a relaxed way on the floor, the boys calm and secure at the table, having their bedtime cereal. The boys that they created together, who are so intricate and perfect and strong. It is more than enough; it is everything it means to be human; it is as good as it gets. She can see that Duane is relaxed, that he is at some level truly comfortable in this moment. Why is he closed to that? Why can't he see it?

She says: Oh! I've found tenants. Two of my classmates are going to move into the basement suite.

Duane's lip curls. You realize they have to pay rent, don't you?

She has, in fact, looked up the going rate, and found that her fellow-students were glad to rent for that, which has shocked and appalled her. She doesn't say this. She also doesn't volunteer that she has moved her boxes into a studio space she's been given, on campus.

In the place where she might recently have felt a bruise or wound at Duane's reaction, she feels almost nothing. Just a little sadness.

▼▼▼

I HAVE A PROPOSITION FOR YOU, Trent says.

He's wearing the new square, dark-rimmed glasses she ordered for his birthday; they look classy, kind of Clark Kentish on him, as she had guessed they would. They're both in their suits, both having come straight from work. They're sitting across a high, square block of ebonized ironwood, having glasses of craft beer while their sushi (well, Cleo's sushi; Trent's teriyaki) is being prepared. They'd ducked into the restaurant because it was the first one that they passed on their way to the car park, but Cleo recognizes it now as a hip sushi joint mentioned in a few lifestyles blogs that she follows.

She can see their reflection in the mirrored wall. They look like they belong there. They look successful.

A proposition? she responds. If it's a game, she's in the mood to play.

You saw the news item about the Lehman Brothers bankruptcy? The Dow dip?

Yes, she says. Of course, she knows about that.

There hasn't been a lot about it, since, he says. It's been kind of ignored, or played down. But here's the thing. There's a whole rack of s&l institutions in the States that are starting to fall over. We haven't noticed the impact up here, but it's sure to hit us at some point.

What do you have in mind? she asks.

I was thinking, he says. We could put the house on the market right now. It's really strong. But I think it's going to go down.

Right now?

Like, yesterday, he says. Isn't your friend's sister an agent?

Sister-in-law.

Whatever, he says. So. Sell the house now. Put the money into the kind of things that do well during an economic slowdown. You don't have to know what these are. I know. And then, when the housing market slumps, we buy up. We buy in a better neighbourhood, something you'd like better, something that would work better for us.

She can see that he's in the grip of some strong excitement, which he is trying, not wholly successfully, to play down.

You're forgetting one important thing, she says. Where are we going to live, till the slump comes?

Aha! Trent says, uncharacteristically. Aha; here's the cool part. We rent something downtown. Or downtown-ish. It'll be small, but renting is still cheaper than buying in Vancouver. And it will be short term. It'll be kind of like being on holiday. We'll eat out a lot. We won't sweat the small stuff.

Okaaaay, she says. And then? When we buy the bigger, nicer house?

Then we rethink, he says. Maybe you take a leave. Maybe I do. Maybe one of us starts up our own business. Maybe we fix it up and rent it to a TV star and go on a long trip.

You don't like travelling, she says.

I'll learn to, he says. What do you think?

Thinking is not something that anyone can do when things are suddenly turned upside down. But she and Trent are always good in crises. Is it because they don't overthink? Because they go with their intuition, their gut feelings, then? And are those more accurate sources of information? That seems unlikely. Nevertheless.

I think you're crazy, she says.

I can show you the numbers, he says.

I'll need to see the numbers.

It is crazy. It's absolutely crazy. And probably not even sensible. But she feels a flame, a warm blue flame, ignite somewhere in her brain. *What if. What if.*

I'll have to think about it, she says.

18

Closing Costs

IT'S THE END OF TERM, and Mandalay has final crits: her classmates and the faculty – not just her own instructor but others as well – will look at her term work and critique it, aloud, while she stands there. She has not yet, even in this final year of her program, got used to crits, used to either the idea or the practice of them. It seems all wrong, a practice of public humiliation.

The challenge of them, the discomfort of them, is part of the practice, though, Belinda says. The role of art is not to be comfortable, but to question, to unsettle.

Mandalay would like to feel comfortable, to feel secure, in one aspect of her life.

She hopes, but is not at all confident, that she has done interesting enough work, original enough work. It has been a lot of years. She hopes that she has taken enough risks. She has often been too tired to push her ideas any further.

She arrives at the room assigned to her a several hours before her allotted time, to set up. She has brought her own mounting supplies. She will bring coffee and pastries from a nearby shop, as is traditional. She has ordered the urn of coffee, the platter of treats, and they will be delivered. She is sharing the room with two of her classmates, whose crits are scheduled just before and just after hers. She likes these students; she likes their work. She is happy to have been assigned the same room.

And Belinda will be there. Belinda will come. She is faculty here, and respected and esteemed by the other instructors, and she will take part. She is not afraid of what Belinda will say.

For her critiques, she is showing a group of three prints she has made in the class. She has chosen the best three, she thinks. They'll make more impact, speak more for themselves, in this grouping. She has worked the grouping out, in the studio, beforehand, coming in on the weekend to lay out her framed prints, to make a sketch of them. (She does not have a phone with a camera, yet.)

Now she attaches them to the wall, in the way that they have been instructed to (in the way she had done when she created a little gallery in a bakery, back in that other life). She measures; she uses a level; she is precise with the hardware. It's part of the process. In the same room, two of her classmates are also hanging their work. She is both conscious and not conscious of them. They are all very busy.

The technical term for her print medium is oil monotype lithograph/relief print chine collé. What this means is that she has prepared a series of plates, etching away the negative space on prepared sheets of aluminum, working from photographs, using both light-sensitive films and tools to incise the surface, applying acids and inks, and then pressing the images to squares of thin translucent paper layered on heavier paper.

It takes a new plate preparation for each colour. She pulled a few prints each time, and then kept the best of each print and discards the rest (or, she will discard them, once she has submitted her final portfolio, which stipulates that she include four copies, for grading).

She has prepared her statement, which describes both her process, using the correct terminology (collage, drypoint, mezzotint, emulsion:

the words have become so freighted, for her, with muscle memory, with the fine oscillations between hand and eye) and the theme of her images. She has written: *Lithography works on the principle that oil and water repel one another.* But that is only part of the truth. In reality the two substances are perpetually disturbed by matter from the environment: natural colloids on the skin.

She has chosen, after all, not only the body surface and clothing, but the textures of the urban landscape that is her home. With a borrowed digital camera she has photographed the features of her neighbourhood: the houses under reconstruction, the half-finished (and, often, indefinitely halted) high-rises as well as the shops and signs and tram lines whose days are possibly numbered. She has photographed the trees where the crows roost and call out, in the park where her sons kick soccer balls and wobble on their new bikes. She has photographed the seawall near Duane's condominium, where they used to walk, a long time ago, between their luxurious and carefree bouts of pleasure. She has photographed the porches of her neighbours, the ones who have watched her sons, over the years, pass by in their twin stroller, on staggering toddler legs, on tricycles and two-wheelers and skateboards.

And on these images, printed only in three colours per edition (though the background paper, showing through, subtly transforms and expands their range) she has superimposed the fierce and delicate textures of the surfaces of living things: skeletal leaves, hands, the tattered lace of a bra she had bought a decade ago, the sole of Owen's first pair of shoes (hoarded, yes, in a box in her basement), the gauze pad – including scabs – from Aidan's recent bicycle-crash road rash.

It's her life that she has mounted there, with acid-free mattes, in Plexiglas frames. But it is also *not* her life. It is something that she has recently been able to peel away from herself, at least from time to time: to hold at arm's length and evaluate.

KAREN HOFMANN

307

As her peers and instructors will do now.

She hangs the last print and steps back to look, and her anxiety ebbs, is replaced by something that resembles pure happiness.

She will do her graduating project next term. She has decided to take on the curatorial studies, because it is her first love, because she thinks it will ladder better into the MFA programs she has applied for, because it is winter and the boys will be in the house more, and it will be difficult to find the space to work on physical projects. She will take that on; she has already got some ideas; she has talked to Amanda and Belinda and a few other instructors, and she will get a start on it over the holiday break.

She has applied to only two Master of Fine Arts programs, the two available in this city. She knows she should have applied to more; everyone has told her this. But if she contemplates moving to another city, which she'd have to do, she becomes essentially paralyzed with terror, and can do nothing.

She surveys her exhibition, her term's output of work. The first crit for her class is scheduled to start in half an hour. She has just time to go comb her hair and brush her teeth and then join the others. She is ready. Let's go, she says to herself. Let's go.

▼▼▼

THE LANDSCAPING COMPANY is going to shut down for two weeks over Christmas, instead of the usual one. The accountant suggests that: It's a great way to save some money, he says. And everyone's happy.

Cliff doesn't think that Juan will be happy to lose an extra week's pay.

Give him a bonus, the accountant says. Grocery store gift cards. We don't have to do the withholdings or tax, so it's cheaper. Also, you can write them off as expenses.

Juan says with the extra time he'll make a trip back to Mexico.

He doesn't mind, he says. Hey, why don't you come visit? he says to Cliff. You and your wife. You can stay with my family there.

Cliff has no answer to that. In what world would it be possible, what Juan is suggesting? Cliff knows that Juan's going short, that it's his, Cliff's, fault.

But he would like to go to Mexico again.

In Mexico on their honeymoon, he and Veronika had gone out in a catamaran to the reef and snorkelled, like he had in Maui, with Ben, a few years earlier, and thought again, that he could be happy to do that for the rest of his life, and not known if he would get the chance to do it ever again.

He would like to see the reef shrimp, which had been featured on a nature show – an underwater nature show, his favourite type. The reef shrimp lived on the coral reefs, like the other kinds of shrimp – the ones with neon blue strips, the glass shrimp, which have transparent bodies, through which their hearts and guts can be seen, working away diligently – so technically they must have had some other name to distinguish them. He thinks that there might be many kinds of reef shrimp, as well. There might be so many kinds of shrimp living on reefs that he could spend the rest of his life just looking at them and still find new kinds.

The reef shrimp on the show had vermillion stripes down their backs and long, jointed, white antennae and black-bead eyes and tails like little fans. They scuttled and swam among the corals and the anemones, scavenging, keeping the reef clean. And the female reef shrimp, they said on the program, did not lay eggs like most shrimp, but carried their eggs inside their bodies, feeding them and keeping them safe.

And when the eggs hatched, the little larvae did not come out a proper birth canal, but instead just burst open the mother's whole abdomen. There was rare, high-definition footage of this happening.

The pregnant female shrimp, stopping in midstep, and then the front of her bursting open, the flaps of flesh and shell or whatever it is, and the larvae in their hundreds spilling out, tumbling and swimming, tiny space creatures with their tiny dot eyes and dozens of legs, and the mother shrimp sort of collapsing into tatters trembling in the current.

It seems the heart of a great mystery. Why do those species of shrimp have to do that, when others don't? It is terrible and awe-inspiring at the same time.

Cleo had said: Cliff, you can probably afford trips to Mexico. Not this year, but next, if Veronika gets a job.

Cleo and her husband Trent had invited Cliff and Veronika to their house for dinner the past Sunday and had sat them down after dinner and gone over finances with them. Veronika was not exactly happy, but willing to do this, because Trent was a professional accountant, and she was getting this service for free. Trent had been clear at explaining how much money they would need every month. Cleo had said: You might find, Cliff, that you're actually doing better. Cleo had made up a chart for them, in different colours. He had thought that they would lose their townhouse but Trent had said no, they could still pay the mortgage. They just wouldn't have a cushion, or retirement savings, or things like trips, without Veronika bringing something in. Trent had written down the numbers, and Veronika had nodded her head, solemnly but not with anger.

He had wondered, then, if Veronika really wanted to be rich. Or if she really wanted just to have a house like Cleo's, with a garage and three floors and no neighbouring walls. Detached.

Maybe he will go to Mexico, again, and snorkel in the reefs. He doesn't really want to see the shrimp bursting. But he wants to see the reef again, to look at it and take it in and know he can't memorize it. It can't be memorized. Just looked at.

▼▼▼

CLEO MAKES ONE OF HER nearly daily visits to the Novabilis site, to check a detail. This time, she's by herself. She cabs to the building, gets out a block away when the taxi is stalled in a construction traffic jam. From the sidewalk she can see the new building, rising elegantly and with a kind of glow. For a moment she forgets the hundreds of hours at the computer screen, the wrestling with intractable engineering problems and intractable budgets, the delicate dances with the whimsy of clients and the whimsy of members of her team, the eighteen-hour stretch of the calculus problem that was, in spite of the cutting-edge engineering software installed on her work computer, apparently insoluble.

For a few moments she thinks, with complete happiness: This is what I do.

She translates the forces in material things – in the earth, the water, the air, into a wall, a floor. She listens to them; she understands them, at some level in her brain – no, more than just her brain, her entire being, perhaps – and translates them into the language of mathematics, which the Egyptians or Greeks or Arabs discovered, so many thousands of years ago, which was guarded through centuries, a holy code. And the mathematics in turn is converted into physical space, matter: the depth of a foundation, the weight of iron, of concrete, the arc of a support beam, the struts and trusses and grids that, hidden, support constructions, raise them up against the piledriver of gravity, the headlock of the winds.

ON THE WAY BACK TO THE OFFICE, her phone pings as if it's gone crazy. There are six different parties bidding on her house. Can you have a look at the new one? the realtor says, several times, in a slightly higher-pitched voicemail each time. Don't have to accept any of them yet, the real estate agent says, but we need to talk. Can you call me back? Can you call me back soon?

▼▼▼

BY COINCIDENCE, Mandalay is thinking about Taylor Gibbons the very moment she bumps into her, near the campus, in the market area of Granville Island. Taylor is wearing a very chic woollen cap – a kind of seventies thing with a brim, angora, it looks like – and large sunglasses, and Mandalay might not have known her, especially out of context, if Taylor hadn't been on her mind.

She had been thinking about Maxwell Gibbons, actually, about his loss of money. It must take a lot of income to maintain that house, the private plane, the cars. To pay for the private school fees and the salaries of the cleaning staff, the parties, the clothes. She has learned from Duane that his personal belongings and house are protected from his business troubles. That's how it works, right? The very rich don't lose everything. But at the same time, that lifestyle must be dependent on the steady flow of large amounts of cash.

She had been wondering what would become of a woman like Taylor, stripped of all those luxuries, the luxuries that must be replenished on a monthly basis. No, that's not quite it. She had been wondering if Taylor would be okay. Is that closer?

She had been trying to imagine what Taylor would be like, without her very nice life, her luxurious house and competent help. Would she be as cheerful, as generous, as chill? Would she have the energy to be effusive and amusing to everyone at her parties? Would she be able to keep up that girlish charm, that self-possession, without weekly pedicures and cashmere yoga pants to buoy her up?

And then Taylor is right beside her in the narrow alley between the converted factory and warehouse buildings.

Mandalay feels guilty. What's the word for what she has been feeling? Schadenfreude. Duane had explained that word to her, actually, when she had seen it in a concert program, once, long ago, when Duane took her to concerts.

It's maybe because she feels guilty that she says: Do you have time for a coffee? Even though she really doesn't want to have coffee with Taylor Gibbons, and is fairly sure that Taylor Gibbons might not even remember who she is.

For a few seconds, the other woman looks unsure. Her mouth, which is about all Mandalay can see of her face, with those giant sunglasses, slackens; she bites her lip. Then she says *Love to!* in her familiar, husky-squeaky adolescent voice.

Taylor is carrying a shopping bag from Opus, which she must have just been leaving. Artists' supplies. Christmas presents for her twins, maybe? Or herself?

Taylor has a latte, Mandalay a mocha and *pain au chocolat* at the French bakery. Taylor tries to pay, but Mandalay is insistent. I invited you, she hears herself say, and wonders why she has made such a point of it. Her coffee and croissant aren't going to make a dent in the Gibbons' fortune, or lack of it, and it might have mattered to Taylor, under the circumstances, to pick up the tab.

It's just hard to imagine.

Christmas shopping? Mandalay asks, wondering if that's okay to ask.

Oh, all done, Taylor says, brightly.

Mandalay wants to ask: Will you be okay? Will our kids still play together? But Taylor's tone of voice and expression don't allow it. She has kept the sunglasses on. Perhaps she has a black eye? But no; that wouldn't happen to her. Would it?

Mandalay can't think of anything to say. There should be online articles: how to have a conversation with your rich friend after her husband has declared bankruptcy. Probably there are, actually.

Mandalay thinks of a couple more starters, rules them out. She imagines suddenly that a lot of people in this city would recognize Taylor, would know what had happened, would feel some sort of avid curiosity or even a kind of gloating. As Mandalay herself had. She must be hiding. She must be trying very hard not to be recognized. She wouldn't have wanted to have coffee with Mandalay, whom she barely knew. It must have seemed to her easier to give in than to turn Mandalay down, and perhaps invite more rancour.

Or she might just be lonely. Or tired. Or showing a kind of grace.

She might want just to be treated like any other mom-acquaintance encountered while out shopping. And that's a problem, because Mandalay doesn't have that sort of life: she never has had, really. The women in her neighbourhood don't really have that kind of life. Or if they do, Mandalay doesn't know about it.

She takes a deep breath, summons her inner suburban mom. Or some semblance, mostly gleaned from having spent time with Cleo.

How are your twins on the subject of chimneys, this year? Mandalay asks. I heard Owen and Aidan discussing whether or not Santa is real the other day. And I *know* that I had the talk with them a couple of years ago. At least a couple of years ago.

Taylor laughs. I know, she says. Galton and Mahalia are the same. Willing suspension of disbelief – I think that's the term.

Is her voice a bit warmer?

Galton and *Mahalia*, though! Malty and Galty. And Mandalay has always thought her own name was bizarre.

This is hard going. All that she can think of is the list of things not to ask: So, what have you dropped hints for, this Christmas? What is Santa bringing the twins? Are you going away? She must not ask anything like that, she knows. Nothing that will come close to the issue; nothing that will sound like a reference to the Gibbons' financial disaster.

All of the social questions she has heard women ask each other. Now she hears the barbs hidden in them. The competitiveness, the secret potential for harm. Maybe that's why she has not wanted to join that group – has stayed in her neighbourhood of language barriers, of minimal social expectations.

Then her mouth opens in spite of her, and she blurts out the thing that she knows she is absolutely forbidden to say.

Are you going to be alright? she asks.

There's a moment's pause, and Taylor runs her tongue over her front teeth, under her lip, and adjusts the frame of her sunglasses, and swallows. Mandalay can see now the fine lines around the corners of her mouth, the thinning of her lips. Maybe those issues have always been taken care of? What is it that people do? Filler, is it? Maybe Taylor can't afford her treatments, and her age, which might be closer to Mandalay's, is starting to reveal itself.

Of course, Taylor says, coolly, brightly. Then: I've just had a job interview. I think it went well! It seemed like such a nuisance to keep up my PD hours and pay those annual membership fees, all of these years, you know? But now it seems like it was a good idea!

A dim memory now of Duane telling her that Taylor had a profession, before her twins were born. She'd tuned him out – he'd so obviously been trying to score points. But what was it? Something Duane considered a worthy occupation, anyway.

I can't remember what you do, she says.

Oh, Taylor Gibbons says, in her bright brittle voice, her lip curling a little. I'm a CPA, that's what I do.

That was it. Mandalay says, and she doesn't have to reach that far to say it: I'm in awe. I am useless at – well, at anything useful. She wonders if it's as boring as it sounds to her, to be an accountant. Or if accountants can make anything near the amount of money that Taylor would be used to having. Or if she minds a lot.

Well, we won't starve, Taylor says. No holiday this year, though. She pulls a wry little smile, and takes off her sunglasses. The skin around her eyes is finely wrinkled, like tissue.

Don't feel sorry for her. But Mandalay doesn't, not entirely. Only a little. She feels mostly something else, a kind of respect, even gratitude, for Taylor's openness. For letting her in. And is this what we want most, Mandalay thinks: To be shown the truth, the inner truth, that we mostly keep guarded from one another.

Taylor stands up. Well, I must run.

Don't feel sorry for her.

She's left her Opus bag behind. Mandalay grabs it, catches her just outside the door.

Thanks, Taylor says, taking the bag. Then: We're not supposed to be getting each other gifts, this year. But I thought maybe Max could relax himself a little by doing some drawing. He used to. But I don't know.

What is needed?

Mandalay says: Give our love to everyone. And take care of yourself.

Overused phrases. Empty with overuse. But she means it; she means it.

I will, Taylor says. Then: Max is afraid to ask you, because he thinks that you'll look down on his ignorance, but he really wants you to catalogue his art stuff for him. You could do it on weekends, maybe? He'll pay, of course. You could bring the boys to play with my two?

And not have to pay a babysitter. The phrase doesn't have to be said aloud. Ha. Mandalay lets herself just be, as those small pieces of information swirl around her, but she's grinning, she realizes, with something that isn't joy, but isn't Schadenfreude either, but maybe some hard-won lens of cosmic irony. Ha. Well, that's interesting.

She watches Taylor's slim form, bulked out artificially in her oversized hat and puffy coat, walk away between the chic industrial-style shops with their corrugated galvanized steel walls, their massive exposed cables and bolts, under the spindly leafless trees, toward the parkade.

▼▼▼

CLIFF MUST DRIVE OUT to West Van and check on the building site, and he finds a free day when it is not raining – in fact, the sun is pouring down; it's a lovely day for a drive. He asks Veronika if she wants to come along, but she can't go: she has a final exam. On a whim, then, he calls Nicki.

No, she can't go. She has a new job. Janitorial. It's good, she says. She doesn't have to have much to do with other people. She works nights, in empty buildings. She is part of a team of two. Normally she could go out to the site with him, but she has a doctor's appointment. She's got a rash and some kind of wheeziness, and maybe it's the cleaning products. She can't cancel.

He drives out on his own, then, west and north: a forty-five-minute drive, in mid-morning. It's a beautiful day, the air more transparent than usual, because it's been raining. He takes the Trans-Canada through Surrey, across the new Port Mann Bridge, with its multitudinous white support cables, which look like crochet thread from a distance, and are thick as his thigh, up close. He drives through Coquitlam and New Westminster and Burnaby. He crosses East 1st and East Hastings, drives up the ramp and across the Second Narrows Bridge. He steers through North Vancouver, up onto the raised section of the highway with its deep chasms and rainforest, its sporadic views of the inlet and small islands, brilliant in the sun, its clematis-infested embankments. He takes the 15th Street exit to Marine and turns onto Marine to follow the coast out to the new development along the cliff edge.

He'd been so surprised to get the contract for landscaping this lot, a year and a half ago it must be now. He hardly ever got contracts like that, because he couldn't bid as low as the bigger companies. Turned out that other contractors had turned it down. Too difficult. Too compromised.

But they needed it; they needed all of the work they could get.

If the owner and architect had just left the site as much as possible in its natural state, it would have been fine. He has seen lots of properties like that. They are fine. But they had wanted a clear sea view; they had wanted terraces and pools, the whole mediated shebang. So they had taken everything out, and the earth had started to slip, which was bound to happen. And then they had brought in some alien ground-cover shrub that was supposed to grow really quickly and have a crazy root system.

He hasn't been able to finish the site; the ground cover has to get established. He wasn't sure they would take at all, the damaged little plants he'd been given. But he thinks that they're starting to grow, now. When he checked on them last, must have been late October, they had started to grow.

They need that site finished. They need to be paid.

There's nobody around. He parks up closer to the house, the boxy cantilevered mass of it, than he usually feels entitled to, and heads for the stairs.

Not much change. On the steep slope below the gabion walls, the imported shrubs flop limply, no bigger (possibly even smaller) than they had been a few weeks ago.

Okay. It's technically winter. They aren't getting a lot of sun, and they are plants from a more tropical zone (though from very high elevations); they are used to more hours of daylight, probably. They've just gone a bit dormant.

The trees he had planted in late summer are not looking any more established, either, though he didn't expect them to. A couple of them are leaning, in spite of the collars and guy cables he has rigged. Without their leaves, they don't even look alive, right now.

In the forest at the perimeter of the site, the arbutus and cedar are still thickly, deeply green.

He starts off down the slope. The soil is gumbo, pretty well. It clogs the treads of his workboots. He slips, a couple of times, can feel the moisture from the mud seeping now through his twill pants. His hands are coated, too, and he doesn't want to, but wipes them on the fronts of his pant legs.

He can hear water trickling, as if he's standing near a little tumbling stream. Lots of little trickles of water, falling.

The December sun is warm on his shoulders, through his quilted vest. That's a great thing. He can hear a nuthatch, and the *cheep, cheepee, tzeet* of a flycatcher, and the hollow water-pipe *cronk* of a raven. The earth smells of rust and ammonia and damp.

He'll go down the slope to the lower boundary and then work his way back up along the edge of the gutted forest, where there will still be roots and shrubs for handholds.

He doesn't like the look of some of the tree plantings. They have been washed out – that's what it is. He finds a spindly ornamental maple that's actually being held up in its guy wires – the soil around its roots completely washed out. Damn it. Damn it.

He stops again to look around, to assess the damage. He won't be able to do much till spring, really.

He feels in his shins and knees the first sign of it, before the sound reaches his ears, before he makes sense of the sound, which is like the sound you'd expect if a very large animal were sucking up concrete slurry and grinding it between its teeth at the same time. But there are only a couple of seconds between, really.

He feels the trembling in his shins and knees, and then hears the sucking and the grinding of stone on stone as the slope begins to descend. He looks up, sees the clayey surface of the mud wrinkle up as the rear of the blanket begins to move faster than the forefront. He sees the useless little shrubs begin to swim toward him, a fleet of small green plants. He sees his staked trees lean and topple and hang in their traces.

He doesn't have time to run, and it doesn't occur to him to run. He is watching a slope surge toward him. He's transfixed by the spectacle; it's so unlike anything he has ever before seen. He has no way to understand it. At the last minute he braces his feet. He waits for it to reach him. He waits to be claimed.

▼▼▼

NOPE, NO HOUSE YET, Cleo says, smiling, moving among the other party guests. Yup, bidding war. Yup, buyers want to be in by Christmas. Yup, movers come Tuesday. Yup, Antigua. Yup, let's hope Trent knows what he's doing!

In fact, she does have an apartment lined up, not in the city, but in the downtown part of their own suburb, in one of the new high-rises. Cleo had luckily been able to negotiate this, through her company's ties with the property developers. Downtown Vancouver had proved, actually, out of their reach. Even with the house sale, the bidding war.

So after their trip they'll all be moving into a rented brand-new three-bedroom condominium with about half the square footage of their house. The developer says that he's holding the property for an offshore buyer who needs a few months to get things together. That he's giving Cleo a deal. She hopes so.

She actually really likes the condo, with its more functional layout, its very modern and easy-to-clean kitchen. Its shiny newness. She has kind of fallen in love with it. And she could afford to stay there, with the kids, on her own salary.

She has been throwing stuff out, so that they can move into a smaller place. Boxes of baby clothes, of toys, of old books, of old projects — not just the kids', but hers and Trent's as well. Dishes and appliances that they no longer use. Her old clothes, too big for her now, which Mandalay had rejected angrily — I don't want your fat clothes! – and which are going out of style, anyway. Ornaments that were gifts. Sewing projects that stir no ambition. The old furniture that filled the never-used basement family room, and the dozen or so shelving units that Cleo had bought, over the years, to store boxes of stuff.

Just think. The basement – almost half the square footage of their old house – had been used for storing *stuff*.

It's all going out.

And then, after house prices plummet – of course they're going to, but even if they don't, they'll be okay – they'll buy a new place, maybe closer to the city, maybe on the train line so Cleo can use public transit to commute. Though maybe she won't take the train, because Sam's going to be commuting with her – he's going to be in a different school, one not too far from her office. Near enough, anyway.

This, she has told only a couple of people: it's the part of the reality she's a little less confident about. But, as Lacey says: Cash is portable. You can take half the house proceeds and split, if things don't go well.

Yup, she can do that.

The party is the yearly Christmas party that Mira and Jim give. It's very crowded. It's difficult to have a conversation. It gets more crowded every year: Mira's and Jim's social circle seems to be able to expand infinitely. They can't be close friends with everyone here though, can they? Cleo used to wonder, when she and Trent were first invited, must be nine years ago, where she stood, in Mira's huge group of friends. She had circled the rooms, trying to gauge where she could insert herself into a conversation, recognizing neighbours with relief. Now she knows a few people, yes, but doesn't worry. She stands with her little plate of crab crackers and pâté and her very large glass of Cab Franc and smiles, and the eddies come to her, they swirl around her, and swirl away.

She sees Trent in conversation with one of Jim's hygienists, the pretty Hungarian one with the very large dark eyes, who Trent always asks for (because of course they are clients of Jim's). Trent looks like he's flirting. He looks happy. He's good at flirting: at the playful thrust-and-parry of flirtatious conversation.

And there is Stephanie, Ocean's mom, looking very current in a hippie-ish dress. Suddenly those are back in fashion, though Stephanie probably bought hers second-hand in the nineties. Stephanie spots her, and swims over through the throng.

Do I smell? Stephanie asks.

Cleo refrains from inhaling. Often, Stephanie *does* smell, a bit, of BO. She is afraid of the aluminum in antiperspirants. I don't notice anything, Cleo says.

It's this dress, Stephanie says. It's vintage. I washed it, but I think the warmth of my body is causing the fibers to release the smells of the women who wore it before me. Anyway, Ocean often tells me that I smell.

Oh dear, Cleo says. Well, apparently I make funny clicks with my teeth when I'm reading. Who knew? Thank god we have fourteen-year-old daughters to set us straight.

Oh, yeah, Stephanie says.

I love your dress, Cleo says, sincerely. She does. It's the real thing. Her own is in a similar style, high waist and floaty sleeves, a lot of embroidery, but only an imitation.

And I love yours, Stephanie says, politely.

And here is Mira, heading toward her now. Mira is in a peasant-style dress also, but floor length, and golden.

They embrace.

Thank you for inviting us, Cleo says. Thinks: Will this be the last time? Because who knows where they will be, next year.

Well, enjoy it, Mira says. It's our last one. Jim and I have decided it's got too big, even for the new house. We're not up to it anymore.

It takes me weeks, you know, to make all of the food. And the clean-up is a three-day job.

Cleo expresses surprise and dismay.

We've been doing it for twenty years, Mira says. It's a lot of work. We thought we might try something different.

It's a neighbourhood institution, Cleo protests. You ought to be able to get funding from the city, for catering and cleanup. Or make it potluck.

Mira smiles. She has a lot of silver threads in her hair, now, Cleo sees. But she is becoming more beautiful, as if moving toward, not away from, some prime state of being. I think we're just ready to change things up, she says.

And now here are Lacey and Cal: Cleo feels a surge of relax-ation – is that the right way to describe it? – an *ebb*, maybe, as Lacey's familiar face comes into view. A feeling of security.

Lacey is not in a peasant-style dress, but in an off-white Angora sweater knit that just skims her chest and hips and ends above her knees. I want that, Cleo thinks, though she knows that on her curvier body, the effect would be quite different. Pin-up, not gamine. She hears Lacey greeting others, her voice bell-like, her remarks clever and bright.

Jim is offering Lacey wine, in the signature giant glasses he and Mira own. Oh, white, please, Lacey says. This dress! And you know I will spill on myself.

Lacey moving through the crowd, in the opposite direction. Everyone looks at her, and most smile. The men all smile, beam. Lacey must greet them all. But she has seen Cleo, has winked. She will circle through and end up beside Cleo. Cleo will just wait here for her.

Then Calvin is saying hi. He's got a chunky piece of glassware in his hand. Scotch, which Jim, curiously, only offers the men. He's wearing a nice black jacket – is it cashmere? – and it has very fine white hairs from Lacey's sweater dress all over it.

She wills herself not to think: Poor Calvin. Because everyone is thinking it – the neighbourhood gossip transmission speed must rival that of fibre optic cable – and because she knows it will show on her face.

Anyway, not poor Calvin. He's doing very well, Calvin is. Like Trent, he is canny. A canny Scot. His brokerage firm, Lacey had confided, is doing really, really well.

How goes the move? Calvin asks.

She makes the expected grimace. Just cleaning out the garage today, she says. You would not believe what was in there. Oh! We pulled out Olivia's first bike, her two-wheeler, and Olivia was remembering that it was you who taught her to ride it. She remembered you putting her on it, and starting her down the hill at the golf course, running along behind and then letting go.

Oh, yeah, Calvin says. I remember that. Claire and Olivia just shooting down that hill beside the ninth! I had them staggered, so they wouldn't run into each other, but I was just galloping up and down that path all morning.

Olivia remembers that, Cleo says.

Hey, Calvin says. Look up. Did you know you were standing under the mistletoe?

Oh, god, how hokey. But Mira hangs those fake fabric mistletoe balls in every doorway.

Okay, I'm forced to do this, Calvin says. Cleo turns her cheek to him as he leans in, but he catches her face in one hand and turns it back, and his mouth lands right on hers, and lingers just a couple of seconds longer than she expects.

Oh my goodness, Cleo hears herself say, in Lacey's bright voice.

Then he's gone, and other people circle back, and it's all Cabo and Cuba and Antigua, and isn't this storm something? I'm hoping that the big maple doesn't come down on the house.

AND THEN AROUND MIDNIGHT, Cleo's phone buzzes and vibrates suddenly, (urgently, she thinks), inside her little retro beaded shoulder bag. Buzzes and vibrates, and she takes it out and reads it (she's going to need reading glasses soon, she notices; she has to squint to read her phone) and she sees that the caller is the security company at the Novibilis building, and when she picks up, the security chief says: You should come down here. It's a disaster. You need to come down here.

And she drives downtown – or Trent drives her, actually, because she's had more to drink than he has. They arrive just a little after one, and there are emergency crews, so they can't get in, but Alex is there, and the developer, and the contractor too, and finally they're allowed to go up, and it is, it really is, a disaster.

The wind had come up off the water – a wind borne from warm, moisture-laden air from the ocean meeting a cold front nosing down from the Arctic – and because this year there was more moisture, warmer air, the wind was bigger, and more determined. It blew in from the coast, where the Western Cordillera shelved under the Pacific plate, where the waters of the Pacific lay, open and shallow, ripe for both evaporation and the unhalted progress of the air currents. This kind of thing was to be expected more and more, with global warming, said the scientists, on the news clips, after.

The new, fresh wind gathered momentum as it funnelled through the Strait of Georgia and into the Burrard Inlet. It entered the channel between the Lions, and was compressed and condensed, and stirred up waves like a mixer. The waves hit the shore at Prospect Point, on the south bank of the inlet, and chomped out great bites of the seawall. Then the wind hit Stanley Park at a hundred and fifty-eight kilometres per hour and raked the tops off swathes of five-hundred-year-old cedars. That footage was in the news for days.

But some of the wind charged straight across English Bay and up Denman Street, and smacked right into the west face of the Novibilis building.

The building did not fall. It swayed a little, as it was designed to do. The ceramic tiles pinned to its shell did not come loose. The great swathes of glass did not shatter, in the wind. But the five-metre gingko trees, the elm and catalpa and parasol pines, in their oversized Mediterranean-style planters – which were made of resin, not concrete, because someone on the team had okayed the sub-stitution by the contractor, and Cleo had not noticed – the two dozen trees and their resin containers were scooped up playfully by the wind, which might have been moving at only a hundred and fifty kilometres per hour at this point, and tossed playfully through the ten-metre glass wall of the atrium. And then, in case it hadn't made its point, the wind sucked up the top twenty cen-timetres of the pond and flung it, along with some rare waterlilies and a pair of five-hundred-dollar koi, through the new opening in the glass.

And it is so bad, so bad, that she can hardly take it in. She can't believe it has happened: her mind just shuts off to it.

She knows the project so well that she can see right away what has happened. She can see that the planters are not as heavy as they were supposed to be. It's my fault, she says to Alex. I didn't double-check that last spec sheet from the suppliers. I left it to Tilly and Michael and I should have checked it. I didn't.

Alex looks at her as if he remembers her vaguely from some-where.

Trent puts his arm around her. Oh, Cleo, he says. Don't look like that. It's only some glass and flooring. It's all insured. And they haven't even moved in yet, so no electronics, luckily.

But she knows: she is finished, in this job. She must be.

She stands in the shattered glass, which looks like expensive crystal snow on the new slate floors. Someone should begin the cleanup. (A disaster crew is on its way.) Someone should....

She sees movement, in a corner: a flash of bright colour. It's one of the fish, the koi. It has moved, slightly. It shifts its tail, again.

She's on it: wastepaper basket, water from the spigot of the fancy black circular lunchroom sink. The animal is slippery, and heavier than she thought. There. In the basket it rights itself. It's too big for the container; it coils itself into a donut. She'll have to fill the sink. And the other?

Trent is nearest it; he lifts it and hands it to her almost ceremoniously. This one is white, moon-coloured. There's a trail of blood, just a thin thread, from its head, but it's also alive. It looks at her.

Into the water, with both of them: the gold and the pale against the black basin. And there they swim, slowly, at first, gasping a little, then beginning slow deliberate circuits. How beautiful they are, how vigorous. Around and around they circle, moving to stay alive, nosing calmly for the opening, the channel that will lead them out.

DISCUSSION QUESTIONS

1. Does the title *A Brief View from the Coastal Suite* have symbolic significance in the story? What could the "coastal suite" represent? Which characters could be said to have a "brief view" of something?

2. How does the Lund siblings' history – their tragic family breakup – affect their ongoing life decisions? And for readers familiar with the first novel, *What is Going to Happen Next*, are the characters better or worse off in 2008 than we might have expected?

3. The city of Vancouver is the main setting for this book: Cleo and Cliff work in the city, though they live in neighbouring municipalities, and Mandalay lives right in metropolitan Vancouver. How does this setting shape the experiences and desires of the characters? Is it significant that it's Vancouver, and not Toronto or Seattle or London?

4. The novel's point of view is shared between three characters: Mandalay, Cleo, and Cliff. Which do you identify with most closely, and why? Why is the fourth Lund sibling, Ben, not given a primary voice in the story?

5. Each of the marriages (or co-parenting arrangements) in the novel contains a great deal of tension. How is this tension related to the setting – twenty-first century Western society? What elements hold each relationship together, and which pull them apart?

6. Each of the three primary couples is formed of two characters with very different backgrounds: geographic, economic, cultural. How are these differences a factor in the relationship tensions? Which of the relationships seems most likely to evolve into something more functional?

7. At one point in the novel, Cleo remarks that she doesn't have time for a weekend getaway with her lover. Why does Cleo, with her already overextended life, engage in an affair? What is she looking for, or attracted to, in Lee? Should she stay with Lee or remain with Trent?

8. Mandalay is at odds with most of the other characters over values and lifestyle choices for herself and her twin sons. What does she want for her sons? Is she naïve or too idealistic to function well? Does her ethos change, during the arc of the story?

9. Cliff, who doesn't have children, views his nephews in terms of potential legacy – someone to carry on the Lund Brothers name. What do their offspring represent to the parents in the novel? How do Cleo, Trent, Mandalay, and Duane – and let's throw in Crystal – view their children? Do these views of parent-child roles evolve over the generations, or are patterns and expectations simply repeated? What does the novel suggest is needed to be a "good-enough" parent?

10. Friends and business relationships feature briefly but significantly in the novel. How are these relationships similar to and different from the familial ones? What do their friendships reveal about each of the main characters?

11. The novel ends with two calamities and a minor triumph. What elements connect all three? Do the outcomes for the characters feel inevitable or surprising? How does the final image of the two fish in the bucket affect our sense of the novel's outcomes?

ACKNOWLEDGEMENTS

Many friends and family members have given me countless hours of conversation about life and writing, and thousands of kilometres of companionship on walks. Thanks especially to Anita, Ernie, Sue, Carolyn, Patsy, Dawn, Leigh, and Susan, and to Julia, Hayley, Max, and Dave, who have all inspired my stories and provided the space and encouragement to work through their shaping. Anita Swing and Carolyn Ives read and gave helpful feedback to an early draft of the manuscript.

Thanks to Anne Nothof and Claire Kelly at NeWest Press for their guidance and sharp editorial eyes.

I am grateful to the office of Research and Graduate Studies at Thompson Rivers University for support in the form of a sabbatical leave and travel support in 2018.

KAREN HOFMANN grew up in the Okanagan Valley and taught English and creative writing at Thompson Rivers University in Kamloops, British Columbia for nearly three decades, and now divides her time between the BC Interior and the West Coast. A first collection of poetry, *Water Strider*, was published by Frontenac House in 2008 and short-listed for the Dorothy Livesay prize. Her first novel, *After Alice*, was published by NeWest Press in 2014, and a second novel, *What is Going to Happen Next*, in 2017. A short fiction collection, *Echolocation*, was published by NeWest Press in 2019. Her poetry and short fiction have won numerous recognitions. Karen is an avid walker, and her writing explores the landscapes, both rural and urban, of British Columbia, as well as the personalities and social dynamics of the inhabitants.